Soul
Siren

Soul Siren

Aisha DuQuesne

Delta Trade Paperbacks

SOUL SIREN
A Delta Book

PUBLISHING HISTORY
Brown Skin Books edition published in the UK as
The Singer in January 2006
Delta Trade Paperbacks edition / February 2007

Published by
Bantam Dell
A Division of Random House, Inc.
New York, New York

Book design by Sabrina Bowers

LIBRARY OF CONGRESS CATALOGING-IN-PUBLICATION DATA
DuQuesne, Aisha.
[Singer]
Soul siren / Aisha DuQuesne. — Delta trade pbk. ed.
p. cm.
Previously published as: The singer.
ISBN: 978-0-385-34074-8 (trade pbk.)
1. African American singers—Fiction. 2. African American
women—Fiction. 3. Serial murder investigation—Fiction.
4. New York (N.Y.)—Fiction. I. Title
PR6104.U67S56 2007
823'.92—dc22   2006021903

Printed in the United States of America
Published simultaneously in Canada

www.bantamdell.com

BVG   10   9   8   7   6   5   4   3   2   1

Show Time

There are three things you have to accept if you're going to read this book about Erica Jones. *This* book, not the one that's due to come out in the autumn by Easy Carson, which is supposed to be an "insider's view," or the quickie bio that's out on the stands now by that journalist for *Vibe*. Mine. All I ask of my reader is that you accept these three things going in. First, Erica Jones loves music. Second, Erica Jones likes sex. A *lot*. And third, perhaps most important of all, she told me everything. She confided in me, Michelle. Her personal assistant, gofer, occasional scapegoat and scratching post, in rare instances her ego booster but at the end of it all, I think—I hope—still her friend. Despite what I did.

I got to see Erica blow people's minds in stadiums, turning an audience into an army when she sang her smash hit "And You Think That Makes It All Right?" She saved the debut of that one for the Apollo Theater, for the place where Billie Holiday, Ella Fitzgerald, James Brown and so many great acts played. "If we're going to try it out, it *has* to be there," she insisted. A hit from the first night, so much so that I thought they were going to tear the place apart. And it only got bigger when she went from the Apollo to Madison Square Garden. I'll tell you about the songs.

And for all the great political consciousness the media gave her credit for, I saw her play the mega-bitch sometimes in the dressing room. But she was full of contradictions—just like the rest of us. The press would call her bullshit names like "R&B's Angry Young Woman" and compare her to Lauryn Hill, and there was Erica on her couch, vegging out and watching *Frasier* re-runs. *Spin* called her "black music's answer to Sinead O'Connor" yet she could be one of the most level-headed gals I ever knew, asking if a piece of real estate was going to appreciate in a certain neighbourhood. She wanted to build a day care center on the site. She was never the diva in my mind. Never.

Then there was Luther. I'll tell you about him, too.

And I have to tell you about myself. Well . . . for the obvious reasons. You must have read about it in the newspapers, everyone has, but at least I can set a few things straight. For those same obvious reasons, this book has been hard to finish, and it finishes with me, not Erica. I can't help that. I don't know what's going to happen now.

Funny thing is, I started this book and did my first interviews with a little tape recorder long before all the ugly business (I can't even remember when, but certainly after the jump to the new label and before work on the *Drum* album). And according to America's gloriously ironic and bizarre system, I still have legal rights to all that material. I thought I could write the thing just from what I knew, what I kept in my heart and my head, but when I finally woke up from my naïvety and realised I should do research, I should interview people, I discovered everyone had an opinion about her.

"Erica Jones can suck my dick!" Easy Carson barked at me over the phone. I'd known then he was a long shot, but

I had wondered if enough water had floated under the bridge to wash away the resentments on both sides. Apparently not. "She can suck my dick," he repeated. Then, thinking he was really clever, he added, "Course she already has, and it wasn't that fucking good a job anyhow! *I'm* gonna set the record straight in my own book, Michelle. You wait. Shit, I made her! I founded this company!"

"But she put it on the map," I argued.

"Erica cares about nobody else but Erica," he shot back, just before he slammed down the phone in my ear.

"Erica Jones is a success not because of Easy Carson or Steven Swann or any of those other guys," Morgan told me.

He said this in that amazing deep voice of his, tugging as usual on his beard that made him look like a jazz sage. Morgan was a "beautiful ugly man" as they say, the kind whose gaunt features made you think he hadn't gone out to see the world, the world had come and steamrolled over him.

"Erica Jones is a success because for someone like her, there couldn't be anything else. She ain't ruthless, she's *driven*. How can folks bitch about her pushing them out of her way when they're supposed to be record producers, promoters, musicians and so on? Can't they do their jobs? What are they there for if not to help her along?"

Morgan, poor gentle Morgan.

(*I am so sorry now.*)

"Erica Jones let full-figured women have permission to be elegant again," said Phylicia Saunders, the designer. "You take an artist like Lil' Kim who just puts it out there with her big tits and her big batty. I think she plays up to guys' immature ideal of a perfect woman when she's in her bikini outfits or lingerie. Erica's got the same type of body, ample breasts and a generous backside, but she doesn't dress slutty. She's sexy."

And I think this is true, even though Phylicia is indirectly promoting herself. For the *Drum* album tour, Erica signed an exclusive deal to wear her costume designs on stage.

"Erica Jones?" laughed a concert dancer who doesn't want me to use his name. "Erica Jones is a succubus. You know, the mythological woman who—"

"I know what it is," I interjected. I didn't need the pedantry.

"Well, Erica Jones likes her raunch," he went on.

And he reminded me of his own special perspective on the show in Minneapolis.

I was, as usual, in the wings, gaping in wonder at how a song, a personality, an image, could bring thirty thousand people (*thirty thousand,* and that's the size of some small towns!) into this bowl of steel and concrete, all for cheering, applauding worship. For her. For my friend. The spotlights swept the sea of faces, the burly security guys pushing back the too-eager types in the front rows, and the imitation Nile Rogers guitar funk for the first song's arrangement blared from the towering black monolith speakers. I watched Erica step out in the Saunders dress that showed off her lovely brown legs, and that sound—that incredible sound of excited worship, the mass voice going *hhhhaaaaaaaa* like when you breathe against a mirror—floated back to the stage.

Erica's smiling face, her large eyes and small wide nose, her white teeth flashing, all of her joy at this response was up there on the jumbo screen behind the band. And she launched into the vocals for her updated rendition of "Buffalo Stance" by Neneh Cherry, a performer she immensely respected. *No money man can win my love, it's sweeeetness that I'm dreaming of . . .* Her new label had argued with her about releasing it as the first single, thinking a cover might not be well received. They wanted the title track, "Pariah," instead. Erica put her foot down. In the end, the cover song hit number five on Billboard and "Pariah" hit the top slot a month later.

I watched her sing seven tunes. Then there was the long instrumental arrangement that allowed for a costume change, the female dancers shaking it while Erica had her break, drank some water to cool her tired throat, towelled herself off and changed outfits. Fifteen minutes. And the male dancer, the one who confided in me and called her a succubus, says Erica pulled him into her dressing room. I can confirm this, because Erica finished song number seven and stepped into the wings, her chocolate brown forehead polished with sweat, a white bar glowing on her skin in the centre of her plunging neckline. Still smiling, still on her thousand-feet-in-the-air high from performing and being adored. "They're so kind tonight, man!" she said, beaming. She squealed with delight, and I saw her eyes flitting around the back of the wings, more energy in her than she could possibly burn off in one night. She saw the dancer. *Contact.*

Despite what you may have heard, I didn't think a lot got past me in my time with Erica, because I was always with her, and I did so many odd jobs, one of which included making sure she hit her cues on the tour, checking that she rested and didn't drop from exhaustion, generally making sure Erica Jones Is Happy. I'd noticed her and the dancer trading looks of interest all that week. Now I passed her dressing room to give a message to one of the production assistants, and the door was open a crack.

"She just yanked me in there," the dancer recalled in the phone interview. "And we're kissing and roaming our hands all over each other, and I didn't think we could do very much. I mean, shit, she had to go on in a few minutes! So did I. People would wait for Erica Jones, they don't give a fuck about me. But if I miss my cue, what the hell am I going to tell people, huh? Who's going to believe me?"

Erica managed to get the zipper down on the back of her dress in one deft move and let it puddle around her ankles, her large breasts tumbling out, everything visible for her man of the moment, from her curvy waist right down to the neatly trimmed wedge of pubic hair. Here was R&B star Erica Jones in her birthday suit right in front of him, and to be fair, what could anyone expect him to do? Resist? He was as hard as a rock in an instant. His costume pants were a tan silk—a deliberately light shimmering material to allow maximum gymnastic movement for the routines on stage, and he was tenting through them. Erica grabbed his sheathed cock in one firm squeeze.

He claims she practically slammed him down on a long table, the kind they put in stars' rooms for decorative assortments of canapés, congratulatory flowers, snacks. He was already topless, as all the rest of the male dancers were, each one a tall proud black man with muscle definition like you wouldn't believe, perfectly formed six-packs and broad chests and arms like superheroes. "Mish, why do half of them have to be gay?" Erica complained to me one night. This one wasn't. She tugged down his trousers to thigh level. The head of his cock was pushing out of his Jockey shorts, the sack of his balls stretching the hem near his leg. Erica snatched up a pair of fabric shears—the kind the costume assistants kept handy to remove any threads, to keep the outfits impeccable. In one brief chop, she cut away his underwear, and her fingers lightly caressed his long engorged penis, veins and blood vessels standing out with his want.

She was wet and ready for him. Erica confessed to me that doing live performances—especially in major venues— gave her not only a high but it made her so sexually charged she had to find an outlet. So I knew the dancer was telling the truth when he said she supplied the condom.

I also knew because when I passed her dressing room

with the slightly open door, I saw her mounted on top of him, impaling herself on that glistening spear of his. I saw his cock disappearing into her as she rocked and rocked, her breasts swaying, her eyes shut tight and her mouth wide open, crying out "Yeaaahhh, yeaaaahh, yeah, yeah!" Her nails dug into his chest, and she looked down at him with a kind of angry hunger. Jesus, I thought, frozen with the sight of them for a moment, unable to tear my eyes away, Erica's buttocks quivering slightly with the momentum. And for all his pose of betrayal when I interviewed the dancer, I saw his expression in that dressing room. He loved it. I saw him pinch her nipples, his wide hand feeling her ass, as if somehow she wasn't real and it wasn't happening to him.

Erica could be larger than life even in sex, her breasts looking even fuller with her wide brown areolae puckered, her nipples hard, a bead of perspiration running down her short flat midriff. I'm just saying as one woman about another, she was beautiful. Without any makeup or today's mandatory photo retouching for CD covers, Erica could be amazingly beautiful.

How many times had I caught glimpses of her in intimate moments like this? Me, Michelle Brown, her PA. PG, more like it. Private Ghost. And as she said, her appetite was all-consuming. It's not like she was so bold as to do things right in front of me, but she was often negligent of the fact that I might be in the house or near the hotel suite of any given week. I have seen Erica Jones intimate in whatever degree of importance or depth she brought to the man or to the occasion—Erica making love when it *was* love, Erica having sex, Erica fooling around, foreplaying, afterplaying, fucking because that's what it was when it was her raw need. And I have to say she was beautiful every time. But then I always thought she was.

I heard the floor director coming up the hall. "Cutting it kind of fine tonight, aren't we, Michelle?"

I stood right in the middle of the hallway, discreetly blocking the way to her room.

"You know who you're dealing with," I said a bit too curtly. Meaning Erica was a professional. Meaning she'd be out there. I could be dismissed anonymously by a few of the press as one of Erica's entourage, a hanger-on, a leech, but I did have the job and the title, and that gave me power.

Fate was kind. The floor director walked away just before he would have heard the loud wail of our star's orgasm down the hall. By the time I stepped back to the door, wondering what the hell I was going to say to move her along, I glimpsed Erica Jones feeling the last reverberations of coming, and then she was scrambling down from the table, muttering shit, I got to get out there. She barely noticed that the sticky condom was still half inside her vagina, and she was literally tugging it off his—

"*She* gets off and then just leaves!" the dancer reminded me on the phone.

As Erica had climbed off, the dancer still lay there, his pants around his thighs, his underwear in shreds, and he couldn't stop himself. On top of him or not, she had brought him to a boil. His cock stiffened and pointed at a new higher angle, and a geyser of cum exploded onto his legs and on his pants. Unconsciously, he grabbed his penis and jerked himself a little, needing to hold on to the feeling for another precious second. Then he saw the mess.

"Son-of-a-bitch!" he barked. "I can't go on stage like this!"

Erica wasn't listening. She had already ducked into the shower and was using the hand-held nozzle to wash between her legs. At this point, I thought, screw it, and I stormed into the dressing room. I had two full seconds of a glimpse at the dancer's now limp cock, still dribbling cum onto his legs and pants, and he looked wide-eyed at me and covered himself with his hand as he sat there like a fool on the table.

"Not interested," I said. And I wasn't. I was intent on doing my job. Protect the Star.

I slid open the glass panel of the shower, not caring about the flying specks of water drenching my T-shirt, and Erica was on her toes as she plunged her face into the spray of water overhead. "I know," she said. She was aware she was running out of time.

"You've got maybe three minutes tops," I scolded and took her gently but firmly by the arm.

"Mish!" she squealed, covering her breasts as she stepped out of the shower, her eyes flicking towards the naked man on the table. As if there truly was anything left for her to be modest about. But her indignant noise made a peculiar kind of Erica-sense. The moment was over. They'd had their fun, and she didn't want him seeing her like that anymore.

"What the hell do we do about your makeup?" I asked.

"Forget makeup," said Erica. "I sweat it off anyway under those lights. I need to get dressed." And she gave me the eye while her hand made a coded gesture: *shoo*. I had to get rid of the dancer on the table.

"Oh, man," he was groaning.

I turned around and stood between him and Erica. One word should give the hint. "Please."

In this business, I tried to be the last ambassador of good manners, and sometimes people were astonishingly grateful for it, sometimes the effort was wasted.

"What the fuck am I supposed to do?" the dancer was whining at me, though I was glad he was finally getting off the table and shuffling to the door. His right hand had grabbed a fistful of the waistband to tug up his pants. "I can't go out there like this! What the hell am I supposed to do?"

"Have more control," muttered Erica, sitting at her mirror.

"Hey!" he yelled angrily.

"Hey, yourself," I told him. "Aren't you on in a minute?"

They were barking his name up the hall, losing their patience, and the floor director was saying, *"You are thirty seconds from getting your ass fired!"*

The dancer uttered the "c" word under his breath and ran out the door.

$\mathcal{L}$ook," I told him when he had finished his rant over the phone, "I was just going to ask some general questions about the tour, about how the crew and the dancers were, confirm a couple of things. I wasn't going to get into all this sh—"

"Well, if you don't include shit like this, then you ain't telling the whole story now, are you, Michelle?" he fired back.

Which is why it's included. I still can't summon much sympathy for him. If he had come first and taken his pleasure inside her, I doubt he would have given any thought that he was making Erica Jones late without getting her off. She had just done a wham-bam to him the way men had been doing it to women since Creation, and I told him so.

"That just explains why you're the way *you* are, Michelle, that doesn't explain her," he said.

He must have heard my sharp intake of breath over the receiver, because he added in a quiet, reflective voice, "But I thank you for saving my job."

"Erica spoke to the director."

"The hell she did."

He was right. I had spoken to him, using her name. Erica was oblivious to the guy's fate.

She still missed a cue during that concert, but not because of her tryst in the dressing room. Thirty thousand fans cheering and calling for her return forty-five minutes later, and Erica was behind the roadies' trailer with her mobile in a serious long-distance conversation.

She was helping her nephew Jake back in Scarborough, Ontario, with his homework, doing her best to remember the original provinces of Canada's Confederation in 1867. "Nova Scotia was definitely one, so was Prince Edward Island, ummm, Quebec, Ontario—oh, shit. *Maybe* New Brunswick? Doesn't your Mom have an encyclopaedia in the house? Vi?" Calling now. "Vi! Violet, I will *buy* you an encyclopaedia, girl, okay?"

She saw the production assistant with his pleading open arms. *Just a minute,* she mouthed. This was Family, capital *F*. She would take as much time as Jake needed.

We lost Erica Jones," opined *Maclean's,* Canada's own homegrown version of *Time* and *Newsweek.* "We lost her because of the blinkered incompetence of a complacent music industry." Harsh but true.

It had started for her up in Canada. She was the fifth child of a reasonably well-off dentist who had a practice in the West End of the country's biggest city, Toronto. We laughed our heads off when we read the publicity bios Easy Carson released for her second album. Then we were appalled. "Erica Jones grew up on the mean streets of Toronto's Jane and Finch district, Canada's own version of Compton." Yes, Jane and Finch used to be known as a poor and rough part of town, but it sure as hell was no Compton.

"Easy, what is this shit?" Erica demanded. "I grew up five blocks from High Park, man!"

High Park. It was one of the most solidly middle-class neighbourhoods in the city, and it's nowhere near Jane and Finch. I knew this because I was one of six black students who went to Sir John A. MacDonald High School, and Erica was one of the others. High school wasn't where Erica first discovered music—no, she got that at home, her gift nurtured by the family piano, her parents and the choir of her local church. But school was where she *knew* beyond doubt she'd become a star. School was also where I discovered what I was, and Erica played a part in that discovery, too.

Easy, however, didn't want to settle for the dewy image of star-struck talented girl flees secure middle-class background. Like his would-be rap stars, Erica was supposed to bloom through the cracks of cement and deprivation.

Easy Carson himself can be a stereotype: the shady black music executive with the grim past. That is sadly part of him. His big joke—his one joke—was that he wasn't a record producer back then, he was a "motivator." To be near him in real life as he said this, you took his meaning, because Easy is six foot one and over two hundred pounds. A black man who gets what he wants by intimidating with his size—or so you might believe. His face is that of a big ebony baby, and I suspect he keeps his hair cropped short just to make you think that. His face reminds me of the actor Forrest Whitaker. The rest of him is a wall of muscle. Some of what you hear about Easy Carson and Easy Roller Records is true, and some of it, well . . .

He tells people today that he got his nickname because his Mom liked Walter Mosley books, and the "Easy" handle came from borrowing the nickname of Mosley's Easy Rawlins. But Carson was born LaMarque Daniel Carson, and when he started weightlifting in his teens a smartass buddy called him "Easter Island," suggesting he looked like one of those dark monolithic statues. Easter got shortened to "Easy." He did have a long juvenile record, mostly for petty break-ins and threatening assaults. And while he calls himself a producer, I know for a fact that Easy cannot read or play one note of music. He wanted—still wants—to make money.

"Easy went into music because he was smart enough to realise he was heading for a prison cell," recalls one old friend. "He says, 'This is the quick way, and it's legal.' Everybody thinks he just glares at you and folks give in, but he's also a sweet talker. *He spots talent.* He gets the creative folks together. People winced at the beginning because he put his name down in credits as a producer, but he worked his ass off to get them the right equipment, to hustle the money for studio time, to promote the shit out of a tune. If he didn't do the mixing, so fucking what? He did practically everything else."

Carson got his start by chasing squatters out of an abandoned paint warehouse on Lexington and then corralling friends into helping him fix it up into a nightclub. "It was typical of him that he ran the joint for three months without giving a goddamn thought to any liquor licenses or building codes or whatever." But this, too, was eventually all taken care of. He found talented DJs to play and used the place to test-drive new artists and groups. A former bouncer told me that Carson's policy was very clear over any trouble at the club, whether gang related or petty squabbles over a jostled arm or talking to the wrong fellow's girl. "Your job is protect the furniture," he instructed. "People can duck and shit. People can get the hell out of the way. There ain't no Blue Cross for our glasses and chairs."

His music label was born in a back room of the club. As late as my coming onboard with Erica, all the equipment for those modest early sessions was still in there—a Zoom

MRS-1044CD hard disk recorder that allowed you to record instruments on 100 virtual tracks (you even had reverb
and equalization on that puppy), a Yamaha S80 keyboard
and two Rode NT2 microphones. That was their whole
kit, and it had cost Easy less than $3,000. Of course, Erica
didn't record with that stuff. Easy's business had grown by
then, and he wanted the best for his artists.

He also wanted to keep those artists around. When contract disputes dragged on, he would sic lawyers on a guy
for taking freelance producing gigs to keep groceries on the
table. I personally saw him fire people when he learned
they were scouting for a job at another label. But no one
has ever offered me a tale of him physically harming anyone.

People actually ask me today why I didn't do anything
about Easy Carson. As if I hadn't thought of starting what I
did earlier. I always have to laugh.

I tell them the truth. Erica took care of Carson in her
own way. She didn't need me that time. And if I had known,
oh, if I had known...

When I met him, Easy was boyishly shy, his eyes nervously checking the ground as he asked how I liked New
York and where I hoped my own career would take me.
"He's clumsy when he flirts," I was told by a woman bartender from the club. "He's got no confidence at all, and if
he gets with women, it's because his friends hook him up.
When I went out with him, he put his big meaty paw on my
thigh and confessed how he really liked me. It was kinda
sad."

He met Erica, in fact, because one of his hangers-on
pointed her out to him at a party up on 127th Street—not
because she was a promising vocalist but in the hopes that
Easy could get her into bed. Like Lurch from the Addams
Family, Carson lumbered over to her, interrupting the conversation she was having with one of the guys from the

group Blue. "I hear you sing. Maybe you heard I produce records."

Erica smiled at his bluster, sizing him up in one look, and said, "I haven't heard of you at all."

"Well, we should fix that," said Easy, and he gave her a toothy grin.

Erica told me later that she wasn't taking the conversation too seriously. She wasn't so naïve as to think a guy wouldn't try to get her into bed by claiming he had his own record label. "But, Michelle, he kept putting his weight on one foot then the other, looking around, biting his lip, I thought: he's either really what he says or the boy's completely deluded!"

Easy talked about how he wanted the label to expand beyond hardcore rap and take on a couple of promising R&B artists. Erica listened carefully. She hadn't heard of his performers, and Carson sheepishly mentioned that he wouldn't expect her to—he "hoped" they would be big. He didn't brag. He didn't name-drop. He didn't even have a business card. He held up one of his huge hands palm forward and begged her to stay put. Then he went and begged the host of the party to go dig out a magazine that mentioned him and his label. She began to think he was sincere. When he actually came back with a little sidebar article with his name in bold, she agreed to meet him for lunch at Sylvia's Soul Food restaurant and talk business. And that was how Erica Jones joined Easy Roller Records.

I don't know what you'd call their relationship. If you stood in the company office's foyer and watched their conversation in those days, there were times when Erica would still be nodding her head like a little girl, saying, " 'Kay, 'kay..." She used to defer to Easy on matters of promotion, on when to bring her album out and why it was better to wait, on how she shouldn't take this or that gig because it made her look small-time. And yet Easy didn't interfere with her sound. I recall one instance when he poked his head in the studio, and Erica put down her Coke and asked, "What can we do for you, Easy?"

"Oh, nothin'."

"Well, it's a pretty small room, and you take up the space of three people," Erica shot back.

And with that, he turned and left. He was her manager, and this is the way she would talk to him. She hadn't yet turned twenty-one.

"Do you tell people about us?" she asked him once as we all piled into his four-wheel and headed out to a gig at a club in Brooklyn.

"Shit, no!" he declared, his baby face scrunched up in disgust at the question.

"You don't?" said Erica, which was her way of saying, *Why not?*

Easy Carson doesn't have an MBA or even a lot of common sense, but he does have cunning, and his explanation gave me one of the best displays of it. "Because, Erica, if I go around town with you on my arm, bragging how we do it, how much fucking credit they gonna give you, huh? That gonna make you look good? Or me? They'll think I front every pussy who comes along and smiles my way, and they'll think you get to open your mouth on stage after sucking my cock out back."

"Can you *please* rein in the gutter mouth?" I asked from the back seat.

I could never stand him talking like this. The fact that he did was a reminder of his emotional immaturity, how he had never learned to talk like an adult male who discarded the crude vocabulary back at the playground.

Easy grumbled that "Hey, Erica asked"—as if he couldn't have put it a nicer way—then made a poor joke about how Canadian black girls were so uptight. We were the only ones he knew. Neither of us was in the mood to challenge this assertion.

I never asked Erica why she was briefly with him because the reason was obvious. She used him. They used each other. Erica claimed that she had genuine sexual curiosity about him in the beginning, and that he was almost sweet in how passive he was.

She says they stopped by the nightclub one evening, and under the flashing red and blue lights, surreal with no music on and an empty dance floor, she undressed him until he stood before her completely naked.

Tree trunk legs, a chest like a menacing storm cloud, wide and dark. *He towers over me,* she thought. She went to embrace him, and his massively thick arms completely enveloped her, his dark brown cock hot against her short belly and so long that its red bulb brushed the under curve of her left breast. When she lay down and opened her legs for him the very first time on the blanket of their coats, the size of him simultaneously scared her and thrilled her. She gasped as more and more of him pushed into her vagina, but she couldn't take him all the way in. She says that making love to Easy was like swimming underneath docks, her shoulders gated by the thick posts of his arms, lying in the shadow of that chest, and he rammed like a bull inside her until a hot stream of his spunk poured into her like a flood. She says she came the first time they slept together, but she never did again.

"You hurt me when we try," she told him.

Easy had dropped his eyes to the floor. Erica didn't go into how he had no concept of foreplay, of seduction, that after a few kisses and a couple of hugs, he was ready for his jackhammer performance. She claimed he was simply too long and thick for her, which may well have been true, and though he lost out on sex, it was an explanation that consoled his childish ego.

They didn't sleep with each other anymore, but it didn't put an end to their sexual involvement. They needed each other for business. By now, there was a buzz in the clubs about Erica, and she had a use for her manager. Carson also knew he had a good thing, too good to get ruined by spats and atmosphere. I suspect what happened between them was Erica's idea, and it was this: Easy had installed a two-way mirror that looked out on the dance floor. "Check this out!" he'd giggle, a kid with a new toy, showing how no one could see into the side office unless he switched a specific set of lights on the glass. Several of us warned him it would be pointless to have it if he didn't shut up about it.

Erica knew about the glass. And it was perfect for her to give Easy a very different kind of performance. She would give him an informal message earlier in the day, "Video night tonight," or ask me to pass it on to him with a word or a phone call, thinking they were both cute. He'd know to be in the club ahead of her that evening.

She brought casual lovers there after hours, never anyone serious. She put something on the stereo system, and as her man of the evening pulled her into a clinch, she always suggested, "No, no, over here . . . It's sexy over here." Here on the black leather couch, where she could urge her man to sit down, and then fall backwards into his lap, pushing herself against his groin. A tug of the zipper, and her dress was a satin halo around her hips, her breasts practically spilling out of her bra cups. Fingers checked her erect dark nipples, pinching them, rubbing them urgently, and as Erica's mouth opened in a gasp, she half rose to ease down her soaked panties, the hand of her lover slipping down from her midriff to her inner thigh.

She opened her legs much wider than she needed to, hooking them behind his ankles as his fingers strummed her clitoris and felt the shining wet lips of her pussy.

Craning her head back to kiss her man, the lift of her ribs like the spread of dove's wings with the arch of her back, and there was the sweet flex of her thigh muscles as she opened her legs still wider, and his fingers disappeared into her vagina.

Kissing him, tasting him, one eye open and staring ahead, her man always thinking it was a turn-on to see the two of them in the mirror. And behind the glass was Easy. I've caught the fingerprint smudges of that wide hand on the glass, evidence that he must have leaned against it, his hungry concentration so intense, his want so close to its object of desire but separated from her, his other fist kneading that huge cock she said he had, brown flesh reddening, veins like tree roots into the black bush of his pubic hair, his testicles contracting into a tight round ball of skin.

And now the couple had progressed to the patch of carpeted floor in front of the couch. Erica's mouth was open in a kind of plea as her face appeared to him upside down, eyes shut as her orgasm made an exquisite warning deep in her core, gathering strength, her fingers clawing into her date's chest as she struggled to raise her knees higher, and her lover's swollen penis sunk into her again and again, Erica's breasts quivering with the momentum.

"See me! See me! Ahhhh—ahhh—ahhh!" she chanted. Her date assumed she was speaking to him, taking it as a prompt to be even more aroused by her coming. "I see you, babe," he groaned back. And with a final groan, the dam inside him would burst. Or a guy would pull out of her and shoot streams of his sticky warm sauce onto her breasts and stomach. Or one night, her man reared up out of her, calling for her to please take him into her mouth, and Erica gripped him in one confident motion and sucked him in, digging her fingers into the base of his cock, making it swell even more as he cried out with his release. Behind the glass, stifling a tortured whimper, Easy unravelled. I could never find Easy Carson attractive, but I think if I saw him that way, the great muscled tower of him naked like that and stroking himself in worship of Erica, I believe I would have found him at least briefly . . . noble. It sounds peculiar to use that word for it, but to me it's right. Or maybe it's because I thought for the longest time we could all be better because of Erica.

I knew what she did in that club for him, or if you want to be harsh in your judgement, *to* him. I knew her little suggestive smiles when her date wasn't looking, her eyes searching for contact behind the glass, how she actually enjoyed him watching her like this and how it reinforced her upper hand in their relationship. Because one night I didn't pass on the message to Easy, and the spectator in the office behind the two-way mirror was me.

*T*he loft space. I am back in the loft space often when I dream. It's peculiar, but I don't castigate myself over and over for the studio. No, it's the loft that plays a loop in my head. Nights when I can see the framed posters of Blue Note album covers for Miles Davis and Thelonius Monk, when I have to involuntarily smile again at the black lacquer bust of Beethoven. What am I doing here? I'm making mistakes. I know enough not to touch the dead body at my feet, but I still make fatal errors.

It is someone else who did this, not you. That's what you have to tell yourself. Emotional detachment. You're going to find what you came for and go, because that's what you do. You're Michelle, and you clean up the messes. You're loyal.

I go through a mental checklist of what I've touched without gloves, still dithering whether to leave them be since I'm a regular visitor here, or to wipe them clean. I opt for wiping them, erasing my presence here tonight. I will be careful, I will be so careful.

And as I rifle anxiously through the drawers wearing my latex surgical gloves, a onetime friend cold at my feet behind the couch, I curse under my breath and chant that I did it for you, Erica, I did it all for you. . . .

Beginnings

It was ironic that Easy Carson, projecting all his gangsta rap executive bluster and never dreaming of backing it up, became a target for Jamal Knight. Because Knight was *the real deal*. As much effort as Easy put into his bad boy front Knight dedicated to his own illusion of respectability. He had a handsome square face of pecan colour and light brown eyes, a thick moustache above his ready smile of caps, and he favoured Hugo Boss suits. I have been told that he owned nice cars but made sure that he never drove himself—not because he wanted to push an image with a chauffeur but to avoid any police harassment. He didn't like being pulled over. If he had to be ordered out of the car, he would suffer it in the role of a passenger. If cops were going to dream up a BS charge then it could stick to someone else's licence and not his own.

Jamal Knight was actually a mere two inches taller than me and not a muscular guy, but he exuded violence in a way that Carson's bulk never could. I was told that he attacked people who wronged him like a rabid dog. The person who told me this walks with a metal crutch and moves in a limping palsy gait, suffering permanent neurological damage. He had made the mistake of trying to attack Knight with a beer bottle over a gang slur.

"Man smiles a lot," says another former associate. "When he stops smiling, someone will bleed." Knight had taken over whole blocks with the old stand-by of the protection racket. When a storeowner lay with his face on his floor tiles and his arm pinned behind his back, Knight often informed him, "Look, even if we kill you, man, you're still going to have to pay."

And Easy Roller Records owned recording studios in Jamal Knight's Brooklyn neighbourhood.

While Easy couldn't relate to women and had trouble asking them out, Jamal thought he was smooth, Brooklyn's new improved Samuel L. Jackson, taking his dates to the Rainbow Room and then up to the Empire State Building roof. Erica told me that she did find Knight attractive, even clever and fun to talk to. He told funny self-deprecating stories, accidentally locking himself out of his house (when, of course, he was never alone) or having to endure brothers who were dull tourists from Georgia on a flight home. But she had also heard the anecdotes of his real business, and they repelled her. "I don't want to go out with some criminal," she said.

Still, she found herself in a long conversation with him in Easy's nightclub when the place was hopping. Erica said that Jamal managed to cast doubt on his reputation by pretending he didn't know about it, that he must be a victim of nasty gossip. I saw him lead her towards the cloakroom, and Erica says that in the darkness, they began kissing, that Knight was a good kisser, stroking her chin and not rushing things. But he thought he didn't have to.

"We should get back," said Erica.

"Oh, come on," Knight told her with a laugh, "I'm not settling for just *that*."

Erica pulled back, and Jamal Knight's face was still trying to be smugly charming.

"Why shouldn't you settle for that?" she snapped.

"I thought there was an understanding," he replied, which pretty much explained everything to her. Not *we* have an understanding, the two of them. He said: I thought *there was* an understanding.

There was a lounge area near the second bar off the dance floor where you could actually hear yourself talk and it was nice to sit and chill. Easy was there with his pals, a few other people, including myself, getting numb on my fifth rum and Coke. I was sober enough to watch Erica march up to us, and in one swift move, she grabbed the old-fashioned grey phone that sat on the bar counter. She ripped the receiver of hard plastic and metal right out of the unit and began pistol-whipping Easy Carson with it, shouting all the time.

"*You fucking son-of-a-bitch!* You pimp me out like that? Where do you get off? *You want to pimp me out?* This how you manage your artists, you lazy-ass fucking pimp? Go solve your own goddamn gangsta shit! You have the nerve to—"

It would have been comical, this girl of about five foot four, wailing that phone receiver on that huge man who was cowering under her blows—if not for her volcanic rage, and the revolting and even potentially dangerous situation he had put her in.

"Erica!" pleaded Carson, and then he shouted, *"Owww!"* Because she had hit him right on the skull, and he was starting to bleed. And still she kicked and swung the phone club in her hand. "Erica, listen, I just figured you two would hit it off, never meant anything by it or—"

"He—said—you—had—an—understanding—" Every word punctuated with a blow of the phone. A couple of the guys came out of their stupor on the couch and rushed forward to pull her off, which prompted, "Get off me! Let me go! I'm gonna kill this bastard!"

Easy Carson was busy panting and holding his head, saying over and over, "I'm sorry, I'm sorry . . ."

I went to bed that night thinking: Well, that's it. They had a deal together, but she'd find an excuse to slip out of it. I proved once again that I didn't have the mind of a record producer or a star. By Wednesday morning over orange juice and toast, Erica said to me, "Mish, let's go see that stupid tree of a man." She wasn't going to break her deal. In the industry, his little stunt would become gossip but any breach of contract would be a point of fact. It wasn't the kind of history you wanted to carry with you when you tried to sign with Warner or Brown Skin Beats. She still needed Easy Roller Records if only for a while.

She confronted him with me in tow, and Easy, doing his best to keep what dignity he had left in front of his staff and buddies, ushered us politely but stiffly into his big office with the plush sofa, the wet bar and the PlayStation hooked up to the forty-inch TV in the corner.

"Erica—"

"Just let me get through this, please," she cut through him. "What I did last night—"

"Was justifiable, babe, completely," he said. "You within your rights, but I'm just sayin' I thought you two would hit it off, I never meant to give Jamal an impression you was—"

"*Easy.*"

He knew he'd better stop.

"I lost it, okay?" Erica gave a great sigh. "That was really stupid, Easy, but I wasn't very . . . smooth about telling you off. It'll make us both look like fools. So this is what we are going to do."

He was listening intently now, because the local media

had heard about the bust-up in the club and was phoning the reception, wanting to know what had happened. He had so far ordered "no comments," which only left the press free to speculate.

"Whatever you tell me, I'm still gonna have that fool Knight on my ass wanting to cut into our business," grumbled Easy.

"That's not Erica's problem!" I protested, but she gave me a look to say it was all right.

"Jamal will leave you alone," said Erica. "You're going to pay him a different way."

Carson forgot himself and lost his temper. "You want me to pay? How—"

"*Yes,*" she hissed. "And you'll do it because it's the smart move. Look, Easy, you are sitting on a couple of these recording studios out in Brooklyn, and half the time you're bitching about the maintenance—the roofs, the plumbing in the johns, whatever. You are going to sell these buildings to Jamal, and he will lease them back to you at very generous rates. You want him out of the music business? Well, I talked him into real estate. Your cleaning contractor, your maintenance contractor, all of 'em, will be your choices. It's a clean break, and it's only going to come around once. Take it."

I could almost see the gears moving behind Easy's forehead. As I said before, Easy was not the sharpest businessman, but he had an animal cunning, and he knew that if Jamal Knight craved respectability, their new relationship meant Knight would no longer have a victim but a tenant. He would gradually learn to solve any problems in the future with lawyers, not baseball bats.

"What about us?" he asked. "What about that whole bust-up in the club? How you gonna sprinkle magic fairy dust on that whole scene?"

Erica frowned as if he was being a bore. "Easy, you honestly think anyone was listening closely to what I was saying?
They were paying more attention to me wailing on you."

"And you did a damn good job of it, babe."

Her voice yanked firmly on the leash she now had on
him. "You *said* it was justifiable."

He nodded, swallowing hard. I noticed that the phone
on his desk had been moved to the bookshelf behind him.

"This is how we play it," said Erica. "You have your buddies leak the word that I was pissed you were going to sign
Kelly—" Kelly was one of the regular backup singers the
producers used. "You were going to let her have a couple of
my studio musicians while I'm busy cutting the album. So I
came in and lost it. You make out that Kelly and I can't
stand each other . . ."

Easy and I both traded looks of startled wonder. She had
clearly thought out all the angles. "But you're not—you're
not going to look good from spin like that!" he argued.

Erica laughed. "I am going to look *very* good, Easy. Your
label gets in the press, a little opera with the R&B, and you
even have reporters licking their chops over the idea of a
catfight. Look, I'd rather play a diva than a chump. Or a
whore. Do I have to say it, Easy?"

Carson met her eyes and then looked away once more to
the blotter. Did she have to say it? That he better not ever
try such an ugly stunt again? No, she did not.

As Erica and I left, I told her how I was amazed that she
had managed to talk Easy into giving up his buildings like
that.

"Thank *your* Dad for me next time you talk to him," she
explained. "Your sixteenth birthday party, he started talking
to me about how the only sure investment is real estate. The
man must have learned something from building all those
houses. Your Dad's really smart, Mish."

"Yeah, he is," I said idly.

Erica had always been sharp—sharp enough to know that once you have a lot of money, you have to learn how to hang on to it. But I was still thinking about the deal she had cooked up for the others. It seemed to me that Carson hadn't properly thought it through. Yes, Erica and I were both so young, but even then I knew it was better to be a landlord than a tenant. Maybe Easy figured selling the studio buildings was more appealing than having his legs broken.

"In six months, Jamal Knight won't be a problem anymore for Easy. I did him a favour. I did us all a favour."

"How do you get *that*?" I asked.

"Mish, all these guys think about is tomorrow, they never think about the day after tomorrow. The authorities are planning this major new road to connect Jervis Street to Stone Concourse over in Bedford Stuy. Guess where it runs through? Anyone reading a paper with a map and a felt marker can draw a line right through Easy's buildings."

"Holy shit!"

"Hey, don't worry, Michelle. Do you honestly believe Easy Carson or Jamal Knight read *The New York Times*? Do you think they even pick up *The Post*? I remember reading about it because I was scouting around in the papers for the new apartment. So in six months, the government will knock on Jamal's door and say, hey, we're taking these whether you like it or not, here's your compensation. Which, of course, will be below market value, but he'll take it because he won't have a choice. And Jamal *knows* Easy Carson would never be aware of this in advance. So Easy will look blameless. Jamal thinks I came up with the real estate scheme to fuck Easy over for his little pimping stunt."

"Isn't Jamal suspicious that you'd want to help him?" I asked.

"We were kissing in the coatroom so I can't look too

pissed at him, just annoyed over his expectations. The guy can understand that I don't like to be taken for granted."

"Jesus, after this, I'll never take you for granted!" I said. Not that I ever did.

Erica tossed her head back and laughed, then threw an arm around me. "Ah, come on, Mish! You're my friend. They were screwing me around, so I got them out of my way." She shook her head. "Men. You always have to treat 'em like pets or children."

Do you know he begged to stay with me? He wasn't man enough for me. . . .

The camera moves only a little as Mr. Jones does his best to keep it on his seventeen-year-old daughter up there on the stage of Sir John A. MacDonald High School. Erica doing a cover of a Toni Braxton song, and she is wearing an ear-to-ear grin because there are amazed cheers and whoops from in between the green and black lines of the basketball and volleyball courts. I was up there, too, supposed to be helping out on backup vocals, though you can barely hear my nervous soprano voice. I was only along because Erica begged me. I'm the one off to the right, out of focus. Michelle, reliably in the background.

I think that might have been the moment when she knew—she just knew it could happen, *would* happen for her.

As with so many other stars, for Erica Jones there had always been music in the family home. Her mother's old LPs and CDs included Chic, Al Green, Luther Vandross, Toni Braxton, Lauryn Hill, Eric Benét, Elton John, Tracy Chapman and vintage Earth, Wind and Fire. I remember being thirteen years old with Erica and another friend, all of us thinking her Mom was so cool as we danced around the kitchen to "Boogie Wonderland." Erica's Mom called it old music, we teased her by calling it prehistoric. But we danced happily away.

Erica's Mom was a singer, able to make incredible harmonies with anything that was playing on the stereo. It was her father who first sat Erica down at the piano, and on the shelf was a collection as impressive as his wife's—only it was mostly classical and jazz. Chopin, Bizet and Beethoven in the company of Lee Morgan, Charles Mingus, Art Blakey, Charlie Parker and Erroll Garner. Before becoming a dentist, Erica's father had tried to make a living with an alto saxophone. But in all the years I stopped by the house and heard Erica singing upstairs, her mother singing something else in her back garden, I never once heard her Dad play that saxophone—always the piano. Erica told me that her Dad used to compose songs, too, but I never heard him play one on that ivory keyboard either. *She* would. Erica's fingers would run along the keys for this or that bit of jazz fashioned by Mr. Jones, and then she would shrug over how Verve or Blue Note simply hadn't wanted it. If I politely asked her father about them, he'd smile shyly and mutter something about "artistic taste being subjective." I don't want you to think the man wore his grief over failed dreams on his sleeve—not at all. He hardly ever mentioned his old life.

When the years passed and Erica had three number ones on the Billboard chart, I was in the Jones house on a wintry afternoon for the Christmas holidays, and I put the question to him. "You and Erica's Mom were always so supportive. Didn't you ever try to get Erica to think of something else for a career? Like a backup, you know? Just in case?"

Mr. Jones adjusted his spectacles and stared ahead at the Christmas tree. "Didn't have to." And when he saw that I missed his point, he explained, "Michelle, she wanted to be a pop star. She was hell-bent on trying no matter what we said. Well, how many years of shelf life you figure they got on the charts? You see them leathery old Rolling Stones, Mick Jagger and that Sting guy and Bono doing their best to claw and hang on to their popularity! How many girls you see up there besides Madonna? And when you do, isn't it goddamn sad?"

I didn't believe this was really accurate or fair, but I didn't interrupt.

"Pop music is a young person's game, especially a young *man's* game," he went on. "You either hit it big right away, or you crash and burn. You're on the clock. Erica's making enough money now that she'll be set for decades if she's smart, and she is. But if she didn't get her break—if it had never happened, or if it came and went in a one-hit blur— there would have been plenty time for her to turn it all around and start again."

He sipped his eggnog and added darkly, "I certainly had to."

There was nothing I could think of to respond to this, and no answer was really needed. I don't think he was ever jealous of his little girl's success. I don't think he could have been more overjoyed. But in his words was a bitter contempt for the record industry machine that assumed its customer must be a child with a Ritalin attention span. This was the dragon his little girl was eager to slay, and she had to take her shot. He knew it.

"That's why you sent her to Morgan," I said.

He nodded gently and echoed the thought. "That's why I sent her to Morgan."

It would be a long while before I learned there was much more to it than that, more than even Mr. Jones knew was going on.

*M*organ would be her "thesis work," as she sometimes called him, while her first big lesson came in high school.

We both learned things about ourselves back at MacDonald High in Toronto.

People don't believe me when I say our high school experience was unique, which means they don't believe me when I say that, despite going to school in the Nineties, hey, we were up in Canada, so no metal detectors or pat-downs in the hall. Why should there be when even in Toronto gun crime used to be so rare? They don't believe me when I tell them we didn't have the American-style caste system where jocks and cheerleaders ruled. It just didn't happen that way. Maybe it's a Canadian thing. Canadian football is so poor we sure as hell were not likely to worship players of the high school version. After all, the national sport is *hockey*. No, in an upscale neighbourhood where folks drove Beamers and Mercedes and lived in five-bedroom houses, the cool kids, as strange as it sounds, were the intellectuals.

The whole thing was reinforced by who was teaching us—a bunch of left-wing expats. I said there were damn few of us black kids, but there were teachers of colour, ones like Mr. Emeruwa who taught us Chemistry. A Nigerian, he got on the wrong side of the Biafran War in the Sixties and lost his job at his nation's embassy in Washington, and he had nowhere to go. There was Mr. Charlton, a man with a ruddy light brown complexion whose South African accent always remained thick, who had killed for the ANC and who had fled to Canada. He used to hold up a textbook in our Political Science class and declare, "This book is published by Praeger Press, and who is behind Praeger Press? The CIA. Question *everything* you read."

And there was Miss Ogis, an exotically beautiful Indian woman, twenty-nine years old, with long black hair and a round face who taught Math and Physics and who coached the girls' basketball team. Every so often, because she was so gorgeous, one of the boys would make a come-on remark, thinking it was a code that only his giggling pals could understand.

Miss Ogis would flutter her lustrous eyelashes at the freshman teenager and say, "Mr. Hart, you make one more stupid comment about *Kama Sutra* or anything else like that in my presence, you will find yourself with so much trigonometry homework you'll be collecting your pension as a senior. Clear?"

She was petite but there was something challenging in those glamorous Indian features that made the boys back off, that in one glance immediately sized you up and found you wanting. She treated Erica no different from any other student, but I think she was irritated by Erica's popularity. In handing back a marked paper, I can remember Miss Ogis raising her voice from her desk, miffed that Erica and Debbie Farmer were softly rehearsing a number for Choir Class, "Miss Houston, can we talk about your grade or do I need to get clearance from the entourage?"

I think that's what influenced Erica's choice at the talent showcase, the Toni Braxton tune. She was being cheeky. And it was in the first term of our senior year when she got up on that stage and blew 'em away that things began to change. I have a copy of that videotape because I'm in it, and it's fascinating to examine the pre-star Erica. The girl smiling nervously, not knowing what to do with her hands, not yet groomed by the record industry. The cheers reaching a crescendo as she relaxes and begins to move around the stage for her second number, doing Lauryn Hill's "Everything Is Everything." "Come on, y'all, sing with me!" she shouted to the students in the gym, and suddenly we were not at a little talent show under basketball hoops and near bleachers, we were at a concert, her first one. *After winter*—

After winter, sang girls standing below, moving with the beat.

Must come the spring, sang Erica, and she let out the throttle on her voice and gave those white kids a gospel wail they had never heard before. *Change, it comes eventu-allyeeee...*

We had agreed that for the show, we'd each take turns backing up each other's numbers, with me bowing out of my chance to be in the spotlight alone. As the applause went on for the Lauryn Hill cover, Deb, who was right next to me, laughed and said, "There is *no way* I'm gonna follow that!"

So while other kids could be the Great Brain or the Stoner or the shy guy who bloomed in Drama class, Erica became The Voice. She was already trying to write songs but she wouldn't show them to anyone except me. I can recall her humming something as we sat in the hall, our backs leaned against our lockers over Spare Period, and I asked, "What's that?"

She flashed me one of those neon smiles of hers and said, "Something of my own. Well, my Dad helped a lot with it really. Mostly the bridge. He lets me use some of his old songs to put in my own." She laughed suddenly and added, "Sometimes I can't remember what I wrote and what he did anymore! You really like it, Mish?"

"Yeah," I answered, and I did. Funny to think that three years later, that snippet of music she sang for me would become "Late Night Promises." "Do some more."

"Nah, Deb's coming," she said, nodding her head towards our friend down the hall. Debbie Farmer, wearing at the moment Erica's borrowed sweater over a peach-coloured top—one that was the same design as the top Erica bought at the Suzy Shiers store on Yonge Street last week.

"So what if she is?" I whispered.

Erica ignored my question. "What do you think, Mish? You really like it?"

"This is what I mean," I complained. "I can barely pass

Choir! Deb knows music theory—you should sing it for
her."

"Michelle," she groaned. "Of course, Deb will like it!
She likes *everything*. It's like ... she tries too goddamn hard."

"She wants to be like you, that's all. You know? Imitation the sincerest form of flattery and all that?"

"I'm sorry, but it's embarrassing," said Erica. "I like her
and all, but, Jesus, girl, find your own style. Doesn't she
know I'd like her more if she thought for herself?"

"Why don't you tell her, then?" I suggested. Then I
added, "In a *nice* way."

Erica laughed. "This is why I love you, Mish. I don't
have to tell you stuff like that. And *you* help me. You make
me think." Her face clouded as a fresh notion occurred to
her. "That shit never bothers you, does it?"

"What?"

"What they say about you when we hang," explained
Erica. Then she dismissed the notion with a wave. "Forget
it, it's stupid."

"Erica," I said, "you trying to spare my feelings over
something?"

"No, no," she said, avoiding my eyes. "They shouldn't
talk about you like Deb. It's not the same ... I mean *you*
don't copy me, so I don't understand the seven-point-five
on the bitch-o-meter. You're just ... quiet. Always scribbling in your notebooks. Now that—that's not fair! I sing
you everything I come up with, and you never show me—"

I clutched my notebook close to my chest and leaned
away from her. "Hey, I didn't ask you about your songs!"

By now Erica was half hugging me, half trying to tear
the notebook out of my arms, and Deb bounded up, calling
out, "Hey, what's going on!"

"Mish is writing porn for Jason Todd to give to his new
girlfriend," said Erica matter-of-factly. "He's paying her to
do it."

"I am not!" I protested. "Shut up!"

"Fifty bucks," said Erica, making up a commission price for my talents on the spot.

And Deb, so trusting, laughed and looked at me as if I would actually make a confession.

I pointed a finger at Erica. "You! You are *evil*. People believe you when you say shit like that, and I don't know why!"

Erica was rolling on the floor, laughing away. "I know! Ain't it great? You have to look 'em straight in the face and talk about it like you heard it on the news."

"You love pulling stuff like that," I said, pretending to still be disgusted with her, but I couldn't. I never could.

Erica, making up stories just to test whether folks would believe her. Erica and her quirky sense of humour, which I suppose is another Canadian thing, when you think of a country that gave the world Mike Myers, Dan Aykroyd and Jim Carrey. And then Erica, The Voice. We reminisced about high school one night over a bottle of rum at her apartment in Manhattan, talking about teachers, talking about old boyfriends, which meant mostly hers since I only ever had two, and I learned something new about that time that helped shape her perspective. She recognised it herself.

"Alex Hardy." She said the guy's name like a swear. "Right after the talent show, he told everyone we slept together a couple of times. The son-of-a-bitch."

Her first taste of tabloid gossip without the tabloid. He hadn't breathed a word about their intimacy until she had sung those two songs up on the stage in the gym.

"You just can't trust them," she said. "They always want to get into your pants, then they want to advertise it."

"What are you going to do?" I said, which was my way of asking: What *do* you do? Because I told you at the beginning: Erica Jones likes sex. A lot. I had seen her appetite outweigh her judgement over discretion plenty of times.

"Never let 'em be able to talk about it," said Erica. "Ever, ever, ever."

It would be a while before I learned how exactly that was done in each case, before I learned all the corollaries of this maxim and what it meant for how Erica treated men, how she lured them in but kept them at bay. I don't think either of us dreamed it would put us both in such hot water.

*O*f course, there was a backlash in school over The Voice, and since we were Erica's crowd, we sensed and felt it first. I remember Deb, Sarah Copps and I all hanging around the Clinique counter in the Eaton's department store at Toronto's best-known mall, the Eaton Centre, when the peroxide bitches as we called them decided to accost us. Jasmine Dorsey, the leader, Natalie Blumenthal and Anna Wakowski.

"Hey, Deb, you did a really good job of imitating the scenery behind Erica," said Jasmine, and she and her friends broke into a spontaneous off-key imitation of our backing vocals. Then they burst into catty giggles—it was how the game was played.

"At least we had the nerve to get up there," snapped Debbie.

"But you backed out of following Erica, didn't you? I know *Michelle's* happy following her around like a puppy dog, but shit, Deb, I gave you credit for wanting to grab some spotlight for yourself."

"I didn't see you shaking your bony ass up on stage, Jasmine. But then I guess you're tired of putting out in the gym. And the lights *were* on that day."

We watched Jasmine's eyes widen.

My one contribution to all this smartass banter was to whisper to Deb, "You got to give her a two-second delay for it to click."

"Shut the fuck up, Brown!" Jasmine was telling me, while to Deb, she said, "You fucking—"

I saw Jasmine reach into her purse for her pepper spray. The story had gone around school that she liked to pull this trick on somebody she didn't like. She would need it, too. Deb was a tall girl with four brothers who had taught her how to fight dirty. She'd scratch the hell out of Jasmine and yank her hair out if she got a fistful. I would be out of luck if the other girls went for Sarah and me. I had never been in a fight in my life, not even in grade school, and my mother would have been horrified if I ever was.

"Just what are you girls doing?"

Miss Ogis. It was surreal to find her here, our teacher, dressed down in a T-shirt, jeans and a denim jacket. She looked even younger in casual dress, and I wondered if she would get carded if she decided to walk into a bar. Her soft yet stern voice made every one of us straighten up even though we were on neutral territory. I don't know if I even hid my relief.

"Jasmine was just complimenting our performance at the show," said Deb, folding her arms and giving her enemy the thousand-mile stare.

Jasmine didn't give a damn about playing along. She said sweetly, "And I was about to give Deborah here a sample of Mace I brought back from my trip to Rochester."

"That's what I thought," said Miss Ogis. "Only I know you won't do such a foolish thing. Not in a public place. And certainly not in front of *me*."

"It's Saturday," said Jasmine, still talking in a mild singsong, "and you're not our teacher here."

Miss Ogis matched her tone perfectly and replied, "That's right, Jasmine, I'm not. Which means I'm free to call the store security and tell them about the five lipsticks I saw you stash away in your purse."

I tried not to laugh as I watched the blood drain out of Jasmine's cheeks.

"So what's it going to be, my dear? You want to show how you're not a lady and have a fight right here by the counter? Or do you all want to take yourselves out on Yonge Street?"

Jasmine gave Deb, Sarah and me a last look full of daggers and turned on her heel. Off she went with her friends in tow. Miss Ogis turned and gave us a curt nod.

"I suppose you think she's worth it," she said.

Deb didn't know it was better for her to keep her mouth shut. "How can it be her fault? She's not even here!"

"No," said Miss Ogis. "No, she's not. Maybe you should think about that."

Roles

Deborah did think about it. I knew something was wrong, that something had profoundly shaken her up when we were playing basketball in the gym, MacDonald versus Danforth Collegiate. Deb badly fouled one of the Danforth girls, which cost us a penalty shot easily dunked through the hoop by her victim. I saw Miss Ogis go over to her on the bench and obviously ask *What's going on with you?* Deb shook her head, muttering a noncommittal answer I didn't need to hear. She kept playing, but her game was off. We lost. And long after the other girls had quickly showered and gone home, I finished up helping to put away some equipment and found myself staring at Deb's back as she leaned against the locker, her dark arms and neck still polished with sweat.

"You all right?" I asked.

"Yeah." Her voice raw with emotion.

"What's going on, Deb?"

"That stupid little bitch..."

"Who?"

She turned around, and I could see all the anger, all the

self-loathing and tearful pain. "Jasmine! That fucking little peroxide bitch. She really pegged it. I'm a joke, aren't I?"

She didn't know what to do with herself so she finally stripped off and grabbed her towel, going for a perfunctory shower. I stood outside the great tiled room, caught up in her rant, doing my best not to look like I was staring at the soap suds running down her long legs and her belly.

"What are you talking about?" I asked.

"Erica!" Deb shouted over the hiss of the water. "I've been such an idiot over her, Mish! I'm a joke. And you know what? It's gonna stop. I'm gonna find my own look, I'm not going to ask her *anything* anymore on how to do stuff and—"

"What?" I demanded. "All because of what that cow Jasmine said? Deborah, get real! She was talking about us singing—"

"It's bigger than that, and you know it, Michelle. Everybody thinks it's so funny—"

"It's not like that," I argued. "I borrow clothes from Erica, she borrows clothes from me, and you—"

"*No,*" she insisted, stepping out and towelling herself off. "You guys swap stuff. She doesn't need anything of mine. She doesn't hang on *my* every word. You want to be part of the Erica Jones fan club, Mish? You carry on without me. Jesus..."

She was frantically getting dressed, and as she pulled out her top from the locker, she noticed it was another one of her collection that she'd copied from Erica's wardrobe. Standing in her bra, wishing she could toss it aside and wear anything else but. She looked up at the ceiling.

"A fucking joke," she muttered again.

"You're not," I said, hugging her now to comfort her. "You're beautiful, you're talented. You know that, you must know that..."

I wrapped my arms around her waist, patting her back,

and she held on to me for what felt like dear life. She was half a head taller than me, my face buried in her hair, her body so warm, and I don't know what it was that made me lose my mind, but I kissed her neck like a close friend, like a sister. And as she sniffed and pulled back to rub her eyes, I had my face very close to hers, and I moved in.

Startled, she stared at me and demanded: *"What the hell are you doing?"*

Oh, God. Oh God Oh God Oh God Oh God—there's no taking it back. Idiot, you're an idiot, oh no—

"Nothing, Deb, you're upset, and I was trying to make you feel—"

"Mish, get your hands off me! What is this?"

Dying inside, I still held her hands and wasn't letting go. She yanked them savagely back even while I said, "You don't understand! I didn't mean anything, Deb, please don't make such a big deal out of—"

"I'm not stupid, Michelle! I know you and Erica think I am, but I'm not! And I'm not a . . ."

"I'm *not* either," I said stupidly, as if a denial could do anything now.

"I can't deal with your shit on top of mine, Mish." And she stormed out of the locker room.

*I*t was me upset now, wailing uncontrollably, facing a worse shame than Deb could ever expect in the MacDonald hallways, and I was still crying when *she* found me in the shower, hugging myself against the wall, wondering how I could come back the next day. Miss Ogis, stepping forward just beyond the sprinkling beads of water, no longer in her coaching track suit but in her formal wear for the classroom.

"You're going to be all right," she said.

"You don't know," I sobbed, "you don't know..."

"Yes, I do," she said. "I heard."

"You...? You heard us?"

She kicked off her shoes and stepped closer to me, putting a hand on my bare shoulder. "Poor dumb Deborah hasn't even guessed the real truth of it, has she?"

I felt my nose running as I stood naked in the pounding spray of water, and it was this that temporarily embarrassed me. Fool. Your nose running while all of what you are will be out there tomorrow for ridicule. I wiped my nose and rubbed my eyes. Hurt and broken, I said, "What are you talking about?"

"Deborah. She dresses like Erica, she wants to sing like Erica...She even copies her gestures. That's why you reached out to her. And that silly girl doesn't even know she's not the one you really want."

I felt my body racked by a new uncontrollable sob of agony and I slid down the tiles of the wall to my knees.

"Come on now, come on," whispered Miss Ogis, kneeling quickly and rocking me in her arms. "Despite what the books say, no one ever died from having an overflow of love to give."

"I'm—tomorrow's freak—for—for Home Room!" I stuttered through sobs.

"No, you're not," she whispered. "You won't be. Honest. You're a beautiful girl, and there is nothing—*nothing* wrong with this need you feel. Or how you want to express it."

Her face was very close to mine, and her fingertips were gently caressing my face. She wasn't clumsy and unaware of what she was doing, not like I was with Deborah.

I could taste the salt of my tears running down my cheeks, and I had forgotten for a moment that I was naked, wrapped up in my own shame and personal agony. I heard Miss Ogis whisper again *Come here,* and she embraced me protectively once more, her hands running down my back. When I sat back against the tiled wall, I laughed self-consciously because her blouse was all wet from the hug, and she shook her head to say, Hey, forget it.

"You don't know what to do with yourself, do you?" said my teacher.

Her fingertips ran down both my breasts and then ever so gently felt their weight, and she held my eyes. "Do you want to know what it's all about?" she asked me. "Do you want to know how it can be?"

I nodded dumbly like a child, feeling the rush of heat between my legs. I sat there, still half in the spray of the shower nozzle like rays of a spotlight, beads of water collecting and running down my breasts, and Miss Ogis—because this is how I still thought of her—sat in front of me, her golden brown face shining with the steam and the spray. Her blouse had become transparent with the water, a gauze curtain in front of two beautiful globes of that light hue, and she kept massaging my breasts with gentle pressure until my puckered nipples felt enormous. I felt like I had collapsed into a dream, feeling expert fingers touch me between my legs, playing with my clitoris, and then her small perfect mouth enveloped one of my nipples and sucked, making me shudder.

When I opened my eyes, I could still feel her right hand pushing into me, but her left had quickly unbuttoned her blouse, her small dark nipples poking over the lace of her bra. Her skirt had ridden up so that I had a tantalizing view of her white panties. She was drenched, but the shower spray couldn't have reached her there.

"Are you sure . . . ?" I was looking towards the door back to the changing rooms.

"We'll be all right," she told me. She withdrew her hand only to unzip her grey skirt and slip it off, tossing it with a lazy throw towards the entrance. Here in our private rain-forest, her fingers were back inside me, and the steady rhythm was at first deliciously pleasurable and then the tingle of my very first orgasm began in my thighs and rushed through me. "Uuuhhmmm! Eeeeeuuuhhhmm! Eeeeuuuhhh!" The sensation I couldn't feel when Bobby Drake put his cock into me with a bull-in-a-china-shop force in a friend's rec room, taking my virginity and leaving me hollow. This was different. Ecstasy.

I watched my teacher slither down into the shallow lake of shower water, me so ignorant, so naïve and without a clue, until she put her mouth on me, and I didn't recognise myself from my moans. As I lay there afterwards, panting and spent, she sat up and smiled, her face so cheerfully grateful that she could give me this, rivulets of water slowly running down her flat belly and the tops of her thighs, a sheen of light on her golden brown breasts now completely visible through the soaked bra. The tuft of her black fur was a vague cloud behind the wet panties, and it was the slight protrusion of her hipbones, such a girlish detail, that made me want to take her.

I lay there as the water sloshed up against my shoulder blades and flowed around my ass and heels, and I stretched out a hand, my eyes thanking her, telling her I wanted to give love back.

"Come home with me," she said. Then she smiled and added, "But not just yet."

She rose to her feet and slipped off her panties, un-hooked her bra, and I beheld the fullness of her, the full flowering of this mature woman. Her straight black hair trailed like a mane all the way down to the small of her back, accentuating the beautiful curve of her round ass. She was incredibly exotic to me. I got to my feet, and I took a bar of soap in my hand and lathered her buttocks. She seemed to swoon and put out her hands against the tiles, and I ran the soap around to her belly and lathered her breasts. We kissed for the first time in a soapy wet embrace under the pounding of the shower water, and it was another first for me. Lips that yielded to mine, that let me coil my tongue around hers in a dance and didn't invade my mouth with a masculine brutishness.

I remember afterwards her buttoning her suit jacket to cover her drenched blouse and squealing over the chill of the wet cotton on her skin. Her skirt was dry enough for us to "escape." I remember her driving me back to her house, both of us very quiet. I remember my first impression of her décor, a mixture of Indian curios, like the multi-armed statue of Shiva, and Fifties-style furniture. You wouldn't think they would go together, but she had blended them well. I didn't know much about Indian culture then, still don't to be honest, but I noticed briefly the depictions of the Indian god Krishna on the walls. He was blue in some framed pictures and black in others. "Those belonged to my ex-husband," she explained. "I should really get around to buying some new things to hang up." But two whole walls in her living room were already completely covered in books, one shelf devoted to feminist literature, another to novels by Hanif Kureshi, Arundathi Roy, Salman Rushdie.

I asked her about a couple of books, still foolishly calling her Miss Ogis, and she smiled and replied, "I think you can call me Karen here."

I was seventeen. I was still in the stage where I blurted out everything that came into my head. "You don't have an Indian first name?"

"Sure I do," she answered. "But I don't use it. I was born here, grew up here, and I'm kind of between two cultures. White people just mangle our pronunciations anyway. Karen's easier. If I get to know you better, maybe one day I'll tell you the other name."

I felt a peculiar shock of hurt. But I was young, holding on to the foolish teenage assumption that intimacy was a leveller, that it made us equals. One minute we were lovers, the next I naturally deferred to her.

"Would you like some tea?" she asked politely.

"Sure," I whispered nervously. And I clumsily stepped forward to kiss her again.

"We have time," she said. "Try to relax. I need to change."

She lived in a bungalow in an upscale part of Scarborough, and when she stepped into her bedroom, my eyes could follow her. I saw her strip off her wet blouse and then slip once again out of her skirt and her underwear. For a moment, she stepped naked in front of a full-length mirror and, seemingly bothered by something about her appearance, she brushed her long hair. I watched covertly as she put on a lacy red bra and a pair of red panties with a flowery pattern in the mesh. I took this as something done for me.

She pulled on a T-shirt and put on a long navy blue skirt with a high slit up the side and then padded back out to me in bare feet, and I was captivated by the mere idea of her lingerie under her casual clothes, by the easy grace of her movements and by the sway of her skirt. When we sat down to drink our tea, she curled up on the couch, and the skirt fabric slid away to give me a view of one gorgeously shaped leg.

"I'm glad you came with me," she said, and we held hands for a moment.

"So am I."

"You're going to have to be careful, you know," she advised.

"I would never . . ."

"No, no, not us," she said. "I'm sure I can trust you. I meant Erica. You're setting yourself up for disappointment."

"I've forgotten all about Erica."

"You're sweet," she told me. "And you have to learn to be a better liar. You're in love with her, and it's excruciatingly obvious."

I was past tears but I still shuddered with embarrassment. "I'm so stupid. Deborah's gonna blab this all over school—"

"No, she won't," said Karen flatly, and I heard the steel in her voice. "Deborah will do no such thing. I'm going to get up in a minute and place a call to Mr. Isham."

Mr. Isham was a history teacher and the vice-principal. It had always been assumed that because they were friendly, Isham and Karen Ogis were having an affair. Now I knew differently.

"He will call Deborah at home, and he will explain that you're very upset, and that she shouldn't talk about that episode *to anyone*," Karen went on. "If she does, we'll hear about it, and she'll find herself not only out of the girls' basketball team but having lost her credits for the semester. They'll be incomplete, and she'll have to spend another year in high school."

"Oh, my God," I whispered.

But she was doing the right thing for me. For all of high school kids' urgent political liberalism, it's still the most relentlessly conservative enclave on a social scale. I wouldn't have dreamed of coming out in school and trying to be who I was. Everyone had heard about a white boy a year ahead of us who came out and said he was gay, and he was beaten to the point that when he could *walk on his leg again* he ran away from both school and home.

Karen did get up and place her call, pulling her bedroom door to as she spoke in a hushed voice to Isham. The next day Deborah avoided me as if I was one of the girl bullies, and it was only days after she stopped imitating Erica that she quit hanging out with both of us altogether. Erica, of course, had always felt a bit embarrassed by her hero worship. As far as she was concerned, Deborah wouldn't be missed.

When Karen returned to the couch, standing for a moment over me, I reached out and stroked her bare leg exposed by the slit in the skirt. "You're right about me..."

She stayed in place, enjoying my caress, and she said, "Sweetheart, it's not too difficult to figure out."

"So how am I supposed to get over this?" I pleaded. "Shit, why would you want me when you know how...?"

"I'm your teacher," she said softly.

"What does that mean?" I demanded, getting irritable. "Haven't you ever been in love? You said you were married and—"

"That was arranged. I was sixteen when I got married. He was okay for a while, but that wasn't love. I thought I found love when I was a little older than you are now, with this girlfriend I had for a while, but...Michelle, it's just too hard. To want someone so badly? Losing yourself and having to negotiate all the time to keep the other person happy? It's just not for me."

"God, you sound like Erica when you talk like that."

"Erica's a very shrewd young lady."

"So if you think that way, what is this?" I asked.

She looked down at me and rested her hands on my shoulders. "This is solace. This is companionship and adoration. This is friendship. You're a beautiful girl, Michelle. You're smart, and you're clever, and you have a good heart. I find you very attractive. Yes, I want you, and we'll see what happens...That's if you can accept what I offer. And believe me, it's something a little more grown up than love."

"What if I fall in love with you?" I asked.

She smiled. "Trust me, you won't."

I stroked her leg, parting the curtain of her skirt, and she looked at me with an amused curiosity. I pretended that I saw the lace panties for the very first time, and I moved from the couch to the rug, kneeling in front of her. I tugged the fabric away and admired her flesh. I breathed in the odour of her, so different from my own scent. When I made her come with the gentle flickering of my tongue, prompting her to joke I was a fast learner, she staggered forward a step, her knees buckling.

We moved into her bedroom, and she seemed even smaller to me now, as if I could gather her up completely in my arms. I needed to take her this time, running my fingers through her sheets of black hair as I nibbled her ear and felt her breasts. I needed my hand inside her so that I could put my face close to hers and examine her eyes shutting tight, her mouth opening and letting out a kittenish mewling. It was the first time I had made a woman come, seeing how the rapture expressed itself on my lover's face after only feeling it for the first time myself earlier. Her black hair spilling onto my shoulder and arm, she held me tight as she fell asleep. I stayed awake and listened to her breathing and worried about school, worried about Deborah's big mouth and Erica's budding career, whether my best friend's dreams would come true. I could never see into my own future, to imagine just what I would be doing with myself.

I became part of Karen's carefully composed life. She had her books, her Indian friends and her non-Indian friends, her classes with us. She still went regularly, to my surprise, to the temple in Toronto, a brief walk from the Yorkville district, where the local ISSKON chapter held its services. What you and I know as Hare Krishnas but what is really not a cult, but a legitimate branch of the Hindu faith worshipped by thousands.

White people didn't get second looks, but I got polite

nods of astonishment the one time Karen brought me along, a young black chick here on a visit. "Hare, hare, hare, Krishna, Krishna . . ." And people danced, a line of Indian girls in saris as young as me bopping up and down in front of us as if they were at a techno-pop concert. A man came around with a kind of lamp, and Karen made waving motions of the heat to her face, leaving a donation of a couple of dollars.

"You all right?" Karen asked, enjoying my reactions to the vivid colours and the thick incense.

"Well, it's not gospel wailing, but it's fun," I laughed.

"Worship should be joyful," she commented. "Only white people make it into a tedious drag."

I returned the favour by taking her to a service of the Second Toronto Baptist Church on College Avenue, which I think must have been an equally surreal experience for her. Karen taught me about literature. She took me to French and Italian movies at the repertory cinema in the Annex district. She opened my mind to all kinds of intellectual stimulation. And on weekends, I rang the bell to the house and once I was quickly inside her short foyer, we kissed like lovers reunited after I'd been gone on a trip.

I celebrated graduating high school with dinner out with my parents and brother, and I celebrated again that weekend with Karen when she took me away to a bed and breakfast in the Ottawa Valley. I told my folks I had won an essay contest to visit the Canadian Parliament under teacher supervision—you don't have to guess who my chaperone was. Looking out the window at the rolling hills of the valley and feeling the silkiness of Karen's golden skin, I knew I had proved her wrong. I was in love with her. And we had cleared the hurdle. I was a graduate, our relationship no longer a risk for her professional career. But I had also been accepted at Yale (Fisk as well, but I wasn't crazy about college in Nashville). My parents were adamant that I should go to a prestigious American university and not settle for Queens or Carleton, or God help me, the University of Toronto, none of which could open as many career doors for me.

"Go learn something," Karen told me at the airport, smiling bravely.

"I'll email you plenty," I promised, hugging her close.

"Look, you have to do this, it's all right," she said, using these words instead of *I knew I would have to give you up one day.*

When they called my flight, I said softly close to her ear, "I love you, Kamala."

Her eyes were moist with tears, and she couldn't speak, her pose of detachment reduced to an emotional fiction. If she hadn't broken in that moment, I do think I would have moved on. Not that I didn't take other lovers, but I always came back to Karen when I visited home, staying at her place, in her arms, briefly picking up where we left off and then parting again. It's why it was so much harder for us later.

Mentor

In the month that I flew out to Connecticut and accepted my room at the dorm in New Haven, Erica boarded a Greyhound bus and rode for about twelve hours on a bumpy seat with shedding upholstery to the Big Apple. The bus wheels turning as she softly sang along with Bob Marley through her earphones: *Open your eyes and look within. Are you sat-is-fiiied—with the life you're living? Uh!*

She stepped into New York at Grand Central Station with her demo tapes and a grocery list of maybe five contacts in the city and no booked hotel room for the night. She says she walked for hours with her pack slung over her shoulder, amazed at how compact Manhattan was. From American television beamed across the border into Canada, you never got the impression that the Empire State Building and the Chrysler Building were so close together, the extent that those lions of the public library commanded a great swath of Fifth Avenue, or how you could look down from the low hill of Madison somewhere between Midtown and the upper sides and see the Twin Towers, because they were still standing back then. Erica Jones was here, but she hadn't yet arrived.

I've always had trouble trying to convey to Americans what it's like to be a black person growing up in Canada, what an interesting milestone it was in Erica's life to come to New York—or in mine. Hell, it's hard enough trying to convey what it's like to come from Canada. There's an old joke that a Canadian will pick up his Coke from a vending machine and say, "Thank you." They think of themselves as middle-class, polite, moderate people. For a long time, my Dad tells me, the most right-wing Canadian politician was still left of any American Democrat. After all, we've got a national health care scheme borrowed from the British. The founders were British and French who never really got along, and the music . . . The music is so painfully *white*.

Bryan Adams and Shania Twain, the Crash Test Dummies and Rush, Céline Dion and Avril Lavigne and Nelly Furtado and Nickelback and the patron saint of Celtic introspective bleating, Sarah McLachlan. The radio by law has to play a substantial portion of Canadian music in a desperate attempt to keep the national culture from going flatline, and to be fair the music industry itself was strong and thriving. But Erica and the rest of my friends hardly ever listened to the radio, because you were either hearing American pop tunes or the tongue-in-cheek Barenaked Ladies or folkie angst. Erica and I spent our weekends hunting for clubs that would play stuff for *us*. They were small scenes that we did our best to support even when they were clearly derivative and amateurish, just to have *something*. You never got a vibe that someone would break out and hit it big. So you couldn't pretend to be cool in recognising them first and having them to yourselves.

I don't know how to convey what it was like. We came

from the second-largest country in the world, but the population is only about 35 million. Toronto is one of the most multicultural cities you can go to—Chinese, Hungarian, Somali, Argentine, Iraqi, Polish, Jamaican, you name it, it's got it. And it's actually the seventh most expensive city in the world to live in, and yet... There was no homegrown black music that could rise to the top and stay on the pop mainstream. If it was black and really popular, it came from Down There. Nothing talked about where we were, what our lives were like at home, it was all Compton 'hood glory or Destiny's Child wannabes.

Around High Park, just off the Polish neighbourhood of Roncesvalles Avenue, Erica and I had both gone to a high school that was predominantly white. So we laughed at the white kids who got their gangsta patter from Eminem and American crime shows, sneering in disgust at them and saying, "Do you honestly believe anybody talks like that? And talks like that around *here*?"

It wasn't so much the incidents of bigotry I recall back home, not that they didn't happen. My father worked as a construction carpenter, and he didn't suffer too often from racism at work or over his hiring—he was just too good at his job. And Erica's father, being a dentist, said if someone had a problem with his black hands going into their mouth, fine, let the bastard's teeth rot. No, what springs to mind is how badly Erica was needed because our kind back then—as far as the popular cultural mainstream mattered—were, for the most part, simply not *there*.

Yes, there's a music network that has patterned itself on MTV and has played some progressive black music, but its producers are a cliquey bunch, and if they don't like you, you never make rotation. Yes, there's the Caribana parade in Toronto with its waves of tourists from all over, but it's a once-a-year gig. I am talking about our own artists getting on CBC shows, getting radio airplay, selling out the SkyDome.

A year after she hit it big, they promptly awarded Erica a Juno, the Canadian equivalent of a Grammy with nowhere near the prestige. The Junos were publicly ignored long before that time when the Brit Awards became a joke over in the UK. But the media tried to appear miffed that Erica didn't bother to fly home to accept hers. In fact, she showed no interest in even having it sent along to her. I have the clip of her interview where our national television network, the CBC, caught up to her at a concert in Boston, the clip that was shown and quoted all over the place.

"Don't give me that (bleep) that I'm dissing my fans— I'm dissing *you*. I'm dissing a music industry that wants reflected glory off things *I* did that they had no part of." She laughed in contempt and added, "You want me to show up and smile for your ceremony? Then you forget that fool hood ornament you give out and pass on some actual *money* to No Big Thang and Jamie Cross and Chantal Fox and play them on CFNY in Toronto. *Then* we'll talk."

You could almost hear the scramble of music journalists as they hunted on Google and Lexis to find out who these artists were that she was referring to. She boosted careers overnight with her diatribe. Because she knew herself what they were going through. She had sent her demo tapes in, she had applied for a Factor grant—that great government financial angel of struggling Canadian musicians—and she had gone to sit-down "chats" with the label executives. She wasn't what they had heard before, and they were not going to take a chance.

So she came to New York because it was New York. And because she couldn't do what she wanted so badly to do in Toronto. "Oh, Michelle, this is not where the music starts," she said as we made our goodbyes outside Union Station, "this is where the music ends up getting heard."

———

I already told you how she met Easy. Her short apprenticeship as backup singer, jingle vocalist, waitress in a Third Avenue diner has all been well documented. What the books and *Rolling Stone* never got right, never heard of at all, was how Erica met Morgan and how he became an influence in her career.

Morgan. His voice always sounding like a bass drum dropped at the bottom of a well. His one nervous habit was to tug on the salt-and-pepper curls of his modest beard as he sat on his piano bench, and he would look at the keys as if he had been waiting to recite a great truth for a long time. Morgan never told me how old he was exactly, but he always looked middle-aged and yet ageless. His freckled caramel skin was etched with character lines, and you knew that wasn't just a name for them with Morgan, that they really were folds and crevices of his maturing character. He didn't have a potbelly or that hard look older men get. In fact, his body seemed to be always straining the cloth of his shirts, and I kidded him once or twice about it to learn if he worked out. This, too, he never told me.

Like everything else, there is Erica's version of their first meeting and Morgan's that you can check from old magazines or articles posted on the Internet. Whoever you believe, the locale and minor details don't change. He lived on the whole top floor of a block above 125th near Fifth Avenue zoned as "artist space" but what really meant cheap apartments with stand-up showers and communal toilets down the hallway. I think Morgan was probably the only tenant who had his own washroom, though he said he took the place because it had a freight elevator that could take his upright piano. On the wall was "A Chart of Basic Jazz Scales," which had columns and rows with headings like C, Db, D, Eb, F, Gb, G matched with "Enigmatic, Chromatic,

Augmented, Whole Tone" and so on. Since I've practically forgotten all of my music theory from high school, it looked to me like a musician's Periodic Table. He says the chart was a gift. Morgan would say that many of his possessions were gifts from friends, like the framed poster for the movie *Paris Blues,* the one where you're supposed to believe Paul Newman could ever jam on a horn with Louis Armstrong, and of all things, the black lacquer bust of Beethoven on its kitschy pillar next to the Sears couch and coffee table.

The freight lift was also the way you got into Morgan's place, and one day, Erica lifted the wooden slats of the guard door and stepped into his living room.

"She walks into my place like she's coming in to buy a paper or something, as if I expect her," Morgan told me, "and she sits down at my piano and says, 'I'm Duane Jones's kid, so that's how I found you, but it's not why you should let me stay.' And she rips into 'A Train' and plays the improvisation off a Stan Getz album I *know* Duane must have. And for three quarters of an hour, she's showing off. The only guy I know who can mimic other pianists that well is Oscar Peterson, who I used to work with. I mean, she did Ahmad Jamal, and if you listen to him, he's all about space between the notes. She did that tinkling Basie, she did Ellington. She cracked me up because she did Erroll Garner, complete with his stride playing and groaning. It was a hell of a performance."

Erica remembers it differently. She claims she never burst in on Morgan and "took over" his piano, but she does admit he's quoted her accurately. And she did play for him.

When she was done strutting her stuff, Morgan took a long pull of his cigarette and said, "Okay, I believe you."

"Believe what?" she asked.

"I believe you're Duane Jones's kid," said Morgan.

Erica's father and Morgan had played together when they

were young. They were bandmates and used to collaborate on song efforts. Morgan would expect his old friend's little girl to grow up hearing jazz legends, and in one line, he let her know that playing them back note for note didn't impress him.

"So what did you come to me for?" he asked, still slumped on the couch with his abandoned book on, of all things, Australia. Morgan had eclectic tastes. His bookshelf had a lot of history, but you could find him reading Agatha Christie novels, a book on the behaviour of bees, a history of the Napoleonic wars.

"My Dad told me I should come to you."

"That's not an answer," replied Morgan. "That's a course of action. I asked about the motive."

"I want to record," said Erica, feeling embarrassed because a big dream like this always sounds ridiculous when you have to blurt it out. "I write songs, but I think I can write them better."

"*Ohhhhhh,* you want to be a star!" said Morgan. "Duane lives in Toronto, right? That's where you're from? Canada? Go home to Toronto, Anna—"

"Erica."

"Gimme a break, kid. I haven't had so much as a post-card from your Dad in five years. Fuck me if I have to remember the name of his kids. I am *not* in the lottery business. I do session recordings. I play with small combos for shit on Wednesdays. I do arrangements. Now and again—very, very rarely—I get asked to compose a little instrumental background music for TV shows filmed here. That's like your wannabe novelist buying his groceries by writing greeting cards. 'Kay?"

Erica didn't move.

Morgan grew irritable. "*What* do you think I can teach you? I do jazz. Jazz is precise. Jazz is *clean*. You can be sloppy all you want with pop music, A-B rhymes, three goddamn chords if you want, and we won't get into the bullshit of rapping—"

"You do music," Erica cut in. "I hear it in my head, new things, scraps of melodies, and I need to tap into it better, use it better."

Morgan nodded with a sigh and told her, "You know, I think it was Elton John or somebody who said he tripped on the formula for making popular songs by using the structure of a hymn. So there you are. All the Zen I can give you. Bye now."

"How about this," said Erica. "You're the only person I know in New York."

"Starbucks. Sixth Avenue, Midtown. Guys will want to pick you up in no time."

She was getting nowhere. So she turned on her heel and stomped back into the freight elevator.

I've heard there is an old Japanese tradition with teaching, and since Morgan read so much, maybe he happened upon it and decided to adopt it. Or maybe in truth, he couldn't be bothered with her that day. The tradition is that the master always says no the first time, the second time, the third, until the student makes such a pest of himself or hangs around so pitifully for so long that the master sees that the student is actually sincere.

Erica haunted a jazz club where Morgan played, a basement joint in Morningside Heights so it could pick up the college crowd, and when he was on a break, she crept over and put one of her compositions over his sheet music. To her surprise, he sat down and started to play her song as an instrumental, then ignored her bridge completely and improvised something completely different, shaking it up, showing her new paths to consider. But when she turned up on his doorstep the very next day, he told her he was busy.

"You're not busy, you're just reading."

"Exactly. I'm busy reading."

"That's busy for you?"

"It is at the moment. I'm also drinking."

"You got a real heavy load there," she said.

"I'm drinking Scotch, neat."

She stopped by his jazz club again. She fed him another composition. He used it the same way. Again, she was refused at his door. When she gave him her first try at "Late Night Promises" out of desperation, he called her at her studio apartment and, without a hello, asked, "I see you've decided to do some work. Get your ass over here."

He was not only her new music teacher. Erica calls Morgan her Professor of Coping. He told her where she could buy sheet music for less, where to go for the best fruit down in Chinatown, where to find meat for curried mutton. He took her on a tour of Harlem music spots like Minton's Playhouse and Smalls' Paradise. He was her guide to New Yorkers' quirky social behaviour. When she asked why everyone instantly apologised after bumping into you on the subway or on the street, he explained, "Paranoia as inspiration for good manners. No one knows what anyone's gonna do anymore. You might get shot. And the goddamn crazy thing is—it works!"

People who knew Morgan say he loosened up around Erica. Even they wondered if something wasn't sparking between the two, despite the difference in age. He liked to go downtown and play chess at the outdoor tables near Washington Square so they could take in the street performers. As he covered his eyes, knowing people could be heartless in their reactions, Erica sang "Late Night Promises" a capella and got five bucks in coins in Morgan's borrowed cap. She was more delighted with the applause than the spare change. She tagged along when he spent hours at the sprawling, endless Strand bookshop. They talked. They talked music. And they mostly talked about what kind of

career Erica would have, because Morgan was beginning to
believe. He did, however, have his reservations.

"Pop music by definition is ephemeral, disposable," he
argued. "Listen: what is this?" And he began to hum a few
bars of something.

" 'Round Midnight,' " she said promptly. "So what?"

"So that lasts. It's delicately constructed, and it'll stand
the test of time. And it's *good* music." To reinforce his point,
he started humming Beethoven's "Ode to Joy."

"I can't believe you cop an attitude like this!" she laughed.
"They're still melodic, they're still popular. And there are
classics that were pop tunes first! When you got started in
music and heard 'Ain't Too Proud to Beg,' did you think
people would still love it later?"

"Hey, watch it," he growled. "Yes, I was around, but I am
not *that* old. And I'm not saying one kind of music's supe-
rior to another. I listen to all kinds of shit. Look, Erica . . ."
He stopped in the park, and she recognised he was being
serious. "It's just that I don't think they're going to *let* you
be the kind of artist you want to be," he said gently.

"Oh, come on—"

"No, you come on," he said, and he dug into his coat
pocket and pulled out her scribbled lyrics to "And You
Think That Makes It All Right?," her blistering attack on
proposed compensation for descendants of slaves. She had
wanted his opinion. "You think you can say the stuff you
want to say?"

"You know my Dad didn't only listen to Duke Ellington
and Miles Davis," said Erica. "We also played Bob Marley
in the house."

"I like Bob Marley, too—"

"They got artists doing political songs all the time," said
Erica.

"No, artists *say* a few things that can almost be called
political," he corrected her. "They're forgotten 'cause they

go into newspapers or magazines. Tossed out the next day or in a week. People hang on to CDs. And their songs are the tamest shit compared to what real people *think*—"

"That's not always true, Mor—"

"Show me the hard stuff, and I'll show a guy that's been slapped down. Or grown tired and faded away. Nobody is saying things in their music as strongly as you want to say them, not in the commercial mainstream in between the Madonna and Snoop and Red Hot Chili Peppers shit. You want to say this stuff, and you want the music to last? To become classics? I don't think they'll let you. I am telling you—you want to be provocative while you climb the charts? Shake your ass, don't speak your mind."

"Morgan, that's a horrible sexist thing to say!"

He rolled his eyes. "Oh, please. I'm not saying that's my opinion. Get a grip. At the end of the day you want to be a *musician*. A composer. You want to say things? Say it through the notes, the chords. Make *music* that's provocative. Forget the words. Any fool can rhyme or paint a placard."

Erica stared at him, refusing to budge from her spot on the pavement.

"Don't give me the hurt puppy dog expression," he said brutally. "You forfeited the right not to listen when you called yourself an artist! You'll get people who won't love everything you do. You'll get asshole reviewers. Suck it up, young lady. The roller coaster hasn't even started. Go prove me wrong."

"Christ, you do sound like my Dad sometimes," she told him, taking his arm.

"Your father was smart," said Morgan. "He got out."

"Then why'd you stay in?"

"For the same reason he sent you to me."

Erica thought she understood. Her father wanted Morgan to teach her how to love the craft beyond the glory. It was a rather bittersweet compliment to his talents, since that kind of lesson is best learned from the one who has failed, the one who stays behind to keep watch, to hold the sacred ground. This was the "Just in case" that her father communicated to me, that if Erica didn't make it, she could keep the music. If she did succeed, then Morgan's training would prove immeasurably beneficial. She walked with her arm linked through his, humbled by the knowledge, both of them saying nothing for a couple of minutes.

"Why don't you have a girl?" she asked.

"What does that have to do with anything?"

"Just curious."

"*Noooo,* you're being nosy," he growled. "And don't think I've never noticed the wheels grinding with you."

"What's that supposed to mean?"

"I want to go play chess," said Morgan, and the subject was dropped.

She admitted to me that she did creep into his apartment late one evening after that walk in the park. The freight elevator didn't tip him off to her arrival because he was in the shower. Morgan stepped out of the bathroom, he told me later, to walk around and get out of the cloud of steaming vapour, towelling himself off as he paced around his apartment with only one lamp on near the television. And there was Erica standing in front of him.

"Hi, Morgan," she purred.

He towelled the nape of his neck, not bothering to cover himself up. Erica told me he was "an impressive hunk of man standing like that." Yes, he was old enough to be her father—he was her father's contemporary, after all—but his body had chunks of compact muscle, his broad chest with a sprinkling of silver grey hairs, his wide smooth thighs the most youthful part of him. His cock was for the most part in shadow, his ball sack visible and hanging down like a tiny velvet pouch.

"What is this?" he said, sounding more disappointed than outraged. "What are you doing here?"

"What do you think?" she asked.

She knelt in front of him, but he didn't move. He looked at her as you would a child acting out.

"Erica . . ."

She reached her hands around and felt his buttocks, surprisingly firm to her touch, her caress working the circumference of his waist until her spread fingers rested delicately on his hips. His penis sprang to life, and he was thin but long. Erica let out a slow, steady warm breath, and his cock stirred, hardening until he was a hot brown pillar, and she saw him grit his teeth but still show no embarrassment or modesty. Or affection.

"This is not," he said firmly, "the way I want or need to be compensated."

She grabbed him—literally grabbed him—at the base of his cock, and while the motion surprised him, tugging him off his heels and forward a step, she didn't hurt him. "That's a shitty thing to say! Take it back."

Amazingly, he said, "No."

Her fingers softened on his flesh, and she began to stroke him, keeping him hard, her other hand feeling the strength in his chest, lightly dancing over the silvery hairs.

"You don't think I feel something for you?" she asked indignantly.

"You want to bring me down just like you've done with other fools," said Morgan. "I know your type. Yeah, sure, hon, it's an enormous compliment that you thought of me for your recreational amusement, but I told you, I can see the wheels turning. It just sticks in your craw that you're getting all these lessons, and I haven't tried to feel you up. Doesn't it?"

She couldn't speak. No man had called her on this in her

entire young life so far, and here was Morgan, naked as a babe but wiser than sin, catching her out. She took him into her mouth.

He laughed cruelly. "Come on, stop. You won't be happy until I fit your definition of an asshole. Everybody must want something, huh? Is that it? So you came out to prove it with me? 'Kay, Erica, I do think you'll become famous. You got the talent. And you've got the attitude already. You don't need folks swarming around you, begging for favours to make you jaded. You're there."

He stood there waiting for her to deny it. She didn't. She sucked him, tenderly cupping his balls in the palm of one hand. At last, she let him go.

"Morgan, I'd believe you if you weren't hard as rock."

He lifted her to her feet and kissed her then, hard, passionate, wet and presumptuous. Erica laughed. Not at him but because his beard tickled her chin. She found herself being lowered onto the couch, and as she felt the muscles of his back, he pushed up her skirt and stripped off her panties, his light brown hand with its pianist fingers pressing on her mound, her juices coming in a tide of astonished lust. Erica was trying to pull her thin top over her head but got as far as her breasts before he entered her in a rush, and she keened loudly. She was willing his hands on her breasts, to feel her nipples as he thrust harder and harder inside her until she screamed, and the echo bounced off the dark brick chasm of the freight elevator shaft.

"Morgan, honey, come into me—"

With a groan, he rolled away.

"Morgan?"

"No."

She saw that his cock was still hard, his chest heaving, the tiny white hairs glinting in the illumination from the lamp, and he wiped his mouth with the back of his hand, his eyes shut tight as he struggled for control. She thought he might ejaculate then and there as he fought his own desire. He had taken her to an exquisite high then had torn himself away from the brink of his own release. She didn't get it.

"You were so good," Erica was whispering. "Let me make you—"

"No…"

"Come on," she said, reaching out to touch his penis before his hand gently but firmly intercepted it. "Is it because of—?"

"No, not because you're his daughter," he groaned. "None of that shit. You got me as far as this, okay? Satisfied?"

"No," she pouted. "I think I'm in love with you."

"Don't be stupid."

She touched his face, caressing his cheek. He allowed her to, but even this tender gesture made him harden even more. His control had been amazing, was amazing. She wanted him back inside her—

"We have work to do, you and me…" He was still panting. "We can do this, but … I'm not going to get the issue … clouded in my head, so don't you…" He took a deep, decisive breath and told her, "We're going to work … on your songs."

Half naked in the near darkness, her hands clasped in her lap, she nodded. She had both won and lost.

She says he made her come again with his hand as she lay there in her dishevelled clothes, and as her mouth opened for a soundless cry of ecstasy, he penetrated her again in one thrust, pulled himself out, and she watched, fascinated, as a syrupy jet stream of cum flew across her belly and another hit her neck just above the collarbone. "I love having him come on top of me," she whispered to me once. "Mmmmphh!"

Morgan kept his word. He helped her with the songs. You would think that maybe his show of integrity would adjust her outlook, but it only changed her view of Morgan. It was special to him, no others. This is how she could still behave the way she did towards Easy later, towards Luther and others right into her signing with Brown Skin Beats. After the success of the first album, she called me and said she'd pay my way to visit her in New York. At the time, I didn't believe she could ever change.

But what brought me down to Manhattan was not only the chance to visit my friend the new star but also the opportunity to investigate what was wrong. Because my friend Erica Jones had actually told me over the phone, "Oh, God, Mish, I met this new guy, and I think I'm in love with him!"

As it happened, she wasn't talking about Morgan.

So I went down to New York an innocent, a babe in those big woods of steel and stone. I am not making excuses for myself. There are people who will tell you that, yes, I was a gentle person, a harmless one. I can honestly tell you that I flew down to New York and never dreamed that I would murder those men.

Shop Talk

I hold an x-ray up to candlelight
of your transparent lies
The roses died two days ago
No big surprise
Tired of needing, emotional bleeding,
of all your disappointments and how you criticise

Don't whisper to me any more in darkness
Don't tell me you'll change in warm sunlight...

The song was "Late Night Promises." Erica's voice, unmistakable, coming out of the speakers of the hired car's stereo as I was chauffeured through the Queens Midtown Tunnel. Not quite a limo, but I could tell my best friend must be moving up in the world, especially since her song had been on top of Billboard's charts for God knows how many weeks now.

After I had pulled my bags off the carousel at LaGuardia, I spotted the young white guy. He was checking a borrowed

Christmas photo of me and holding up a cliché strip placard with MICHELLE BROWN neatly printed on it in felt
marker.

"My name's Justin, and I got your ride for you, Miss
Brown. Oh, here, let me get that for you." I detected an
Alabama drawl. "Miss Jones says she's real sorry she can't
be here, but today's supposed to be big for laying down the
backing vocals on the eighth or ninth track. Maybe track
seven, I can't remember exactly."

I made a nervous laugh, my usual preface to an intrusive
question. "So, like, who are you with?" Common sense told
me the guy couldn't possibly work for Erica. I knew she'd
only just signed with someone, but she wasn't that big yet.
"You with the record company?"

Discreet smile here. "I'm with *a* record company."

That's about as much as I got out of him about his employer. He was chatty about everything else. Yep, this is
Manhattan, Manhattan's the best. So he lived somewhere in
the city? Hell, no! He couldn't afford that. He lived out
in the Bronx with a couple of other guys for roommates. At
the corner of 57th Street, I got out of the back seat at the
stoplight and jumped in up front, confiding to him it just
felt too weird being driven around like that.

"Now aren't you a breath of fresh air!" he chuckled. "I've
had folks thundering and hollering at me because they didn't
send a stretch job with the tinted windows and the mini
wet-bar inside. I guess it's true what they say about you
people."

"You people?" I echoed, instantly on my guard.

"Canadians."

"Oh! Yeah, I guess it is, eh."

"You guess it is, *eh*? I love that!"

He pulled the car into the narrow parking strip in front
of a sumptuous hotel, and I looked up and saw the gilt logo
for the Lockwood-Tremblay. This was the brand spanking

new luxury job along "Museum Row" designed to rival the Plaza for views of Central Park. There's got to be a mistake, I told him. I sure as hell wasn't booked in here. In fact, I didn't know where I would be staying that night, presumably in a sleeping bag on the floor of Erica's closet of an apartment up past 135th Street or in Midtown or who knows, maybe out in Queens if she were so lucky.

"They're expecting you."

"I can't be staying here," I insisted.

"I don't know if you're *staying* here," he said with a shrug. "Miss Jones said bring you to the party, and she'd come as soon as possible. Look, don't worry about it. Go on in. Your name's on the list. Nobody's going to give you no hassle."

I was staring like a fool at the doorman, waiting like all doormen in one of those ridiculous outfits that are a cross between a Beefeater uniform and the wardrobe for an organ grinder's monkey. He wore a rather benign expression on his face, considering I'd arrived in faded jeans and a sweater over a tank top with my knock-off Fendi luggage. I thanked him as he pulled on the large brass handle that formed the "L" of the "TL" logo and walked in.

Ssshhhheeee-it. Thirty-foot-tall mirrors, oxblood wingback chairs and framed sepia photographs of old New Yorkers. Yes, I had had passing brushes with luxury before—I'd gone into the King Edward Hotel in Toronto, and, yes, my parents did take my brother and me to restaurants with napkins of linen instead of paper. But this wasn't like creeping timidly into the lobby of the Plaza or the Waldorf Astoria as a tourist and maybe splurging on the seven bucks for a lousy bottle of Evian by the fireplace. I was twenty years old, and someone had my name on a list and was expecting me. I thought the best way to limit embarrassing myself was to find the youngest clerk behind the front counter and appeal to his pity.

"Look, I'm supposed to be here," I explained after providing my name, "and I don't know where I'm going."

"*Here?*" The blonde girl in the navy blazer poked her finger downwards as if to mean "this spot." It didn't seem such a stupid idea when you thought of how I was dressed and what little information I had. For all she knew, I had come for day work. "Hang on. Brown . . . No 'e'?"

"That's right."

She tapped my name into her computer terminal. "Yeah, here you are. Floor twenty-one. Here's your swipe card, and if you can please return it to us when you leave. Elevators to your left."

"What room?"

"Sorry?"

"What room?" I asked again. "You said *floor* twenty-one."

"The whole floor, Miss Brown. Mr. Swann has booked all of Park View C for the weekend." Sensing the enormity of my ignorance, she leaned in and said, "Umm, *do* remember to hand in that swipe card. It's got a sensor in it. It's not like it'll set off the doors at Bloomingdale's or anything, but the security guys come after you outside, and people feel silly forgetting."

"Thanks," I said. "Uh, who did you say booked it?"

"Steven Swann," she said, smiling and slightly shaking her head in surprise. As if she couldn't believe I didn't know my host.

*S*teven Swann. Yes, I knew *of* him. I didn't know I'd be sharing the same oxygen with him two and a half hours after escaping New Haven. And I certainly didn't expect Erica to know him.

Jesus. Steven Swann. One hundred and seventy-five pounds of fair-haired, blue-eyed teen girl dream worth at least twenty million in soft drink concert sponsorship and athletic gear endorsement, and that wasn't counting posters, T-shirt sales, television appearances or the "likeness" licensing for a kids' board game. I haven't even got to the albums yet. Twenty-three and already incorporated. I learned later that a rumour was out he was supposed to do one of those live appearances in Times Square that afternoon. A *rumour* had sent ten thousand of the devoted jamming West 43rd Street, which brought out the cops with their crowd-control rails and a couple of mounted patrols. The Lockwood-Tremblay management were probably crossing their fingers he didn't poke his head out a window.

He had a little more respect than Justin Timberlake and Britney Spears for not starting out on some God-awful Disney Mousketeer show. But he was still a refugee from one of the boy bands, Trust. Remember the song "Ashamed of Us" that climbed the charts for six weeks about five years ago? He was part of that. When he signed as the first white solo artist for Brown Skin Beats (and didn't that just ensure *reams* of pop music criticism), the label waged a detailed PR campaign to build up his musical credibility. It suddenly emerged that Steven had toiled away as the real creative force behind the band with little recognition.

"Stevie did a lot of our choreography on 'Small Wonder,' " said fellow bandmate Tyler Shaw, which no doubt came as news to Luba Kauffmann, who planned the steps of the video shoot and who went on to actually block all the routines for Trust's concert tour. And there was producer Jake Monkhouse telling MTV Base, "The bridge for 'Ashamed of Us' is all Steve. We really slaved on that one until he came up with it. I mean, it's just flippin' inspired!" But if you talk to enough people, you learn the bridge was written and even the arrangement set before Steven walked into the studio.

And none of this mattered.

Erica had to use her creativity to scale the mountain. Having proved his bankable potential with a hot boy band, the mountain for Steven came with a ski lift. His creativity was invented for him. Ever notice how no one bothers to ask certain stars how they came up with their hits? It's a dead end query if the songs are written for them. Instead reporters ask how they "feel" about their tunes, what they're "trying to say." Believe me, it's something else to take in a "creative" meeting in which a couple of producers sit at the boardroom punching CD decks of potential tracks to record, the talent nodding or shaking his head. Cut to the talent waxing rhapsodic six months later over how "I was going through a real difficult stretch in my life, just broke up with my girlfriend, and I wanted to say . . ."

Steven was a master at this sort of thing. When he took off into mega-stardom, he began this habit of putting little Zen sound bites into his interviews. Someone would ask him about the relentless media attention, and his answer would be (boyish grin, hanging his head a little in early George Clooney heartthrob style): "Yeah, it is relentless, but this is part of the price you pay, man. So like, I just dive into it. I think handling media attention is like the story of the guy who put his hand over a flame, and somebody asks him, 'Dude, what's the trick?' And he shoots back, 'The trick is *not minding.*' "

By the time someone figured out that the clever anecdote had nothing to do with the question, he was already talking about something else. I know the British tabloids absolutely loathed him, and that was because he had played them for fools. *The Sun* and *News of the World* and the others always claim they can't be fooled, or will get theirs back in the end. It didn't exactly happen that way with Steven. First, his people carefully "leaked" fuzzy, grainy photos of him with a boy of about four years old while he was on tour in the UK. Out went the story that this was Steven Swann's love child with an old English girl-friend, and certain sources on the peripheral circle told tales about how he was completely devoted to the little tyke but wanted to protect him from the paparazzi. More photos—Steven taking the boy to the London Zoo, buying him toys at Hamleys. Funny thing was, the American papers never matched copy on these daily episodes.

The reason being that the record label clued them in it was all nonsense. Check the photos. The kid's always blurry and if you looked carefully, it was a different kid each time. Soon enough it emerged that the child in the original photo was a desktop amalgamation of a bunch of composite features. And when asked, Steven said, "I never claimed I had a son. A few friends wanted me to visit with their kids because they're fans, that's all. And I did some work for a Big Brothers association."

Played. Perfectly played with no one but themselves to blame. The tabloids swore vengeance, tried to take the spin that they were victims of a publicity stunt, but they couldn't connect the dots back to him.

The ironic thing was, in all my short years of witnessing the pop world Steven Swann was the most *authentic* guy I met.

*D*rambuie."

There I was, having walked into the enormous cavern of Park View C of the Lockwood-Tremblay hotel, my bag over my shoulder. Catering staff made their rounds with silver platters of drinks. Guests were decked out in everything from track suit chic to formal wear, laughing and talking, while Steven Swann's cover of Peter Gabriel's "In Your Eyes" played through the stereo speakers. (I never much cared for this version, since Steven's voice sounds thin and whiny compared with Gabriel's robust heartbreaking vocals, and instead of Youssou N'Dour for backup, he gets that Algerian singer.)

Here I was at this party where Erica hadn't arrived yet and I knew absolutely no one. I had found myself standing next to a gigantic fountain with an ice sculpture of two elephants spouting creamy brown liquid out of their trunks. For a brief moment, I was captivated by this whole garish display. I reached out a finger to the cascade as if I were about to touch a hot stove.

"Drambuie," explained a gentle voice next to me.

And there he was, shorter of course in real life than you'd expect, maybe half an inch taller than me, smiling pleasantly and offering me a clean glass. Blue eyes with their sincere glint, and I swear it was like peach fuzz on his upper lip, even though he was twenty-three. He'd been cast as seventeen when he did that guest shot on *Smallville.* It helped at the moment that he was wearing jeans, too, with a T-shirt for the Lobos, the football team from his home state of New Mexico. He swept a comma of blond hair out of his eyes and tipped his glass into the waterfall of the fountain, taking a quick sip.

"Hi, you must be Michelle, Erica's friend. I'm Steven."

I nodded, staring at him. You know the gears in your head that make you say stupid things in nervous moments? The switch got flicked for me right then, and I pointed to the elephants and the fountain of booze. "This must cost a fortune!"

Idiot. Who cares?

"Awww, no," said Steven, scoffing at the bizarre thing. "You want to know something? Not even the label is picking up for this. We tell the liquor distributors, the flower guys, the movie studios we're having a shindig, and they send us out freebies. For a three-second shot of this on *Entertainment Tonight,* it's worth the gallons getting pumped through here. My idea."

"No kidding?"

"Honest. My MBA has to be good for something. Here, let me show you around. We're just kicking back. More people are coming, and things'll liven up a little. You missed Elton John."

"He was here?" I asked in disbelief.

"No, I'm kidding. We had to settle for Elton's 'significant other.' Or at least he claimed to be that guy, I can't be sure. Don't know how he heard about it. Couldn't get him out the door fast enough. *Fuuuuuck!* Come on. You want something to eat? Sure?"

Slaps on his back and handshakes as he guided me through. Pink bounded up and gave Steven a hug, offering me the quick finger-fold wave, and then she was off in the crowd of celebrators. There were at least two Ms. Js, the high legend arriving with her hair in ringlets, wearing Givenchy and a large entourage and sweeping in for a few minutes, and then the party hit a Lo, who poked her head in at the door and saw that the legend had possession of the field. She quickly left. Better than Mariah, who I was told wasn't even allowed up. "Why should we let her in?" said one record executive. "She's turned down our label too many times!"

We passed a young star of *Scrubs* talking to someone about how he was setting up his own production company to develop scripts. Sitting on a pool table was a legend of Seventies R&B leading three session musicians in a game of "I Spy" with Sambuca shooters. It was one o'clock in the afternoon. Steven played good sport and downed an offered shot in a single gulp, arching his eyebrows and smiling at me as if he were the indulgent father of them all. We went down a hallway, and he opened the door next to a wall of frosted glass. "And we got a pool here . . ."

Which hardly described it. There were two pools, both heated, according to Steven. A modest regular one, and then an oversized Jacuzzi, and the Jacuzzi was full, no one wearing suits. A chorus of "Hi, Steve!" and seven hands shot up to wave in greeting. My host made a poor joke about how MTV was due by later, but they probably wouldn't be allowed in here. I saw a huddle of kneeling white and brown bodies on the wet stone, and in my ignorance, I actually thought someone might be having a heart attack. Steven cocked his chin for me to go and have a look—he wasn't worried. I walked over.

There was an Asian girl on her back, her head resting in the lap of a white man, and when she turned her face I could see she was a supporting star of a prime-time drama. Since there are very few Asian girls on network TV, you go ahead and guess which one. A black guy was pounding his dick into her, and he had one of the longest I'd ever seen, which figured because I was told later he really was a porno star. She'd taken him on a dare, and now she was screaming until her cries bounced off the echo chamber walls of the pool room. She couldn't care less if anyone watched, her knees up, her small breasts jiggling. She had a nice little body.

Steven caught my look.

I pulled my eyes away and tried to be cool, but it's one thing to read about star shenanigans and another to see them happen. "You get yourself a couple of Roman columns and pass out the white bedsheets for togas, and you're all set."

He rolled his eyes and laughed. "Come on! It's not that bad. It's a party. You're going to Yale, aren't you? You telling me you never go to any wild parties off campus, Mish?"

Mish. Only Erica and a few close friends ever called me that. The boy had done his homework.

"I'm just kidding, Steven," I answered. "I'm not a prude, really. Hey, when is Erica going to show?"

"Tell you what, I'll go phone the Easy Roller studio and check. We'll see what we can do for you." The way he patted my arm belonged to a flight attendant off to fetch an extra pillow. "Look, mingle, and I'll catch up and let you know. Don't worry."

I smiled politely and put some distance between me and the pool room. To hell with it, I could use another drink. Minutes kept passing, and I was hit on by three guys, each of whom started off the conversation by saying, "Hi, I'm Bill/Frank/Sean, I'm a vice-president..." When each one found out I was a mere college student, the guy would take it as his cue to rattle off the list of celebrities he knew. Who talked like this? The artists I met were on permanent scope, guy or girl, their heads bobbing neutrally to whatever I said while their eyes went tick-tick-tick around the room. I could say this for Steven Swann. He focussed his attention on you when you spoke with him.

I walked into what looked like a display kitchen of some kind, with two large serving islands in the middle, spotless gas burners and immaculate trays of silverware. This room, too, was wired for sound, and there was a guy in here alone with his back to me. He wasn't listening to the Goo Goo Dolls playing in the main foyer, he had on this salsa jazz stuff. And he was playing along with the percussion. He *was* the percussion, more like it. He got sounds out of wooden spoons you wouldn't believe. He made an entire orchestra out of the hanging pots and skillets. I must have watched him for a full minute.

Thoroughly enjoying himself, he didn't hear me come in and only stopped when he turned and saw me. Then he burst into a loud self-deprecating laugh.

"I was bored," he explained.

"What are you? From *Stomp*?"

"I used to be," he said, and I saw that he wasn't kidding.

Yes, he was. He'd been with the American homegrown production of the show a long time ago. He thrust out his hand for me to shake. "I'm Luther Banks."

It was strange. Steven Swann and Luther were both about to become very important figures in my life, and they were poles apart in terms of physical looks and natural charisma. Steven had a model's beautiful blankness, but Luther's *café au lait* face was all about character. A half-moon scar, very faint, just above his right eyebrow, his black hair perfectly cut, a neatly trimmed goatee that framed a crooked smile. His eyes, people said, always looked a bit sleepy, half-lidded, but Erica would later remark they were bedroom eyes but not a pair that *wanted* you, more like they held an expression as if you've both just finished the dirty deed together. Those eyes took everything in. Steven Swann played on his fresh-faced delicacy. Luther had a masculine ruggedness to him that implied a natural quiet leadership. I liked him almost immediately.

I shook hands with him and said, "Hi, I'm—"

"Michelle Brown. Yeah, Erica said you were coming."

"Everyone's expecting me, but no one can tell me when she'll get here. Hey, how could you tell who I am?"

"I don't want to be rude, but you're kind of dressed down, and not in an arch, designer 'street' way."

I was back with embarrassment as my theme of the afternoon. "I didn't know I'd be coming to this. People keep asking me what I'm working on, and I have to say Jane Austen. English lit as a minor."

"Don't sweat it. I put in two years at Juilliard, and I'm treated like a Martian. The new democracy in music! These days everybody wants to be a DJ, but they can't play a note. They think they'll just string something together with samples on a computer."

"Umm . . . Should I know who you are?"

He laughed again. An endearing belly laugh, sincere and

loud. "*No!* You mean am I in Steven's league? *Nooooo!* My big mistake was giving away my best songs to other artists, so there was bugger all left for my first solo album. And Brown Skin Beats put it out more as a nice gesture and a thank-you. There was no marketing support *at all*. The CD makes a nice coaster, though. Hey, listen, we don't have to talk about the music business just because you're at this party."

"That's a relief. It's all a little intimidating. Like eating at the grown-ups' table."

I stepped over to the window, where Central Park was a square of green in a forest of shiny needles. "This is my first day in New York," I said, announcing it more to myself than to him.

He flipped a ladle into the stainless steel sink and dusted his hands. "Then come on. You shouldn't be cooped up in here. You're a tourist, for fuck's sake." When I hesitated, he said, "This thing's going to go on until three in the morning, trust me. Let's get you some fresh and smelly, lung-choking New York air. What do you feel like doing? Anything you want. I live here, so you come up with the ideas."

I was concerned for two whole minutes about whether I was being picked up, but the conversation kept circling around to Erica. Erica's career was going to Pluto. She was going to be *huge,* he assured me. She had great instincts, and the hooks she came up with for her tunes...Luther's daily bread was his producing, in addition to his song-writing, and he had worked on or mastered five of the tracks for her second album in progress. He said he'd put in enough time that he knew how far she could go.

"If, of course, she doesn't fuck up."

"What's that supposed to mean?" I leaned my face into

the wind and tried to pick out Liberty Island. Not very original of me, wanting to go up the Empire State Building, but Luther was a good sport about it. "What do you mean *if she doesn't fuck up?*"

"I mean your friend has a slight case of John Lennon disease."

"I don't get it," I said.

"She's bursting to tell the world all these things she wants to say, and she's going to be raw about it. She's cynical about the issues, and that'll sell, sure. Beautiful young artist pointing out ugly shit going on in the world? It'll play *big*. But she's also cynical about people. They say Lennon was the same way. He'd go off on rants when he was younger. Shit-scared that his ambition and talent made him a phoney, so he projected all that out to other people. Now, your friend doesn't harangue folks. She's found more creative ways to use people just to prove shit to herself."

It was the most interesting way I'd heard yet for calling Erica Jones a slut.

"The trouble is," Luther went on, "eventually artists like Erica run into smooth talkers who will know exactly what buttons to push and what they want to hear. And she'll get snared. It's good that you came down to visit, Michelle. Honest. People starting out in this biz, they need friends from their old lives to ground them."

"She's doing well," I argued. "She's already famous. Is there any reason to worry?"

He nodded.

"You sound bitter and burned," I suggested.

"Oh, I am," he admitted, nodding. "I've been burned. But I'm not so spiteful that I watch others poke their toes into the fire. They've got all kinds of ways so that you never realise there's smoke coming from your head—until it's too late."

He laughed ruefully and said, "You know how I ended

up producing? Didn't have much of a choice. I signed my deal with my music publisher, thinking I was the cleverest S.O.B., and then I took a second look at my submissions quota—so many tunes to create and turn in per quarter. And it was ridiculous, no way I could crank 'em out. Fine, said my publisher. I breach my contract, they feel justified in cutting off my advances on stuff turned in already."

"Bastards," I said politely.

"Oh, but it gets better. If you don't read the fine print, you may find out—like me—that you, the writer, are responsible for getting the cuts."

"Cuts?"

"Uh-huh. It's biz lingo for getting an artist to record and release your song. Well, lo and behold! Your publisher has turned you, through the magic of a signed contract, into their salesman. *They're* supposed to be the ones securing the artists, and unless you're a hot producer with a thick Rolodex, the water's going to get a bit deep. I got good at producing for the sake of survival. When my publisher came back to me one day bitching over my submissions quota, I said go ahead and cut me off. Fuck you. I just made more off my work for Busta than you pay me for three quarters."

"I'm sure Erica's situation is different."

"It is. And it isn't. Know what I'm saying?"

I gave him a noncommittal nod, my eyes on the Manhattan skyline.

Even up here on the 86th floor, you could hear the traffic and the symphony of car horns. Sure, I know the history—how New Yorkers built *up* because they had limits on building *out*. But you still couldn't resist the psychological effect and marvel at how shrewd those original architects were. To get up here or up any of those sparkling towers made you feel differently about your lot in life, made you think of possibilities. It made you ambitious *to keep the view*. In

Toronto, you've got to take a ferry out to Centre Island or at least stand at Harbourfront to get a sweeping view of the tall buildings. In London, as a tourist, I couldn't get a half-decent view of the capital unless I stood on one of the bridges of the Thames. In both cases, though, you're on the ground. You're forced to tilt your head respectfully up instead of enjoying the temporary illusion that you can dominate it all, take it all in from a high vantage point.

Erica must love it here.

"We should get back," said Luther.

"Do we have to?" I bleated like a little kid.

He laughed. "Erica's going to turn up and worry about you." With a groan, he added, "And I've got to put in a few more social hours."

"If you're not having a good time . . ."

"You can tell you're not in the music business," he said. "A certain amount of shmoozing is required. Doesn't matter whether you like folks or not, it's business. These parties are where folks can scout out the hottest video director. They take a barometer reading of who's still got clout. They pick up stock tips. Whatever."

"Wow, you just gave me a whole lecture about Erica's cynicism. I didn't see that much wheeling and dealing. People were getting wild back there. The booze is flowing. And in the pool—"

"Sure, sure, a lot of 'em play hard," said Luther. "But the ones fooling around and making asses of themselves have shown up for the entertainment. They don't have an agenda. Didn't you notice it was either the old stars who've made it, or young up-and-comers who think it's their turn in the candy store? The young ones are playing, Michelle, but their managers are on the clock. Read *The Hollywood Reporter* and daily *Variety* over the next couple of weeks, and I'll bet you see five deals where you can trace all the players back to this party."

"So what's your agenda for being there?"

"Me?" He tried to laugh away the question. "Oh, I'm one of the fun-seekers."

"Beating up pots and pans?"

"Party kicked off about noon. Quarter to one, I played a demo tape of a song I wrote for somebody connected to Black Eyed Peas. By two, somebody was asking my advice about World Music, and if I can track down these Azerbaijani horn players I know, I've got another album job."

"So you're working the room, but you're warning me how if Erica's not careful, your colleagues will eat her alive?"

"I never said don't swim in the deep end. I said she has to be careful. If money talks when bullshit walks, then flattery *sings*. There's a reason why they have the expression 'music to my ears.' "

Distractions

We beat Erica to the party by half an hour. A swarm of people hovered near the door for the newest bright young thing, ensuring that I wouldn't get a chance to greet her for about fifteen minutes. Lots of hugs, lots of kisses on both cheeks. Then Erica gave a big squeal as she spotted me, and we hugged.

"You're here!" she yelled. "You're finally here! Oh, girl, we are going to have so much fun! Look at *you*!"

"Look at me? Look at you! You're the one in the Chanel suit."

"Borrowing it," she lied. As I stayed on, so the suit stayed in its place on the rack of her walk-in closet. But this was an Erica who still felt slightly embarrassed by new wealth. She tugged on my arm and whispered in my ear, "Can you believe this shit?"

"Hey, it's your ball, Cinderella."

"I don't know if all this is . . . necessary."

"Your friend Luther was telling me how a lot of deals get cut at parties like this."

"Luther," groaned Erica, but she had this smile on her

face, which I came eventually to understand was reserved just for him. Interest? Affection? Definitely something going on between them. "Luther's paranoid about the business. He talks about the deals 'cause that's all he sees."

"I don't know," I offered. "He didn't sound like—like a salesman or anything."

"Oh, no, he's not that at all!" she said quickly. "He's a fantastic producer. He's great, really. But he bitches a lot about the labels, and he's always trying to warn me. I say, 'Luther, I *can* get a lawyer, man.' I think he's a little burned out if you ask me. Listen, honey, I don't want to talk about him. You meet Steven yet?"

"Yeah."

"So what do you think? Come on, tell me, tell me, tell me—"

"This the one you phoned about?"

She nodded vigorously, still with an ear-to-ear grin. The way Luther had talked about Erica, you would think he was involved with her. Wrong. Funny thing was, the way Erica talked about Steven, you'd think *they* were an item. Wrong again. I think at best, she and Steven had a vibe going, and that was about it. It must have been obvious to Brown Skin Beats management, because they were pushing Steven her way, with Luther thrown in as a bonus. The message seemed to be here's what you can have if you cross the street to us: hot talent to collaborate with, hot producers and whatever else you want. But keep in mind, when I came down, Erica was still doing her peep show routine for Easy with his two-way mirror, and that whole sordid business with gangsta Jamal Knight was about a month in the future.

"He's smart, and he's funny, and, thank God, he's talented, and he's already *there*, Mish," she was saying. "He's made it. It's awkward with anyone else now, you know? Ever since the first album took off, I've had a couple of dates, and guys just look at you strange. They're either scared puppies, or they're horny as hell to nail a pop star, or they think you're going to ramp them up to the six-figures. They must be dreaming if they think I've made that much money!"

"You will," I offered.

She didn't hear me. Still holding my arm, eager to gush about the new love of her life. "But Steven knows what's going to come my way. He's been through all that bullshit with the negotiations and the marketing idiots. He's been so helpful, and he's really caring. He's got genuine charisma. Don't you think so?"

"He seems nice."

"Hang out with us tonight. I really want you to like him."

"Okay, but Erica, I got to go somewhere and change. I feel hopeless dressed like this."

*S*he insisted we jump in a cab even though she lived only a few blocks away from the hotel. When we walked through her front door, I saw how she could afford to splurge. A white carpet as pristine as fresh-fallen snow lined the four-bedroom apartment under ceilings twelve feet high. The windows in some rooms went from the floor all the way up, the views not fantastic but still impressive enough with their corner panorama of Manhattan. One wall in the living room was completely covered by a shelf unit with a 36-inch-screen television, DVD player, stereo plus sleek Sanyo machines I couldn't even identify. The pictures on the walls weren't prints. They were original paintings, chosen carefully to go with tables and chairs in blond wood and the gigantic white sofa. The second bathroom leading off Erica's walk-in closet held her only ego wall. Here she kept her double-platinum award for "Late Night

Promises" and a poster for her first big concert in New York.

"You've arrived," I gasped.

"You like all this?"

"It's . . . a grown-up's place," I joked.

She laughed, knowing what I meant. I had spent so many summer hours with her in Erica's room in her old family house, listening to music, trying on clothes and simply talking. When this holiday was over, I was going back to New Haven, Connecticut, to a dorm room or an apartment with roommates off campus. And here was Erica, done already with a twenty-something's rite of passage as far as apartments go. No more roach-trap dives with a suitcase to rest your TV and pots and pans borrowed from Mom.

"You're rich," I said.

"No, not yet. But I'm doing okay. We better get you changed so we can get back."

She led me into the second bedroom and showed me the en suite bathroom I'd have all to myself. I hurried to open my bag and find the couple of dressy ensembles I'd brought along for nights on the town.

"Mish?"

"Yeah?"

"Do you think sex changes when you get a lot of money?"

I had to laugh. "You're asking me? You're the one with the cash! You tell me how it is."

"Hey, I told you I really don't have a lot of money," she explained. "I bought this place, and that's got to be it for a while. I'll have to work my ass off to hang on to it, you can be sure of that. No, seriously." She bit her bottom lip and steered us back to the issue on her mind. "You think if you'd got a lot of money, you'd be different with someone?"

I settled on a silk blouse with a leather mini. I could have slipped into my one cocktail dress, but instinct told me that hanging with Erica would mean other chances to impress. Next party I'll make an entrance, I promised myself.

"Different how?" I asked her. "You mean you'd be actually different in bed?"

"I don't know," she answered, and I watched her struggle to put it into words. "Maybe when you can have everything, you think you should..."

I know what you're thinking as you read this. Those guys she fucked during breaks in performances, the guys she picked up before and after concerts in all the cities along a tour. But success didn't give Erica Jones a healthy sexual appetite—it was already a part of her.

"What are you trying to say, sweetie?" I prompted, laughing. "You think you'll come louder on satin sheets instead of plain cotton whites?"

She slapped my arm playfully. "I have _got_ to stop telling you shit. You're terrible."

"Hey, I don't understand, that's all. This is pretty insecure for you."

She shrugged, sitting down on the little bench where she could try on a dozen or so shoes. "I know. Remember I told you how I hear the music in my head? I mean, it must be like that for you with writing, isn't it? You get words or notes or whatever, but you're happiest when you're putting it together."

"Yeah...?" I didn't know where she was going.

"When you make love, don't you feel like you're creating something?" she asked me innocently. "I don't mean _babies,_ I mean...You're in the moment, and you want to make music physically. I don't know how to say it, Mish. I think when it comes down to it, we're all just ultimately _alone._"

"This is good," I joked, "you're in the mood for a party, sure."

"No, no, I'm not depressed, I'm fine," she told me. "I'm

just making a point. You're with a guy, and no matter how tender he tries to be or, hell, when he's just giving it to you, and it's *ummmph,* good, you're still so inside yourself when you come. Just once, I want to find a guy who makes me want to write out a chart after he makes my toes curl."

"You're talking about love," I said somewhat dismissively. "You're only dressing it up in different words."

"No, it's not just love," she said, shaking her head. "Well, it is, but ... Look, I know creative people are selfish. You have to claw and fight your way to steal somebody's time to listen to your demos, and that means somebody else loses, and you miss dates and friends' birthdays because you're trying to get there. You're climbing and climbing, and you think just a little bit further. So now I'm almost there, and ...."

I thought I understood. She wasn't worried about being alone at the top. She was worried that this was who she was. This is what she did. She made music. She would go on making music, and any man who wanted to be with her had better accommodate *her.* Erica Jones, force of nature. And how did she get the man who would make her happy? Of course, she had the regular concerns—finding a guy who wouldn't be a submissive doormat but not a control freak either, one who let her breathe. She knew already you could have great sex without love, but she was beginning to wonder if she could find a great muse, and what's love got to do with it?

All I could think was: you need a good woman, darling.

*P*arties. You never notice how the steady arrival of people increases the pitch of everything. The music, the air, the reflexive increase in the stereo volume, even the crash of the ice as the bartenders fix a new drink. That afternoon in the hotel, I had been in my jeans and tank top, and now I was here again, looking around in a tan silk blouse and a short black skirt, and I heard voices layered over each other. I found Erica in the room with the billiard tables and the pinball machines, her arm wrapped around Sheila Tammany of the group Black Canaries, both of them singing along melodramatically to "I Have Nothing" from *The Bodyguard*. Erica was hilarious as she parroted each one of Whitney Houston's gestures: *Stay in my arms if you daaaaaare, or must I im-ahhh-gine you there*...

We burst out laughing when Steven made his entrance. He was carried like Whitney in Kevin Costner's arms, only the arms holding him in this case belonged to a tall muscular black guy. As Steven got down, he introduced his "rescuer" as Odell, the lead dancer for his upcoming concert tour. He had a dark complexion and his head was shaved, which helped deflect attention away from how long his face was, but it was a nice face. He was reasonably handsome. You could see he had a dancer's vanity, standing in a way that showed off his arms and chest. Sheila was suitably impressed. Erica was polite, having met him before. Odell made me a bit self-conscious, focussing all his attention on me. I felt distinctly set up.

"Steven's heavier than he looks," said Odell. "Now you... You're so petite, I'll bet I could lift you over my head like a feather."

"Bet you can't," Erica put in quickly.

I gave her a look: *Don't encourage him.*

"I believe you," I told Odell.

"No, you don't," he said with a grin. "Come on, I'll bet you were a dancer in school, too, weren't you?"

"Not at all," I lied.

"She was a singer," Erica volunteered.

My eyes were pleading: *Will you stop.* Erica mischievously shook her head: *Nope.*

As he gripped me by my hips, I sprang off the balls of my feet so that I wasn't deadweight for him. He lifted me high in the air, and my squeal was lost in the cheers of the others below. As he brought me back to earth, I had to slither down his chest, staring into his eyes.

"Told ya," he said, as if it were me who had contradicted him.

I said I needed a drink after my "latest flight," and he rushed off to fetch me one, saying don't go anywhere. Erica linked her arm through mine and led me away, assuring me Odell would find us no matter where we were on the floor. "Didn't think you'd go for a guy like that," she teased, "but he'll be good for warm-up action. I'll find you a better one, I promise."

"He seems nice," I said. "Comes on too strong, but..."

"You can do better. Odell's the kind of guy who if you're doing it in front of a mirror, the man's watching *himself*. Oh, shit, there's Easy. I better go do some baby-sitting before we have a real scene on our hands..."

She was off. I didn't know all the politics of their relationship yet, not then. When Easy Carson had arrived with Erica, I had watched his baby face light up for a couple of friends then shyly look away as he lumbered in. He and Steven Swann gave each other the barest of nods. Spotting Luther, I drifted over to him to ask what the friction was all about.

"Carson thinks that Brown Skin Beats wants to lure Erica away from Easy Roller Records," explained Luther. "And he's right."

"He is?"

"Mmm-hmm. Carson only signs his artists to two-album deals. His 'short leash' policy has meant that his rappers, his singers, his producers all got to worry about job security. But it's a double-edged sword. He's never had a star break into the top ten before. The distributors aren't going to love *him*—they think it was pure luck he found Erica. They don't want to buy in with him, and that means he can't throw cash and goodies at Erica to keep her happy."

"Erica cares about other things besides money."

He wore this look of patience on his face as if I were hopelessly naïve. "All right. I'll put it another way. Forget the perks and the trinkets, Easy doesn't have the cash to back her *as a star*. To keep her on top, he's going to need to spread around the green for the image consultants, the producers, the tour machinery, all of it. Easy thinks if he just hangs on to her, he'll get the investment somehow, and he's jealously guarding his stake."

"What do you mean?"

"Steven offered to sing backing vocals on 'Pariah'—title track of the second album. That little cameo alone can shoot an artist into the top twenty or thirty on the charts. Keep in mind, all this was being talked about a while ago—nobody could be sure how well 'Late Night Promises' would do. Easy gave Steven a flat no. Didn't matter his voice would be perfect for the track, or it would help Erica, or even that she wanted him on it, Easy interprets the help as the label wanting to swoop in. And he doesn't want to owe Brown Skin Beats any favours."

"That's too bad," I said.

"Not at all. Steven sang the vocals anyway."

I looked at him and burst out laughing. "How . . . ?"

"*I* produced that song," said Luther. "Maybe Carson's bullshit works on other people, but I'm not going to have that asshole march into a studio and tell me how to put together a track."

"Won't he recognise . . . ?"

"Uh-uh. I told him I'd get a sound-alike session vocalist. No contract involved, nothing legal, and I have sign-off authority under *my* contract for how the job's done. This is all about publicity anyway. The label execs can act coy when they're asked, and when the time is right, they'll confirm it. There's not much Easy can do now anyway. He went ahead and released the single, and there's how many thousand units pressed and hitting the stores on Monday ... ? Tough luck, sucker. He'll look like a fool if he wants it remixed for the album."

Someone dimmed the lights, and the towers beyond the dark expanse of Central Park shone through the windows. Then the stereo cut out, and there was the unmistakable *squelch* and *ooooooo* of a microphone turned on for an amplifier. I hadn't even noticed the DJ's board and gear being set up in a corner. Luther and I politely turned to see our host's entertainment.

Steven had everyone's attention, Erica already hovering like a presidential wife off to the side. I noticed he'd changed, too. No more T-shirt with ripped sleeves, patched jeans and Nikes, now he was in what looked like Jean Paul Gaultier stuff, neon purple tie over crisp and very loud button-down purple shirt, a diamond ankh pin glinting in his lapel. Erica's pretty white boy was a hell of an actor. Because I watched him walk like a panther in that suit over to whisper something in his bodyguard's ear. A pat on the fellow's arm, a nod that said: *Get it done.* Steven the boss. Then, as he picked up the microphone and began to speak, he fell right back into the nineteen-year-old's head bob and tug at the collar, as if this was the teen dream's first necktie.

"Hi, everyone, I'm Steven." Nervous eyes down. You could almost hear him counting the pause—two, three, four, look up. "Hope everyone's having a good time. And thanks for coming out to celebrate my second birthday of this year." Laughs and applause, a couple of hooting whistles. "We thought since you're all here, we'd make you our 'victim test market.' We're releasing two versions of the 'Skankin' Around' video next week, and we thought we'd show you the, uh, director's cut."

The tuxedo and designer dress crowd gave out a big frat-boy cheer. *"Whaaaa-heyyyyyyy!"*

Steven coyly protested his innocence. "Don't y'all be like that! I'm a decent guy. Ahem. Anyway, there are two versions. And we're going to play the hot one for you tonight. A special video that's only going to show in the clubs. Now I know you guys didn't come out here to watch a screen. So I thought if I asked our choreographer, Luba Kauffmann, very nicely—naw, shit, I begged her—to round up some of the dancers, they could give us a live demonstration tonight!"

And the howling and clapping became thunderous.

"Give it up for Luba, people!" shouted Steven, pointing to a small skinny woman in black slacks and a zipped-up leather jacket. "She's worked with and learned from the hottest ones in her trade, man—Marty Kudelka, Travis Payne. Send her some love, folks!"

Polite enthusiastic cheer for Luba, and you could just make out Steven shouting to kill the overheads. One of those enormous television projection screens for lectures came down, while all at once we saw a row of scantily clad dancers posed in the glow of red and blue spotlights. *Boom, bidda-boom-boom, boom-bidda-bidda-bidda* as the percussion for Steven's new single roared out of the speakers, and the dancers snapped into action. If I had to describe Luba Kauffmann's style of choreography, it had those impossible athletic moves that Justin Timberlake used in "Like I Love You," only more sexed up, far more suggestive—

Steven was on the projector screen, nude on a king-size mattress with a brass rail headboard, fan blades spinning lazily overhead for the shot down as he sang out his angst.

And, yes, a woman's head obscuring his privates as she mimed fellatio. Clever boy that he was, he didn't divide the attention of his audience, singing live in the shadows while people took in the raunchy image of him on the screen.

You're just skankin' around—

Image upon image upon image, no attempt at narrative, the director doing a couple of tribute shots to Madonna's "Express Yourself" with guys wrestling in a downpour and Steven walking over to a blonde girl bathed in blinding white light on luminescent sheets. And then no-name actors were penetrating the girls in quite graphic displays. Back to Steven, walking away from the camera nude, girls in the audience squealing over his little ass as he went into a washroom and acted out shaving.

On the beat, the female dancers tore away crotch patches on their male partners—doing a Super Bowl Janet. Every one of the guys a hung horse. Back to the main theme as our live Steven marched into view at last only five feet from the impromptu circle of guests, his necktie gone, shirt unbuttoned to his navel. *Just skankin' around*...And I have to admit there was something sexy about that white, immature flat chest with low pecs, his physique almost androgynous.

People couldn't believe the spectacle. They stared openmouthed. The girl dancers were shedding more clothes until they were completely naked, and the guys mimed stroking their pussies. On the screen, we were already into soft-core territory. Steven danced out of the spotlight, now in shadows but still identifiable as the naked dancers moved from the Timberlake staccato poses to more fluid, almost Spanish-style movements, bodies dipping and arching, writhing and breaking apart only to come together again.

It was a club video, so I knew it was going to go on this way for about ten minutes.

I took a walk.

I found a small area that looked like a "green room" with a couple of plush chairs and a television. This one was set up with a multiple DVD player, and there was a bookshelf stacked with videos and movie boxes instead of bound volumes. I found the remote and clicked on a video of Mya doing her little striptease and tap dance show.

I hope—you have—an appetiiiiiiite, she sang. *So baby, will you come and spend the night!*

Odell found me.

"If you're the lead dancer for the tour, why aren't you out there?" I asked.

"That one's a little too rude for me," he said. "I get to do a much more toned-down version when we hit the road."

I smiled. "Lucky you."

"So what are you doing here?"

"Thinking," I answered.

"Oh? 'Bout what?"

"How Brown Skin Beats and Steven wasted good money. Because that video director doesn't have a clue what sexy is." I pointed the remote at Mya on the screen. "This—this is sexy. There are some classic videos that are sexy as hell, and they beat anything going on out there."

Odell came over and sat down on the arm of the chair. "Well, a few in the crowd seem to agree with you. Luther split."

"He did? But I thought Luther and Steven were friends. Luther's done some producing and writing for him, hasn't he?"

"I wouldn't exactly call them friends, but they get along all right. Hey, I'm probably giving you the wrong impression. Luther split because . . . It's not that he didn't like the show. He just ain't crazy about how much *Erica* likes the show."

"Ahhhhhh."

I found it amusing that Luther felt thwarted by a display

of Erica's more than healthy libido. I liked Luther, liked him immediately, but he better get used to how Erica was.

Odell wanted attention. He was rubbing my shoulder, leaning in to me and saying, "Go on. You show me out of these what you think is sexy."

So I flicked through the videos and gave a shout of victory as I discovered En Vogue's anthem: *Whatta man, whatta man, whatta man, whatta mighty good man!* And like the amateur film critic I was, I tried to explain how those girls looked sexy as hell during the verses, all the while Odell keeping up his painfully obvious and relentless seduction.

"Can I sit down?"

I smiled. "Perfectly good chair over there."

"*Or* you could sit in my lap."

Oh, what the hell. He wasn't Karen, but he was here. He had a nice angular face with his shaved head and smooth dark skin, and he struck me as gentle. I hadn't been with anyone else since Karen, still wondering if my bad experiences with guys meant I hadn't found the *right* guy, or if Nature had sent me those jerks to drive the message home. I gave up the chair and sat down on Odell's knees. He linked his arms around my waist, and I ignored this, clicking the remote onto George Michael's "Freedom."

"Shit, who put this collection together?" he complained. "Some VH1 fool over fifty years old?"

"You're telling me you don't like Naomi Campbell up there?"

"I'm not saying that, no. Sure, this is sexy. I wouldn't think you'd find it sexy."

"What? Because I'm a girl? You've got a very narrow mind. Okay, yeah, they're all models, but look at the details, the way the water beads on Cindy Crawford's skin, how gorgeous that chick is when she pulls the sweater over her head—"

"You like that, huh?"

His fingertips on my leg, just brushing under the hem of the skirt. He was nuzzling my neck, trying to kiss me. I shook my head in a slow, gentle manner, and as his chest lifted for an exasperated huff, my hand covered his and moved his fingers farther up the inside of my thigh. His face betrayed its confused surprise, and he thought I was teasing him. He tried to kiss me again, and once again, I averted my head.

"I don't understand you," he whispered.

"You don't have to," I replied. "Just let this be enough for now. . . . Okay?"

"Okay."

I guided his fingers to my pussy, feeling the tips of them through the layer of my cotton panties.

"Any other videos you like?"

"Mmmm," I moaned, and struggled to fast-forward to Kelly Rowland in her red cap singing "Can't Nobody." I could feel Odell's erection on my hip like an iron bar through his trousers, but it was his hand, his hand—

Trying to be nonchalant. "Check this out," I said. "See, the way I figure, they were trying to go for the sexy kitten side of her with that video where she's on the beach, but I think she's drop-dead beautiful in that white number in the alley by the fire escape. Look how she bends her knees and sinks like that—"

See I'm the only one that can love you, babe, you're not that big a foooool.

Kelly Rowland. And he was inside my panties now, whispering a joke about how he never knew videos could be like porn, two fingers burrowing inside me, and I gasped and then leaned back against him, saying Come on, it's not porn, Snoop Dogg is porn, this is erotica. Ashanti now, riding her elephant, and Odell thought I was getting off on the shots of the poster-boy type walking in barefoot and shirtless to tickle Ashanti's toes. I couldn't tell him it was that lovely girl in the sun and the sea. *Aw baby when you come to me, I'll make it so you'll never leave* . . . Fingers slipping out of my vagina to play with my clit, then pushing inside me again, his other hand fondling my tits through the silk, and he was caught up in it now, in the minimalist arousal, a brief glimpse of bare skin, both of us watching intently, keep watching, keep watching . . .

And then Erica's video came on for "Late Night Promises," and I hadn't seen it in a while. Erica singing, Odell doing things to me, and I couldn't confide that I touched myself this way when I played my very own copy of it back in the dorm. "Lyrics."

Erica in perhaps the only overtly sexy video she ever made, her first and last surrender to how she would be depicted. One of those too-handsome brothers from Central Casting played the boyfriend in this one. He gripped the tails of a white dress shirt she had on and knotted them under her breasts, leaving her midriff bare. Odell's fingers moving faster, but keeping a steady rhythm, me panting as Erica sang: "Lyrics—" Keening now as I pressed the rewind button to get that achingly beautiful shot of her stomach again, the swell of one of her breasts, and it didn't matter that I had seen my good friend naked before, changing clothes in gym or in her family bedroom, she was there on the screen, only two buttons done up on the dress shirt, and, oh, cut to a shot of Erica raising her lovely leg as she slips on pantyhose and, ohhh, cut to Erica after school years ago when I saw her date Alex Hardy unbutton a shirt just like this one and slip his hand in to feel her tit, the way she kissed him, her full lips like tiny red pillows, and *I knew* what I felt for her, what I had to avoid telling myself. Cut to the video with the "boyfriend" turning down Erica's collar. A gesture with such a sexy, casual intimacy about it, then soft dissolve to her close-up for the bridge, and I looked down at my bush of tight pubic curls and the strong brown pad of flesh that extended from Odell's thumb, his fingers inside me, wracked with sobs and shudders, coming against Odell's hand as Erica tortured me with her voice on the screen....

Bling Bling

*W*hat was *supposed* to be three weeks of sightseeing and shopping and decompression in New York was rapidly turning into my internship in the pop music industry. Erica and I took in a few local wonders, The Met and a quick pop into Grand Central Station and Chinatown. And Erica's new celebrity opened a couple of unusual doors for me as a tourist. I don't think I could have afforded lunch at Gotham Bar & Grill if Brown Skin Beats hadn't picked up the tab and Luther hadn't invited me along—more "wooing" of the star to their side. My peek at Rockefeller Plaza included standing on the sidelines *on the inside* of the NBC studio while Erica was interviewed for the morning show. My friend. And all during these weeks, I helped dig through her apartment for lost sheet music or scribbled lyric notes. Mish, can you check my appointment book over on the desk? What did I do with that blue top? Shit, been looking for this for *ages*—thanks, Mish. They're letting me have final say on these photos. Mish, don't you think they're a bit too sexy? My Dad's gonna freak. (Erica nude but lying on her stomach, looking over her shoulder back at you some-what imperiously, like the viewer had just intruded.) What do you think? *I trust you.*

When the three weeks were nearly up, she said to me, "Listen, I'll pay for the extension on your ticket. Just stay a few more days, will you, sweetie? It's been so good having you here."

"Erica, I'm over my budget. Hell, I'm broke. I keep this up, I'll be dipping into my stash for next year's course fees!"

"Girl, I'll pick up the tab, don't worry."

"Look, I know you're getting royalties, but you can't be making that much."

She offered a reassuring smile, celebrating her own private Christmas. "I'm playing tonight at Brownies, and I'm getting a nice fat wad of money for it. We're good for a month—more than that, even. And the way that label is chasing us, I don't think I'm going to have to pick up a check in a restaurant for days!"

Us. I don't think she meant it in an egomaniacal "royal we" sense, she was already beginning to think of me as part of her personal team. After two days of settling in, I was the one who woke up first in the guest bedroom and shuffled my way into the kitchen to turn on the coffeemaker. My friend was putting me up, so I paid her back through little things. I wrapped a scarf over my "morning hair," threw on some clothes and took a quick elevator ride down to hit the shop on the corner. It was a combination newsvendor and café with great apricot-cinnamon croissants and a supply of Erica's morning reading: *The Times, Newsday, Daily Variety* and, on Thursdays, *The Village Voice.*

Before the star greeted the day, I found myself munching on scones and reading the papers myself. I marked things I knew she'd be interested in, a review of one of her concerts, or how Roc-A-Fella Records was doing in a business sense. I was her amateur press clipping service. I had her clothes for the day hung up and ready for her in the walk-in closet. Consciously, I told myself I was a good friend. Unconsciously? Maybe I wanted to be indispensable.

Erica was a sleeper who didn't like to rise until "the crack of noon," but I could usually roust her a bit beforehand. I remember stepping into her room one of those early days, and there she lay, the sheets and duvet pushed aside like crumpled clouds. I listened to her breathing for a moment. I took in the sight of her. The large eyes were closed, the sensual thick lips slightly open. I marvelled at her body, how it captivated me in ways that Karen's didn't. Karen's petite frame and exotic glow were so different from this luscious girl lying here, all her features so full and ripe. Her dark heavy breasts spilled to the side, and the nipples were erect, making me wonder if she was aroused by a dream. I admired the curve of her waist leading to the slope of her beautiful bum, and as she stirred with a moan, her legs shifted. I could have reached out a finger. I could have teased that glorious clit in one stroke. I was tempted. I was terrified.

I did nothing. I patted her arm. Like a friend. And I said, "Hey, it's 11:30."

Never self-conscious about her body around me, she groaned and muttered a recital of desperately needed items like a doctor from an *ER* episode. "Nescafé in an IV push, 10 ccs of orange juice plus ten minutes of CNN ..."

I socked her over the head with a pillow. "Oh, get up. You look too damn good for a rock 'n' roll suicide."

One month turned into two. I went back for four days to Toronto to see my parents and have a passionate reunion with Karen, and then I was back in the Upper East Side, saying hello again to clothes and my hair curler left behind— like I lived there, not in a dorm in Connecticut. I don't know exactly when the turning point was for her, but the clincher came when Erica, Luther and I were just hanging in her apartment one afternoon, finishing up lunch, and she tossed me the cordless phone. "Mish!" she hissed at me, as if the person could hear her right through the Caller ID display. I had to play palace guard to fend off Easy Carson.

She had been slowly starving him of his casual sex "video nights" in the nightclub, perhaps because the first album had taken off so much that she was getting a lot of media attention. And Steven Swann was an unlikely candidate for her to fool around with in front of that two-way glass. Easy, however, was holding on for dear life to Erica in a business sense—just as Luther predicted.

"Look, Michelle, I *need* her here, understand? Five days of rounding up the press and the TV guys, and I got my whole starting line-up for this appearance, you know? We got Trevor Nelson from England over here, man!"

Erica, listening in on the extension, vigorously shook her head: *No way.* But she already knew I understood. To put in an appearance with the other Easy Roller artists would now make her look small-time. Carson had Erica and one other R&B artist on the label, which meant most of his "line-up" would be his rappers who couldn't break the charts. Luther muttered how he had his doubts Carson could bag Nelson anyway, let alone if the guy was in town.

"Easy," I said in a calm voice, "if you got your whole crew, you won't need Erica there."

"Yes, I do! Come on, Michelle, she's the top-seller for the whole fucking label—"

"Well, then, you didn't plan this very well, now did you?" I argued. "You get all the media out, and you don't check her schedule for—"

"*Fuck* that. What is this diva shit? All my artists promote *each other,* girl, you understand me? You don't pick and choose what fucking publicity engagements we set up—"

"Where is that in her contract, Easy? You're telling me she's at your beck and call?"

That made him really lose his temper. "What am I talking to you for, *bitch*? You're her fucking house guest! Put Erica on the line. Now."

"Why don't you stop calling me names and listen for a moment," I said, doing my best to keep cool. "I can't pass you over to Erica because she's not h—"

"Well, where the fuck is she?"

"If you wait a minute," I went on, "I'll tell you. Erica took a flight back to Toronto. She wasn't feeling well—her guts have been bugging her. We're guessing maybe it's her appendix or some—"

"Why didn't she just check into a hospital here?"

"Oh, right! Like she can afford the health insurance you got in the land of the brave and the free and the incredibly poor? She's Canadian, Easy! We got a *proper* national health system where we're from, and instead of spending a few thousand bucks for an overnight stay, she can go home on her flyer points and talk to her GP *for free*."

In the background, Luther and Erica's expressions went from surprise to silently cheering me on.

"Okay, then gimme the number for her place in Canada," he demanded.

"Get real, Easy!" I told him, beginning to enjoy myself. "I don't have the number of every goddamn hospital in Toronto! She said she'd get back to me."

"She's not answering her mobile," snapped Carson.

"They don't allow you to have your mobile phone on in a hospital."

"This is *bullshit*!" said Easy. "This is bullshit. You have her call me when you hear from her." And he hung up.

Luther and Erica were both still looking at me in amazement and were now free to burst out laughing.

"You do know," said Erica, "in case you ever get sick

down here, you can just show doctors your Ontario Health Insurance card, right?"

"Yeah, but I bet Easy doesn't know that."

"Clever girl."

In truth, I'd learned from the master. That whole business with Jamal Knight's busy hands and Erica's idea of the real estate swap opened my eyes quite a bit.

"She's good," said Luther. "She's damn good."

"Good enough to bring her on board?" she asked him.

This was like Mom and Dad talking about you at the dinner table when you're seven. "Hey, what is all this?"

Luther shrugged at Erica and said, "Your friend, your idea."

So I looked to Erica.

"Sweetie, what you going to do when you get back to Yale?" she asked me.

I laughed in mild confusion and disbelief. "Go to my courses, try to get an apartment for myself and live off campus. What? What are you two getting at?"

"What about after you graduate?" Erica pressed on. "You're taking English, Michelle. I mean, what are you going to do with that?"

"You're doing a great imitation of my mother, Erica, but what is all this?"

"Dummy. I'm saying you don't *have* to go back. Why don't you stay and work for me?"

I was flabbergasted. I truly was. Like I said, on an unconscious level, perhaps I was creating a job for myself, but I don't know. When the offer came, I was sincerely surprised.

"Doing what?" I asked her. "Erica, I don't know anything about the music business! What am I going to do?"

"What you're doing now as my friend. You're handling phone calls, getting my wardrobe set, helping me with stuff, keeping the idiots off my back. Mish, I'll pay you to do it.

As a matter of fact, Luther thinks we can actually get Brown Skin Beats to spring for your salary as part of the contract. You'll get an office of *your very own* right downtown so that you can deal with all the suits, the marketing and the publicity guys. You divide your hours between here and there."

"How can I stay? I'm a Canadian—"

"Don't worry about that," said Erica. "BSB has an office in London. On paper, you're going to work there for a couple of months and then get transferred to New York, personally assigned to me." She arched her eyebrows at me as she laughed and said, "I'll be your boss! And, hey, I'll be a great boss. Who else is going to pay you to go shopping?"

And that was how I stayed.

*I*t was a case of Strange Days as we made the transition from Easy Roller Records over to Brown Skin Beats. The second album, *Pariah,* was supposed to be Easy's coup, but Erica was merely running out her time on the clock with him. Luther produced it, and he worked often for BSB. One of the singles released from the album featured Steven without credit, a BSB-signed artist. And Easy's tight fist on his wallet made BSB's promotional team leap on another contractual loophole.

"Easy was never obliged to promote his artists," explained Taurian Shaw, who fled the label to become a presenter on *The Cherry,* the weekend hip-hop chart show on the BET cable network. "I tell you, Easy Carson's idea of promotion was to say, 'Well, you can have a couple of gigs at the club.' *His* club. So he got you coming and going. You wanted to do a tour, he'd say, 'You go find money for a tour, man. It's your album.' When Erica slipped away from him, I just told him you got what you fucking deserved, man, always thinking small-time."

So just as I could tell Carson off, saying that Erica wasn't obliged to show up for his grand event, so, too, he could opt out of backing a tour for the second album. But with Erica hitting it big, he was scrambling like mad to organise a tour. Too late. Brown Skin Beats did it already. They couldn't use the name of the album in newspaper advertisements and posters, or play clips on television and radio commercials, but it didn't matter. They pushed *Erica Jones* in name. Once Erica got up on the stage, she could sing whatever the hell she liked. They were her songs. And the thinking at Brown Skin Beats was, fine, let Carson rake in his cut from the tour for *Pariah*. We're pushing our girl who has already signed with us for her next three albums.

And in the background was Luther, always. Tall and charming and with an energy to him, a vibration, like the kind she brought into a room. Those sleepy eyes and that somewhat crooked smile in his *café au lait* face. His powerfully toned arms doing his little *Stomp* percussion thing at the hotel party. Funny how Luther and Steven both dressed sharp, but had their different approaches. Steven didn't mind being a clothes horse for the big designers, but he still picked his wardrobe off the rack. Luther said he got enormous satisfaction picking out a fabric from a bolt of cloth and having it tailored to him. And it showed. He always looked crisp and sharp, and despite his rat-a-tat drumming when bored, he sat down in a chair with a panther's grace. I've seen other girls look at him across a room. A woman would swallow hard. She'd scope the joint, checking to see if he was alone then move in—

And get nowhere. I inevitably drifted over to him at these parties. "Luther, I'm a wallflower because that's me. What's your excuse? I saw that girl. She's gorgeous!"

"You have her then, Michelle."

"Maybe I will."

I don't know why, but in those days, I often made sly

references like this in front of him. I felt safe. I sensed that
Luther wouldn't have behaved weird around me had I come
out of the closet, and when I eventually did, he proved me
right.

"I'm too busy to get involved these days," he explained
in a weary voice.

"You are so full of shit!" I laughed.

"What? You think a guy can't be too busy for sex or not
want it sometimes?"

"Not at all," I said. "You're not too busy. You're waiting."

Cautious now. "Waiting? What am I waiting for,
Michelle?"

"For her," and I tilted my head over at Erica talking with
Ginuwine.

He folded his arms, and it was difficult to tell if he was
annoyed or impressed with me for being so perceptive.
"Now how did you suss that out?"

I shrugged at him. I couldn't very well tell him that I had
made a life, hell, I had even started a career out of waiting
for her.

They were friends, according to Erica. It was good for a
change to have a male friend. She didn't think she had had
one before. Morgan could have been one, but her relationship with Morgan was ... complicated. And it would get
even more complicated when ... Well, I'll get to that. Luther
had shepherded Erica around Brown Skin Beats. Before she
hooked up with Steven, it was Luther who was her guide
to the next rung in the business. At three in the morning,
he would ring her up and say, "Yeah, I know it's late, but
you've got to hear this!" Senegalese music. Or a piece of hot
demo from Jamaica. Or what if the bridge to the track they
were working on went with *this* chord? And Erica would
cuss him out, it's three in the morning, for God's sake.
Then: "Let me get my headset." I would stagger bleary-

eyed into the living room to find Erica in her robe, sitting at the desk and listening to him as she scribbled out a chart.

"Do you think Luther's for real?" she asked me once. "You don't think maybe he's being nice because he's like, you know, the company's babysitter for me, do you?"

I was flabbergasted. It had never occurred to me to have this suspicion, and I went with my first impulse. "Erica, no! No, Luther's all right."

Luther loaned her books. He always said here, I want to loan you this, but he never asked for it back. A coffee table book on Moroccan art, a paperback called *The Holographic Universe* about how reality isn't what we think it is, a novel by Salman Rushdie. She would thank him warmly and ask what made you think of me for this one? And his reply was usually something like "You can get inspiration from all kinds of places." When we visited his apartment, I discovered well-thumbed copies in his bedroom of the same titles. You sly dog, I thought. You didn't see the book and think of her. You think of her all the time, and it makes you want to go out and buy her these gifts.

I couldn't figure out whether he wanted to influence her thinking or—well, no, I think he actually wanted to share these things with her. He had the happy expectation that she would respond to a volume or a CD the way he had, or better still, her sentiments would flow from her fingertips to the ivory keys, creating something new and dazzling. Because of him.

In those early days, I can think of only one occasion when they allowed the natural chemistry between them to boil to a froth. He had phoned her up with an idea, always needing to communicate to her immediately, and once again I was a half-asleep witness staring down the long hallway at the two of them sitting side by side on the bench at her baby grand. Erica not even bothering to change, having buzzed him up still in her robe. I heard her murmur, "Shit, Luther, at four in the morning, I'm dead, man."

And he said, "Okay, put your hands on mine. You'll remember the pattern later." An obvious ploy, really, just to get her to touch him. And so she rested her hands gently on his as they played the notes.

When he finished his piece of composition, I heard the note resonate for a couple of seconds in the cavernous living room, and in that moment, they looked at each other.

"We ought to stop," said Erica. "We'll wake Mish up."

He nodded, cleared his throat nervously. "There's, um, something I've been meaning to give you—"

"You don't have to—"

"No, of course I don't *have* to," he interjected, laughing gently. "I want to. You know, Erica, I would have loved to be there when you first arrived. Watched it all come together for you. I would have liked to have taken you out somewhere to the Brooklyn Bridge or something and say, 'It's all going to happen.' And you shaking your head, saying, I don't know. But then, I guess you'd never do that. You were always sure, weren't you?"

She didn't answer. She merely stroked his arm affectionately. Down the hallway, I understood what he meant. It would have been nice if she had needed somebody for that kind of reassurance. She never did.

He fished out of his pocket a gold wristwatch. "My granddad worked as a barber in Woolworth's for twenty-five years, and when he retired, they gave him a gold watch. He said to them, look, this is great, but I've never had much money to give my wife anything nice. Can you trade this in for a lady's watch? They said sure, and my grandmother wore it until the day she died. I never had a sister, so my parents gave this to me. And when I was really down and out, I had to sell it at a pawnshop. The Japanese were supposed to be scooping up things like this back when they were flush with cash. And I felt sick as soon as I'd done it. I mean, shit, I'm not going to be broke forever, and instead of eating soup for a week, I'd given away a little piece of my family. I stewed on that for quite a while, and then I got a couple of songs published, made a bit of money, and I actually tracked this damn thing down to another pawnshop up in Rochester. Bought it back."

He held it out for her. "I want you to have it."

"Luther, honey, I can't—I can't possibly accept this—"

"Course you can," he replied. "Don't you understand? It's done its trick for me. I don't need it anymore because then I'm just holding on to it, it's just a possession. It should go to somebody who can look at it and give it a new meaning. If you ever lose everything, babe, you can get it back. You know it, don't you?"

"Oh, Luther . . ."

He understood her better than she thought, because she did worry about losing it all. Wouldn't anyone? When you get all the way to the top, you have to ask: how long can I go on? How can I re-invent myself again and again to keep them interested? Erica had an ultraviolet sense of humour sometimes, and she once joked: Fame is like cancer, man— *how long have I got? Instead of it eating from the inside, it eats you from the skin to your bone.* Here was Luther, who knew he couldn't give her the grand gesture of a night on the bridge to say all this is going to be yours one day. It already was. She didn't need him to introduce her to influential people. Her name could open those doors now. So he went the other way. He went small. And with that modest grandmother's watch, he told her: when it all gets too much, think of me.

As she leaned forward to kiss him on the cheek, her left breast fell out of the panel of her robe. She laughed and was about to cover herself up when his hand cupped her flesh in one smooth, confident gesture. She watched him as he watched her, his fingers exploring that full ripeness, his thumb moving to stroke and tease a large, puckering nipple, the areola swollen. She could see he was hard, his cock straining the crotch of his trousers, and she darted her hand forward to unzip his fly. In only a second, she had popped him loose. From my hiding place down the hall, I gasped and almost gave myself away. God, he was big. A light brown pillar of flesh blue in the semi-darkness, and Erica licked her middle finger and touched the side as if she were moving to pet a delicate bird. His cock stiffened in a spasm of desire. Both of them were leaning anxiously forward, Luther massaging her tit for minutes on end, her brown nipple like a teardrop clinging, Erica driving him wild with one finger barely touching his girth. It was practically a duel.

Then it was spoiled. He asked her, his voice raw with need, "What . . . what are we going to do about Steven?"

She squeezed her fist around him for the first time, and he groaned.

"Don't worry about Steven."

"Erica . . . I want you all to myself."

"Luther, aren't we friends?"

"Good friends," he said, and took his hand away. She didn't bother to cover herself up. "I want to be more than that."

"We can be," she answered.

"You mean like you're friends with Steven?" He was irritable now. He stood up and pulled away from her, adjusting himself and zipping up his trousers.

"Luther, I care about you, I do," she assured him. "I think I love Steven—"

"Then what is this?" he demanded, his voice climbing an octave with his hurt.

She shushed him, still thinking I was asleep down the hall. "This?" she echoed in a whisper. "This is sex. You telling me it's okay when a guy *really loves* a girl and plays around, but if a girl does it, it's wrong?"

"Hey, that's not me, I think it's wrong for both," he told her.

"You've done it in the past, though, haven't you?" she said, smiling, trying to lighten the mood.

"And I was wrong about it then, too," he said.

She chuckled and softly closed the lid on the piano. "That's pretty damn convenient after you've had your fun! Don't be so serious. Look, you're here. Come to bed."

She went to kiss him, and for a moment, he was nearly swayed. Then he retreated again, pushing her gently from his body. He was still hard, though. "I'm going home. I still want you to have the watch, Erica."

She thanked him. They traded good nights, and I heard her exasperated sigh as I stole back to my bedroom. I know he hadn't given up on her, but for now, he was leaving the field wide open for Steven Swann, who would be happy to take her.

*S*teven. At first, Erica's involvement with her new man was worth only a gossipy line in the press. Steven Swann was "seen with" Erica Jones at such-and-such a gala. She didn't want to go to any premieres where they'd suffer Death by Flash Bulb on the red carpet. It was her choice, a reflection of her ongoing policy of keeping her private life private. You can know my politics, sure. My sex life is none of your damn business. But Steven...Oh, that boy was clever. He had a whole stealth campaign in mind like a corporate takeover, and it was a long while before I understood his agenda. If she would be discreet over public appearances, he would cool things right down when it came to the physical.

It was as if circumstances conspired to keep them from

sleeping with each other. The two of them getting hot and heavy backstage when Steven did a guest appearance on one of those *Unplugged* shows, and there's my cue, babe, got to run. Steven in Erica's apartment, both of them down the hall in her bedroom, and she told me that she was stripped to her waist, his white hands fondling her tits, rubbing them in circles over her nipples as he smelled her hair and kissed the nape of her neck. And then I had to be the villain, not that I wanted to be that time. I took a call long-distance from New Mexico mentioning a family emergency, the relative tracking Steven down to Erica's place. Days later, he told us it was all a false alarm—

Keeping her waiting. Keeping her off balance.

Erica hadn't felt so teased since she first took up with Morgan, only Morgan had come off as aloof, detached. With Steven, she knew there was interest there. "If he doesn't make some time for me soon, I am going to rape that boy!" she joked. And all that anticipation, that pent-up hunger for him did the trick of motivating a public possessiveness in her. She flew down to perform a couple of duets with him for the Florida leg of his mini-tour. She was his date for the runway show of the latest Anna Sui designs. The "seen with" references in *People* graduated to the first big lies about Erica in the tabloids. A chauffeur claimed the pair got frisky in the back of a limo. I was surprised by how Erica treated the story with good humour. "Mish, I know it wasn't me because it's so damn tame. If they knew what I really got up to!"

But they didn't. They never did. The dancer she took during that instrumental break in the concert got fired, re-hired on my say. The studio vocalist she made time with in Seattle discovered his bookings would dry up if he breathed a word. The chiropractor she liked for a while and then tired of was introduced to a new flame. Gratitude, favours, threats—we used them all. Sometimes Erica picked up the phone, and as time went on, she left the cleanup more to me. *Never let 'em be able to talk about it,* she had told me that night we reminisced about high school. *Ever, ever, ever.*

But here was Erica now, gushing about Steven to *E*! "He's utterly amazing. He brings such intensity to his work and to everything. And when he looks at you, you just want to melt into a puddle." Erica, whose lyrics had been called "excoriating" for her songs about the environment and Third World debt, reduced to clichés you could read in *Seventeen*.

"So you're saying he's off the market?" laughed the interviewer.

"Definitely off the market," replied Erica, giggling. "Hands off, girls. Back away from the prize."

And perhaps most peculiar of all, I know for a fact that Erica *still* hadn't slept with him when she was making these comments.

Of course, he finally did "make time for her." He took her back to his place that wasn't very far from her own. Steven had bought up two of the massive stable spaces at Park and East 66th Street, the kind that had been purchased a while back and converted into trendy art galleries. He'd converted his into a sprawling six-bedroom townhouse. The son of successful painters in artsy Santa Fe, Steven could discuss home decoration and furnishings in a manner that prompted Erica to joke once, "Do you know how gay you sound when you talk like that, honey?"

I liked Steven at first. I found him more physically attractive than most men, especially white men. And when he dropped his guard, you could talk to him about all kinds of things on the news, and he was *informed*. His whole inarticulate, talented shy-boy act seemed a natural post–Timberlake progression in the pop world—the new improved image for teenage girl consumption. But the image grated on you after you had drinks with Steven and were reminded how bright he was. He'd tell you how *The Atlantic Monthly* did a great piece on the forgotten Balkans. "Get a load of this bullshit France is pulling with their airlines," he'd say, his wide screen tuned to Bloomberg more often than it ever was to MTV. Teenage girls don't like their poster boys brainy. I asked him once if he thought he would have ended up a corporate lawyer if he hadn't been spotted for his first band.

"Fuck, no, Michelle," he laughed. "You know what I wanted to be? I was going into politics. My high school in New Mexico had this big campaign over desert wildlife preservation, and I actually wanted to be a senator. You believe that?"

When it came to sex, I know he wanted Erica. He approached her as he approached everything else, plotting his moves, leaving little to chance, but his appetite was as raw as hers. On the night he invited her over, he was kissing her at the door, and they didn't stop kissing and fondling each other until he had backed up all the way into his bedroom.

"I want this to be special," he told her. He jumped on top of a footstool and hit a button on a strange box that had been specially attached to his ceiling with drill screws. "I couldn't believe that shit when he hit that compartment," Erica confided to me later. "I mean he was like some villain out of a James Bond picture or something!" Because she had discovered that her gorgeous white boy was into kink. Nothing heavy, pretty mild stuff, but perhaps when you go to bed with dozens of girls and can pick and choose, your attention turns to method, not frequency. I suppose I'm not the person to ask. And Erica always said that black men in her experience didn't stray too far from regular lovemaking. "It's always the WASPs who go in for the leather and bondage stuff, isn't it?"

I told her I didn't know.

Steven wasn't into leather. What he pulled out of that

special compartment was a set of *solid gold manacles*. By now, Erica's jaw had dropped. It wasn't just the escape artist's expensive jewellery, either. Her boyfriend had a whole elaborate rig set up. Along with the handcuffs, he had pulled down a kind of swing suspended from heavy ropes. Erica told me she didn't know whether to laugh or run for the door.

"And who do you expect to hold prisoner in that thing?" she demanded quietly. "Me?"

"Nope," he said, flashing his patented naughty boy grin. He handed her a gold skeleton key.

She watched him unbutton his shirt and toss it in a ball in the corner. Then he clicked shut the first cuff around his left wrist, stretching out his right arm for her to help him do the rest.

"You say you want it to be special," she reminded him. "But you had this gear all *built in*. Seems to me you've done this plenty of times."

"Not with anybody else, no," he quietly insisted. "I didn't set this up to be with somebody, just for myself."

She stared at him, hanging by his wrists, his toes just brushing the ground, and she didn't understand. He wasn't at all embarrassed by his helplessness but by what he was about to tell her.

"Non-tactile masturbation," he explained in a whisper, smiling shyly. "I got this idea that . . . that I could bring myself off just mentally, not touching myself."

Erica posed the obvious. "If you're alone, how do you get out of this thing?"

"There's a way," he said coyly.

She folded her arms and looked at him. "I don't believe you. You *must* have been fooling around with a girl with this set-up."

"Swear to God."

Erica laughed. "Let's see you do it, then. Make yourself come for me."

"I didn't say I'd got it to work!" protested Steven.

And now she was roaring. "Well, this is a pricey way to test your theory, isn't it, sweetheart?"

"I got the green, babe."

"All right, then," she said huskily. "Let's see if you're making any progress."

He said she would have to finish undressing him. It would be the first time she would see him naked.

She stepped up to him slowly, savouring the moment, and she unbuttoned his fly, zipping it open just enough for his jeans to sag a bit down from his waist. Then her finger-tips slid over the smooth skin of his hipbones, the almost feminine delicacy of them, circling around to his ass. She rubbed his cheeks, and the slight momentum made him sway a little in the manacles, all his weight going into his shoulders, and his breathing started to quicken. Erica told me she actually closed her eyes as she tugged down his trousers, drawing out the anticipation, her blind hands slipping off his boxer shorts and enjoying a two-second sensation of his balls and cock in the fabric.

She opened her eyes.

Still dressed, she unconsciously touched herself between her legs over seeing him like that. Muscles swelling from the exertion of his captivity, wrists above his head, and he was breathing hard through his mouth now, ribs flexed, and then the vision of his strong legs unable to find purchase on the floor, the way his feet dangled...All of him, his chest and even his legs so smooth right to his hard cock, pink and thick, the circumcised tip a vivid red. She had to fight the impulse to sink to her knees and gobble him up in her mouth. She wanted to trace her hands over his body and feel its strain. But more than this, more than all of this, she wanted him to make good on his promise. She wanted him to come through his own will and fantasies.

"You still got your clothes on," he reminded her.

"Umm-hmm."

He laughed, understanding, knowing what she wanted. He gazed into her eyes, and Erica read such lust in those sparkling blues, she swore she could see every play of their bodies in his imagination. He actually got harder in front of her. She looked at him chained like that, Steven almost going for a literal gilded cage, and it triggered something dormant and perhaps unrecognised until now. She told me later she didn't even suspect how aggressive she was sexually until she had Steven Swann at her mercy, that what she was about to do was perhaps an extension of those quick fucks she went after with stagehands and dancers. "I fuck angry," she joked about herself. And no man until Steven had challenged her by giving himself up so completely to her control.

She didn't caress him. She didn't masturbate him, not yet. She looked at that beautiful boyish skin, the smooth small buttocks, and she went around behind him and slapped his ass as hard as she could. At first, she burst out laughing. It was ridiculous. Even Steven laughed as he yelped. And then it wasn't funny anymore, because she saw the strain in his shoulders, the way his wrists shook in muscle spasm, and she slapped his ass again until his cheeks were a bright red, and her palm actually hurt. And his penis was darker with the surge of blood, thrusting skyward. She came up close behind him, gripping his ball sack and feeling the tender fuzz of his testicles, and she sank her teeth cruelly into his shoulder blade. Steven yelled his pain through gritted teeth, asking her what are you doing, what are you doing? Erica replied by raking her nails down his chest.

"I'm going to make you cry," she said. "Go on and cry for me—"

"No," he said, and she couldn't tell if he was being defiant or playing along.

She understood the swing on the ropes now. She came around to face him. Erica was a reasonably strong girl, about Steven's height, and she could just grip him by the buttocks to ease him into the seat of the swing. Steven let out an almost sexual gasp of relief because some of the strain had been taken off his arms. But she wasn't done with him, oh, no. She brought her lips to his and pushed her warm tongue into his mouth, and he didn't suspect a thing as she took the long nail of her middle finger and drove it into the soft skin at the base of his cock. She could feel him like thick rope, feel the skin of his penis stir and be pulled even more taut. Amazing, she thought in that instant, because except for the kiss, she had given him no gesture of affection, no kindness in her hands at all. She kissed him again and pinched his nipples hard, and this time her cruelty summoned the tears. She didn't want to mark his face in any way, still conscious that their looks were part of their bread and butter, but she grabbed a fistful of his blond hair and yanked hard.

"I'm going to bite your balls off," she threatened.

Pleading with her. "No . . . no."

In a rush, she stepped back from him and undid her trousers. Her wedge of black fur visible, her bra about to be unhooked, she says he was crying again, yanking hard on the gold chains as his cock swelled and ribbons of cum fired out of him. "Aw, shit, aw, God! Oh, Jesus . . ." Coming and coming as the tears ran down his cheeks. And she stepped back to him and wrapped her arms around his neck.

"Fuck, that was amazing," he said. "I didn't think I could . . . I thought we'd do this with me inside you."

"No, that was cool," she laughed. "And we're not done, honey."

She grabbed some tissues from the bathroom to clean him up, her index finger and thumb giving the head of his penis a mild squeeze to release the last bit of his essence. Steven was blushing fiercely, saying he had to get out of the cuffs now.

"Your arms tired?" she asked.

"No, no," he groaned. "It's just . . . I got to pee."

"You don't have to get out of the cuffs," she informed him.

"Erica, I can't do that in front of you."

"Yes, you can. I'll just get a glass or something."

"Erica—"

"Hey, if you got to go, you got to go."

His protests went on for a moment, but she kept ignoring him. I remember squealing a bit when she told me this part, asking her: Jesus, what do you want to help him pee for? And Erica lifted a hand and said: no, no, listen. It was *so* intimate. Her hand on his penis while he was bound like that, guiding him as he released himself this way, wiping him off again and having him completely vulnerable. Steven actually started to get erect again as he finished.

Time to play again, and this time she felt him all over. She wanted to wrap her arms around him from behind, feel his buttocks against her middle. She stood in front of him again, dropped to her knees to smell his musk, teasing his cock with her tongue, her helpless prisoner. His arms cuffed, there was a heightened eroticism to her guiding him into her pussy, penetrating her without an embrace. They laughed like children as she clumsily did her best to climb into the swing with him, but it was better without it, Erica coming around and doing it doggy style with him, relishing the suspense of whether he could hold out, arms taking his weight again, toes finding the carpet, and Erica pumping her hips like mad, her legs drenched in her own juices. These times were for her, and she felt like she was on a precipice, about to be swept into open air, orgasm after orgasm holding her aloft.

She heard a metal scraping, a clink of a mechanism, and before his hands were even pawing and squeezing her tits, she laughed at how, yes, just as he'd said, there was a safety device, an escape mechanism. She was down on the floor on her hands and knees, and it wasn't so much how his cock slipped so easily into her yawning, juicy pussy that drove her over the edge as the final pay-off of his hands, his chest, the brush of his thighs behind her legs, the enveloping at last of his whole body so long denied by the manacles. Such *heat* from his belly and thighs. The tiny blond hairs on his legs. He flipped her over, and with her knees on his shoulders he buried his face in her hair, a sheltering cocoon of smooth white skin, pale flesh filling her up and surrounding her, and she liked the perfect eternal youth in that white boyish face, commas of blond hair that fell and tickled her forehead, the hollow in his pale neck and his delicate collarbone, and skin on skin, white against black in an obscene yin and yang, luminescent blond pubic hair, the softest down, meshing with her fine dark curls, and look at how those blond strands are getting slick with her lubrication, their bellies together. She felt she was screaming with each quake of her body, Jesus, Jesus, don't stop, don't stop because no one had ever got inside her like that before, his pubic hair *like soft down* and Steven exploding inside her, and, sweet Jesus, those shiny cuffs just setting us up for the main event, oh, yes, a fuck as good as gold. . . .

Dogging It

Saturday night, and social life and business are mixed up again as we're all gathered at Morgan's. As I told you before, I liked Morgan. I liked the way you'd come up the freight elevator into his funky loft above 125th Street and smell his rice and peas in a big pot on the stove, cooked up the way his mother had made it. I liked his gravelly, world-weary voice, and the way you could talk to him about anything, and it was usually *good* talk that prompted you to challenge your assumptions, only with Morgan, you didn't have to shell out for expensive latte at a Village café. I borrowed books from him often. A whole gang of us came bounding through his elevator that day, hiya, Morgan, hey, how you doing, man? Zen Master nodding to us and getting out his herbs from the kitchen cabinets. As I walked in, I patted the bust of Beethoven on its pillar, my regular salute, and then I heard Morgan say, "Mish, get your paws off my *Nation,* honey."

I'd picked it up from the table and had immediately started flipping through it. "There's a piece in here by Christopher Hitchens I want to—"

"Uh-uh. Wait your turn."

"Busted," laughed Luther.

Everybody was in a good mood, Odell along this time and playing bartender. I don't think anyone happened to notice the open Scotch bottle and the glass on the table next to the magazine. It was five in the afternoon. Huh. Luther was saying something to me, trying to tease me over *The Nation*. Never realised you were one of them humour-less left-wingers, Michelle—

"Yeah, she's also a lesbian," piped up Odell with a toothy grin, thinking he was clever. "Trust me, I know."

I shot him a look full of daggers. Thanks for announcing to the world I haven't put out for you yet. Luther's face offered me sympathy, and he picked up a Cassandra Wilson CD and went over to Morgan to say, hey, I didn't know you had this.

It was one of life's little coincidences that Luther was also one of Morgan's protégés, both he and Erica treating him like a cross between the Grand Old Statesman of Jazz and a wise father. It wasn't hard for me to pick up that for Erica, there was more to their relationship. Luther had come into the place, tapping Morgan gently on the shoulder in the kitchen with the rolled-up copy of *Downbeat* he had fetched for him. Morgan kept his eyes on the pot he was stirring and muttered a short, gruff "Thanks." As Luther had gone to take off his jacket, Erica had leaned in and kissed Morgan on the cheek, and the old misanthrope deigned to give someone his attention. Her eyes holding his, and *click,* something else promised there.

Business first.

For the third album, Erica and Luther thought she was doing well enough now to take a couple of risks. "I don't want to do self-indulgent shit," Erica had complained to us. "People start to lose it and get sloppy. Or they go the exact opposite way because they feel the pressure to crank out hits, so they do really lightweight easy hooks. I don't want to make something that sounds *dated* after two years."

The answer, she thought, was jazz. But not covering old songs and tunes the way so many artists had done ever since Linda Ronstadt started the trend (with Natalie Cole, Bryan Ferry, and how many others following after all the way to the *Red, Hot & Blue* Cole Porter anthology and after *ad nauseam*). No, no, she said. She wanted a *clean,* sleek jazz sound, not swing orchestration but combo cool. *"Dream of the Blue Turtles,"* said Erica. "Classic stuff. No, really! Whatever you think of Sting, you got Branford Marsalis on that album, along with some kick-ass arrangements."

When she confided this idea to Luther and me, both of us looked at each other with the same thought. Brown Skin Beats would not be happy. No label likes risks. They like sure things. They had a stellar R&B talent on their hands giving Alicia Keys, Jamelia, Missy Elliott, *et al.* a run for their money, and their artist was going to deliver something that might make the loyal fan base go *huh*? We delicately played Devil's Advocate. Luther suggested the album better have lots of high-profile guests on it to create a buzz. He said there better be one sure-fire regular hit thrown in as in-surance to open it right on the charts. No, no, said Erica, raising her hands, she didn't want to play it safe. This would be her *Off the Wall,* her *Miseducation* and *Sgt. Pepper's* and *Joshua Tree* all combined. She laughed at us in disbelief.

"Come on, guys! Just because our parents liked some-thing doesn't mean it's shit. Think about stuff you can remember your Mom and Dad putting on that you still like. You like it for a reason."

You could almost hear Morgan's voice in that argument, and he was the obvious next step. So we visited him bear-ing gifts that night, bringing them out after dinner. Erica saying here you are, chief: an Alesis ADAT system. Not the most advanced one but good enough for Morgan's purposes.

He wasn't a technophile anyway, and Luther had to show him how to work the board and the computer software. The man was thrilled. This was plenty sophisticated for him. People don't know that while the ADAT was considered mostly for demos, Alanis Morissette had recorded all of *Jagged Little Pill* on it.

"This is really something," said Morgan. As he rubbed his salt-and-pepper beard, I thought he looked genuinely touched.

"And it'll come in handy," said Luther, "when you're helping us with arrangements."

Morgan didn't have to be asked twice. He played it cool, but he was secretly tired of scuffling along on piano bar gigs and doing occasional composition work for television. Jazz labels like Verve and Blue Note had long since stopped returning his calls. They wanted young artists with fresh sounds, and Morgan's work was dismissed as either too "derivative" or "conservative." If they wanted a sound like that, they had whole back catalogues of Miles Davis and Charlie Parker. Here was Erica and Luther telling him: We are grateful. We haven't forgotten you.

"I got to write my Ma and tell her I found work," he joked. "Let's open another bottle and talk about what you want." And as Erica and I fetched glasses from his open-plan kitchen, we heard this rapid machine gun fire jazz playing on the keyboard.

Welcome to the blue house! sang Luther. And he and Morgan had already adjusted the computer to give them an alto-sax accompaniment: *da-da, da-da, DA-da! Hello from the small mouse!*

When they were done bowling us over, I asked, "What was that?"

"It's the theme to *Bear in the Big Blue House*," explained Luther.

"It's on the Disney Channel," supplied Morgan.

"You watch the Disney Channel?" asked Erica.

Morgan pouted his lip. "I *do* have grandchildren, you know."

"And I have a son," Luther said briskly, heading for the kitchen to fetch some ice.

Erica pressed him for more. "You have a son? I never knew that."

Luther shrugged. "Trey. He's about three now. I don't get to see him much."

"Oh. I'm sorry."

"So am I. It's all right, it's just...His mother didn't—well, she didn't like the feast or famine deal with my child support when I was, uh, trying to climb my way up in the biz," he explained.

"I'm sorry, Luther," whispered Erica.

"It's okay. She moved him out of New York, so what are you going to do? My work's here. Can't chase them across the country because she decides to be somewhere else. I go down south when I can."

"We gonna play music or talk music or what?" complained Morgan.

"Keep your pants on, old man," said Luther, handing him a drink and a slap on the back in that order. "Here, we'll give you something in neutral and see what you can do with it—" He tapped at a few keys on the computer, and we suddenly had a generic jazz bass and drums in four-four time ascending and falling *dum dum dum dum dum dum dum dum*...

"Please," groaned Morgan, a cigarette dangling from his lips, "don't insult me."

Dum dum dum dum dum dum dum dum...

One relaxed brown hand came up, tapping out a staccato Morse code on the ivory keys: *Da* (Pause) *Da, da, da, DA*. Luther, Erica and I were all laughing now as we recognised Duke Ellington's "C Jam Blues." Luther went back to the computer, cackling that "Ah-ha! Dad wants to go to a higher level on the PlayStation." He fooled around with the bass line, and Morgan kicked into a smooth rendition of "Now's the Time," a lot of his improvisation around the melody borrowed from Oscar Peterson. The tune blew Odell away, and Morgan said, "You never heard no Charlie Parker in your life, boy?"

"I know Charlie Parker. He's old school, right?"

"*This* is Charlie Parker," said Morgan, as if hushing him in church. Then he quit "Now's the Time" to play a bit of a haunting bluesy number that sounded vaguely familiar to my ears. I couldn't quite place it.

Luther was captivated as well. His brow furrowed, he smiled at his friend and said, "Who's that? I don't recognise that." His voice was mildly teasing, as if perhaps it was one of Morgan's own works.

"That," said Erica, grinning at her jazz sage lover, "is Duane Jones."

Her eyes met mine briefly, and she saw on my face how it came back to me, one of the pieces she had casually played on the family piano years ago in high school. Of course.

We were all respectfully silent as Morgan kept playing his old partner's composition right to the end.

"To Duane Jones," said Luther, raising his glass in a toast.

"To Duane Jones," the rest of us echoed.

*M*organ played a few more snatches of this or that jazz legend for Odell. Erica and I stood in the kitchen area, leaned against the counter by the sink, watching the men. I knew by now that I wasn't destined to be one of the breeders, but Luther's revised status as a parent endeared him even more to me. As bizarre as it sounds, considering how

I felt about her, I actually considered him a good match for Erica. I wasn't about to push them together, but I was curious why Erica hadn't chased him as she had blatantly chased others. After all, Luther might "want her all to himself" but men will settle for having a taste of Erica before giving her up to rivals.

"He's smart, he's responsible—I mean he's doing his best for that little boy of his," I said, ticking it all off for her. "He's mature—"

Erica downed her drink and gave me a patronising pat on the arm. "Mish, I know you mean well, but God save me from complicated men."

So she was not about to be hung up on Luther Banks. Luther, however, was still very much interested in Erica. After all the analysis and talk about bringing in not just studio pros but real jazz session musicians who could record together instead of laying down individual tracks, we all said our good nights. Odell made his pitch again to see me home or better still why didn't I have a nightcap at his place? What was the big deal? I told him I had to get up for a meeting. We were milling around, finishing our drinks, and Erica didn't go for her jacket slung over her chair. She told me she'd see me back at the apartment. I shrugged and said fine, and it was Luther giving her a second curious glance. Watching and not at all happy as she stood next to Morgan, who was already pouring them both another drink.

As the wooden slat door closed the freight elevator, I glimpsed Erica's hands sink under Morgan's belt and pull out his shirttails. She was caressing the skin on the small of his back, Morgan smiling and keeping his eyes ahead, a flicker of pleasure there as if the entire evening had been a prelude for this sensual reunion.

He must have caught it just as I did. Luther.

"You okay?" I asked.

"Yeah," he muttered, and as the freight slowly descended, his eyes gazed ahead, still burning on the image of them together.

I think he was disillusioned with Morgan as much as with her. He had this face . . . You could paste it on a boy of twelve who catches his father walking out of a hotel with a woman who's not Mom. Morgan was a teacher, a mentor for him, so that there was always a deference no matter how casual the business conversations or just shooting the breeze. Involvement with Erica shrank the old master down to life-size and made every wrinkle, every mole and crack in that craggy bearded face abruptly visible. He would be touching Erica in a moment. He'd be kissing Erica. The idea of her with Steven Swann was unpleasant, but Luther carried around a private amused disdain for Steven. Erica and Morgan? Too much. All the other men he guessed that she'd been with were abstractions, but Erica and Morgan . . . It was a screwdriver twisting and burrowing in a knothole in the mind, driving him crazy, the way it could drive me crazy when I stopped to consider it.

"It's fucking sad, really," said Luther.

"What is?" asked Odell, casting his eyes warily at me. He had a glimmer of what was going on.

Luther sounded like he was talking to himself. "We're supposed to be macho and think, wha-hey! Good for you, man, you get yourself a sweet young honey when you're coughing away in your fifties or whatever. But it's kind of pathetic. You still look like the girl's Dad."

"No one cares about age difference anymore," I put in quietly. "And you can't tell me you think that's such a big deal to you."

"As a matter of fact, Michelle, I do have strong opinions on it, yeah." Luther clucked his tongue once more in disgust. "It's not fucking dignified, man. It just ain't."

*S*ummer, and Erica and I had our first flight in a private jet, visiting Steven's ranch home on the outskirts of Santa Fe, New Mexico, on a long weekend. It was the four of us, really, Odell coming down as my "date." Steven and Erica had so casually invited him down without asking me first, believing that he and I were on a parallel track of relationship. I said before that Erica told me everything, but by now you must have figured out I never told Erica everything.

Steven plunged thoroughly into his role of playing host, offering nuggets of local history and pointing out the city's various art galleries. "Here you go," he said. "The place they once said looked more like a prairie dog village than a capital." He used his celebrity son status to get us all a tour of the Bonanza Creek Ranch, where Western films were shot. There was Erica and me, two city girls who grew up near rolling green Ontario hills and lakeside skyscrapers, standing around and gazing at white adobe houses and a desert horizon. As we strolled past saloon doors and hitching rails for mounts, Steven remarked, "Hey, I thought every little girl went through a horse-loving phase." We told him that would be true if we were a couple of white kids who could hit the Bridle Path in Toronto's very exclusive mansion district.

When we arrived at his gigantic house, he led us in a rapid march past a gaudy lounge, suggesting, "Okay, close your eyes." The room had the décor of a Tex-Mex restaurant: bull antlers in a plaque, framed "Wanted" posters on the wall, and one of those L-shaped combo couches in a tan colour aimed towards a giant television, plus there was a wet bar with colonial period stools. Ugh. Odell asked if Buffalo Bill threw up in here or something. "I know, it's awful," admitted Steven, "but I keep it for photographers from *InStyle* and other mags."

Image. The irony was that Steven, the kid with two gallery-showing artists for parents out in New Mexico, really was an American Civil War and Wild West buff. Talking up a storm to us about that great Ken Burns mini-series, and how it was "staggering, man" the ineptitude of the Union generals in the early years and how Crazy Horse was one cool dude. But he kept his interests mostly on his bookshelves and on the racks of his DVD collection. Steven didn't like the idea of fans knowing exactly what his home looked like, so he had created this showpiece, furnishing it with bric-a-brac of ordinary people's misconceptions of the Old West.

His *real* taste in furniture leaned towards the plush but modular, tans and black tones with track lighting and framed artsy photos of Spain on the walls. He had sculptures on glass tables that looked like scale models of Gaudi architecture, all seashells and pebbled stone and curves. There were chairs and stools that picked up on his love of the West, but they were clever designs with period fabrics. Steven always had to be clever.

"Whoa," I said. "No IKEA chairs or Klimt posters for you, I see." I thought of my fellow dorm residents at Yale with their wannabe bohemian tastes.

"Please!" laughed Steven. "I don't do that Swedish particleboard shit. So what are we going to do?"

"It's your ranch, Hoss," joked Odell.

"You're right, it is! Okay. Simon says we get drunk. And then we all get laid."

Erica flashed a look at me, smiling away, her eyes shining with half-anticipation, half mild apprehension over what he could have in mind. She had always been uninhibited, but Steven was turning her into his special breed of daredevil. I had flown down, rehearsing in my head a careful speech that would keep Odell from sharing my bed, but our host had just dropped a big hint that he had group sports in mind. . . .

*L*ate. Post-pizza. Post-Tequila, Scotch, gin, vodka and a case of the inexhaustible Drambuie supply Steven was still working on from the catered party. All of us drunk, only two of us—the professional singers, Erica and Steven— able to hold a note in this state, Odell and I butchering the Santana and Rob Thomas hit on the stereo: *And it's just like the ocean under the moon, well, it's the same as the emotion that I get from you* . . .

Steven declared this our "Wretched Excess Weekend." With a burst of energy like a kid off his Ritalin, he led us into the pantry. He tossed a big jar of olives like a football to a wide-eyed Odell, a tin of caviar to Erica and a spray can of whipped cream to me. From a cabinet, he brought out a serving tray like a cheese platter of drugs du jour—mushrooms, pot, 'ludes, Ecstasy. Erica set the tone for all of us. "We don't really need that, honey," she suggested. "Just light us a couple of joints. Let's keep it soft."

It was Odell who scooped up a handful of drugs and stuffed them in his pocket, muttering if not now, later. He pissed me off doing that. "What? You hit a buffet and you stuff rolls and lamb chops down your pants, too?"

"Oh, chill out, Michelle," he whispered as Steven and Erica danced to the music. "You know our boy gets choice stuff. If you two don't want to party, fine, but *I got other friends,* you know."

I shook my head in disbelief. It never ceased to amaze me how when you get into the circles of the famous or the so-called elite, people could behave out of raw, shameless Id. They acted like they walked out of a cartoon. I got other friends, he said. Translation: And won't they be impressed when I bring them Steven Swann's dope. I wanted to tell him: Look, you've made it. You're the head dancer on his tour. And now you're not content with name-dropping, you need to offer drug samples? He put a couple of things back to mollify me and kissed me on the cheek. I gave him a noncommittal rub on his shoulder.

With the way he behaved, I was surprised he hadn't hit on Erica yet. "Oh, he has," she told me when I asked her. It was a while back and he was so obvious, she'd have nothing to do with him. But he'd left her alone after his single attempt, which also baffled me.

"Mish, there's nothing I can do for his career that Steven hasn't done for him already, so I'm not *useful* to him. If a guy wants sex, he'll stick it anywhere he can."

"Oh, thank you very much," I said.

"Oh, sweetie, don't be like that. Didn't we both have guys who treated us like that in school? And I can see the boy's just a stopgap for you, too. It's so obvious there's no heat between you."

Yes, she and Steven had invited Odell, but she claimed it was Steven's idea, and she couldn't find a way to cut his good friend out. Guys don't always pick up on these things as well as women, she said.

"Okay, we're fed, we're watered!" Steven was shouting now, holding up a bottle of Tequila. "To the armoury!"

To the *what*? We followed him into a room of dark wood panelling and display cases. It gave the three of us a sobering jolt. Guns. Lots and lots of guns. Our host was the all-American boy all right.

"These are my babies," he declared, setting the Tequila bottle down on a small end table. He casually opened the door to one of the cases, and Erica and I traded looks. Shit, shouldn't he keep these things *locked up*?

"We got the whole Wal-Mart collection in here," said

Steven, his words only a bit slurred. "Plus, check this out, check this out! These are Iraqi issue—confiscated in the war, man. Plus the best street shit converted to full automatic. And look at this, a *plastic* M16 gun, only the barrel is metal. They got agents that use this!"

The pop star who wanted to play spy. He was waving the things around, scaring the shit out of us, Odell saying in a voice that got higher and higher, more insistent: "Steve... Steve. *Steve.*"

Steven, oblivious: "I got Civil War rifles around here someplace."

"Put the fucking gun down, will ya, man?"

And Steven replied, "Will you relax, Odell? You guys want me to show you my place, I'll show you my place. Jesus, I'd expect this from the girls, but you're a guy for fuck's sake—"

Which was a telling comment, I think.

I watched Erica. She was as rattled as the rest of us but trying to sound calm because she thought this would get through to him. "Please, Stevie, you're making everyone nervous, babe."

"Sorry! Sorry, sorry, sorry." And he placed the weapon back on its display rack.

"Thank you," snapped Odell.

"Okay, it's over," I cautioned him. "Let's just get out of this room and have another drink."

"I'm fine, I'm cool," he assured me, his voice still betraying his adrenaline.

We went back into the living room and all had another couple of shots. I felt the lift again, a silly weightless freedom.

"Here, different toys," said Steven, and he picked up these white balls we hadn't noticed before and began juggling with them.

"What are those?" I asked.

But he was giggling away, running into the second

lounge back near the kitchen. Odell made a smartass crack that just our luck, they'd be grenades, but Erica and I obediently followed our host. We asked again, what are those things? Steven had that laugh you get because you find your own joke hysterical first.

In a Vegas lounge lizard voice, he announced, "These are *luuuuuv* eggs!"

And in mid-juggle, he tossed one to me, one to Erica. They were indeed eggs, small plastic ones.

"What are you supposed to do with those, man?" asked Odell.

Once again, the maturity level dropped another ten points to primary school age. Steven's eyes flicked from Erica to me, and the three of us burst out laughing. Steven pulled out a remote. Erica gave a mild shriek and then laughed again as the egg in her palm vibrated.

"You've heard of immobilisers, well, this thing mobilises!" said Steven.

The four of us were really gone now, that giddy I-drink-because-I-think-I'm-thirsty, feelin'-no-pain drunken state. Everybody was talking at once, everybody talking over each other. And Erica, with a coy mischievous glance from me to Odell, unbuttoned her trousers and shrugged them off, ditching her panties as well. There she was with her well-endowed backside and her pussy fur on display, and Odell was gasping, "I don't believe this shit." We all watched as she deftly inserted the egg into her vagina. Steven, his eyes coy as well, hit the button. Another squeal from Erica.

"Gimme that thing," she said, pretending to reach for the remote. "I don't need you guys anymore!"

All of us were laughing hysterically. And Erica pretended to walk with great difficulty into the living room, asking what's the range of this thing? Fifty feet, said Steven chasing after her, two triple-A batteries of heaven. Kissing and nuzzling her, stripping the rest of her clothes off as she collapsed onto a scoop-like chair, a mod design with a deco-rated buffalo-hide cover. *You have got to try this, Mish, it is something.* Steven tossed the other remote to Odell, but I caught it before he did, trying to make it look like I was teasing. Oh, no, you don't. And, no, I didn't. I didn't want him having that control.

Still hovering in the kitchen as our host and hostess got it on. He tried to kiss me, and I brushed cheeks with him and pointed. There was Steven, stripping off now and on top of Erica. Odell and I both hypnotised but for different reasons, my date for the weekend scarcely believing that Steven would take her right there in front of us. Odell call-ing out: *We having a dogging party here or what?* And Steven muttered something about guess so, man, "Wretched Excess Weekend! Whooo-hoooo!" and I saw the star unbutton his Calvin Kleins, his white cock impressively thick and flush with blood as Erica lay under him, that lovely layer of baby fat around her belly, bringing her knees up with not an ounce of shame. Steven was rubbing himself against her, the tip of his penis running over her clit, timing his ama-teur electroshock therapy with his strokes. "Mmm, mmm, mmm, mmm—"

He looked over at me with mild astonishment, and I didn't understand this until I felt the slightest pressure of Odell's dick against my pussy lips. I was barely conscious that he had opened my blouse. I didn't recall him unzip-ping my skirt. My small tits were hanging down, swaying slightly as Odell filled me up from behind, and he was so big he couldn't get himself all the way in. I was gripping the edge of the counter top already, and I felt pleasure and a twinge of discomfort over his girth. Steven still watch-ing me, hungry over *me,* and I was surprised at how much I enjoyed him seeing me naked. Odell was nothing, my "beard" who didn't have a clue, but Steven... This was a change, feeling turned on by a man's attention. It had been a while. And beyond Steven's wolf eyes, beyond whatever Odell could do for me was the stimulation of my girl on that buffalo-hide scoop chair. My beautiful love was in her glory, head rolling like a doll's as the alcohol and the pot lifted her. She didn't notice us until Steven whispered she should look.

"Fuck, Michelle," she said, her words slurring, "it's like a goddamn tree trunk, girl!" And she cackled away, sheer delight at being vulgar. This was Erica. Politically brave and brilliant, caring and generous, with a mouth some-times like a sailor. *"Make 'im bigger, hon."*

None of her attention on me, just on Odell, ramming himself faster and faster inside me to show off while her eyes grew wider, and I looked over my shoulder to see why. I don't think it was so much that throbbing brown pole, and I admit I'm biased because the sight of it didn't interest me much, but she liked the pattern of his abs glowing and perfectly defined, the way the sweat rolled down his chest in a cascade of a single line like a tiny waterfall. He was pulling out of me, wanting to turn me around and set me on the counter. Make 'im bigger, hon. And I decided to give my girl a thrill.

I pressed the love egg against his testicles and hit the re-mote.

The vibration made Odell's cock harden even more and thrust at a higher angle, and he let out an almost feminine gasp. A fountain of cum shot out of him like shaken-up champagne, slapping across my tits and up to my neck. Steven and Erica thought this was hilarious, Erica turned on but still laughing at my prank. But Odell had a face like thunder. He looked at me as if I'd betrayed him somehow, cheated him out of something. I wished I could have come out and said, *No, you may not come inside me. No, you should give a damn about what pleases me.* I didn't. I muttered something like, "Oh, calm down. You got off. And you look like you enjoyed it."

His eyes strayed over to Steven and Erica. Maybe it was the proud black man super-stud thing. He didn't want to look like he couldn't control himself in front of Erica—or in front of the white boy.

"Come on," I muttered soothingly again, and kissed him on the lips.

Steven rolled off Erica, both of them still laughing, and Steven saying, "Come on, man, take a joke. I'm gonna get Erica to do that to me. I bet I come like a rocket! What are we going to do for an encore here?"

I grabbed some towelling and ran water over it in the sink to wipe off my chest, passed a couple of fresh panels to my shock victim.

"I wouldn't mind seeing some girl-on-girl action," said Odell with a smirk.

"Don't be a pig," Erica said right away.

I wasn't surprised or hurt by her words. In fact, I was clucking my tongue in disgust and stepping away from him.

"What?" said Odell, holding his hands open in a pose of innocence. "What? What did I say?"

"Sure, Odell," I told him. "We'll do that right after I see you give Steven a blow job."

Steven affected a Southern drawl. "Odell, my man, yours just ain't a gentlemanly suggestion."

"Why not?" he laughed.

And Erica looked at him, her eyes slits, demanding, "What are you thinking, man? I have to get Michelle off because you can't?"

Steven was rolling again with giggles.

"Hey, you're out of line with that shit," Odell snapped, and I could see the word forming on his lips: *bitch.*

It's not as if I had been enjoying myself with him. Maybe she was more observant than I thought.

Odell grabbed me around the waist, trying to pull me into a clinch. "Come here."

"What?" I said. "You gonna fuck me now to *prove* something?"

"Hey, they want a show, let's give 'em one, babe. Get me hard."

"Get yourself hard," I said, slipping away from him.

"Well, this is losing its charm," said Erica, closing her eyes and pretending to fall asleep.

"Odell, why don't you take a shower and go watch TV or something, man," suggested Steven. "You're bringing the party down."

Odell was searching for his trousers. "Oh, I'll do better than that, dog. Throw me the keys to the Porsche. Fuck this shit, I'm outta here."

"Doesn't have to be like that, *bro*."

"Oh, yes, it does, bro," he shot back, buttoning his shirt. "This is a party for three, I guess. I'm going back to New York."

"Yeah, you're going home *coach*," said Erica.

"Fuck you," said Odell. "Gimme the keys, man—"

"Don't," I piped up. "This is stupid. We've all been drinking. Odell, why don't you just go and cool off—"

"No! No, I've had enough of this bullshit. You two playing cock-teases while—"

"*Hey!*" Steven, raising his voice and losing his patience.

"Let 'im go, Michelle—"

"He's been drinking, Erica!"

"I can drive fine," Odell was saying.

"And I don't give a shit if you can," Steve cut through him. "You're not wrapping my car around some trucker's rig! You want to go home? Go and walk, asshole. You're twenty minutes from an Exxon. You can call yourself a fucking cab into the city."

Odell shook his head, tucking in his shirt. "You're a spiteful prick, Swann."

"You don't know the half of it," answered Steven. "You're fired."

We heard the door slam behind him.

Steven clapped his thigh. "Forget him, ladies. Let's have a good time. Michelle——" He tossed me the remote in his hand and gestured for me to toss over mine. "Odell's got one poor imagination. I got a much more fun game in mind."

And he handed the new remote to Erica. With a glance and a lift of her chin, she instructed me to put the egg inside me. I didn't care that Steven was watching. I would have done anything she told me in that moment. I pressed the egg against my wet lips below and slowly pushed it in. It felt a hell of a lot better than Odell.

"You," Steven said to me, dropping his voice to a lascivious whisper, "get to critique our performance. If you like what Erica's doing, you give her a reward. And maybe, just maybe if you're fair and just, she'll give you one back."

And when we were past the giggles, and Erica saying, Aw, Michelle just wants you for herself, me telling her no, show me what you got, girl, I watched my best friend. She stalked her man, her fingers sliding up his leg to cup his ball sack. Massaging him there in a way I didn't think possible, a manner both sensual and utterly lewd at the same time. His penis came to life like one of those flowers turning towards the sun, blooming from a half-erect pink to an unbridled crimson, and Erica extended her tongue to give it a lick like sweet ice cream. I hit the setting for *one,* and she sat back on her calves for a moment to revel in the thrill. She returned to a slow embrace with Steven on the floor, the two of them rolling around like the lovers in *From*

Here to Eternity but no beach and no crashing tide washing up to them. Then Erica got that look in her eye, that look that said she was about to pounce, shoving her pubic mound up to the inside of Steven's thigh, remembering my trick with Odell and putting the egg under his balls, and I hit the two setting to drive them wild, Steven rubbing his cock on her belly. And I was there, I was there—

Feeling an intimacy with her I still can't articulate properly. I was forgotten and yet I was like human background music, at last able to give her pleasure, and I couldn't help myself, my hand reaching down to play with my clitoris. It didn't matter that she only received, that she wasn't giving back, her remote now abandoned a couple of feet away on the rug. Erica slipping Steven's white cock between her luscious brown breasts, her lips coming down to suck two inches of him in, and then his penis sandwiched between her tits again, Steven's hands running through her hair, Erica moaning as I jumped a setting right to *four.* The egg inside me, only giving a pleasant fullness, no vibration, just my finger rapidly strumming my clit, and now Erica was down on all fours, and for the briefest instant I saw her mound between her legs, and then Steven ducked his head in and began to deliciously work his tongue on her lips. *Five.* Maximum.

"Shit! Oh, shit, *uuuh, uuuh, uhh!*"

I gritted my teeth to stop the torturous keening escaping my lips, my eyes shutting completely as I tipped in slow motion onto my back on the carpet. I felt tears rolling down my cheeks, and then a warm mouth was kissing my lips, seeking entry, requesting a dance of tongues. I died on that floor, loving her, my eyes opening to see Steven's closed lids, one tentative hand cupping my left breast. My eyes looked past him to Erica, lying on her side, happy and spent, offering her silent permission. She was making a temporary gift of him to me. I shook my head and mouthed the words: *It's okay.* Taking the egg out of her vagina, she gave me this goofy expression like Can you believe what we're doing here? We're crazy. Two girls going wild. She was so blind.

She called him back to her.

I watched Erica finish him. I watched her fingers jerk him off then guide him inside of her, pumping her hips to make him come quickly. Steven's face contorted into a silent cry, never looking more like a boy than in those seconds of ecstasy. The three of us lay on the rug, each very quiet, and then Steven slowly got to his feet and made a casual remark about fixing us some more drinks. As if we'd been playing tennis out on his courts, nothing more. Erica got up next, saying, "Shower then hot tub. You guys in?"

"Yeah, sure," I said.

"Mish, you thinking about Odell?"

No.

"Don't worry about that asshole, sweetie," she went on. "He's nothing. We'll get you a guy. Right, Steve?"

"Hey, you're the one who was endorsing the egg."

"Shut *up!*" Laughter, and then she was off to the shower.

I slipped on my blouse and did up a couple of buttons. As I padded back to the kitchen, Steven looked at me as if I were still nude, holding out a rum and Coke.

"Thank you," I whispered.

"No problem," he answered. "She's really something, isn't she?"

I lifted my drink in a toast gesture and said, "Yeah, she sure is."

"So are you."

He saw me blush, taking it for a come-on, and I think he wanted to get a slight rise out of me, see how I would react. He must have known I was tempted to have him after Erica gave me permission. It was one thing for her to send him to me, another to learn he was interested.

He added, "I just meant Odell doesn't deserve you. Forget him like Erica said."

"Thanks."

"Look, you're clearly going places," he said, coming out of the kitchen still nude and casually scratching his balls, "Erica's doing well, so you're doing well. I know there'll be big things in store for you. Look, I never lie. At least, I never lie to my friends. Forget Odell. Jesus, the guy's my lead dancer for the concert tour."

"Meaning what?" I asked, confused.

"You're practically an exec, Michelle," he explained. "Erica got you that office at BSB. You think Odell's got one somewhere? His office is an Adidas bag! In the whole pecking order, the whole fucking entertainment industry caste system, you were dating *down,* honey. Him leaving is a good thing."

Heat

"*There was a real vibe,* I mean, a real crackle of energy with the whole team when we were doing *Drum,*" Luther told an interviewer on one of those shows about the top-charted albums of all time. "You know how these artists go on in movies or music, and they say, 'Oh, no, man, we had no idea how big it would be.' I can't BS you, man, we knew!" Loud, happy laugh, deep from the gut on this one. "Come on, Erica wanted an epic, and damn if we didn't set out to help her make one."

He was right about the atmosphere during those sessions. Morgan had assembled his "dream team" of unknown legends to record live on five of the tracks, and meanwhile, Luther was working with the African choir. There were heated debates during the mixings over some of the effects used, mostly between Morgan and Luther, but they both *cared* so much, they both felt how important this album would be. Erica had the final say this time, having fought so hard for so long with the label over creative control, and she wasn't going to give it up. But instead of her flamboyant public style where you knew exactly how she felt on war, Muslims or corporate oil pollution, when it came to the music, she was unusually reticent. She waited for the men to shout themselves hoarse, tire themselves out and then appeal to her. With one sentence, she could settle the issue.

One afternoon, Luther and Morgan crossed swords over the arrangement of a bridge. Finally, they turned to her.

"What do you think, babe?"

"Erica, there's a reason the strings come in that early for—"

"You're both wrong," she said.

We waited.

"The reason the arrangement doesn't work is because *the bridge* doesn't work," she said, staring at the control board and rubbing her temples. "It sucks."

We all looked at her blankly.

"You wrote it, honey," I said.

"I know," she said. "Still sucks. Give me ten minutes, guys."

The two of them looked at each other and obediently stepped out of the booth. I moved to leave as well, but Erica stopped me. "No, you stay, girl."

"What for?"

"Keep me company, tell me what you think," she urged me. "You're the only one not yelling." And within fifteen minutes, she had rewritten the bridge.

It was something to see, however, the three of them putting it together. Morgan doing keyboards on the title track with Luther's own feverish percussion, using a peculiar mix of household objects and Third World instruments, the two of them trading looks as if they were simply jamming. Whatever Luther felt over Morgan's involvement with Erica, he must have forgiven him or excused him. There was child-like joy between them in that studio, a bond never in serious danger of fraying over petty jealousy.

Erica was the centre of it all, the cause of the tension, the magnet that pulled them back together. As the tracks slowly coalesced into her defining album, the musical style like a spine on a book, we all watched her vision mature. When you make something that well, even the creator gasps a little.

"This is going to go through the roof," I whispered in quiet awe one day in the studio.

"This one," said Erica, allowing herself a faint smile of pride, "is for my Dad. He gave me so much for this."

Yeah, I thought, I imagine he did. Maybe it took a Duane Jones putting in his time in clubs with his alto saxophone to clear the road for Erica Jones. Most people would say no, it was Duane Jones going through dental college and bringing her up right, sitting her down in front of the family piano. Erica always told me she learned more about composition from her father than anyone else, and that included Morgan.

"If I never do another album," said Erica, "then I'm glad I finished here." But of course, she would and did. Never mind the Grammys, we knew what she wanted, and it was a CD that was a must-have classic, that will still hold up decades from now. "This one's for my Dad," she declared again.

One of the most popular tracks off the album turned out, of course, to be "It Was a Pleasure to Burn," even though we couldn't get airplay and the networks told us flat out not to even bother making a video for it. Erica said she didn't care. "You'll see," she laughed. "Mish, folks can tell the difference between horseshit and roses." I didn't know what that spontaneous aphorism was supposed to mean at the time, but I found out later that radio stations across Europe were playing the hell out of the cut. Erica tried to cover her surprise and pretend that she expected it all along. But I knew she was genuinely surprised when she heard fans chanting the opening line at a concert. That's when everyone was sure of an underground classic.

On the album, Luther sampled a bit of this atmospheric track from Art of Noise that must have been close to twenty years old, "Instruments of Darkness," that had this brooding malevolence. It sounded like the theme music for an army of evil. And then Erica started the vocals quoting the first two lines of a book we took in high school, Ray Bradbury's *Fahrenheit 451,* taking those famous lines in a new direction:

> *It was a pleasure to burn.*
> *It was a special pleasure*
> *to see things eaten,*
> *to see things blackened and changed.*
> *A future not earned*
> *to see the ignorant fuckers beaten*
> *where fools with inadmissible lies*
> *have history rearranged.*

In concert, she often recited these lines in darkness, the stage lights killed for the brief moment of suspense, and after the tour dates in Boston and Chicago, she couldn't get through the second line without a huge cheer of expectation welling up from the stadium.

*W*hen Steven came back from finishing the tour to promote his new album, *Slummin',* he called me. After a quick chat about what Dallas and San Diego were like, I turned the conversation to Erica's itinerary and how he could catch up to her perhaps—

"Mish, I need to see you."

"What's up?"

"Just want to talk." He wouldn't say about what. "How soon can you get over here?"

He'd mildly flirted with me in the past, but I heard his personal assistant in the background on the other line, and I had no reason to expect trouble.

When I got to his townhouse, sure enough, his PA was working the phones, giving hell to a dry-cleaner as if her livelihood depended on it, which it probably did. Steven sat at his desk, watching CNN while leafing through a prospectus for a new all-gay television network trying to get a launch out of San Francisco. "I must be hitting some interesting markets to have my people send me shit like this for investment," he commented.

"You, uh, don't want to see an all-gay network?" I asked innocently.

"Doesn't matter what I want to see," he said, tossing the folder aside. With his blond locks and wearing a bright red Versace jacket, he looked like Gordon Gekko's nasty little son. "These assholes are too thick to remember gays only represent ten percent of the population. Sure, we all watch *Will & Grace,* but that doesn't mean they got a lock on the entertainment industry or that I want to watch queer cooking, queer soaps or queer porn after eleven. If you only ever hover at ten percent, how can you build market share? Idiots."

"Thanks for the advice on the stock portfolio," I said. "Why did I haul my ass down here?"

"Odell."

That was a bolt from the blue. He certainly hadn't called me after our sexcapades in Santa Fe and Steven firing him. Maybe Steven would take him back as friend and employee, but I wasn't interested in seeing the guy again. And I hoped Steven hadn't called me all the way over here just to talk to me on Odell's behalf.

It wasn't that at all.

"About halfway through the tour, just after Erica came out to visit me in Florida," he explained, "Odell got through on my PA's mobile and left me a message. Says that Erica's been fucking this old duffer on the side and how she's willing to take even a shrivelled-up black cock over my sad little white dick. Nasty shit like that." He shrugged. "I know the guy's pissed at me for kicking him out, but he was a lousy friend, and he wasn't that hot a dancer anyway. Still—"

He looked hard at me. Waiting for me to defend her, to explain.

I tried bluffing my way out. What else could I do? Sure, I was surprised. There were ways of erasing the no-name fellows Erica slept with, but I had somehow never considered the prospect of Morgan being an embarrassment to her. Morgan was *inside*. And for Erica and Morgan, sex was just sex. He was one of the most unsentimental creatures you could ever meet, and so long as he didn't have to meet Steven Swann, he couldn't have cared less that Erica was with *him*. I had never looked at the coin flipped over. I never thought I would have to cover up for Erica and lie to her boyfriend in addition to the press.

"Steven, what are you expecting me to tell you?" I asked. "You're going to take Odell's word for it? A guy who wants to get back at you?"

"If I took what he said, I wouldn't want us to talk."

I lowered my voice to a whisper. "Jesus, Steven! We're doing it in front of each other out west, and now you're getting worked up over her *maybe* screwing another guy?"

"It's not the same thing," he said. He was damn calm about all this. Perhaps he didn't want to show the pain or anger in front of me.

"It's not a big leap," I countered.

"So Odell's telling the truth."

I didn't answer. My face said: consider your source. But I wasn't making a strong denial.

"He gave me a name for the guy and an address, told me the jazz bars where he plays. You might as well tell me, Michelle."

His personal assistant was calling across the room that somebody was on line two.

"Look, I'm sorry," I said. I was talking too fast, part of me sincere, part of me acting. *Because I was glad he had found out.* I just couldn't show it. So I was the great lady of the theatre the same way I had to perform for dozens of executives or producers or lovers who wanted Erica's time. Time that cut into my portions with her.

"This isn't the way you should have—no, sorry, that's a stupid thing to say. What I mean is, I don't think she ever intended to hurt you. This thing with Morgan she's got, it's almost as if she fucks him out of gratitude, I don't know, she always says sex is like food or wine, but I think she's putting on a guy's attitude because—"

"*Michelle,*" he interjected. Then the boyish smile again, the one he thought could smooth everything over. "It's okay. I wanted to know, but . . . I forgive her."

"You do?" I said in mild astonishment. What I wanted to ask was *why?*

Not even a tight-lipped expression of hurt on his face, no sharp intake of angry breath, nothing. And not because he already knew. There should be some betrayal of what he was feeling, even an infinitesimal one. The most I could hear was the soft clicking of tumblers, the calculation of angles. Was he past cold hate, planning a humiliation for her because of her cheating? Mild panic in me for all of two seconds. No. That wasn't it either.

"I forgive her," he repeated.

Line two was still beeping away.

"Sorry, I got to take this," he said.

I don't know why he'd asked me over instead of confronting her with this. And to the best of my knowledge, he never did bring it up with Erica.

He said he forgave her. You say that about somebody, you imply the sin is done and in the past, not to be repeated. But if he wasn't going to talk to her about it then Erica could go on seeing Morgan. Here was the golden boy offering me no sign of how he could prevent this. He must have known their casual trysts would continue. I walked out the door not having a clue what was on his mind. If I had, perhaps things would have turned out differently.

Two weeks later, Erica had me type up a press release announcing her engagement to Steven Swann.

*N*ow *you're dressed in black, when I left you were dressed in white. Can you fill me in?* . . . Craig David's voice floating out of my computer speakers as Luther's latest email popped up on the screen, complete with a little webcam movie attached. Luther in London, putting himself in self-imposed exile. He told me he made one last-ditch attempt to persuade Erica that Steven wasn't good enough for her. She said Steven must be good enough for him, what with his paycheck for producing Steven's *Slummin'* album.

"You did *Drum* out of fear, didn't you?" he asked her.

"Excuse me?"

"You did—"

"You're full of it, Luther—"

"Oh, yes, you did, Erica. You know damn well that hooking up with Steven means you're not going to do important work anymore, you're going to churn out fluffy pop tunes because you'll be surrounded by it every goddamn day! It's Steven, Erica. The guy asks to put a song together the way you write up a balance sheet."

"Oh, great, so I have to meet a higher standard than you

set for yourself!" she told him. "How can you say that when you're *his* producer? Are you a hack then, too?"

"Don't confuse work with life, Erica. I do his albums then I go home to my own place. They got a saying in Hollywood: even shit has its own integrity. And when I compose *my* work, I don't hear Steven Swann's crap coming out of my music. You don't have to do this. You going to play wife for him? What about all the things you believe in? You think you can write another *Pariah* after you marry a white—"

"Oh, here it comes," she said. "That's what this is about—"

"No," he insisted, "no, it's not. But you think Steven Swann cares about anything past himself and what NASDAQ closed at on Tuesday? You're going to pass around your talent the way you—" He stopped himself abruptly.

"The way I *what*?" she demanded. "Go ahead and say it, Luther! The way I pass around my body?"

"I wasn't going to—"

"Yes, you were!"

And he was. But he didn't want to say it because he knew it wasn't fair. Luther told me this later, that guys these days, well, at least, any enlightened guy doesn't think of women as "sluts." He knows it's a double standard, even though he may seethe about how a woman carries on— mostly because she's not carrying on with him. Funny how girls will still call you a slut to your face.

"Say it, Luther! You pick on the music 'cause it's an easy target. I am so tired of you thinking you're going to rescue me. You come on like a Jehovah's Witness at my door, man!"

So much anger and frustration and sexual electricity between them, and they didn't know what to do with themselves, how to resolve it. He rushed forward to kiss her, to tell her sorry. Taking her face in his hands and then putting an arm around her waist to hold her in, but she pushed away from him, hard.

"What are you doing?"

"Don't be with him!" he cried. *"Be with me!"*

When he moved forward to kiss her again, she grasped him tightly as if she had to breathe him in, as if she were flying up out of the depths of a deep pool where she couldn't hear sound, let alone music. Tongues searching each other, his hands running over her breasts—

A tortured "No!" She broke away, declaring angrily, "I decide! You hear me! You come on like you want me to be better, get higher, but you're just telling me what to do! I don't need controlling shit like that from—"

"No, I'm n—"

"What is it between us?" she snapped. "You say 'Be with me'? Okay, let's get it on now!" She was tugging her blouse out of her skirt, still raging.

"Why are you going to marry him then if you can be like this?"

She stared at him, unable to answer. She said she loved Steven. She'd told me as much. When it came down to it, Erica thought love was someone letting you have so much independence that he "checked in" on you every now and then. That was how Luther put it when we talked about it later. In Erica's version, she "just froze. We're yelling at each other, and it's spontaneous and hurtful but you're speaking what's in your head, and then he asks me *that.* Oh, God, Mish, somebody asks you why you're marrying a guy, you don't stand like a deer in the woods! What if he's right? Maybe I've been full of it all this time, talking big when I've sold out?"

So Luther flew away. Erica and I had a night of videos, ice cream and soul-searching, but Luther was gone. What did it matter how she felt about him if he was out of the picture? Erica threw herself into parties and gigs, evenings of lovemaking in Morgan's loft, as if to persuade herself that life didn't have to drastically change after marrying Steven.

*L*uther's emails came to me like notes in bottles bobbing along the Net. In one MPEG, there he is—webcam held by a new friend—drumming a couple of Rubbermaid pails in Leicester Square. Two London policemen walked up and demanded if he had a busker's permit. "Who says I want money?" demanded Luther. "Do you *see* a hat on the ground with coins in it?" The cops looked mildly embarrassed over this commonsense logic, and one turned to say right, you there, stop filming this. Cut to Luther, smiling in bitter amusement, "Do you know, Mish, this is the country with the biggest amount of CCTV surveillance in the world? No shit! Here, you got to see this . . ."

His emails to me were full of gossip about Damage and Artful Dodger, the nuances of pecking order in the DJ scene and how the white artists in the label offices walked around with attitude, talking like they had an entourage when there'd be no one in step behind them. "Goddamn hilarious, Michelle," he wrote. These performers had an incredible chip on their shoulder regarding American airplay and markets. *We don't need them,* but of course, they desperately did. The hottest black artists had a "we're-all-in-this-together" view, going in with the assumption it was going to be a bitch of a climb up anyway. He liked London, Luther said. Wouldn't want to live there, however.

He sent maybe seven emails a week to me. During his entire trip, he sent about two to Erica. When I asked her what he had to say in them, she informed me in a distant voice, "Oh, he's landed a couple of producing gigs over there. He says he's writing a lot."

He had told me the same thing in an email, that he was writing music. Hearing songs in his head and getting them down. He didn't ask at all about Erica's wedding in seven weeks.

Luther had London. Erica had her engagement parties around town, thrown by the label and friends. And I had my own little celebration . . .

Karen wore this bewildered, delighted smile at LaGuardia as I came to pick her up. She'd never been to New York before. As we recognised each other across the distance of the terminal, there was so much immediately communicated in a millisecond, such a quiet trade of feeling. We hadn't seen each other in ages, trying to make up for it with emails and occasional phone calls, but they were poor compensation. She wore this little calf-coloured fringed suede bolero jacket over a white T-shirt and one of her long denim skirts, and I took in the sight of her lovely golden skin and the curve of her hips, that mane of midnight hair down her back (I made her promise me she'd never cut it). I felt something I hadn't experienced in months: complete unmitigated lust.

The torch I carried for Erica could have a roaring flame or quiet embers depending on the star's genius, her occasional tantrum and her manipulations of guys. Odell had been just me fooling myself. And I hadn't tried at all to check out New York's thriving lesbian scene. Karen . . . This will be simple and pure, I told myself. Karen was *here,* and she was here for me.

We exchanged quick "Hi's" and goofy, euphoric gazes into each other's eyes, missing each other so much, and then I didn't care that the driver of the Brown Skin Beats car was five yards away, I held my lovely older woman tight and opened my mouth to hers, muttering, "God, I want you so badly. It's been so long." And our tongues met and remembered their feverish play.

Our driver kept glancing at us in the rearview mirror so much I thought we would have an accident. Karen and I were stroking each other in the back, murmuring to each other and laughing, catching up. Karen telling me scraps of news about the silly politics up in Canada that only we would care about, what was happening back at her school. I pointed out Big Apple landmarks, and as she craned her lovely neck up, I saw the girlish wonder in her eyes, and the way she looked at me with a new respect . . . and something else.

"Boy, you must really know your way around," she said.

I knew I was showing off a little. I used to defer to her so much when we were home, but now I was guide and host. I gave her hand a squeeze. "I can't believe you never took a trip down here. There's so much!"

"I'm looking forward to it," she said, touching my cheek. She arched her eyebrows at the Chrysler Building and said, "I don't know. The relatives were always bugging me to come visit them in London or India. Just never had a good enough reason. Until now."

We kissed.

"How is this going to work?" she asked me gently.

"What do you mean?" I whispered, one eye on the driver to see if he was eavesdropping.

"I mean you're living with Erica, right?" She saw a spark of mild hurt in my eyes, but she raised a hand, indicating she didn't mean it as a reproach. She knew there was nothing sexual going on between her two former students, that I was simply the personal assistant. "Am I her guest as well? Where am I staying, honey?" A nervous laugh here. "I didn't even try to book a hotel."

I could have put her up that night at the apartment. Erica was in Chicago, doing a couple of benefit gigs, and she wasn't due back until later in the week. But—

"I didn't think you'd want to be her guest," I replied. "I

thought maybe it would be awkward...It's not as if she's your favourite person."

Karen said nothing. Eventually, the questions would come. Had I put my feelings for Erica aside? How could I have when I had dropped out of school and begun a whole new career path that depended completely on my friend's indulgence and references? Karen never ever got openly cross, her anger and resentment always on a slow simmer when it came to our few squabbles. But she wasn't about to spoil our reunion this soon. I half-wondered if she would bring up the issue during her visit. She always claimed that she could be patient. I know you'll change, she once said to me, but Erica never will.

"I got you a hotel," I went on. "I pulled a few strings to get you a corporate suite the label puts out for."

"Look at you, the smooth operator!" she laughed.

"No, that's a friend of mine, Luther. He's the angel who helped. You're going to love this place, sweetheart, it's like it was made for you."

And for Karen, the Library Hotel was perfect. The car pulled up at the corner of Madison and 41st Street in front of the brick and terra-cotta restored building, and I grabbed her bag and walked arm in arm with her into the mahogany-panelled lobby. The place has more of a feel of a private club than a hotel, with a "Writer's Den," a "Poetry Garden" and reading rooms. I had told a white lie in the car. Yes, Luther had got me the corporate suite, but he also helped me arrange to get her the hotel's "Erotica Package." We took the elevator up to the "Love Room," where Karen clapped her hands and burst into giggles at all the cliché fuss: champagne on ice waiting, a dozen roses, strawberries in low-fat Cool Whip.

"Yes, I know," I said with a mock groan. "*Your* copy of the *Kama Sutra* is in the original Indian! But, hey, you get to keep the robe."

"Oh, God, come here, baby," she said, rushing over to me. "All of it's so...kitsch!" And she burst out laughing and kissed me quickly.

I was tugging her T-shirt up in a frantic rush, my hands eagerly pawing her breasts, ducking my head down to gently bite the nipples puckering hard out of her bra cups. She was unbuckling my pants, and it became a race of hands, hers reaching between my legs as I kept massaging her nipples. Such golden skin, and the way her silky soft black hair fell like it belonged on an exotic dark animal. So incredibly, astonishingly, delicately feminine with her petite physique, yet having such confidence in her touch.

I sat down on a chair, wanting her to sit in my lap, straddle me, but she knelt at my feet, her hand still exploring my vagina with my legs rudely open, working me so that I convulsed and gripped the seat to steady myself, my teacher, my lover, like an idol, like a doll on her knees, and my eyes strayed to the way she overlapped her feet behind her as she knelt, the smallness of her toes and even beauty in the arch of her foot, the way her breasts were flushed and full, awaiting my hand. As I started to come, I half-jumped, half-collapsed out of the chair to the rug, my body wracked with spasms of overwhelming ecstasy, Karen's mouth covering my own, my eyes losing all sight of the room under that shroud of midnight hair. "I got to have your pussy," I rasped. "I've got to taste you!" Too long, far too long since I had quenched my thirst from between her legs. We were both crying as I went down on her, the rise of her rib cage as her back arched, as sweat glistened on that luminescent skin, made me swear love eternal to my Kamala, made such a damn liar out of me.

*Y*ou can't see the park from here, but we're close enough to walk," I yelled apologetically from the kitchen.

"Are you kidding?" she called back. "This place is amazing!"

Back in the apartment. Karen and I making love again in my bed, making it special and memorable in a way that no hotel suite ever could.

I heard a noise out in the living room but didn't think anything of it, went back to firing up the blender. I squealed because I had to quickly shut it off. *Fool.* Forgot to put the lid back and nearly made a mess out of my Destiny's Child concert T-shirt, the only thing I had on at the moment. Margaritas done, I sipped my own home-made brew and smacked my lips on a finger. God, I'm good, I said, and I headed to my bedroom with a glass in each hand. "You tell me if this is the way you like 'em!" I called out.

I walked in just in time to see Erica and Karen, frozen like they were caught in a snapshot. Erica was three feet in the doorway, jaw almost on the floor, staring at Karen completely nude and rubbing lotion on her leg. We were suddenly back in high school as Erica blurted out, "Miss Ogis..." Because she hadn't known her as anything else.

Karen pushed back her long mane of lustrous black hair and said nonchalantly, "Hello, Erica. Congratulations on your success. Michelle, could you please hand me that towel?"

I was still holding the Margaritas like an idiot, paralysed by my two worlds colliding. Erica picked up the towel and handed it to Karen, who wrapped it around her waist. Then Erica smoothly took both drinks, passing one to her former teacher and downing the other in one swallow.

"These aren't bad," she pronounced. "You got more?"

"In the blender," I said in a deadpan voice.

"I should get going," said Karen. "There's a show at the Frick I want to see—"

Erica waved that away. "No, please, don't go on my account. Stay, um, Miss—"

"Karen."

"Stay, Karen, please. Hang out. I don't have to be here. I could go to Luther's or Morgan's." She laughed nervously. "If you two need—well, if you want the place to your— umm." Erica turned to me to explain. "We got back early because BSB sprung for a flight. They want to add another night on the front end to Madison Square Garden, so the union boys on the crew put their foot down over the days off, and getting back early was the only way we could— oh, you guys don't want to hear about all that. I'm sorry I barged in the way I did. Karen."

My lover smiled at her. "Not at all. You've got a lovely home."

Absolute pin drop stillness. All of us staring at each other.

"I should get dressed," said Karen.

Erica and I both remembered our manners and left her to it. Making our way to the lounge, I hung my head as I mumbled, "I'm really sorry, Erica."

"No, no, sweetie. This place is your home, too. But..." She burst into a kind of whispering squeal. "*Miss Ogis?* You seduced our teacher?"

"Other way around, actually—"

"*Whoa!*"

"Look, I can tell you all the gory details later, but she's right next—"

"How long has this been going on?"

"Erica!"

"Okay, okay." She stepped forward to hug me. "As long as you're happy, I guess. Didn't you think you could trust me? I mean that you're... Oh, shit, Mish, you hooked up with Odell so I figured..."

"Odell was nothing," I replied. "Odell was persistent. And he just ended up being my Saturday night dildo."

She laughed softly in surprise. "Wow, I guess some of me is rubbing off on you."

Karen knocked behind the closed bedroom door, giving a loud hint she wanted to join us in the living room.

"Okay, ladies, I've brushed my hair and fussed with my makeup as long as I can. You two caught up? Is the coast clear now?"

"Always was," said Erica, and thrust out her hand for a proper handshake of greeting. "By the way, I still think you gave me a shitty mark on that Calculus final."

Pressure

Erica did her best to play co-hostess and tag along with us on a couple of shopping excursions. She went along when Karen begged me to take her to *The Producers,* the bizarre musical they made out of the Mel Brooks film. I saw that movie for the first time on her DVD years ago in Toronto. Karen always was one for tasteless humour that skewered the sentimental. Erica was very quiet during our lunches and in the shops, and Karen assumed it was because the star wasn't the centre of attention. I told her she was being harsh. "She's trying her best, but it's not as if you two have a lot in common."

"Okay," she laughed. "I'll try not to be such a bitch around her."

As it happened, Erica found work to do, and we saw less of her. Having my friend walk in on us made me give up the whole pretence for others—and for myself—that I was a straight. I took Karen to my office at Brown Skin Beats and introduced her as my "girlfriend," which could have meant anything. But work colleagues spotted us holding hands in public, and people seemed to take modest pleasure in thinking they had pinned me down. I never knew I was such a cause for water cooler speculation. I didn't call myself lesbian or gay. People stuck these labels on me in conversations at parties, and the bolder ones asked, "But you were with Odell. What was that all about?"

No wonder Erica had kept a hermetic seal on her private life up until Steven. What I was, whatever I was, opened the gate for a few morons to make snide comments to my face, but I would have to deal with it. Instead of the well-worn "must be on your period" you were informed that you were being unfair to a marketing guy because "You *do* got a real problem with men, don't you?"

Karen told me that when men gave her a hard time, she went home, ran herself a bubble bath, opened a bottle of gin and put on her DVD copy of *The Last Seduction*. God, I had missed her. She was dropping not-so-subtle hints that she was considering taking a sabbatical in Vancouver, that sure, house prices were through the roof, but she had a family connection through the Indian community out there for a cheap short-term apartment lease. There'd be room enough for two if I wanted to return to school and do a year at the University of British Columbia. Rocky Mountains *and* Pacific Ocean—think of it, honey. And I'd say Empire State Building and Broadway, streets where Walt Whitman and Langston Hughes and Billie Holiday walked . . .

"You could write out there, sweetheart. You *used* to write."

I told her I'd collected enough publishers' rejection letters to paper my walls. She wisely didn't press me on the issue.

It was around this time that I got an early hint of what trouble I was going to have with Morgan.

I was having dinner with Karen in Greenwich Village when I got a call on my mobile. I didn't recognise the number, but it was the manager of Clint's, a basement jazz bar on Avenue A. He explained he was trying to get hold of Erica, really, but maybe I could help. Is Morgan still playing there? I wondered. Morgan was playing tonight, said the manager. *He* was the problem. I said I'd get there as quick as I could. Karen insisted on coming along since it was an emergency, and I spent the whole cab ride apologising to her, saying I didn't have a clue what was going on.

We made our way down the steps to Clint's and opened the door to a fog of strong cigarette smoke. Hardwood chairs and little round tables, the joint didn't offer much to look at—except for the spectacle of a piano player with caramel skin and a salt-and-pepper beard, a fallen soufflé of a face etched with character lines brooding over the keys and playing perfectly. His playing wasn't the problem. You could tell from the menacing gleam in his eye and the curl in his lip that he'd been drinking. The manager said he'd grown abusive with the folks sitting in the tables close to the stage. The bass player and the drummer didn't know him well enough to indulge him, and they had walked out before the second set.

"I don't want to tell him to get off," explained the manager. "If Clint was here, he'd shut the damn lights off the stage and tell him get the hell out. I can't do that to him, Michelle. It's Morgan, you know?"

"I understand," I said.

"I don't know what his problem is, but . . . Look, you're here, can you calm him down for me?"

At the moment, Morgan was playing Vince Guaraldi's signature theme to the *Peanuts* cartoon, which inspired mixed applause from the sparse crowd. "Don't fucking applaud when I'm in the middle!" he growled. "This ain't a football stadium. See, you idiots don't know Dexter Gordon, but you know this shit."

Jesus.

Karen watched me watching Morgan, not having a clue about the back history of all the principals involved in this little drama, or why I should be saving this guy from making an ass of himself, why I was here instead of Erica. I could have told her this is what I do, sweetheart. I clean up the messes of others. And Erica Jones can't be seen trying to talk her lover down from 30,000 feet after so many Scotches, not that she wouldn't try if the manager had reached her. Better that I was here. So, no, I didn't explain to her in that moment. If she needed me to later, sure, but first things first.

Morgan spotted me by the bar. He gave me a sloppy grin and interrupted his own playing, putting on a lounge act voice as he announced, "Here, folks, since we have a special guest in the audience—I won't say who—we'll play you one of my own tunes."

And he started the first bars of "Hurt Me Again." What the hell was he talking about, his own tune? It was Erica's third song on the *Drum* album.

"You'll hear it soon enough everywhere," he told the crowd as he played. "It's nice to hear your music at airports or in stores, even if the fuckers rip you off—"

He laughed boisterously, leaning back too far, and he fell right off the bench. I don't understand how you can play music that well but not be able to keep your balance. Didn't matter, the show was over. Karen, the manager and I were all rushing to help him, the manager saying, "That's it. This is too embarrassing..."

As we grabbed Morgan under his arms, pulling him up, he said, "Hello, Mish, who's your guest?"

This wasn't like him. This wasn't like him at all. We were going to bundle him into a cab when he straightened up and held his balance for an impressive moment, no stagger, no swaying. He turned to the manager and declared, "If

you're going to cheat me out of my pay for the gig then
don't give me this false courtesy shit that I can have a ride
home—"

"You are *so* out of line!" said the manager, losing his patience.

"You cheat me out of my mon—"

"Take him home, Michelle!"

"Come on, Morgan," I said, trying to hustle him out the
door and up the stairs. As the autumn bite in the New York
air made us all wide awake, I said, "What are you doing,
Morgan? You shouldn't go around saying Erica's songs are
yours."

"They are mine," he insisted.

I studied him. He said it with such matter-of-fact direct-
ness, I couldn't dismiss the claim as wild talk on a drunken
tear. Erica had never said anything about co-writing the
tunes on the album with him. The only time she had ever
collaborated with anyone was with Steven, and that was to
write some backing vocals for his *Slummin'* album—unless
you counted her Dad helping a sixteen-year-old Erica at
MacDonald High write her first unpolished tunes.

"Do you want a cab or not, Morgan?" I asked sharply.

"No. Thank you, no."

"Good night then."

I was irritable. I didn't know why I had bothered coming
out for him and what I had accomplished. And he had just
dropped this bombshell that I sensed he was quite willing
to repeat while sober. I kept cursing under my breath because cabs wouldn't stop for us. Karen said, "Look, let's forget about the ferry ride tonight. We had a nice dinner, that's
something. Let's just go back to the hotel—"

"No, hon, I promised you Staten Island, and—"

"Mish, it's okay. It's getting a bit late for that, and it'll be
cold."

"Fine," I snapped. "You want the hotel, we'll go to the hotel."

On the subway, she sat staring ahead and furrowing her brow. "There's no truth to what he was saying, is there? That he wrote those tunes, and she stole them."

"Of course not."

She didn't say anything else on the subject. But I could see she was still wondering about it. And I was wondering how big a problem this would be.

I called Morgan the next day, thanking him sarcastically for ruining my evening. He was unrepentant. "I didn't invite you to the bar, darlin'," he laughed.

"You embarrassed the hell out of me," I said.

"What? Your cute friend never saw a drunken musician before?"

"What you said: about Erica's songs. Don't go saying things like that—"

"I'm perfectly entitled," he rode over me, "when they're true. And now that you bring it up, Michelle, you're with the label. I think you should have a little talk with your BSB friends about adequate compensation."

"You got paid for the arrangements, Morgan."

"But not for the compositions."

"Erica wrote those songs, Morgan."

"The hell she did. We were messing around with those tunes since she took her Greyhound down here. They're mine as much as hers. A joke's a joke, and I know this is her time now in the spotlight. I'm not asking for any credit in liner notes, but I *do* want the money."

"You weren't as drunk last night as we thought, were you?" I asked.

The pause on the line was all the confirmation I needed. Damn it. Maybe he got drunk enough to build up the nerve for his stunt, maybe he knew Erica would be unavailable.

He wanted to show me . . . Show me how it could get very, very embarrassing.

"Why are you coming to me with this, Morgan? Why don't you take it up with Erica?"

"I think you can figure that one out," he replied. "We're all fond of Erica, Mish, but this is business. I thought that's why she and Luther came to me for the arrangements in the first place, because they're *our* songs, and I'd give my own babies tender loving care. You handle all the damage control, Mish, you can handle this."

"I can't go to the label and tell them you wrote those songs!"

"Oh? Because . . . ?"

"Because of the fucking obvious, you know that. You said yourself, this is *her* time."

"Then get it another way."

"And we pay you on the basis of what proof, Morgan? Your word?"

"I can show you my original charts, Michelle, if you like. I can go and pull my old demos. But I think you know I'm not lying. I created for that girl. Now you can be creative for me. Find the money, darling."

He hung up. I didn't know this man anymore.

That was Headache Number One of the week. Headache Number Two would turn into a full-blown migraine.

I was with Karen in the Jacuzzi of her room at the Library Hotel. The water bubbling away with lavender soap, hot enough to melt both of us, and my lover flashed a smile and went, "*Eeeeeep!* Whose idea was it to make it this hot?"

"Yours."

She rose into a crouch with a short pant over the temperature, and I was mesmerised for a second by the vision of her body. "Don't move. Just don't . . . move!"

"Why?"

I told her to look at her arms. In the confines of the washroom and the bubbling lavender froth, steam rose in elaborate curlicues from her limbs, wisps of it rising from her thighs as if her lovely golden body had been taken out of a forge. Look at the steam, I said. Ribbons of it, flowing away from her skin and dissipating into nothingness, steam from her skin. Her breasts and her stomach were glowing, burnished by the water from our private hot spring. It made me nostalgic. I asked her, you remember the first time we made love? *Oh, yes,* she said. We kissed tenderly, a bead of water from the bath falling from her chin onto my leg . . .

"I remember," she whispered. "You still excite me so much." And she turned my face so I could look at myself in the bath's mirror. "This is what turned me on. I couldn't help myself."

In the glass, I saw myself, nude. I didn't recognise the girl that had captivated her back home. I only saw a young woman with light brown skin and shoulder-length black hair, breasts that were firm but small and thighs that still needed toning. I made a mental note to myself to increase my workouts. I personally think my mouth is a little too wide, my forehead a little too low, and people have told me my eyes were my best feature. I know I'm not beautiful, and I've never liked looking at myself naked. Karen was beautiful. She could have had anyone, and I always thought she overlooked the physical when she loved me.

"Look at that beautiful woman," she said now, pointing to my reflection. "You never see it. Sometimes it's so charming that you don't, but sometimes it's like you wish you could erase yourself completely."

I took her hand and brought it to my lips. "But you do when you fall in love. You lose yourself in the other person."

She kissed my head and wrapped her arms around my

neck. She smiled. "I've never wanted you to run away from yourself completely. That's not love, honey."

I was about to answer her when my mobile rang, bleeping away from its resting place on the sink.

"Don't answer it," groaned Karen.

"I have to," I said, sloshing water as I reached for the phone. "Technically, I'm supposed to be at work."

That was the whole point of being a star's PA, being constantly available.

"Let 'em leave a message," said Karen.

I rolled my eyes at her and clicked on the phone. The caller ID already told me ERICA. Yes, I had to take it.

"Mish..."

She was upset. Luther had flown home to New York, had emerged from Kennedy Airport that morning, and she was all worked up about his return. They had spoken briefly on the phone, their conversation strained, and she realised she had so many unresolved issues, and, damn it, she was supposed to get married in a few weeks! Could I see her? No, not at the apartment, why don't we get coffee at Edgar's on West 84th?

"Okay, I'll see you soon," I told her. "Don't worry."

Karen rose from the bath, her golden skin dripping and getting the floor all wet as she snatched a towel and padded out of the washroom. I shut off the Jacuzzi so we could hear each other, pulled the plug and grabbed a towel.

"Okay, you're pissed," I called to her. "She *is* my boss."

"Do what you have to do," she told me. "It was a nice moment."

"Karen, I won't be long."

"Just do me a favour and ask for her itinerary for the rest of the day. No, never mind, I'll be at the Met. I can spend hours in that place—"

"I said I won't be long."

Naked, she snatched up her brush from the night table and let down her long curtain of black hair, vigorously brushing away, clinging beads of water on her thighs and down the small of her back.

"Who works like this?" she asked the walls. "You're not a doctor or in real estate! Who does these hours and drops everything for—"

"I do."

"Look, I don't pretend I understand this," Karen started. "But—"

"What do you mean you don't understand this? What is *this*?"

I was a bit annoyed with her. As good a time as we'd been having, I sensed that her normal reserve had been set at a cooler temperature all during her stay. Karen didn't like being out of her element.

"This business, this world!" she replied. "Don't you think they lay it on a bit thick here? Everybody's such a drama queen."

"Not everyone."

Karen laughed. "You're working for one of the biggest, Michelle."

"That's not fair," I said as I got dressed. "You've never liked Erica. She's . . . got this personal thing, and she's upset."

"So? She's a big girl." Karen put on her bolero jacket and reached for her purse. "What are you jumping in for? Lovers' spat. We've had them. Jesus, what am I saying? They're not even lovers, according to you! And she's got a fiancé! I feel like I'm watching the two of you in the MacDonald hallways again."

"Meaning what?"

"Meaning she should have got this nonsense out of her system when she was seventeen. Darling, does she really expect you to come running every time a man gets bored and wants a little time to himself? Besides, from what I hear, Erica is perfectly capable of finding her own amusements."

"The only way you heard that is from the parties I took you to."

Karen shrugged in mild confusion. "So what? What's the big deal about where I heard it from?"

I sighed. I didn't bother to explain why I was defensive over the point. I had gone to a great deal of trouble to make sure Erica's sexual adventures never circulated beyond the Manhattan and LA party circuits.

"Look, Michelle, it can't possibly be your job to pass her the tissues and be a shoulder to cry on when—"

"It *is* my job," I said impatiently. "I'm her personal assistant, for crying out loud! *Personal* assistant. That is what I do. I book things for her, I make out her schedule, I pick up her dry cleaning if she needs me to, and, yes, Karen, I'm also her friend!"

She stared at me in shock, and then I saw her face blush with hurt and anger. Like all calm and reserved people, her rage could be volcanic. "Oh, God," she said.

I waited for the explosion. The earth was shaking under my feet, but it was only Karen's voice that trembled. She wasn't going to yell at me. She wasn't about to get into a screaming match. There was a crushing finality in her tone and words, and the worst of it was that I was prepared to accept her verdict.

"I thought you were past this," she said to me. "I worried about it, of course, when you took the job, but I thought, hey, playing gofer for Erica Jones and putting up with star tantrums and whatever would *cure* you. The bloom would be off the rose. Boy, am I a fool."

I couldn't say anything except "Listen to me, Karen, I love *you*. I do!"

"Yeah, I think you honestly believe that," she said, her

voice climbing an octave as she rubbed a tear away. I moved to embrace her, but her eyes warned me off. "You won't change. You'll *never* change. Do you actually live and wait for her to have you? That she'll change her mind to-morrow?" She shook her head to answer her own question. "I suppose I should count myself lucky. You have so much love in you, Michelle. You must have for this much trouble. I suppose I should be grateful you let me have a bit of it. You gave me just enough to think I was rich!"

"Kamala—"

"No," she sobbed quietly. "No, I'm going home. I'll know that you mean what you say when you finally come back to Toronto. Maybe we can still do Vancouver..."

"Kamala, my job's here! My life is here!"

"I know," she said, finally unleashing her temper. "You gave up school for that *slut*! You gave up a *life* to take care of her. I'll know you're serious when you come home, and you're ready for us to take care of each other."

She walked out of the hotel room and left me standing there. I didn't know what to do. I knew her well enough to let her be for a while. There was nothing to do at that moment but get to the café to console Erica, to give her advice that would sound as hollow as I felt.

*E*dgar's Café on West 84th Street. Rich desserts, and hot cider in the winter. Edgar Allan Poe lived a block farther east on 84th, hence the name. My best friend was at a table in the back, nursing a cup of coffee, dressed down in the hope she wouldn't be recognised in public. The grey sweat-shirt and black Gap jeans worked, but it would have helped if she'd taken off Steven's engagement ring, its blazing dia-monds like a lighthouse beacon for autograph seekers. A huge rock on her finger to constantly remind her of him, and here she was talking about Luther.

"He's going to be expecting something, I know he is," she told me, shaking her head and blowing her cappuccino. "Barely sends me a word while he's off in England, but I know it's not over for him either."

"You're the one who said he'd had his chance," I reminded her.

"I know, I know," she said, rolling her eyes. "But there's such *heat* there, Mish. It's worse than when Steven was putting me on hold, making me wait, thinking I didn't know what he was doing. Don't get me wrong, I love Steven, but sometimes he's too clever for his own good. It's like all the hunger's gone out of him, and he's got to have games. I worry sometimes if I'll . . . Well, if I'll keep him interested. With Luther, it's like the two of us can't help it. We're burning up, and we don't even know what it is! Then something happens or one of us gets stupid and stops to think about the repercussions. It could be so great, but . . ."

"But what?"

Erica blew on her coffee again and offered this sad smile, one that belonged on one of those Venetian Masters' paintings, a smile that said there was so much behind the eyes. "People call *me* angry. I think sex and love and creativity are connected. Don't ask me how, this is about as metaphysical as I want to get. It's a gut feeling. And Luther, he's been so angry at the business for so long. You've heard him carping, we all have. But what I really think he's angry at is . . ."

"Himself?"

"No—nothing that predictable. He's trying to pull something out of himself, flush it, make it, I don't know, but he's not going to be satisfied or happy with anyone until he's done. I know I sound selfish, girl, but I don't want a seeker. I want someone who's settled, who's got it out of his system. I do enough searching of my own, damn it! As a matter of fact, I think that's what Steven likes about me."

I wanted to laugh at this warped logic. She was my friend, so I said nothing. She didn't realise she was saying in other words: *he likes that I'll grow, because he's rich, successful, and with me, he doesn't have to grow any more.* She was going to have a fine marriage of convenience. The old-fashioned term would mean more with them than with a French politician and his wife. There could be dancers or jazz sages for her in between concerts, and in addition, Erica could develop politically and emotionally while Steven Swann kept his eye on how many vintage guns he collected and how well his mutual funds did.

I read over these lines, and there's a judgmental, cruel tone to them that's not entirely accurate about the way I felt then and there in the café. What I saw was my beautiful girl groping towards an ideal, not sure of what she wanted and having so much love to spoil on whoever would be her choice. I lived for these small intimacies that gave me a window on her dilemma. Karen had up and left. She couldn't understand how half an hour of coffee on the Upper West Side with Erica could send me to happy oblivion, could erase my own self-disgust at those failed novels Karen suggested I try to salvage. I went off to the ladies' room and when I came back, Erica was scribbling on a large white napkin with the café logo on it, writing one of the first verses for "Burn My Letters." One minute we were reflecting on her love life like any other pair of girls at a table, the next she was writing the song that *New Musical Express* in Britain called "a scalpel peeling back the soul." I wish I could have explained it to Karen. Erica is larger than life. She's larger than my life.

I rang Karen's room the next day and left a message. She didn't return my call. When I showed up at the front desk the following day, I was told she had checked out. Her ticket was a special open-return, and I knew she had kept her word about going home. I considered booking a flight to follow her, I really did. I could always stay with my folks. But she was demanding that I return *permanently,* so that any romantic gesture of turning up at her door in Scarborough would have rung hollow after a few days. As I stepped out onto the corner of Madison and 41st, it wasn't one of Erica's songs that played in my head but a tune by Vonda Shepherd, the chick who sang for the old Ally McBeal series, only her real stuff on her albums has always been so much better. Tears in my eyes as I sang off-key: *I'd rather take a blow, at least then I would know, but baby don't you break my heart slow . . .*

Karen . . .

I loved New York. I loved the feeling of being important, as artificial as it was and dependent on a house of cards of office politics and a friend's loyalty. But Karen was right. My life here had its price. I didn't even know what I could do if I returned to Canada. I had dropped out of school, never completed my BA. My guess was that the recruitment pages in *The Toronto Star* or *The Globe and Mail* still had few advertisements for PAs to pop stars.

But that wasn't why I stayed put.

We both knew why. And all I needed was an excuse to rationalise it to myself. Erica provided me with one.

She came home to the apartment in dark sunglasses, her eyes puffy and bloodshot from hours of crying. When I asked her what was wrong, she told me.

"Stev—Steven's called off the engagement!" she said, her body wracked with sobs. "He—he doesn't—he won't see me! He doesn't want to see me!"

"Oh, shit," I said and put an arm around her, walking her to the couch.

"What am I going to do?" she wailed. "Mish, God, it

hurts so much! He—he won't see me at all! What did I do? I love him. I don't understand!"

I kept rubbing her back, telling her it would be all right. But I wasn't sure. The papers were full of news about her engagement and the speculation on the wedding date. For the first time in her career, she had been open with the media about her personal life, and it was only because she had felt safe, secure. Now that the door had been opened, it might never be shut. She could be made to look ridiculous. She might be portrayed as spoiled or gullible. We could both remember the reams of nonsense printed about Jennifer Lopez's on-again-off-again romance with Ben Affleck. We could both recall dozens of other celebrity couples in music and movies, their dirty laundry suddenly getting the spin cycle on television. Erica was in real trouble. *Steven* had called it off, and it wouldn't take long for that detail to get out.

I wasn't going to fly home for quite a while.

Risks

I had to go see Steven. Understand, please, I was her protector, her chief architect for damage control. It was one thing to persuade a flight attendant in Chicago that he shouldn't open his mouth and no one would believe him. This was Steven Swann, who had more money, a bigger profile and an image-making machine behind him of his very own, not just the publicity department at Brown Skin Beats. Nothing could hurt Erica more than to be made to look ridiculous in her personal life. If she dumped him, fine, but *he* was the one breaking it off. Erica was too caught up in her pain right now to help herself. Why, she even thought she could win him back. Steven, however, had always shown us that he stuck to every decision he made. It was over between them, and I had to know why.

He wasn't at all surprised to see me show up at the townhouse. I didn't bother with a greeting as I stormed through his front door.

"You played her," I said.

"I did not 'play' her," he insisted. He did his bashful Tom Cruise laugh, the one that said I know you want to take me to the woodshed, but you can't bring yourself to do it, can you?

"You did. You played her."

"Mish—"

"Don't call me that. *My friends* call me that."

"*Michelle,* the engagement was real. I was in love with Erica, but we—we want different things. It just wouldn't work out."

"So you can't be honest with me. I thought your big thing was you never lie."

"I don't lie," he said, and he actually giggled over this. "I just change my mind, babe."

I tried again. "What was it?"

"You want me to be the bad guy, fine," said Steven. "How about I didn't want to settle down? I'm a big star, so I want to have as many girls as I can have. Will that do? You don't like that one, we'll come up with another."

"Steven . . ."

He folded his arms and squinted at me. "What did you come here for, Mish? Was it for Erica or was it for you?"

"You've lost me," I said.

"Oh, I think you get what I mean."

I didn't say anything. I was genuinely confused.

"I think you're relieved as hell that I've broken it off with her," he said.

"You've hurt my best friend. You guys didn't fight. You didn't have any major problems. You said you forgave her for Morgan. So now you do this, and it comes out of nowhere. I want to know why."

"Well, maybe it's over you, Mish," he said.

"Yeah, right."

He took a step very close to me, and I could feel his breath on my cheek. "We both know the truth is I've wanted to slip into your panties ever since you became Erica's girl Friday. And we also both know you'd like me to.

That Saturday night at my house out west? That was very enlightening."

"I'm gay, Steven. You know that."

"I think you're versatile."

I laughed in his face. "You've got a hell of an ego, Steven. That's it, eh? You're one of these guys who thinks he can *turn* a girl like me with his magic wand?"

He rested a hand on my shoulder. "Not at all. I'll be flattered to be your exception to all that pussy."

"Not interested."

"Yes, you are. I don't fool myself. You want me because Erica had me, and part of you wants to know what kept her coming back. Seeing us go at it wasn't enough. *Annnnnnnd* in your twisted, pretty little head, you think you can 'help' her by us getting it on. You want to prove what a creep I am, even if you can never tell her."

"Wow," I said. "You come up with all that just to get with me? You're forgetting something anyway. She wanted to give you to me that Saturday night."

"We were all pretty drunk. And giving me away ain't the same as taking me, is it?"

"Boy, do you lay it on thick."

He shrugged. "You haven't gone for the door. You and me, Michelle—neither of us likes people very much, do we?"

"No," I said. "No, we don't. But I love Erica. She's my friend."

"Yeah, don't we all love our bosses!" he scoffed. "Cut the shit, Michelle. You are relieved it's been called off, aren't you? You couldn't *stand* Erica gushing on and on like that, making a fool of herself. She was one step away from being a joke. She'd be carving our initials in a heart on a tree or something next. Come on! Yes, maybe she's a pain in the ass when she's fucking dancers backstage or picking up guys like stray cats, but when she's single, she writes *hot,* and her mind's like a laser, man. I have to say I did admire her shit. When the news gets out to the press, yeah, she'll look silly for a day or two. So what? We'll both do another album and make more money."

"So it was business," I said. My lips tried to make it a question, but it came out as deadpan confirmation. "The whole time you were together, it was business."

"Not the whole time. She was a *fantastic* lay—well, you of all people know that. You saw. How good are you? It's not like I can go by Odell."

"Fantastic," I shot back. "For the right girl."

"I'll add revenge to your motivation," he said, chuckling again. "You *want* to pay her back, I know you do. You *hate* the hypocrisy, you hate that she's crying her eyes out when you know she cheated on me. And guess what? The hilarious thing is, I didn't fuck around on her at all! And look at what a villain you're making me out to be. Fucking hilarious."

This was getting me nowhere.

"Please, will you tell me what it was all for?"

"Make it worth my while."

I looked at him hard, dragging out the suspense a little, but both of us knew it was going to happen. I was in a short grey wool skirt, and in two seconds, I reached under the hem and pulled down my panties, offering them to him as a trophy. He smugly shook his head and tossed them aside. He gripped me by the waist, lifting me like a dancer to the perch of his desk. My skirt rode up, and he had a view of my pussy. We didn't kiss at all. His fingers slid up the inside of my thigh, and then he was fingering my petals, stroking me and summoning my juices. Slipping inside me, then out again to tease the bud of my clit, back inside my vagina to sink a little deeper, explore a little more. Two of his fingers inside me now, pushing and retreating, his eyes locked with mine, his face very close so that he could listen to the sound of my ragged breathing. He wanted my heart to flutter. He wanted response.

Withdrawing his hand, he reached out and ripped open my blouse, laughing at my shock.

"Don't worry, Erica left a couple of tops here. You can wear one home. Hey, maybe she'll even ask you how you got it."

I didn't even see the pocketknife in his hand that sliced between my bra cups. My tits were suddenly exposed, and I felt this stab of exhibitionist pleasure. I don't know why I felt it now and not when we were out west, maybe because I was still acting with Odell, playing a role. My tits swelling for him now...Before I could say anything, his mouth greedily sucked in my right breast past the dark circle of the areola, prompting me to moan. He took that as encouragement, circling his tongue around my nipple and closing his teeth down in a gentle bite. God, I thought only Karen could do this well. Once again, he interrupted himself and opened a drawer to the desk. He pulled out a very big gun. A .45 actually.

"Jesus," I whispered.

"Relax," he laughed. He emptied the magazine into his hand.

"Show me there's nothing in the chamber," I said, because I wasn't an idiot.

He turned and pointed the thing at the wall. It made a soft click as he squeezed the trigger, and I jumped. "Here, feel it." And he plopped it into my palm. It felt heavy.

Then he scooped it up again and put the barrel in his mouth. Crazy, he's crazy—

Then he put it between my legs, and I understood why he had sucked it. Warming up the metal. Nudging the hard barrel against my hot gates, slowly, slowly...

I said as bravely as I could, "I'm not sure I like this game."

He ignored my nervousness, saying, "Feels weird, doesn't it? Feels like it could still go off. Like having a bomb next to your flesh."

The barrel against my pussy lips, his other hand playing with my clitoris, and my vagina felt the pressure of the gun and allowed it *in,* that metal tube harder than any guy's cock, Steven, it's Steven's gun, inside me, penetrating me as I whispered *you sick fuck* while he laughed, while I actually covered his hand with mine to help guide that slick hard barrel a little farther into my pussy. I couldn't control my breathing. Now his other hand was cupping my left tit, massaging it, lightly pinching my nipple between two fingers, sending a tiny electric current of pain through me, and as I yelped, I heard *click.* And so help me, my juices were pouring out onto my thighs, helping it to glide in and out of me with such ease. And *click.* I must have been out of my mind at that moment, my brain telling myself not so much in words but feelings that, yes, I could have him this way. As if he were torturing me, taking me by force. *Click.*

"What are you hoping for?" I demanded in a whisper.

He didn't respond, only smiling. My hand reached down and clawed at his zipper. I had him out of his briefs in a minute, that smooth white cock that was now a throbbing crimson, its red tip glistening with a bead of pre-cum. It had been years, literal years, since I had *wanted* a guy's dick in my hand. Poor Odell never desired at all, and here I was, jerking Steven, rubbing him to get him harder, the barrel inside me like some obscene violation, and, Jesus, sweet Jesus, my shirt open and my breasts exposed, my skirt up with my vulva on display, and half-clothed like this it was so much more erotic, his mouth greedily sucking at my tit as my fingers slid along his white shaft, and *"Eeeeuuuuhhh!"*

Coming, coming with this gun barrel in my pussy. Coming with the barrel inside me nearly up to the trigger guard. *You sick fuck, you sick fuck,* just do me like this—

I wondered what else he had in store for me.

"So now that we've had the foreplay, what's the main event?" I said huskily. "You gonna strap yourself into your golden harness?"

"That bitch has got such a big mouth," he laughed, and he growled as I increased the rhythm of my hand. "Bang, bang!" he whispered back.

Click.

His hand at the desk again, and then he was handing me a silk Hermès scarf. I didn't know who it belonged to, Erica or someone else, but it didn't matter. He put the gun down on the desk, and it made a dull clatter of lifeless metal. He was holding the scarf out for me with two hands, wanting me to take it. And I knew instinctively what he wanted. The guy's really twisted, I thought. And he doesn't know how *motivated* I am . . .

He stripped off in front of me, and what I saw was familiar, prompting a replay of old images from the Santa Fe weekend. The boyish flat chest and narrow hips like a sixteen-year-old's despite his real age, the arms and legs with their muscles toned from hours of practised choreography for videos, and that tight pale ass. His pubic hair a peculiar shade of dirty blonde, its silken curls lovely to touch. My hands were stroking his back and his buttocks even before he had his jeans off. He had this beautiful boy androgyny about him that was keeping me wet. It made me desire a man for the first time in ages.

He lay down on the couch and watched me discard my clothing. I held the scarf in front of me for a moment like a veil, my breasts and belly seen through a lens of expensive silk, and then I wound it around both my wrists, snapping it tight, making it an enticement and a threat.

"You're crazy," I told him. "People have died doing this."

He cackled, stroking himself while he watched me, so turned on by just the idea. "You afraid you won't be able to stop?"

"I'll bet you've done this before," I retorted. "But I bet you never handed yourself up to someone who might actually like to kill you."

He bit his bottom lip, letting out a long stream of nervous air and tension in his lungs.

"Do it."

I took his shaft in my hand and put him inside me, felt male flesh, hot and alive, fill me up. "Ohhhh . . ." Groaning, grateful that I was on top and able to direct the pace. I wasn't on my back and just a receptacle for some guy's indifferent thrusting. This wasn't Odell, no, he felt much better than Odell. I pumped my hips, revelling in the sensation, and Steven felt so good inside me, my eyes shut for a moment as his hand roamed up my stomach to my breasts again. I kept the momentum going, coming very quickly once and rocking and swaying, and as I felt myself almost swoon, I looked him in the eyes. Without a word between us, we knew it was time. He lifted his head off the pillow just enough for the scarf. I pulled. Tight—

Pumping my hips again, Steven doing his best to help me, trying to lift his ass a millimetre off the cushions and brace himself against the back of the couch, but he soon fell back, letting me drive. His face was getting redder and redder, and, Jesus, I could *feel* his cock swell inside me and seem to lengthen with his arousal, his eyes glazed and into it, wanting to go to dark places, telling me with a crazed look to tighten the scarf, and his face kept darkening with the rush of blood. He was goddamn huge inside me, and for two seconds of this lustful insanity, I felt him like that gun barrel, and the muscles of my vagina closed around him as I pictured Erica—not him, Erica—in that golden get-up of his. Naked, bound, vulnerable, glowing with perspiration and slight fear over what I could do. Steven's eyes rolled up inside his head, and then he was shooting inside me, spunk firing off in hot streams. A choked voice: "Fuuuuuucckk, eeeeeahhh!..." Me, in simultaneous orgasm with Steven Swann. He floated down first as my noose on him went slack, and our eyes met again. With a sudden hardening, he shot one final time. Son-of-a-bitch. He saw it in my eyes.

How tempted I was.

I loosened the scarf. As soft as it was, there was still an angry purple ring around his neck, not quite a rope burn but dark enough for gossip. I pumped my hips once more selfishly, leaned down and sunk my teeth into his neck, sucking hard with my lips to mark him. That didn't bother him either. I got off him and felt my knees buckle under me, sliding down the end of the couch to the rug. I didn't care about leaning against his legs, no emotional attachment presumed in this casual contact of our bodies. I was back to my quiet dull emptiness, and Steven...Steven was goddamn Dorian Gray with a new coat of paint slapped on.

I showered in his washroom, and he stood in the doorway, naked, watching me through the clear glass sliding door. He sat down on the toilet, and I was busy lathering my legs, barely noticing that his hand was suddenly full of sticky lube. He was masturbating, his cock reddening as his fist shot up and down with an urgent rhythm. I stopped what I was doing for a moment to watch, pressing my tits and my pubic mound up against the glass, fascinated because he needed to come again. He shot a ribbon of milky spunk across his hairless white chest and sagged against the toilet cabinet. Strange. He hadn't wanted to come into the shower with me. He didn't ask me to come out and fool around again. He had made himself come in seconds just from watching me.

"Now tell me. Why'd you do it?"

Naked and sticky, his eyes half-lidded in that peculiar drunken afterglow of masturbation, he looked at me and seemed to be taking my measure. The man-child with the MBA who could give the Wall Street sharks a run for their money. Then his face brightened, and he was gracious in victory, quite willing to be candid now that the deed was done. His voice dropped all its feeling. Like shedding a skin. Fucking reptile.

"Do you know how many albums *both* of us sold the week that Erica broke the news of our engagement?"

Jesus.

"You know how much play *Drum* got on MTV Base that week? No, no—better point. You know how much play they gave *Slummin'* on MTV Base? They've put it in the Hip-Hop category for the charts as well as Pop."

The water was still running. I stood behind the glass door in his shower. I was like an outsider in a rainstorm looking through the window of an exclusive restaurant. Only there was nothing palatable in there. Cascades of lather were still rolling down my belly, and there were suds over my hands as I unconsciously squeezed the bar of soap. Steven was hard again. Horny as hell. Horny and oversexed even as he explained his nifty little plan that exploited my friend and employer. A flood of images played in my head as I stared at him, trying to imagine how Erica would handle this confrontation. My beautiful friend could be so much stronger yet occasionally so much more vulnerable than me. I thought of the way she played Easy like a keyboard in his nightclub. I soaped up my breasts. Steven was jerking himself off again.

"You wouldn't just do this for album sales," I argued.

For a moment, he wasn't with me, his eyes closed, his cock hard and thick as his left hand cupped his balls. "No..." Then eyes open, not looking at my face but at my lathered nipples. "No... But the cred I got."

"Credibility?"

Bastard.

"You got to be shitting me," I said, half to myself. "Why didn't you just *write* something that talked about the same stuff she does? Or just sing one of Luther's songs?"

"Guilt by...association, baby." Laughter mixed with a grunt of pleasure. "Who is gonna believe a white kid from nice upscale suburban Santa Fe is sincere when he sings about the poor of Brooklyn, huh? You look at me, you think I can pull the Springsteen? All that aching social conscience shit? I keep my mouth shut, and I must care because *I'm with her.*"

"And now you're not."

He came again, gentler this time, his cum oozing down his penis, and I saw the endorphin rush snap him to attention.

"And now I'm not," he echoed. "But it's all good. The numbers don't lie. And neither did I, Michelle. Not once."

I turned the taps off and slid back the glass panel.

"You fuck with me on this, you'll lose, Michelle," he warned. "It's not too difficult to leak the word about her skankin' around."

"Please don't quote your songs, Ste—"

"Michelle, I *know* you paid them or hired them or made them go away. Her guys. Her casual flings. I'll just put in a higher bid to bring 'em all back."

"Wasn't thinking of it," I answered, towelling myself off. "I just wanted to know why you're doing this. Erica made her own bed with you, and she'll have to lie in it. Where's that blouse you promised me?"

I let the damp towel fall to the floor of the bathroom,

and damn if he didn't get hard again. I walked out, crossing back to the main lounge, where my panties and my skirt still lay on the floor. As I finished zipping up the skirt, Steven came out and handed me a red top. Sure enough, it was Erica's, one she'd bought while shopping with me at Bloomingdale's. I put it on, not caring that my nipples poked through the thin blouse and cast dark shadows under the fabric. He'd made shreds of my bra, so I'd have to go without. As I squeezed my feet into my shoes and slung my purse over my shoulder, he called out to me.

"Mish! Catch."

Tossing me a set of keys. I caught them out of reflex, staring at him from the door. He stood naked in the living room, his cock still half-erect, wearing that naughty teen hunk smirk of his.

"You were right," he said, pausing for emphasis. "You're a *fantastic* fuck. Let's party again sometime."

I slammed the door behind me.

I went for a welcome-home drink that night with Luther, and he told me stories about his stay in London. He said that after a few weeks, just before he got his major producing gigs for the British artists, he checked out of his hotel and went to stay with a new friend up in Hackney, sleeping on the floor of a spare bedroom with a borrowed duvet. He said it was as if he were going into hard training for a sport event of his own creation. He had to let life there permeate him, let go of tourist urges and old habits and breathe in curry smells, diesel, stale beer and brick. He said he could sense new textures in the music he wanted to write. He wanted to work on a big canvas, not another *Drum,* but, sure, his own landmark album in a way. He couldn't stop smiling, his face aglow with the enthusiasm of the convert.

"Luther, you talk about it like you're a UNICEF worker in the Third World!" I kidded him.

"But it is in a way, and they don't see it!" he laughed. "They got these, um, what do they call 'em? Council taxes. Say you rent a place. You're paying this council for your street upkeep, your trash collection, you know, the whole infrastructure thing. It's not just folks who own houses or property, and I got friends there telling me how you might rent a flat and pay more in council tax than a guy with a mortgage!"

"So this is Socialism?" I asked. Okay, I was ignorant. And naïve.

"Don't you get it, Mish? They're not putting everyone on an even level, they're sticking it to the down-and-outs in a back alley way! The poor dumb bastards rioted against what they called a Poll Tax years ago, and this is just the same thing with a different name. It just kills me when they get self-righteous about the rich and poor in America. I say, look at yourselves, man. Look at these row houses with not a stitch of green grass out front. Do you know you got to pay a *fee* to own your television there? You believe that shit? They say it's to support the BBC. And I tell 'em yeah, but I don't watch BBC1, man, 'cause it's shit. What do I want to *pay* to watch snooker or ten-year-old movies from over here for? They don't care. There's a *meanness* to the place."

"The way you talk about, it sounds like you didn't have a good time at all," I said, a bit confused.

"Are you kidding?" he answered. "I had a blast! No, this is the thing. It took me out of myself. It gives you perspective. You go over to Europe, some other country, and you try to write music about it, but you can't escape yourself. And so you end up creating something unique but still *American,* you know what I'm saying?"

He shrugged and gave a shy half-smile, embarrassed that he had slipped into a lecture. "And you, umm—"

Quick cough to clear his throat. "You discover what's important to you."

He speared the pecan pie with his fork and took a bite, waving to me as if to ask what did I think?

I said, "You haven't asked about Erica." I paused then went for it. He'd find out eventually anyway. "Steven's broken off their engagement."

He looked shocked. "He did?"

I nodded. "It hasn't hit the media yet. I think Steven's waiting for the press to notice they're not showing up together at places, and then he'll make a statement."

"And Erica?"

"She doesn't want to make a public comment. Well...I talked her out of it."

Luther frowned for a moment, his expression betraying a chivalrous flare of anger over how Swann must have hurt her, and then his face was calm, unreadable. He didn't look on Steven's exit as an opportunity for him.

"I had a lot of time to think about Erica. Get some distance and turn it all over in my head. I think I understand a little more about what drives her."

"Oh?"

"Yeah."

"You're not going to share?" I prodded.

Luther was cryptic. "Not now. We'll see if I'm right. Best thing I can do for Erica is leave her alone. We're attracted to each other, but...I'll keep it professional. Otherwise we'll just give ourselves a world of pain."

I settled for that answer for now. I had my own suspicions. I think Luther was a lot deeper than your average guy whose big revelation for his woman would be: *Oh, we're mirrors, we're the same.* I don't think he had her completely figured out. But he had found a piece of her psyche on his adventure in London. Sleeping on the floors of friends' apartments, watching the football yobs march through the street like so many over-aged teenage boys, feeling the waves of quiet resentment over being black, being American, being *there,* he was alive, awake in a way that pulled him out of his streetwise complacency with Manhattan's roughest shocks.

And Erica: auditioning lovers and settling on Steven to escape the mundane prevalence of ordinary living. Because if you can create something beautiful it's a high that surpasses all others, that convinces you that *you matter.* She'd had crap jobs waiting on tables or working a telemarketing phone for all of five minutes after high school. No more anticipation of success—she was successful. She'd made it. But we still crave anticipation, we need it, and we will go looking for our personal suspense in lovers, art, work, anything to shock us out of our wide-eyed sleep.

I know he was still in love with her. It was all there in how he talked about her, however briefly, and his own work. He had defined his own restlessness and taken the cure. She was with him in London without knowing it, touching him in everything he did when he sat down at a keyboard or walked into a studio. But she—and I—didn't know yet if he had left her there.

"You told me you wrote a whole bunch of music," I reminded him politely. "You going to play me any of it? We going to hear some of it soon?"

He shook his head and gave me a sad smile. "No."

$\mathcal{T}$hree days later, I changed my life irrevocably when I went back to visit Steven. I can recall actually sitting hours beforehand at a table in the Dean & Deluca café on Prince Street and fingering the spare set of keys he'd given me. A special security key plus one Yale key for the top lock. I considered changing my plan. There had to be alternatives, but I couldn't see any, and time was an important factor. It wouldn't take long for the media to get a whiff of blood in the air, their intuition kicking in that something had happened. If I were going to pull this off and save her, I would need to do it soon.

And so I put the keys back in my purse. I intended to use them.

When my own personal "zero hour" hit, I used one of the last semi-clean Bell payphones you can find in the Big Apple. I called Steven's townhouse to make sure he was home—I didn't dare use my mobile in case of any permanent trace record later. He answered frostily, and just from his tone, I knew he must be in his home studio. Steven always liked the option of re-recording his vocals in his own time in his own space, no pressure from engineers or producers or anyone else when he was at home. This would be perfect. I hung up without saying a word and looked for the nearest subway station for the journey from SoHo to the Upper East Side.

It was clear he wasn't paying attention to his security monitors as I let myself in, and I mentally patted myself on the back again for my good luck. I wouldn't need to chit-chat now or make up an excuse. I could cross the living room to his desk, and I won a bet I had with myself that Steven would be careless. Yes, indeed. The drawer with the gun was unlocked.

But no gun.

Shit.

Come on, I thought, my heart pounding. Where would he leave it? Knowing his huge ego and casual sense of invulnerability, it would probably be in plain view. From where I stood, I could see the little red bulb he'd had installed that meant he was recording, a warning for any house guests staying over. His studio had all the bells and whistles, right down to professional soundproofing, not just the layers of cork board Easy Carson had stapled up in the back room of his nightclub. Come on, I told myself, you don't have forever.

Where the hell was it?

I looked to the designer coffee table, each of its legs a gaudy replica of a Fabergé egg, the top a sheet of thick glass with a small trick chamber for a pen—no kidding!—that had a diamond stylus. Celebrities he liked could autograph his coffee table. I looked to the bookshelves. A copy of *Bury My Heart at Wounded Knee,* a copy of Shelby Foote's three-volume set on the American Civil War, still in its shrink-wrap and probably a gift. Damn it. Where ... ? Then I spotted it resting on the stereo cabinet.

It looked different from the last time I'd seen it, but from its size and weight, it had to be the .45. You would think I'd know, having been intimate with the damn thing. As I checked the magazine and shoved it back home, there was a metallic *clack* that never penetrated the studio, and then I snapped a round into the chamber. I tossed the gun into my handbag and took a deep breath. *Just don't be an idiot,* I warned myself. When you pull it out, make sure you release the safety. Do it quick. Do it without hesitation.

God bless America. In Canada, it's harder than you think to get a handgun. There are rural places like out on the prairies and such where men have rifles, either for sport hunting or killing pests on their farms. But if you want a pistol, you make a written application and the Mounties, our federal police, interview you in your home. And you better have a damn good reason for wanting one. None of this "right to bear arms" shit. You *must* keep it under lock and key at home, you *must* transport it in a sealed case in the back of your car to and from the firing range. Like Britain, guns get smuggled in and sold on the black market, but the odds of getting shot in downtown Toronto are a lot less than if you were walking around Detroit or even Beverly Hills.

In a way, Luther was my unwitting accomplice for Steven Swann. He had taught me how to shoot.

He wasn't a gun freak the way Steven was, not at all. Growing up in one of the more affluent neighbourhoods of Brooklyn, he never saw a gangbanger until he began producing. I asked him once about it, and he looked at me with this peculiar expression as if he'd just returned from Beirut.

"It's fucking Mars, Michelle. I'm sitting in the back of a limo with Chester K and a couple of guys from Furrr, and this Audi pulls up at the stoplight next to us. All I can see is a hand in a white jacket sleeve making signs at Chester, and I can't hear anything. Chester gets out of the car and pulls out this honking big Magnum! But the Audi rips through the stoplight and tears off before he can do anything, thank God. When he's inside and sitting down again, I'm saying, 'Son-of-a-bitch, man, how can you live like this?' They're all laughing at me, and he says, 'Got to get the word out, dog.' "

Luther rolled his eyes to the ceiling. "I said to him what word? And he started in on this whole thing about how this is *real life,* and I didn't know it. I said, 'No, Chester, real life is buying groceries and going to the park and making music if that happens to be your job. You think *real people* go around like bandits capping each other?' He looked at me as if he hadn't heard a thing I'd said and told me, 'I'm the genuine shit, Luther. I ain't posing.' And I told him yes, I know. I went to his label management the next day and told them I'm out. I'll finish up Chester's album, but don't *ever* ask me to work with this guy again because I don't want to be standing next to him when his head gets blown off."

Still, Luther had purchased and registered a gun. A semiautomatic just like Steven had, only his was a Smith & Wesson, I think. And on a whim of modern chivalry, he'd insisted on teaching Erica and me how to use it because we were two single girls living alone in Manhattan. Granted, we were on the Upper East Side, but we were alone. Erica, he said, should buy herself a gun. "No fucking way!" she told him. But she couldn't resist her morbid curiosity to experience what one felt like in her hand. Neither could I. So there were the two of us wearing those clear protection goggles like they have for surgeons and dentists, Luther standing behind each of us as we took a turn to heft the weight of the thing and squeeze off a few rounds. It sounded jarringly loud, even through the protective headphones.

The next time I saw a gun, it was Steven's, and he was nudging it inside my pussy.

And now I had it smuggled in my handbag.

I took a breath to calm my nerves and walked over to the recording studio. I stared at him through the glass. The dimmers were on low in the room so that he was almost in shadow, and at last he looked up from the control panel and noticed me. I gave him a puckered half smile, my brow furrowed, as if to say: *all right, I did have to come back. I don't like you, but I enjoy fucking you.* I couldn't look too eager for him.

He smiled back at me and killed the music as I walked in. Folding his arms, he remarked, "Well, I guess it wouldn't be very sexy of me if I played it smug."

"No, it wouldn't."

He paused a moment over his board, at last saying, "I knew you had fun. Let me finish up here, and then we can have a couple of drinks."

I watched him work for a long moment.

"You expecting anyone else this evening?"

"No," he said, his face clouding for a moment. "Why?"

"Just hoped we'd get some privacy, that's all."

"You have me all to yourself."

Shoot him. Shoot him now.

I couldn't just yet. I felt strangely detached from my

intention. I didn't feel sorry for him or have this big attack of morality that, yes, killing was wrong. I wasn't even nervous. I was so calm that all my outrage seemed to have drained out of me. I was too collected. Ending him would be like exterminating a pest. As bizarre as it sounds, I needed my righteous indignation back. I wanted to feel something, so I kept talking to him.

"Hey, listen," I said. "When we were doing it the other day, and you had me strangling you . . ."

"Yeah?"

"Did you think about where you were? That you could die in that room?"

He shook his head, thinking I was making a joke. "No."

"But you could have died, Steven. That would have been it. *Your spot.* In your home. And it would have been a hell of a way to go."

"I trusted you, Mish. Wasn't that a turn-on for you? You know, taking me to the edge and all that? My life in your hands?"

"Maybe it was a bigger turn-on for you than for me," I suggested.

"Yeah, maybe," he said in a casual voice. "You can tell yourself that if you want to. If we got to play games, honey, okay, we'll play games."

He hit a button on the panel, and as I heard a flood of music, I took the second to dig into my handbag and release the safety.

"You're gonna love this," he told me.

I heard the distinctive bass line from "It Was a Pleasure to Burn." He was weaving it into the mix of his own new single.

I couldn't believe it. "You think Erica will let you keep permission to do that?"

"Does it matter these days?" he shot back. And then:

"But the beauty of it is, I got it during the engagement! She waived royalties on the use. Oooh, oooh, check this out, it's my idea—"

And before the bridge was an instrumental section with a strange sound. I couldn't place it. I sat leaning against the dynamically futuristic desk he had in there for his mixer boards and equipment, my hand still touching the gun in my unzipped handbag, and the situation was absurd. *Guess that noise,* as I stood waiting for the right moment to pull out the Colt and shoot him.

"It's this kid's squeal in a day care run backwards," he explained. "Sounds like a girl coming, huh? I pick up all kinds of stuff to throw in."

He held up a palm-size Sony micro-cassette recorder, punched the play, and, yes, there was the kid in a long joyous giggle, *"Eeeeee!"* He had done an amazing job of sifting out the ambient background noise around it for the mix. He hit the play for the new track, and there was the bass and the keyboards again, plus his creation.

I shook my head at him. "You're a real heartless bastard, you know that?"

He made a horse whinny of a laugh and fell back against his chair. *"Fuuuuck!* Gimme a break, Michelle. These rappers borrow from Sting, Phil Collins, Bruce Hornsby, who the fuck knows how many other half-buried corpses from our parents' rock and roll, and you want to get pissy over me using a bit of Erica? Alicia Keys took classical piano, and what? You think Mozart is bitching? That's what I'm going to do, you goofy chick! These white suburban wannabes *like* the brothers' music. *I* like the music. I'm not going to apologise for putting my own spin on it or 'watering it down' or whatever you want to call it to speak to my kind. What, I'm a thief because I talk to *my* own target audience using their licks? Bullshit."

I was captivated for a moment by his impromptu diatribe, maybe not so much by his argument but by the fact
that for once, Steven was being sincerely *passionate*. He
wasn't pulling his pretty boy Zen aphorism shit, wasn't being condescending. He actually believed.

"I love the hypocrisy, man," he said with a wide grin.
"Music is music—so goes the big politically correct chant.
Except when *we* go to the well and want to pull up a bucket
of African rhythms or Indian stuff or whatever the world
music flavour is this month. Let Paul Simon and Malcolm
McLaren burn in hell, huh?"

"That's a nice speech," I countered. "You're always saying you don't pretend to be what you're not. And then you
pull that engagement shit to look good—"

"Not this again—"

"Yes, that again. *That's* hypocrisy."

"No, that's marketing," insisted Steven. "Look, I let you
in on what I only *hoped* folks would think. I can't be sure.
And I never came out with any statements about Erica's
politics or crusades or any shit. I never stuck my nose into it.
People made their own conclusions about my credibility—"

"You said the album sales—"

"Hey, do you think that says something about me? Or
about them?"

I couldn't answer that one.

"What do you think they'd say about you if they found
you naked with a scarf around your neck after sex?" I asked.

"Oh, we're back to that," he answered. "You're talking in
circles today."

"Come on, really, what do you think they'd say?"

He stood up, his fingers drumming along the leather
sleeve of the Sony tape recorder, and he reached out to
stroke my cheek. "They'd say...That Steven Swann. The
guy was coming and going! Get it?"

"You're a riot," I told him. "I wish you begged me for your life."

"Why?" he laughed, backing up a step and glancing down at the mixer board. "Would that have made it more erotic?"

"No," I said as I withdrew the gun from my handbag, "but maybe I would have felt something. Maybe I'd change my mind about this."

He stared at me, his mouth slack and his eyes wide and completely bewildered. No cleverness in him at all as he faced the barrel. I fired.

It wasn't like in the movies. There was a cannon roar in my ears, and the ugly muzzle of the thing spat flame and a tiny cloud. In a fleeting instant, Steven grew a bright red dot in his forehead and cried out, short, sharp, and without hope. Then he appeared to suddenly faint, falling to the side, hitting the control board and slumping to the floor. His right hand flew back and dropped the tape recorder, his other hand fanning out to complete the spread eagle. And all the while, Steven Swann's voice sang inside the studio. The tiny green light indicators were like an ever-changing bar graph popping and falling with the vocals and the bass.

I paused a minute to make sure he was gone. I wasn't interested in the ugly red and black hole I had made in his head, I watched for a change in his expression, a stirring of movement. But his face was frozen in its shock.

I had come prepared with a thick flannel cloth and a medium-size makeup pouch inside my handbag. I wiped my prints off the gun and slipped it into the pouch, zipped it closed, and as I slung my handbag over my shoulder, I realised I hadn't even checked through the glass of the booth to make sure Steven was right, that we were alone. When I turned no one was there, and my body shook in spasms of jangled nerves. *Now get out of here,* I ordered myself. I took another flannel from my handbag and wiped the inside and outside knobs of the studio door, but I didn't care about my prints being in the rest of the apartment. I had been a regular visitor here with Erica, no suspicion aroused by that. Best to wipe down the front door, though.

Then I was out on the street. I took a short ride on the subway, and half an hour later, I waved goodbye to the makeup pouch as it made a soft splash in the East River. No more gun. Yes, the cops would figure out that Steven's gun was missing, and that it was probably the murder weapon, but there was no reason I should make life easier for them.

I went home, and Erica was out. I felt the need to take a shower. I liked mystery stories, and I liked cop shows, and I remembered reading that stuff from guns, powder or whatever, can contaminate the shooter. I must have stood under the hot spray for forty-five minutes, obsessively washing my arms, my hands, my face and my neck, as if I could cleanse away both Steven Swann and what I had done to him. I wondered if they'd found him by now. I wondered if it made the news yet.

I told myself I was right to do what I did. He would have ruined Erica's career, at the very least tarnished her reputation, and he did it not even out of cruelty or revenge over her sleeping around. He targeted her like he was a goddamn plant manager needing to get rid of a few thousand workers on a factory line. She had loved him. She had opened herself so completely to him and even opened up her personal life and her feelings to the world. For him. For the likes of him.

I hated what he did to her. I hated him.

And I hated that Steven made me come.

Questions

I don't need to go over how huge the fallout was from Steven's death, do I? First the headlines and quotes from shocked friends and BSB management and then the lurid speculation about who might have killed him. The leading theory for fifteen minutes was that the murderer was a secret gay lover—probably pushed by that contingent of fans and press who cynically believe *every* celebrity's gay and in the closet. Then there was the candlelight vigil outside the townhouse off Park Avenue, Fox News showing kids who said, "Steven's music was about peace, man, and we can't forget that." As if "Skankin' Around" had a message.

Erica hated the idea of playing the grieving fiancée. The label's publicity department very politely and steadily kept nudging her to make a statement until I watched her explode in their offices. "I am *not* going to stand in front of a bunch of fucking cameras and cry my eyes out like, like— some beauty queen getting her crown! Steven's dead! He's *dead*. Do you understand that? You don't have to patronise people by giving them a show! You think they have to *guess* how I feel?"

And her hands were balled in fists as streaks of tears poured down both cheeks. What they couldn't get in front of a camera was wrenched out of her in this private confrontation. As she rushed out the door, I remember one executive appealing to me.

"Michelle, talk to her, will you?"

I turned on my heel and stared at the guy. "How old is your mother?"

"What?"

"You heard me," I said. "How old is your mother?"

He actually had to think about it. "Seventy-three. Why?"

"When she dies, remind me to send a camera crew to *your* house."

I hurried for the elevator to catch up to Erica.

I know, I know. Who was I now? I had detached myself completely. It was another Michelle who had gone over to Steven Swann's apartment that night and exacted a revenge for Erica's humiliation. I swear to God that when I looked at the newspapers the morning after, *Newsday, The Post, The Times,* I felt a ripple of genuine astonishment and grief for him. As if killing him hadn't been real and only the papers made it so. To be completely honest, I didn't feel a pang of guilt for Erica's desolation over his death. It struck me as a *wish* for a genuine grief, no more substantial than the zircon pain over their break-up. Maybe because we both knew that, as righteous as she sounded in that BSB office, she wasn't about to divulge the fact that, oh, yeah, by the way, he broke up with me only a couple of days before he was shot.

Yes, I was detached, disconnected from what I had done. I couldn't even summon impatience over Erica's mournful sobs, bringing myself to tell her snap out of it, girl, he dumped you, he was a bad person. We don't wish him dead, but he doesn't deserve this many tears. (I did wish him dead, and I had made it so.) Erica cried. I held her. I held my beautiful luscious star, and I basked in the warmth of her body, I let her tears cascade down her face until they touched my lip, and I revelled in their sweet salt. There were dreadful nights when she was close to exhaustion, already in her nightie, and I came into her bedroom out of sincere concern. But as I held her close and she rocked in my arms, barely knowing me, I could feel the press of her pubic bone through her cotton underwear against my thigh. My face in her hair, her breasts crushed against my own in her grief, I felt closer to her than even in the intimacy of our sex games with Steven's toys at his house out in Santa Fe.

After I finally coaxed her to slip back into her bed, whispering, "Sleep, Erica, come on, sleep, honey," I went back to my room and my own en suite bathroom. I sat nervously on the sill of the tub. Shivering, gooseflesh on my arms, hot needles in my legs and feet, my panties so drenched, I was peeling them off me. It took only seconds of stimulating myself to reach orgasm. If she had kissed me, God, if she had tilted her face up, her generous breast escaping the silk the way it had so "accidentally" freed itself for Luther, and what if she wasn't wearing underwear, if I could feel the tight curls of her wedge of fur against my skin? Erica, oh, God, Erica, if I only could comfort you the way I want to . . .

*E*rica didn't go to Steven's funeral. The family organised it, and they didn't deign to inform her where it was. His parents were called all kinds of names over this snub, including "racist" in the press, but Erica said she could understand how they didn't want the funeral turned into a circus. "He must have told them," I remembered her whispering in the apartment.

"Told them what?"

"That he broke it off," she explained, her voice dead of feeling. "He must have told them it was over."

She never raised the subject of him again. Within a week of the funeral, MTV and Fox were talking about something else, and while I heard rumours that *Vanity Fair* had assigned a reporter to delve into the shooting, even the cops weren't knocking on the doors at Brown Skin Beats anymore. Life had to go on. The dewy-eyed girls who had made up Steven's fan base had given him candles that burned brightly but not for very long. When it came down to it, Steven didn't inspire any moments of pause among household strangers the way people were stunned by the plane crash that killed Aaliyah. With her, you thought, my God, too young, so much potential, an *innocent* talent. No one could ever say Steven Swann was innocent.

Steven's death, however, prompted one significant decision in Erica's life. She didn't talk about it with me first. And I never saw it coming.

*B*rown Skin Beats was one of those corporate cultures that loved their frills. As you walk in the marble-floored lobby, you pass a full-service cafeteria and an open plan bullpen for junior management with large aquariums of tropical fish. Somebody had ripped off this décor from the Bloomberg offices. My corner office was small but it was mine, and I also liked to take advantage of a large gym in the BSB basement. There was a room with rowing machines, stationary bikes and other equipment, plus a dance studio with a balance bar and full-size mirrors. Since Erica was my boss and I made up her schedule, which meant I pretty much made up my own, I liked to go down there in the afternoon when no one was around and do some stretches.

It was three o' clock when I strolled into the studio, expecting to find it empty, and there she was. This tall young woman who couldn't be much older than me on a stretching mat. Her skin was a *café au lait* shade, and I had a generous view of it as she sat in skimpy shorts, her long shapely legs in a "V." As she sank down to press her elbows on the floor, her oversized tank top was pulled by gravity, and I saw the divide for two magnificent full breasts. Her hair was cut short, framing an oval face with lustrous dark lashes, hazel eyes and a smile of brilliant white teeth. She gave me a friendly smile as I came in.

I waved back and draped my towel over the balance bar. "I didn't think anyone else used this space in the middle of the afternoon."

"Oh, I'm sorry," she said quickly. "Did you book it for yourself? I'm new. I haven't learned yet how things are done around here."

"No, no, it's fine," I said, and I introduced myself.

"Jill Chandler," she replied. We shook hands.

There was an awkward pause where both of us didn't know whether to go on talking or share the space and do our separate exercises. I decided for both. I took up a position close to her side and began doing knee bends, sinking my weight and sending my right leg back in a long stretch.

"So what are you going to be doing for BSB?" I asked politely. "You in marketing? Production?"

"I'll work with Erica Jones."

"Oh." A small but insistent warning rang in my head, like those annoying alarm clocks that buzzed over and over again.

"Yeah," she went on. "I'm going to tag along on her public appearances, go along to the concerts with her. She's decided she needs physical therapy because the touring can exhaust you. It's brutal."

"Tell me about it," I chuckled.

"You're *that* Michelle, aren't you? You're her PA. Wow. Been waiting to meet you." And then we were shaking hands again.

"Why, uh, why would you be waiting to meet me?" I laughed.

Jill went on stretching. I had stopped what I was doing, listening closely to her now, but I was very distracted by her movements. She was twisting and curling her body into the most flexible poses I'd ever seen. They resembled yoga stances, but they were somehow more energetic and suggestive.

"Oh, it's just I heard you were really nice," she said.

Aha. A diplomat.

She looked at me out of the corner of her eye with a slightly embarrassed smile on her face. "They say you make a lot of the big decisions when it comes to her, and ... I mean they did say you were nice, but I know you're important around here. I was hoping we'd hit it off. You know, new job, first impressions."

"Hey, I'm a kitten," I replied. "I'm glad people told you that, umm ... what *are* you doing there?"

She stood up, blowing air from her lungs with her exertion, and there was a glow on her forehead and neck now. Her perspiration had an almost sweet smell to it.

Smiling at me, she said, "It's kind of hard to explain. It's one of the reasons I usually duck out to use a gym all by myself. This is kind of an ancient African form of exercise and meditation, it's uh—" She lowered her voice to a girlish whisper. "Kind of an African Tantric yoga."

"Get out!" I blurted, laughing. "Come on, there's no such thing!"

"No, really," she said.

She gave me the African name, but I couldn't remember the multiple syllables, and then she touched me lightly on the arm for emphasis, reassuring me the art actually existed.

I felt a sudden electrical charge, wondering if she was flirting with me. But my radar was never any good with women. Men were obvious. Girls were subtle and more difficult to read.

"It's wonderful stuff," said Jill. "You should try it sometime."

"Hey, Sting, I'll just watch you for now," I joked.

She shrugged an okay and knelt down again on her mat. Then she was falling back on her knees, arching her spine until her shoulder blades touched the floor. A swan neck and such beautiful graceful arms, her thighs so toned and perfectly sculpted.

"Well, you're just standing there staring, so you might as well get down here with me," she said.

"Pardon me?"

"Come on, we'll do some regular stretches. Hey, I give a real good workout."

"I'm sure you do," I said.

And for the next forty-five minutes, we exercised together. We gripped each other's wrists and see-sawed forward and back with our legs spread out. We took turns holding each other gently around the waist as one of us raised a leg high. We ran in short sprinting bursts around the studio to keep ourselves pumped. I told her that was enough for me today, I was going to hit the shower. Jill still had reps to do on the weight machines, and then she'd head out for a jog down several blocks of Fifth.

"Go with God," I panted, towelling my neck.

As she waved a goodbye at the door, saying she'd see me around, she passed Luther and traded brief hellos. Luther, wearing a tank top and sweatpants, spotted me through the glass in the door and walked into the studio.

"Hey, how you doing?"

"I'm okay," I answered. "Made the mistake of trying to keep up with Wonder Woman there."

"She is something. How you holding up?"

"Me?" I asked in surprise. "Why? Holding up under what?"

"Steven's death. Everybody's been so focussed on how Erica's coping with it, I wondered if anyone bothered to give a damn that you were hanging with him, too. He did take you along with Erica to Santa Fe, and I got the sense you two were on good ter—"

"I'm fine, honey, I'm good. I don't know if I could call Steven and me friends, but..."

I shrugged, wondering what else I could tell him. Typical Luther, the one guy with the thoughtfulness to remember others were affected. Being smitten with Erica never gave him blinkers. But I was at a loss to come up with anything to confide for his trouble.

"I understand," he said, not truly understanding at all. "You kind of packed it away, haven't you? I've noticed that about you. You're so quiet, it's like you think you'll waste your emotions if you express them in public." He gave me one of those sideways grins of his. "In a way, you're the perfect fit for Erica. She's so out there, so extroverted, she just gives it out in a tidal wave, and you, you're..."

"A dripping tap," I suggested.

"No..."

"A birdbath?"

"You don't have to be so closed off about Steven, you know," he tried again. "Especially with me. We're friends, aren't we, Michelle?"

"Course we are, sweetie."

"Right. Look, it sucks. Big time. I'm not sure I completely liked the guy, but I worked for him and with him, and I respected his drive. Steven was always so go-go-go, you know what I'm saying? And in the middle of the night, even I'm sometimes so *pissed* at the son-of-a-bitch who took it all away."

I thought I better give him a little of what he wanted to hear. "I am, too," I said in a small voice.

"We go on," he said, still in rallying mode. "We go on and make music and do business. I think it's a good thing Jill's come on board. I doubt Erica will need her that much, maybe for the odd wing nut, but she's got the same kind of *zing,* doesn't she? She's really charismatic in her own way. And she seems to know how to be there for Erica without cramping her style."

I didn't know what he was talking about anymore. "You've lost me," I said. "What do you mean 'cramping her style' ? She told me she's Erica's physical therapist."

Luther's mouth grew from a tight-lipped line to bubbling laughter. "Must be Jill's idea of a joke."

"I don't understand," I said, and I still didn't.

"Well, maybe Jill was trained once as a physical therapist, I don't know," answered Luther, "but that's not why she's on the payroll now. With what happened to Steven, Erica thinks maybe it's time she got some protection. Jill's her new bodyguard."

*S*o Erica had picked up another shadow, one right beside my own. I met Jill Chandler again that very evening. Erica's limo collected me at the office, and on the leather seat waiting inside was the newest member of the team. As the car rolled towards our apartment to fetch the star, I asked Jill about her little white lie. She confirmed Luther's notion that, yeah, she had a bit of an off-beat sense of humour, and besides, it paid to be discreet about her work, even when folks would eventually find out what she did.

"It's never good to come off as a big enforcer type or throw your weight around," she explained. "I've seen some women try to pull that in this line of work, over-compensating for all the sexist shit they put up with. But look at me. I'm not that big, and I'm not *really* that tall. It's just better to play it low key."

It made me wonder how she ended up in her line of work to begin with. Jill said she'd been a New York police officer for three years, and after the brief joy of graduating from the academy she had hated every minute of being on the force. A grind: the ungrateful public, the hazards, the politics, all of it. So she got a job with a high-profile corporate protection service, and after two years of walking two steps behind oil executives and bankers, realised the business depended completely on good customer relations and rapport with clients. When she set up her own bodyguard service, she took an impressive number of clients with her.

"What about all that African Tantric Yoga stuff?"

There was a wicked glint of mischief in her eyes. "Oh, that's real. I wasn't making that up."

I leaned forward in the seat, making the leather upholstery crunch, and I opened the mini-bar. Helping myself to a tiny bottle of Johnnie Walker, I tossed her another one and told her, "I see I'm going to have to keep an eye on you."

"Oh, we'll get on like a house on fire, you'll see." She dropped the little bottle into her slim spaghetti-strapped handbag, explaining, "Can't drink now. These are *my* working hours."

The car rolled up in front of our building just then, and Erica came down. At Madison Square Garden, I would have normally been watching the audience or Erica dazzle her fans. I had to stay alert and close by for any sudden chores, but tonight the show ran smoothly, and I watched Jill instead. Oddball girl, sure, I thought, but she's nobody's fool. Look at her scope out the crowd from the wings, ignoring the usual boisterous fans in the front rows, letting security do the mop-up on them. Jill training her eyes on exits, backstage corridors, places where the disturbed might find access. And when the show was over, hovering over Erica's right shoulder, one step behind—able to stop anyone from chasing after the star but close enough to intervene if trouble jumped out of the blue ahead of us.

When we went out on tour, most of the nights were uneventful, but early on—the second show in Detroit—I saw how Jill handled trouble. A white guy with a face full of stubble and eyes frosted over with an angry blankness moved out of the crowd and started bitching about how Erica wouldn't let him see their child, why are you doing this, Erica? Completely made-up insane stuff. His hands extended to either shake her or choke her, and Jill was suddenly *there,* blocking the man's way, folding his wrist in on itself and spinning him forward and then back in a wide arc. She sent him hurtling to the concrete with a dull thud.

People were shouting things like holy shit and somebody call the cops, and Jill's calm tone held a demand instead of a polite question: *Erica, you okay?* Erica not moving, staying put exactly as Jill had insisted in their agreed-upon contingency plans. You do as I say when there's a problem, Jill had told her, or I can't keep you safe. Erica was probably fixed in her spot more out of shock than anything else, just as I was.

We asked her later: what the hell was that?

"Oh," said Jill, her voice casual, "a little police takedown, a little aikido. You two did well. I'm glad neither of you panicked."

The minor incident barely rated a paragraph in the entertainment pages, but it was enough to secure Jill Chandler's job for a while. The problem for me was that Jill Chandler wouldn't be satisfied with standing around and playing sentry.

*M*ichelle? Call me when you get this, please."

Morgan. Again.

Morgan had begun to treat the message space on my mobile like he had squatter's rights there, calling me at all hours to "resolve" his royalty issue. I told him we'd discuss it when I got back to New York. He kept calling. I left a message on his answer machine that royalties were out of the question, but, yes, I was checking with the management of Brown Skin Beats to see if I could get him some kind of "bonus" for his work on *Drum*.

Funnily enough, the decision came down to Luther. His stock had soared since his producing gigs on a couple of Britain's hottest R&B stars, and BSB got smart and brought him inside, giving him a fancy title like "associate creative director" or some such thing. He still did what he did, only now he scouted talent, he assigned producing jobs, and he had budgets to manage. He made more money. Not enough to party like the stars, but he would be comfortable. When the tour reached LA, he was in town over a movie-scoring thing for one of the label's acts, and he took me aside to discuss the Morgan issue.

"Mish, why do you want me to sign off on giving him more money? Yes, he's family, but he got a fair price on *Drum*."

I considered taking Luther into my confidence. Before his jaunt to the UK, I could have predicted which way he'd go on the issue. He would have called Morgan crazy or a liar over the songwriting credits. He would have taken Erica's side hands down. No way he could see her objectively. After London, well...Integrity was very big with

Luther. He would have raised a huge stink, gone digging for where the bodies were buried, found out if Morgan was right. And if Morgan was right? Well, his shiny spanking new job with BSB wouldn't stop him insisting on public reparations, future credits in liner notes and in publishing, and if the label wanted the matter ignored, he'd say no and go public.

I had to lie to him. "I'm getting stick from one of the musician unions."

"*Morgan* went to them?" Luther could scarcely believe it. He knew Morgan was never one for politics in music or for organisations.

"It's real complicated."

"Well, what does Erica think?"

"I haven't told her," I said. "God, Luther, you know it would break her heart to know he complained. She'd pony up whether he has a case or not! She wants to be such a good friend to the masses over equal pay and rights, but I'm the one who does her books, man. Please. BSB's got deep enough pockets they can afford it. And you'll want the option of using Morgan again, won't you? If the label brass gets wind of this, they'll put him on a shit list and stamp him as a troublemaker. You won't get to use him if that happens."

Luther pursed his lips thoughtfully and scratched his chin. "That's not *exactly* true. I use who I want when I'm producing, it's in my contract. But if we bring him in for somebody else's album... Yeah, you're right. Erica doesn't need this shit right now anyway. And I don't know what's up with Morgan these days. Maybe he owes money or something. Maybe he's burned out."

He told me how Morgan had performed his drunken jazz player routine at another one of his regular gigs in Morningside Heights. The way Luther described it, I was sure our friend had, at least for now, not spouted off about "his" songs on an Erica Jones album. Good. But self-interest aside, I was as concerned as Luther about the man's steady decline.

What did I say early on about Morgan? That Erica's father had wanted him to teach his little girl how to love the craft beyond the glory. I called it a bittersweet compliment to Morgan's talents, since that kind of lesson is best learned from the one who has failed, the one who stays behind to keep watch, to hold the sacred ground. Why now? Why come apart now? He's tired, I thought. We'll pay him off, and maybe he'll get back on an even keel. We'll be able to talk to him and come around to his place like old times.

I was hanging around with people who booked a corporate jet on weekends and who bought themselves Bulgari watches when they had the blues. Cheques cured worlds of hurt. Morgan still lived in a dump of a loft with a freight elevator, his furniture on creaky boards and his double bed past a beaded curtain, and people thought this was cool because it reminded them of the movies. Bohemian chic. Morgan was probably sick of having lived like this for the better part of his life. Okay, I thought, we can fix that. Naïve yet tarnished as everyone else, I thought Luther's sign-off on the additional money would solve my biggest problem. I was cynical.

And I should have known better. Erica had told me how her father, good ol' Duane Jones, and Morgan had a real bust-up before Mr. Jones quit their band and headed off home to Toronto. Sure, they had kind of patched things up over the years, and Erica went to Morgan with her Dad's blessing, but she knew the stories of how Morgan could be a real spiteful son-of-a-bitch sometimes. He could really dig in his heels when he felt like it. I was about to discover what that was like.

*T*here was a break in the tour when we flew back to New York, and Erica worked on a couple of tracks for the latest album. In the morning, I had a window to go over regular business with her like cover art designs and shots for a new magazine spread. When Erica worked on recording she could spend hours without breaks, without meals, and on Tuesday, I begged my way out of sticking around and returned home. I had two D'Agostino bags' worth of groceries in my arms and my key ring in my teeth as I opened the door. There was Jill, feet up on the desk in the front lounge, pensively examining various objects pulled out of the drawers.

"Make yourself at home," I snapped. Erica thought her bodyguard should have a key, though she told me she had strict rules on Jill's use of it.

"Hey, I'm sorry, I thought you two were at work," said Jill. "I didn't think anybody would be back for hours."

"Sorry to disappoint you. What are you doing?"

I put the bags down and took a couple of tentative steps over to the desk. I noticed now that there was a common link between all the objects she had pulled out and was checking. They were all the gifts that Steven Swann had ever given Erica: a plush toy animal, expensive jewellery, a boxed CD set of the best of David Bowie, an Hermès scarf and so on. Erica had shoved the things away after his brutal admission that he couldn't love her anymore.

"A pattern," said Jill. "I'm looking for a pattern."

"A pattern of what?" I asked.

"How Steven thought. What he liked, what he was into, what turned him on."

"So you let yourself in to *our* place? Go to Barnes & Noble and get his bio if you want to learn about him! There are dozens getting released now. Or Erica can loan you a couple of his albums. You need HMV, not our desk." I took the groceries into the kitchen and began putting them away.

"Steven's killer is still out there," said Jill, raising her voice so that I could hear. "For all we know, maybe the killer wants to go after Erica, too. The best way I can think of for preventing that is to catch the person first."

I came out of the kitchen and gestured with a cup, offering her tea. Might as well be civil. No thanks, she muttered.

"I'm sure the cops are still investigating his murder," I said. "It's not like they need you to play Nancy Drew for them."

She nodded, conceding the point. "Yeah, that's true. But I have one client, one long-term contract. And so I've got one case. I can devote a lot more of my personal attention than they can."

I drifted back into the kitchen and poured tea for myself, nervously taking a sip before I gave it a decent chance to steep. What was she doing, sticking her nose into Steven's murder? She was supposed to be a bodyguard, not a private detective. Trying to keep my voice calm, I called out to the living room, "And you think the best way you can catch the guy is understanding Steven?"

She waited for my return before answering. "I do. I shouldn't be alarmist about this, Michelle, but I think Erica, you, Luther, a couple of others could be in real danger. It's so obvious that the killer was someone who knew Steven well. He must have been someone in your inner circle."

"You're scaring me," I said. I didn't have to lie about it either.

"See, I shouldn't have said anything," sighed Jill, taking her feet off the desk. "Now you *are* going to worry. Look, I still have friends on the force, and they've given me access to the file. I'm looking into it. And, yes, you're right, the cops are still investigating."

"But you said yourself, they can't devote all their attention to it," I replied, letting my voice quaver a bit. "Shit, you mean his killer could be one of *us*? I just can't believe it. Look, I'm sorry I was catty with you when I walked in. You do have to help figure it out, don't you? The cops get murders every day, and they—"

"Oh, they'll find a suspect eventually," she argued.

"Why so certain?"

"Because of the gun."

The gun?

There was a flutter of nerves on my insides like startled pigeons being chased from a square. "What do you mean the gun? I thought they never found a gun."

"Oh, not the murder weapon," said Jill quickly. "No, they didn't find that. Swann had all kinds of guns all over his house, and they found a .45 under his pillow. The cops, they, uh . . . How can I put this politely? When the forensics guy put the barrel close to his nose to smell if it had been fired recently, he—uh—picked up something else."

Stupid. Stupid, stupid, *stupid.* Showing off his collection, all his BS talk about the Old West, his rifles and even a goddamn flintlock in his display case, and it never, ever occurred to me that Steven would have more than one handgun. I had thought the pistol looked different when I picked it up. I knew what she was going to tell me.

"Swann owned a couple of .45 Colts, and from what I hear, he liked to do the whole John Woo thing sometimes out at his property in New Mexico," explained Jill. She raised her index fingers at me. "Bang, bang, bang, bang! Boys with toys. When he was in New York, he split up the twins for home protection, and he must have been playing some kinky games in his spare time. The lab found traces of vaginal secretions on the barrel of the gun."

I couldn't say anything. She took my reaction for regular shock. At last I ventured, "Where, um, where did they find it?"

"Swann had it under his pillow."

Keep a poker face. Don't react.

"The cops are interpreting that as a fearful response," said Jill. She didn't sound convinced. "They think he must have been threatened either by a crazed fan, or maybe there's a gang with hip-hop or rap ties that didn't like him and made it clear. So he felt his life was in danger, and that's why he kept a gun under his pillow."

"But . . . you don't think that." I wasn't asking.

"No, I don't."

"Why not?"

"I've thought it through," replied Jill. "If you're in fear for your life, yeah, sure, maybe you sleep with a gun under your pillow. But here's a young guy making gazillions, and he doesn't hire a bodyguard. The others have bodyguards, the Jacksons, the J-Los, the action stars. What was Erica's response to Steven's murder? *Hire me.* And Steven didn't beef up security at the townhouse."

"He had a burglar alarm already, didn't he?" I tried to sound as ignorant as possible.

"Yep. One of the best. Which leads to the next obvious thing. If the cops are right, and he's killed by someone threatening him, why no forced entry to the house? The cops come back to me with some half-assed reply that he must have known who was threatening him and been trying to talk his way out, let bygones be bygones. That's a bit of a reach, don't you think?"

"I wouldn't know."

"It makes far more sense that either he invited his killer over since the door was unlocked—which is less likely, I mean, hey, we're in New York—or the killer had her own key."

I shrugged. "Why? Why does that follow?"

"Steven was in his recording studio when he was murdered. There was no sign of a struggle. Here's a victim who supposedly doesn't feel safe enough in his own home that he sleeps with a handgun, *but he doesn't bring it along with him when he's in a sound-proof room.* He's working on tracks. He's mixing. He's playing back stuff. And what's more, he's playing it back for someone else."

I was really astonished now. And getting nervous. "How can you be so sure he was playing stuff back for someone else?"

"This little Sony micro-cassette recorder had fallen out of his hand when he was shot."

I didn't get it. "So?"

"So no patch cord from the tape machine to the board," said Jill, smiling in wonder that I didn't make the jump in logic. "You're mixing sound, putting together your song, and you whip out a little tape recorder to suddenly hear something? That presumes you need it. He didn't scribble down any notes on paper, and he didn't have the tape recorder hooked up or one of the micro-cassettes popped in a deck."

"Maybe he was about to," I suggested.

Jill sucked on the tip of her index finger, looking pensive again. "Maybe. I doubt it. I think he was playing something for his killer, and she shot him right afterwards."

"You keep saying 'she.' *She* killed him."

"Do I?"

"Yeah," I said. "Why can't it be a guy?"

"Goes back to those vaginal secretions on the gun barrel," offered Jill. "Like I said, the boy liked his kink. *That's* why he slept with that gun under his pillow, it was a little joke he was having with himself. I think perhaps he took it too far, and the girl got righteously pissed off. She came back later and showed him a new place to stick it. Vengeance for a sexual assault."

Oh, Jesus.

"It's only a matter of time before she's found," she went on. "Big pop star like that, of course, he'd be working his way through rows A to M at his concerts, but I'm sure they'll find a match eventually, sooner or later."

She was right. I had to take a big gamble.

"Jill. It doesn't necessarily follow that this girl was his killer."

"No?"

"No. Because . . . because if I gave the cops a DNA sample, they'd find out it was me."

"*You?*"

I nodded.

"People told me you're . . . Never mind." She let out a long sigh. "Shit, Michelle. You know I have to go back to the police with this, don't you? And you're going to have to talk to them, too."

"I know."

She looked at me, just looked at me. Waiting. "I visited Steven at the townhouse two days before he was killed," I said. "We had sex. It wasn't rape. There was always an attraction between us, and he started laying it on thick about how he knew Erica had guys on the side, but he planned to be faithful to her *after* the wedding. And he would expect the same of her. He figured if she could play around before the wedding, he should sow a few last oats of his own."

"And you decided to be one of them. Help him cheat on her."

"Don't judge me, Jill," I snapped. "You haven't worked for Erica as long as I have. You'll see plenty of shit. Yes, maybe you've worked for other celebrities, but she is *insatiable*. And it's not in your job description or mine, but you *will* be expected to cover up for her and make excuses for her, and sometimes you'll be in a corner and have to watch. She's the star. It was a hell of an ego boost for *me* to have Steven Swann say let's make it, honey. Yes, he was twisted. The gun was his idea. He said to me, here's a *real* dildo for you. It wasn't loaded or anything, and I let him do it to me. And the scary part is, I did get off on it."

Jill didn't answer for a moment, and then she said in a small voice, "Well, that's not a crime. Still. They'll want to talk to you."

"Okay. Please, please don't tell Erica about this! She was devastated over Steven. She may have fucked around on him, but I think she genuinely loved him. I'm sure of it. No good will come out of talking about his private little quirks now."

"No, I suppose not," she said, nodding slowly.

I realised I was making a mistake and quickly added, "And you know I don't want to lose my job."

Her head was still nodding, deep in thought. "Course. Of course you don't. Let's go talk to the cops."

*T*he police questioned me for two hours down at a station house that looked like a set from *NYPD Blue* or something. Drab green walls, an interrogation room with busted plastic chairs and a Formica table, and posters that were woefully out of date with the temper of the times. One had a pen-and-ink drawing of a blond, blue-eyed boy in a Fifties-style shirt with tears in his eyes under a slogan that read: ARE YOU LOST? DON'T KNOW YOUR WAY BACK HOME TO MOMMY AND DADDY? In the hall, a skinhead type with multiple piercings in his face was led past me in shackles. I watched but couldn't hear Jill talking to a plain-clothes detective. She nodded towards me, shrugging her shoulders, and then the detective was pointing.

After a few minutes, I was led into the interrogation room and had to sit across from a ginger-haired sergeant of detectives who cracked his knuckles and frowned at me. "If you're a lesbian, what did you sleep with the guy for?"

Jill was in a corner of the room, watching. "Holland, don't be an asshole," she piped up.

He gave her a dirty look, grimacing in a way that was supposed to tell her he was *allowing* her to be here. It was a courtesy that she could stay, since she wasn't my lawyer. She was only a former cop and my current work colleague.

"At any point, did he, uh, use any restraints on you? You know, tie you up? Or, umm..." The cop cleared his throat noisily. I figured he enjoyed the seamier aspects of this case but he was too button-down to talk about it without embarrassment. "Look, did he hit you or anything? Did you hit him?"

"Why are you asking me that?" I demanded. "What does that have to do with someone coming along later and shooting him?"

"Goes to motive," said the detective.

Jill walked over to the table. "They found this contraption of his. Solid gold handcuffs on chains." She passed me a blown-up photograph of it.

"There's an apparatus for, um, holding up his weight," the detective added.

Jill rolled her eyes. "An apparatus! Jesus, Holland, it was a fuck swing, okay?"

"No, he didn't use that with me," I said. "I heard he had it, but—"

The detective pounced on that one. "How did you hear about it?"

Jill and I traded quick looks. She knew I was lying when I said, "Parties. People talk."

She didn't contradict me.

"And that got you interested in him?" asked Holland the Prude.

"Is that important?"

"Maybe."

"No."

"Sounds like you two were playing pretty rough."

"He didn't hit me. But he did want me to use a scarf on him."

Now it was the detective's turn to trade looks with Jill. They explained that the pathologist had discovered bruising on Steven's neck, and, yes, the obvious conclusion was he was up to some kinky sex days before his murder.

"So because of that, I'm a suspect," I groaned.

The detective leaned back in his seat, scratching his uncombed mess of red hair. "I'm inclined to rule you out. Especially since you decided to come forward."

"Why?" I asked.

"If you had wanted to kill him, you could have done him in with the scarf, and it would probably be written off as death by misadventure. It happens. People get stupid. They play dangerous games. Now if he had wanted *you* in the scarf or maybe snapped you into those cuffs, well, perhaps you'd want to erase him for mistreating you. But Miss Chandler here tells me that you don't look like you're physically injured in any way, you don't appear to have suffered any trauma, physical, psychological or whatever."

I waited, expecting to hear more. He sat in his chair and simply stared at me. "So that's it?"

"Unless you have something else you want to tell us."

Strange how you can feel the compulsion to volunteer something.

"No," I answered.

"Then you're free to go," said the detective. He handed me a business card in case I thought of anything else.

Outside the precinct house, Jill saw the question forming on my lips: why? Why didn't you give up Erica as Steven's other playmate?

"The same logic that says you two had consensual sex and no one got hurt—much—goes for whatever Erica did with him, too," she explained. "It rules her out as a suspect on that score. Cops enjoy gossip like everyone else, and I'm not about to confirm for Holland that Erica Jones gets hot over guys chained up. I'm her bodyguard. The way I see my job, it's not just about the physical threats. Besides, Holland can be a bit of an asshole."

She paused a moment then added nonchalantly, "I notice you didn't mention anything about Erica and those handcuffs either. That's how you heard about them, right? She told you?"

"Yeah."

"Oh, well. She was his fiancée. You'd think the cops would have asked her about them when they questioned her anyway, right?"

I said I didn't know. When Erica had emerged from her own interview with the cops—hers at our apartment—it was one of the few times she was actually reticent with me. She didn't feel like talking about her own inquisition. And I didn't press.

"Did they?" I asked. "Get nosy with her about the cuffs?"

"No, they didn't," said Jill. "I asked her about it at the time. But *you* couldn't have known that for sure before Holland spoke with you."

I stopped and studied her. I wondered if she were somehow testing me. Or playing games.

"You're very loyal," remarked Jill in a breezy voice. "That's rare. Hey, I guess we should get back to Erica at the studio. Why don't you wait here, and I'll bring my car around."

She was sniffing around a lot for a bodyguard. I didn't know how I was going to get rid of her, but I resolved to find a way. The funny thing was, I never did, and when the issues over Steven's murder cooled down and began to fade, I was glad I hadn't.

Attractions

Life went back to what passed for normal in the pop music business. Any remaining friction between Jill and me dissolved as we went about our separate jobs, and we even developed the camaraderie of the entourage. You need it when you work on big headliner tours. Things turned a corner in Boston when Jill and I went to fetch Erica in her dressing room after the show, and too late, Jill opened the door without knocking. I should have warned her: Erica gets horny as hell after concerts. There she was, naked and dripping with sweat, one of the white stagehands eating her pussy while a black sound guy was fighting to control coming into her mouth, Erica bleating and squeezing her eyes shut as her release made her belly and breasts shudder. She didn't even notice us come in.

"Oh, shit, I'm sorry!" Jill said, slamming the door shut.

"Chances are, she didn't hear you," I said in the tone of the veteran. We walked back towards the wings of the stage, watching the roadies tear down the set and pack up. "Told you you'd see plenty of shit. Tomorrow night it could be another guy—or guys."

"She's crazy," said Jill. "There's all kinds of nasty stuff going around out there."

"She's spontaneous in the moment," I explained. "Doesn't mean she's not *selective*. She has these guys checked out."

"She does?"

"Who do you think gets to ask the difficult questions?" I replied. "You'll probably get enlisted to help."

"This doesn't bother you?" she asked.

"You're not going to call me Erica's pimp, are you?" I asked. "I've heard that one before. From guys usually."

"Good Lord, of course not!" she laughed. "What I meant was, it doesn't bother you what she's doing to herself? She's one of the nice ones. I've had to baby-sit some real creeps, and she's not bossy, she's not a diva. She's smart and fun and talented, and she's just folding in on herself. Hell of a way to grieve."

"She did this stuff before Steven died," I pointed out. "She's simply doing it more. I'm hoping she'll come out of it. And, yes, it does bother me. It breaks my heart."

"Maybe she needs one steady guy, a good guy," remarked Jill.

I shook my head, forgetting myself for a moment. "I can't stand that pop psychology stuff that says a guy will solve all your problems—"

"Hey, I'm not saying that."

"It's the *kind* of love she needs," I argued. "Erica's more complex than anyone knows..."

The truth is that I didn't look forward to the time when Erica would move on and find another steady guy. Her casual screwing around meant that I was her reassuring continuity. I was the one she confided in and relied on.

I didn't notice for a moment how Jill was looking at me. It was disconcerting how she studied everybody and everything so intensely. To fill the pause, I added, "Erica is very choosy."

"Yeah, I get that."

Yes, it did sound ridiculous after what we'd just seen.

"It's remarkable how you love her," said Jill. "As a friend, I mean. You've known her since high school, right? She's very lucky to have someone like you who's got her back."

The compliment made me blush. "Thanks, I guess."

"We're going to miss our flight if we don't get moving. You think they've finished by now?"

J was surprised as well at how the tension seemed to dissipate between Luther and Erica. No awkward pauses, no hidden meanings in casual conversation. They were friendly to each other and fell into their easy rhythms of working together on the songs. For a while, I couldn't figure out what was going on. She had become as reticent about him as he was over her—at least this is the way they were with me, perhaps because I was a friend to both of them. If Erica wanted to try again with Luther, she seemed resigned to the fact that he was no longer willing. A reminder of that—a surprise to me—was that Luther had hooked up with Jill.

He told me about it over dinner one night. Ever since I had met him at that first party in the hotel, Luther and I had a "brother-sister" kind of friendship. It was so relaxed and easy between us that there was hardly a blip on the screen for Luther when he learned I preferred women. He liked having female friends when there was no burden of sexual tension. I think it demonstrated a guy who could genuinely appreciate women. And he confided in me. We were in this Peruvian restaurant called The Courtyard on 57th Street, all candles and Tapada paintings and Inca-style jugs for decoration, and he rolled out the tale of how Jill went after him with a vengeance. He wasn't bragging. He said her attention just blew him away.

"She has a small house out in Brooklyn, and she wants me to help her repair her kitchen roof," he explained, smiling shyly as he studied his red wineglass. He had done his share of carpentry and handyman work years ago before music paid the bills. "She says she had this leak from the washroom upstairs, and the water's collected for who knows how long, and she's got this big hump coming out of her ceiling now. I say, 'Well, get yourself a good contractor, honey.' She tells me, Hey, big producer-man, maybe you make the big money, but I can't afford some guy to come out for x-hundred bucks! I need a tall guy and an extra set of hands and blah, blah, blah, she gets me out there."

Right where she wanted him. Jill's house in Brooklyn, he said, had echoes of both Erica and Morgan in its decoration. Great shelves of books, every picture hung on the wall in black and white, discerning choices in plush white furniture. But her bedrooms and basement all had modest towers of boxes stacked and gathering dust, as if her work and solitary life never allowed her a chance to settle. Jill greeted him at the door in a tartan shirt with the tails knotted, showing off a nice midriff and cut-off jeans, instantly handing him a rum and Coke.

"This better be my first and last unless you want everything crooked," he joked.

"Well, do the job right, honey, and you will be rewarded."

He let that one go by without comment. She asked him if he wanted some lunch first, since he'd come all this way, which only confused him further. We'd better get to it, he said.

"Oh, we're okay for time, I did the Polyfill in the ceiling holes already."

Then what did she need him for? She couldn't be sure she had done the job properly, she explained. And she knew it would take her forever to paint the ceiling all by herself.

With a sigh, he said let's start—the sun will go down soon enough. Yes, they'd have the lights on, but natural light always helps.

They were chatting about nothing important, just work and artists they liked, movies they ought to see together. Painting a ceiling, they were bound to get drips and drabs spattering them thanks to gravity. Jill soon had plenty of white splotches on her bare legs.

"Damn, I thought life would be easier if I wore less," she told him. "Instead of wrecking my clothes, I thought I'd just take a good bath. I mean I was going to paint naked if I had to do it all by myself, but this stuff is drying hard. I got to scratch it off my skin. Ugh." She came over to him with a wet cloth and washed a tough stain off his forearm. "See?"

He couldn't resist. "Hey, you can still paint naked if you want. I'm not stopping you."

She patted his face with her hand and said, "Get back to work."

As they kept at it, Jill said it was funny talking about painting naked, strange how people could get about their own bodies. She'd heard a story about Steven Swann, how he'd actually paid to have a gold set of manacles suspended from his bedroom ceiling. Luther said it wouldn't surprise him in the least.

They were done about a third of the way when Luther noticed large cracks emerging in the stucco plaster. "Jill, when did you do the job with the Polyfill?"

"About an hour ago, why?"

"Look at this," he told her. Pushing the paint roller over the filled-in holes had disturbed the repairs. All their hard work was crumbling apart.

"Shit!" she hissed. "What do we do?"

And perfect timing, there was a modest but ominous *crack,* Luther dropping his brush onto the newspapers on the tiled floor and thrusting up two hands to catch the buckling ceiling. *Jesus,* he muttered, and Jill was saying, Oh, God, oh, this is just great. Defeated, she clapped her hand on her lovely bare thigh and told him you might as well let it go, just let it come crashing down. Luther was telling her not to give up, they could jump in the car and hit a hardware shop to buy new plaster board sheets, but right now she should fetch a bin before they had a gigantic mess all over her floor.

"No," said Jill.

"What?"

"No," she said, flashing a smile of dazzling white teeth at him.

He didn't know what to think as he gazed down at her from the short stepladder, hands over his head, playing Atlas. "What do you mean no, Jill? Look, my arms are getting tired and—"

She began to unbuckle his trousers.

"Jill, what are you doing? I have to let go of this thing, and it'll break into a gazillion pieces on our heads unless you go get a trash can or something—"

"You're not going to drop it on us, are you?" she asked. She laughed as she pulled his trousers down to his ankles.

"Jill! Come on, my arms are getting tired. What are you—"

"Luther, I'm counting on you, babe. Don't let my ceiling cave in, just keep your arms up there." Her hands caressing his legs, giggling all the time as her fingers stroked his thighs and dug under his Jockey shorts to grip his buttocks.

He couldn't help but laugh, but he felt completely vulnerable. "Jill, this is crazy—"

"Just hold your position, soldier. I want to talk to little soldier. Hi, there." Tugging down his underwear in one smooth yank, her mouth sending a hot breath on his testicles and the thick girth of him springing to life.

"What's this *little* soldier crap? Jill, my arms—"

"Hold still, baby."

Laughing all the while as she rested her head and moaned happily against his thigh, feeling the heat of his cock against her cheek, her fingers tracing the globe of a buttock and then reaching up to find hard muscles in the small of his back. He felt ridiculous even while he was aroused, his laughter taking a bit of energy out of his hardon, until she slipped off her shirt and pushed his cock between her two large breasts, rubbing him between them. When she brought her mouth down on him, he couldn't take it anymore—

As if ducking away from a bomb explosion, he bent over to shield her from a rain of plaster and paint. Both of them laughed helplessly as shards of plaster dropped off the scarf around her hair and Luther's shoulders. He had obediently kept his position on the stepladder. Jill helped free one leg from the trap of his bunched trousers and underwear, and he jumped down to take her in his arms. Filthy, dusty, white speckles over writhing brown bodies, Luther slipping her jeans over her narrow hips to reveal she was wearing no panties at all, and he lifted her with those strong biceps muscles that could drum congas and barrels, raising her high enough that he could enter her in a wet rush. He moved her to the kitchen counter, Jill's ass sliding on a drape cloth over gas burners as Luther pounded inside her, wrapping her arms around his neck, his broad back, whispering hoarsely, "Bed—Bedroom..."

He said she made love like no woman he'd ever had before. I asked him: This African Tantric Yoga stuff? Yeah, he said, looking away at his glass again. He couldn't remember everything she did, feeling so swept away, but it was amazing. "Her middle finger would fire out like a shiatsu therapist or something," he said, and she'd spear a muscle in his groin, light pressure at the base of his cock, making him feel like a steel bar. Fingers massaging his glutes as he thrust inside her, unravelling him and making him feel like he was about to come, only to have her hands withdraw and the tide subside, her expert touch discovering a new point, sending a fresh charge through him. Gazing down at her, spatters of white paint on her lovely brown skin, her breasts heaving, touching him and making him feel so powerful, more attractive than he ever saw himself except in his days of drumming on stage. His muscles expanding and contracting, biceps and abs chiselled and defined just as her gorgeous athletic body showed him what she could do.

We're like two zebras, dirty like this, she laughed, cupping his balls and running a nail down the inside of his thigh past an island of hardened white paint. It made him shiver with delight.

They showered together and cleaned up for their second bout, and as the ochre sunlight spilled into her bedroom, they were like children at play, Jill setting the tone, contorting herself for her amusement and to drive them wild. Lying on top of him faceup as he sagged his body against her headboard, his cock inside her, Jill touching her clit as she craned her neck back to bite his lip and tickle herself with his goatee. She slipped her tongue under his, his hands rubbing circles around her nipples as her right hand reached around and found this exquisite point in the nape of his neck, and *uhh*... His chin on her shoulder, looking down at her glistening beautiful wetness under her one finger, loving to watch this woman stimulate herself, the way he disappeared into her under those tight black curls—

I had never listened to a guy describe sex from his point of view, and to have a guy like Luther, who would never be crude about it, who created a picture of the two of them with words and who talked about Jill in ways both lyrical and tantalising...I was fascinated. I could see her as she felt him start to come, moving her hips just enough so that she could reach down with her small hand and grip his engorged cock, her vaginal lips still encasing the crimson head, summoning a cry out of him he had never given in any intimate encounter before, burying his cock into her again in slow motion that made them both spasm violently. And then another tender kiss, her fingers on the nape of his neck—

"She made love like it was choreography," said Luther. "You know I don't want to sound sexist, Mish, but some girls, they expect you to do all the work. They let things be *done* to them. Jill is one of the most sensual women I've... I mean, Jesus, it's too bad we couldn't have something."

"What do you mean?" I asked.

He looked pensive for a moment. Then: "I told her the truth. I told her she ambushed me, took me by surprise, not that I'm complaining." He chuckled a little, and the pensive expression returned. "I know I said I thought it best to leave Erica alone, but...I don't know. I think I'm not as over her as I thought. Jill's nice. She's great, really. But good sex doesn't mean a guy gets mush in his head right away and falls in love."

As they lay side by side in afterglow, she had kissed him, two fingers delicately stroking his penis, trying to awaken it again as she said baby, it's okay. She wasn't looking for anything serious. It would have been nice if they could see each other for a while, but if he didn't want that, well, life was too short for vanity. She didn't feel scorned at all. She hadn't had her toes curled in so long, and she had really needed him. Luther said he felt strangely flattered.

"Stores must be closed by now," he had said to her. "What are we going to do about your kitchen?"

"It's all right. My contractor's coming tomorrow." And as he sat up, she added, "I can't afford a set of golden hand-cuffs."

J couldn't say a damn thing," laughed Luther, ordering another round for us.

"She's kind of like Erica in a way—needs sex, but not men," he laughed. He sighed in exasperation. "What am I doing, Mish? Do I carry around a magnet that picks up girls like this? No, that's not fair, I chased Erica. You think I'm a fool for still holding out for her?"

I told him I didn't know. It was the safe answer, the diplomatic answer. I wasn't really thinking about it at all. He couldn't have known how I had disconnected from our conversation. My mind was frozen on the image of them together, the idea of Jill Chandler in an intimate embrace, all this sexual prowess for which she dropped beguiling hints and he had now confirmed.

"I think sooner or later, we're going to have to have it out," Luther was saying. "Erica and me. I thought she and I were cool, but I can feel it building again between us. *Drum* just skyrocketed, and now the label's pushing her hard to get me in on the album after the follow-up—"

Jill. But Jill's straight, I thought. Isn't she? That first day I met her, I could have sworn she was flirting with me, not that I'm the best judge of the lesbian mating dance. After all, I hadn't slept with anyone since—

"Which means we're back together in the booth, and we got all this unfinished business . . ."

Why not Jill? God knows I needed to get laid. For the first time in quite a while, I was thinking of someone else without the perverse notion that I was somehow cheating on Erica. If Jill wasn't interested, it could prove excruciatingly awkward for the short term, but according to Luther, she seemed able to glibly detach emotional investment from sex. Just like our boss.

In my own strange way, I had learned to do the same. Loving Erica, but finding physical release with guys like Odell all the way back to pimply fools in high school. Karen had been her only worthy rival.

If Jill could find me attractive, it would certainly keep her mind off snooping in places she shouldn't. Morgan was calling me again. I would have to do something about that man.

Jill handled security. I had a lot of access given my position with Erica, a lot of power, but it wouldn't hurt to have someone like Jill firmly on my side.

What had she said to Luther? *We're like two zebras, dirty like this.* Those beautiful bodies speckled with paint. Crazy chick letting the ceiling fall in, putting him to the test as she went down on him. I wondered what she looked like naked. I wondered if she'd feel inhibited being with a girl—

"I said are you okay for a ride to the *Vanity Fair* thing tomorrow?"

"Sorry? Oh, yeah, honey, I'll be fine. I got to run a couple of errands for Jill first and then I'll catch up to you guys."

"For Jill? What do you got to do for Jill?"

"Nothing," I said, drawing a blank. "What are you talking about? I got to shop for Erica's present for BSB's president— he's got his birthday coming up. And marketing is bugging me to go through those 'video autographs' for the charity kids. You know what my days are like, Luther."

"I think you must be tired, Mish. We should call it a night."

Well, well, I thought. Look at me. First the woman's stirring me up with her intrusive questions and now I'm actually contemplating the idea of being with her. Here I am excited by the idea of getting Jill Chandler into bed.

———

*O*nly a couple of weeks before my dinner with Luther, I was in Seattle on the tour when I had the impulse to phone Karen in Toronto. It had been a long time since we talked, only emails that said nothing important except that we missed each other. Neither one of us ever referred to our last argument in the Library Hotel.

I heard laughter first as the line was picked up, then: "Hello?" A female voice but not hers. More tinkling laughter in the background, Karen's unmistakable voice, and the anonymous girl ordering her playfully, "Go! Go to your corner!" Karen saying *Hey, that is my phone, oh, Jesus, it better not be work—*

Just before the receiver was passed, I hung up. The girl who answered, she sounded so young.

*M*y seduction of Jill began with modest thoughtful gifts. Stuff from the Body Shop because "Hey, I was picking up stuff for Erica, and I thought you'd like this." An Eric Benét CD she might enjoy. I progressed to having my workouts at the gym coincide with hers, though I could never bring myself to join her on those punishing jogs. Jill certainly couldn't guard Erica 24-7, and her deal allowed her certain days off. While she was there for most concerts and public appearances, Brown Skin Beats and the concert promoters were obliged to fill in any gaps. As Erica's PA, I learned Jill's official routine as well as my boss's, so I was there and ready with a suggested evening out when she was available. We went out to dinner. Frequently. We hit the movies together, and there was a night when she fell asleep during a boring European picture, and her head rested against my shoulder. I stroked her short hair, and her eyes opened slowly. She didn't complain. She muttered an apology and went back to watching the screen. I thought: *Contact.*

One night after dinner, I invited her to walk back to the apartment with me for a nightcap, knowing we'd have it all to ourselves. Erica was doing a shoot for a video in the West Village, and I knew at this hour she'd be holding a cup of hot chocolate near a line of trailers with blazing white lights and police crowd-control sawhorses. They probably wouldn't wrap until five in the morning. Knowing Erica, who was a good sport and very patient when it came to filming the videos, she'd probably go out for breakfast with the dancers and crew. I had the run of the place.

I went to the stereo and put on the old *Acoustic* album by Everything but the Girl, Jill watching me as I said, "Yes!" Loving the cover version that Tracy Thorn sang of a Tom Waits classic. *Will I see you tonight on a downtown train . . .*

Then I fetched bottles of gin and tonic water, deliberately bringing all the fixings to the white carpet. Sit down on the floor next to me, I implied, shortening the distance between us. Jill plopped herself down, and I stretched out, carefully arranging the cascade of fabric of my sarong. She smiled at me and did a couple of leg stretches, saying the walk had done her good. She told me how much she'd always liked "Erica's and your place."

"It's Erica's, she owns it," I corrected her.

"Sure, but I can see little touches of yours in the decoration. It's your home as much as hers, right? Hey, what are you trying to do, get me drunk?"

Two-thirds gin, one-third tonic. I laughed and said, "Yeah. Maybe I'll get the truth out of you."

"Oh? What do you want to know?"

"Look, I don't want to give you the impression Luther has a big mouth," I said. "But he's my friend, and we're fairly tight."

"Yeah?" she asked blankly, not knowing where I was going with this.

"Did you, uh . . ." I was on the verge of giggles. "Did you really force him to hold up your ceiling while you pulled his trousers down?"

She rolled on her back, laughing. "Ohhhhh, *that!* Damn right, I did! When I want something, I make sure it can't get away!"

We both laughed for a long moment, and I topped up our drinks. Jill said Luther was fantastic in bed, but he had made it all too clear they wouldn't have any future together.

I was consoling. "Well, Luther, he's the brooding type. Only happy when he's miserable."

She shook her head dismissively. "I don't know what it was with him. We did it, and then he couldn't get out of my house fast enough. Maybe he just didn't like the package when he unwrapped it."

"Are you fishing or what?" I said. "You know you're beautiful. You kind of look like Sade to me."

She burst into giggles. "Please!"

"No, really."

"You're as bad as Erica. She thought I looked like that black actress from *Clueless,* you know the one. What's her name? Oh, help me out here. She pops up in TV shows now and then, Stacey something—"

"Stacey Dash—"

"Stacey Dash, yeah. It's because of the shape of my face, I think. It's so oval."

"It is not," I insisted. "You're very pretty." I took a chance and leaned in to her, kissing her cheek near her mouth, getting close but not so close I'd frighten her away. As I pulled back, I paused. Our mouths close enough together to taste each other's breath, our eyes staring at each other.

"Let me, um, ask you something," she said with a self-conscious laugh. "Our going out lately ... Have I been going out on dates, and I don't even know it?"

I leaned in and tenderly pulled her full bottom lip between my teeth, sucking it and then kissing her. After a second of indecision, her lips returned the sweet pressure.

"I got to tell you this is new to me," she whispered when the kiss was over.

"You mean you've never been with a girl?" I asked.

She looked down at her hands demurely, shaking her head. "I wouldn't know what to do."

"You got to be kidding? You and your yoga? I figured if you did that, you must have done some experimenting in your time. And from the sounds of it, you rocked Luther's world!"

"Yeah, but being with a girl," she started again. "I wouldn't ... I mean I don't know if ... "

"Let me teach you ... "

She watched me in fascination as I reached out and took her hand, bringing it first to my mouth to suck her middle finger. And then I guided it under my sarong. I pushed on her finger to nudge it between my pussy lips, directing her silently in my desired rhythm, and then with my other hand I was cupping her breast, my fingers stealing under her jumper. Her flesh was warm, her nipple already puckered and waiting for my touch. I needed to see her. She kept fingering me as I gently lifted the jumper over the swell of her breasts, taking in the sight of those lovely buds, Jill's mouth still open in fascinated arousal.

"Kiss me ... "

As she leaned down to join our mouths, I felt her finger slip into me all the way. She kissed me quickly at first, shyly, a smile of brilliant white teeth flashing as her eyelashes brushed my cheek. I was still kissing her and didn't even notice the sarong suddenly parted like curtains on the rug, my pussy and legs exposed.

"Can I taste you?" she asked me. So shy. Like I was all those years ago with Karen.

I cried out with the contact of her mouth. Her hot breath on my clitoris eliciting a moan even before I felt the wash of her tongue. God, she had such instincts! The way her tongue probed between my lips, her fingers strumming my clit. I opened my legs wide for her, lying back and enjoying myself in a submissive way I hadn't felt since . . . Yes, since Karen. She made me come but didn't relent as I finished, returning her hand to my pussy and letting her mouth explore my bare stomach, kissing me between my breasts. I couldn't strip for her quickly enough, and she still had her thin jumper pushed above her tits, the large areolae swollen, the nipples jutting out. It was more erotic in a way, seeing her like this, still clothed but the layer peeled back. Her chest was bigger than I expected, her breasts round and full and reminding me of Erica. That was it. That was what exhilarated me in those first wild embraces. The target of my seduction seemed to offer me the physical best of my lovers, the girlishness of Karen's small body and the ripeness of Erica's, with Erica's sensual aggressiveness.

"Oh, God, you're so beautiful," I whispered, and I lifted both my hands to cup her tits, to knead them and fondle them.

She looked glassy-eyed for a moment, as if frozen in pleasure. And then she said softly, "Can I trust you?"

I didn't understand. I would have nodded yes to anything she asked me in that moment. Yes to everything. Sensuality. Release. Joy like you've never had with a man, baby. For the first time in my life, I think I was making love with a sense of hope. I loved Erica, and I knew I would go on loving Erica, but I needed an outlet for my own physical cravings and frustration. I liked Jill. I thought on that night that I could develop real affection for her.

"Will you . . ." My turn for shyness. I sensed a magic in her, a prowess that both tantalized and intrigued me. "Will you do things to me?"

Her mouth on mine in a sudden hungry rush as if my request was a granting of permission. I felt her straddle me like a man, climbing on top of me with almost a masculine assertiveness, snuggling down to crush our breasts against each other's, Jill flicking her tongue out playfully, running it over my bottom lip just before she sank her teeth into it, rubbing her pussy urgently on my thigh. "I don't know if this is going to work on a girl," she murmured almost in apology, and she took my right arm and raised it above her head, nibbling the sweet spot just below my armpit. All at once she rolled onto her side to spoon behind me, left hand coming around to finger my pussy, right hand pressing against the small of my back, still tasting my skin below my arm.

I felt myself opening up to her as I heard her whisper *you're so wet* and the actual slurping sound of her fingers on my slick labia, her fingers on my back sinking down, slithering down, making their way down, down, down to the very top of the cleft between my buttocks, and it was like she hit a massage point or something *there*. So intimate just at the top between the cheeks of my ass, and now Jill's breath on my neck, tonguing me just behind the ear, my voice squealing surrender, "Oh, fuck me, baby, fuck me hard, please, please fuck me hard!"

Like a nimble cat, she scrambled to the other side so that she could face me, dexterously switching hands, and back she went to that delicious point just at the top of the cleft in my ass, three fingers inside me now plus a warm wet tongue alive in my mouth. Coming in short cathartic spasms now, *aah, aah, aah,* opening my eyes to look at her as I felt my mouth open in wonder as well, saying again and again like a chant, you're so good, so good, baby, and in one violent quake, I held her tight as she rammed most of her hand into my greedy pussy, thumb on my clit, pumping my hips as I gritted my teeth and cried and cried.

I lay back with such a sense of grateful release, stroking her hair, saying, "For someone who says she's never done this before, you sure know what you're doing."

She looked modestly down at the sheets, covering half her face in her hand. "I like . . . giving pleasure. I just always thought it was weird, you know, the idea of lying flat on your back and letting a guy do stuff to you. I can't enjoy myself unless I'm pleasing my partner. It's all intuitive for me."

"So how can I please you?"

"I'm okay," she said, kissing me reassuringly.

"I want to see you come," I whispered.

"I . . . don't know. I'm sure you'll think of something."

"Well, what do you want, sweetie?"

"Do what you want with me," she said. And when I hesitated, she added, "No, seriously. I can't come unless I know the other person's enjoying him—herself. It's my hang-up."

"You are straight," I laughed. With one hand, I gently insisted, "Now lie back and think of England."

"Shut *up!*"

But I was busy opening her legs. I smelled the enticing odour of her pussy. I probed with my tongue, I teased, I offered long, warm, wet strokes that worried that lovely bud of her clit. The tension in her legs seemed to gather in a ball, Jill's fingers running through my hair. As she rose on the crest of the wave, her thighs began to close on my face, and she apologised in a high-pitched sob, spreading herself for me again as she flew back on the pillows. I was lapping her furiously, and when she cried out, a new tide of her juice flowed with her orgasm. I wanted her as swept away as I had been for her, my tongue still lathering her, and then the fingers that were in my hair softly caressed their way down to a point on my neck, tapping, gently tapping. I didn't understand at all what she was doing. It was almost distracting me, and then as I sucked her clit into my mouth and began a rhythm with this mischievous technique, thrilled with her moans as she bit her lip, a bolt of lightning went from my neck down my spine and to the core of me. I was crying suddenly like a little girl, curling up in a fetal ball, still sucking Jill but touching my own pussy as my vaginal muscles contracted with a furious impulse. The two of us coming simultaneously, Jill getting off from striking at the very heart of me.

We kissed and fondled each other in after-play for a good hour, no words between us. Then she fell asleep. She seemed to fall asleep easily, little tossing and turning, not so much drifting off as suddenly collapsing into slumber. I traced a fingernail down from the mound of her breast, over the shadows of her ribs to the sweet fleshy portion of her hip, circling around to the softness of her ass. God, she was beautiful. She made love like a *Cosmo* magazine fantasy about massage therapists, those deadly *Kama Sutra* fingers of hers finding erogenous zones you never knew existed. She woke up and kissed me as if we'd been lovers for a while, asking groggily, "You okay?"

"Yeah. I didn't mean to wake you."

I was a little embarrassed, but I couldn't stop.

"What's wrong?" she asked.

"I need...I was watching you sleep." She had caught me masturbating.

For some reason, it made her smile. The flash of those brilliant teeth nearly drove me over the edge. "You getting off on actually watching me sleep?"

"Yeah."

"You want some help?"

"Yeah."

We kissed a short kiss on the lips again like familiar lovers. One more short kiss, then a long one as I kept strumming my clitoris, and there was a rustle of the bed sheets as her hand massaged my breasts then settled on a point between them. Kissing me, her other hand resting on my pubic bone. Her touch so light, no more than the weight of a coin. She told me later that all kinds of disciplines had identified these points on the body—acupuncture, chiropractic, cranio-sacral therapy. It was getting warm below my navel and between my breasts, and her voice was a dirty lullaby, *keep touching yourself, baby, you look so hot touching yourself, I want to taste your cream,* and oh oh oh, bringing my knees up and shedding tears as whatever she did to me this time happened.

Her mouth on me was exquisite, perfectly timed.

$\mathcal{S}$he found me half an hour later, standing naked in the doorway of Erica's bedroom, asking once again if I was all right. I felt her arms drape around me, felt the wedge of her fur on my buttocks.

"I have a confession to make," I said, turning to her.

She raised her eyebrows at me, still smiling, still on a high from our making love. She waited.

"I think I was a major bitch to you when you first showed up," I said. "I guess I felt threatened. I've worked with Erica for quite a while now, and I . . . Well, I wasn't prepared for someone else to work with her so closely, day in and day out."

"Seems to me you got over it," she laughed and hugged me close.

"Yeah, guess I did. I know it sounds silly now, but I feel guilty over how I behaved."

"You *are* being silly. We both got our jobs to do."

"That's right," I agreed. "You're right. I have to share her now."

In the darkness of the apartment, there was just enough light to see the fog of confusion on her face. I didn't think what I said was so odd.

"That's not the way I look at it," she said after a moment.

"No?"

"Erica has to share *you* with *me*."

She smiled at me in the darkness, our faces close together, and then she added, deflating me a bit, "Look, I don't want to give you the wrong idea or lead you on. I like you, and this blew my mind but . . . I'm not looking for a serious relationship right now, guy or girl. I think I'd like to try this again—" She kissed me tenderly, briefly. "—And soon, but I also like how we've become friends. Would that be too weird for you? Hooking up when we need it? Some people have said to me, 'Jill, you treat sex like a guy,' like I'm a callous bitch or something, but I don't know. I can't be objective about myself."

"It's a two-way street," I said, stroking her hair. "What if I'm really frustrated, and I need you for a night? You going to be there for me? Or will you tell me you've 'done a lot of soul-searching,' and you've found yourself now. That you're straight?"

"Honey, I don't think I'll ever think of myself as that after tonight."

Fair enough, I thought. Things were promising. Her talk about not wanting anything heavy but asking permission to sleep with me now and then—who was she kidding with that? We'll see how it goes.

She led me back to my bed, and I was happy. I felt the euphoria of infatuation. And I also felt: *I'm home safe and dry*. She's with me now. She asked me if she can trust me, and now she believes she can. Even if we don't get involved, if we never sleep together again, there shouldn't be any more questions about Steven Swann's murder. Dead ends on all the roads to evidence, and the one persistent, relentless individual who once still gave a damn now likes me naked. Jill's on my side now. It's over.

I was wrong. I was wrong about everything.

I was in my office when the phone rang. Morgan. *Ugh.* He didn't bother to say hello. What he said in that gravelly tone was: "It's not enough." Blunt and to the point, and I wondered if he'd already been drinking.

"What's not enough?"

"Your little kiss-off remuneration, my dear. I've got my pocket calculator out, and I can work up a rough estimate of what Erica's going to make on her royalties."

"Morgan, we had a deal."

"Yeah, based on what we *thought* the songs were worth. Seems I underestimated your girl—or rather myself."

I let out a long breath. "I can't go and up your price again for the arrangement work. It's a done deal, and you were paid. BSB's going to wonder what the hell I'm thinking if—"

"Then get it from one of their other 'special' funds," he snapped sarcastically.

"What? So you can come back and bleed us again?"

"I think I'm letting everyone off pretty easy considering what you'll make off that album. And you know I can sink it with one phone call to *Rolling Stone* or one of the other mags. Doesn't matter if they think I'm full of shit, they'll print it anyway—"

"You keep threatening us, Morgan. No one will buy it, they'll dismiss it out of hand."

"Not if I go to court."

"You do that, Morgan, and you know you'll lose every friend you've got. You won't even get gigs in basement dives anymore."

"So you're threatening me now?"

I sighed in exasperation. "No, Morgan, no, I'm not! We're *friends*. Why are you doing this? I can talk to a couple of people around the office, see if we can get you more arrangement work, maybe even a producing contract on one of the B-artist albums—"

"I don't need help getting work, Michelle," he said indignantly. "And doing more work isn't payment on work *already done*."

"Why are you coming back to me with this shit, Morgan? Why do you want to hurt her?"

"This isn't about hurting Erica," he said. "Michelle, do you think she's the first blazing hot talent to find her way into my elevator, demanding my help?"

"I'm sure she's not."

"Don't patronise me, darlin'. No, she's not. She is, however, for the record, the *best* of them, but that's not the issue. They all come up, and I do my stuff and I teach 'em, man or woman, don't care, and I give all of myself, you understand? I put it all out, and I get stupid time and again. Each time, I think it will be different. They go away, and I hear snatches of my own stuff coming out of their tracks, and I *try* not to be petty. Not one has ever cut me a cheque except Luther. And Erica and Luther had me do the arrangements, and that's good. But that shouldn't be my compensation! They didn't put it to me that way when they asked, and if they had I would have told them to go to hell. So don't ask me to be bend-over-backward grateful over what's reasonably *my due*! Everybody's great buddies until the money rolls in. Guess what? I'm a professional, too."

I didn't say anything for a moment. Any bitterness he'd ever shown us had always been mitigated by his self-deprecating charm, his bearing and easy grace that seemed to be echoes of a Blue Note Birdland world we admired, but only as spectators gazing back in time. He admitted that he enjoyed all our attention, treating him like a holy relic and national treasure, but when a relic is locked away, it gathers dust. He was sick of it. Recognition would be nice, but cash you can spend. I could see his point—no, not about who wrote the songs. I couldn't bring myself to believe that, not yet—I thought maybe he was owed more for how he helped her, plain and simple.

It was a debt of Erica's I couldn't repay. And Morgan had lately been evolving into another jazz cliché, hell, an entire music industry cliché. The gifted but anonymous player who starts to let himself go a little, who uses just enough drink that he's not out-and-out pathetic but does become a self-fulfilling embarrassment.

"Morgan. We can talk about this. I can't give you an answer over the phone. Let me check a few things out first. Why don't I swing by your place tonight?"

"Okay. But if you'll excuse the pun, Michelle, don't bring me any late-night promises."

I had a grim queasiness of familiarity in my stomach as I took the subway up to Morgan's place. In some ways, I prepared better than I did with Steven, but a high percentage of me didn't know what I was actually going to do. I carried the intent, but I didn't have the means. I sat on the train, trying to concentrate on the tune playing through my portable CD player's headphones. Vonda Shepherd again. I listened, aptly enough, to a song called "Soothe Me" with its achingly sad lyrics and mournful piano, a song of regret for a lonely wanderer through the streets of New York. It made me think of Luther and Erica, and Luther and Jill, and, yes, of course, I couldn't hear it without thinking of Karen. *And, darling, I love you, but I swear that I'll be goo-ooonnnne by the time you figure out what you want . . .*

Sacrifices

*M*usic. Messages in music everywhere, and as the freight
elevator made its slow crawl up a tunnel of brick and darkness, I heard "Pariah" without the vocals. It was playing
from the ADAT through the speakers. The melody was carried in a different key, but there was the same unmistakable
bass line. He might as well have painted me a billboard. As
I undid the chain and slid back the wooden slat door of the
elevator, Morgan ambled over and handed me a drink.

"You're behind," he said and lifted my glass in a silent
toast before he handed it over. Tonight it was gin.

"These days you give yourself a pretty good head start,"
I answered.

"Oh, let me guess," he said coolly, "you think I have a
problem now, and it's because I'm pitying myself, is that it?"

"Not at all," I replied, taking a small sip of my drink. I
wanted to keep a clear head. "I think you're getting slack
on your own discipline, though. You're the one who always
lectured Erica about creative people, aren't you? People
bitch about the big corporate octopuses and how hard it is
to get your foot in the door and get a label or an agent,

whatever, and they never consider the idea that maybe they fail because they suck. You said it was easier to compose excuses than music. You said if it's so goddamn good, play it in the street, and people will get magnetised. They'll come to hear you, and you'll know."

"Yeah, I probably said shit like that," he admitted. He shook his glass to ask if I wanted another. I was barely halfway through my first. "What's your point, Michelle?"

"That you don't need to do this. Bring out new stuff."

"Maybe I don't *have* new stuff!" he barked. "Maybe that's the best stuff I'll ever come up with."

"Don't yell at me," I said in a low voice.

"Maybe it's my best stuff, now and forever," he said, eulogising himself on the spot.

"If it is your stuff, Morgan."

"You actually believe I'd lie about it, don't you, Michelle?"

"I think you're looking back on a career and feeling a little desperate," I said. "I think a person can start out with a lie, and after a while they get so good at repeating it, they start to buy it themselves."

"I defer to the expert," he said cryptically.

"What?"

He crossed the floor to light himself a cigarette. I watched him, not knowing what to think. If he was making it up that he helped Erica write those songs or composed them himself then he was contemptible. If he honestly, sincerely believed Erica had ripped him off then I had to question how I'd been handling this. I hadn't brought in the cavalry on this one.

There was *no way* I would have taken this to the Brown Skin Beats management. Too political, and they would have had me for breakfast, made me a fall guy. I could still go to Luther and ask: is it possible? If not, help me show the guy he's wrong. But like I mentioned before, I didn't know where Luther's head was these days, and he had this integrity thing. If I thought Morgan and Erica could talk this out, I'd push them together, but Morgan said he didn't plan to take it up with Erica, she'd just deny it. He was taking it up with me. I had sense, I did damage control—

"Talk to Erica, Morgan. She's reasonable."

He shook his head. Not an option.

"You still want her," I said.

"Huh?"

"Is that what this is all about, Morgan? That you feel left behind? Steven dies, and she no longer feels like spending nights here?"

He laughed at me. "Yeah, sure, Michelle. I give away my material out of love then I decide I want royalties on them, but I do that out of love, too . . . ? Mmm-hmm, you got me pegged. Interesting logic, dear."

"I don't think love is ever rational."

"Love!" he groaned. "You got me confused with Luther's hurt puppy act. Have I ever given you one sign that I'm sentimental? No? Right. Then please get me the money."

"You're in love with her," I insisted. "Why come to me with this? Why don't you go bug Erica and talk to her about it? Because you want me to open the door for you again."

"No, I want you to cut me another cheque."

"You're in love with her."

"Michelle," he said, shaking his head, and fool that I was, I thought he was about to protest too much. "You're right on one thing. This does have to do with love, but not mine."

"What are you talking about?"

"If I go to Erica, stubborn girl that she is, she'll tell me to fuck off. 'See you in court, man.' Now you, Michelle, you're calmer. You're perceptive. You watch, you listen, and you know she'd be making a mistake. You want to protect her.

You always want to protect the person you fall in love with."

"Wha—what?"

"You're the one who loves Erica, so *that's* why I came to you, baby. Oh, that's cute—you're blushing. Swann was such an idiot, of course, he didn't notice, and Luther? Well, Luther's a good boy. Kind of slow when it comes to people, though, and then he wonders why he gets fucked over in contract disputes..."

I couldn't believe it. I stood there, listening, and he had taken the wind out of my sails. I never thought anyone could have guessed. Yes, I was passionate about how I protected her, I was Erica Jones's quietly aggressive advocate, but she was my boss and my friend. I'd always thought I hid my feelings well.

"Too bad she likes guys, isn't it, Mish?"

I was ready to spit blood in that moment, and I couldn't even put my finger on why, maybe because he talked about my feelings as if they were a dirty little secret.

"Okay, I'm in love with her, I'm not ashamed of it," I told him. "So what? Before, I didn't take personally what you're doing, Morgan, but now you're making it personal. You're saying your little shakedown is aimed at me."

"Naw, I'm just dealing with the person who has her interests at heart."

"And you're banking on me to cover up for her again. Because I love her."

He turned away to light himself another cigarette. "Hey, if you do what you do out of love, then it's not so bad, is it?"

"You're right," I said.

He had his back to me. He had turned his back enough that he was vulnerable, and this was the alarm that rang through my mind. *Do it now when he'll never see it coming.* There was a statuette sitting on a low coffee table, a modern figurative thing like a Henry Moore sculpture, and I picked it up and raised it high, bringing it down in a savage blow to the back of his head. He grunted a little and staggered. I hit him again, hard. He fell to his knees, and now I was shuddering in panic. *Jesus, I have to finish him.* I hit him the third time, the last time, and he collapsed to the floor.

It was done.

Morgan was dead at my feet, and I paused for a moment. Part of it, yes, was the gruesome selfish instinct that I hadn't finished the job properly—that he might stir, moan, display some signal of life. And part of it was because it was Morgan. He had been a better man than Steven Swann, and out of some perverse impulse of respect for the dead, I thought I owed him a few seconds. I had seen dead before, the way that people appear smaller than they were when you knew them, as if the soul had weight and *volume*. Whatever Morgan was supposed to be, it was gone and his body wouldn't finish it. I felt a disconnected sadness, a peculiar objective pity for him as if I was merely an assigned executioner given the job of his time. With Steven, I admit I took some pleasure in it. But Morgan . . . If only he hadn't kept making threats. If he had honestly cared about Erica, he would never have made threats like that.

That hardened my resolve again for the cleanup.

In my purse, I had brought along a set of latex medical gloves. Some killer, I thought to myself. Brings gloves but has to improvise the murder weapon. *Shut up.* I had brought wiping cloths. I took a deep breath and got on with my task. I considered removing the sculpture, leaving the cops with no evidence in the same way I had denied them Steven's gun. It was too bulky to carry away with me. And I had come over, thinking I'd have to make his death look like an interrupted burglary. It looked more plausible to leave the object there. Yes.

I fished his wallet out of his trousers, pocketed the cash. Not much. I hated doing that to him. It sounds perverse, but I felt genuine revulsion for desecrating him like that. Still, it had to be done. I rifled through the drawers of the chest in his bedroom to make it look good. I knocked over the black lacquer bust of Beethoven that sat on its cheap pillar stand near the couch. Another regret, destroying that charming piece of kitsch. But I needed it to look like he had struggled with his attacker.

All this effort wouldn't be good enough, of course. I couldn't protect Erica by simply killing Morgan. I had to erase Morgan's threat. I went over to his desk to search for charts, notes, whatever implied a connection between his compositions and her work. *I wrote those songs,* he told me. Well, no one would ever hear his lies again.

Sitting next to his computer was a loose pile of books, a couple weighing down a padded envelope with a printout clipped to it. Jackpot? No. The printout was a letter from one of the big production studios. Morgan had composed something for *Easy Death in Queens,* the latest "cutting edge" cop drama, and it turned out they didn't need it. I opened the envelope. Inside was a music chart with a CD— I assumed it must be the demo. The funny thing was that the address on the envelope was written in Morgan's own handwriting. Hmm.

There were certainly items of minutiae I didn't know about the music biz, and maybe this was one of them. After all, I had come into the game as Erica was on her way up. Maybe composers had to send their stuff off like writers with a self-addressed stamped envelope, an "SASE" as it's called in the book publishing game. And before I gave up the idea that I was going to be Maya Angelou or even the black Danielle Steel, I had opened the mailbox countless times back in Toronto with letters written on the front in my own handwriting.

Focus, girl. This was nothing I needed to worry about. Erica wouldn't have done theme or background music for a television show. I abandoned it on the desk, putting it neatly back where it was. I couldn't reseal the envelope, but it was reasonable for anyone to assume Morgan would open his own mail.

I turned on his computer. I didn't expect to find much, but there could be damning correspondence. He didn't— I mean *hadn't*—gone in much for email, so that made the hunt a little easier. I checked the ADAT. Again nothing.

I was starting to get anxious. His body was cooling on the floor only twenty feet away from me, and I couldn't stay here. If I was going to find what he was talking about, I had better do it fast.

A car's headlights swung in an arc across the ceiling, and then I heard the engine stop. *Shit.* The sound of doors opening and then closing with a metal crunch, low conversation, and, Jesus, there was only the freight elevator as my way out.

Calm down. I peeked outside the window. Carefully. Whoever they were, they hadn't come to see Morgan.

Their arrival reminded me of one additional problem. I knew I'd be an unlikely suspect in Morgan's murder, but after my close call over Steven, I thought I'd better give myself an alibi. How? I had to think fast. I went over to Morgan's computer and started up his broadband connection. After a few seconds, I typed in the link for a sound effects archive website—Luther used it, that's how I'd discovered it. They had what I needed, and Real Audio Player waited only for a touch of the mouse. Perfect.

I pulled my mobile phone out of my handbag and impulsively called Jill Chandler. Who better, I thought. Let her be the one.

"Michelle?"

"Hi, what are you up to?"

"Kind of . . . finishing up a date," she said sheepishly.

Oh.

"Listen, Mish, I should have talked to you about—"

"No, hey, I'm sorry! I just wondered if you wanted to take in a movie with me, but if you're with someone . . ." And behind me, the computer speakers played the ambient noise of a Cineplex crowd.

"No, no, he's got to go early," said Jill. "We can still do it. What do you want to go see?"

And on her side of the line, I heard footsteps approaching and a deep murmur of "Call you tomorrow, 'kay?" The smack of lips pecking a cheek. *Luther?* Interesting. I thought it was over between them.

"Michelle?"

"Yeah. I'm . . . Well, we don't have to see what's here. I just got the idea by passing this theatre. Loews in Midtown is showing that British thing."

"The one with Hugh Grant in it?"

"They all have Hugh Grant in them, Jill."

"Sure, sure," she laughed. "Give me about an hour, forty-five minutes if I can catch a fast train. We can always get coffee first if we're in between the shows."

"Perfect," I said. "See you then."

And I'm covered, I thought as I clicked off my phone. Plenty of time to jump on a train and link up with Jill.

But I still had to find Morgan's incriminating material.

Hurry *up*. The desk. Maybe he had whatever he'd need stashed away in the desk, and I took a deep breath as I checked the drawers. Locked. Before panic set in, I pulled out the long drawer under the green blotter, and sure enough, a key sat squarely in the middle in plain view. Makes you wonder why one would bother, but people are creatures of habit. It was the bottom drawer that held the goldmine. More and more padded envelopes, each and every one addressed to the loft in Morgan's own handwriting.

I opened them all.

And looked at the charts for "Drum," for "Pariah," for "Hurt Me Again" and others. Some, of course, weren't what Erica called them, they had different names, but I could read music well enough to recognise the songs. "Son-of-a-bitch," I whispered softly to myself. He had told me the truth.

She is bigger than this, I told myself. She simply doesn't know it. After all, she didn't need Morgan to write "Late Night Promises." She certainly didn't steal anything from him for "It Was a Pleasure to Burn" because we took the Ray Bradbury book together in Grade Eleven back in MacDonald High, and I was there when she was fooling around on the piano and hit on the tune. Maybe they had collaborated on a few of the other songs, and they had a spat over who did what and should get the credit. Morgan writing things down shouldn't prove anything.

But it would damage her.

She is bigger than this. No one has to know. No one will ever know.

I stripped each envelope of the charts, notes and little cassettes and sifted the contents carefully. It would look ridiculous if his files were completely empty, and I would have to leave some behind. *I was very careful.* All this time I worked in the latex gloves, and though they were beginning to feel uncomfortable, I kept my discipline and left them on. It wouldn't matter if my fingerprints were on the freight elevator or a couple of items of furniture—Erica and I were both regular visitors. But I had to be sure his desk wouldn't betray me.

I couldn't know Morgan's music, but I knew practically every nuance of Erica's, and it didn't take me long to divide what was hers and what was his. I went over to Morgan's gas stove, lit up a burner and pushed the chart for one of her minor tunes on the *Drum* album into the blue flame.

As the page blackened and curled, and a tiny orange fire started, I realised my mistake. It was too late for this one, and I left the ashes in the little gutter around the element, but the others... The others I would save. I would save all the other charts.

She would need proof if she ever worried and was sleepless that it would come out. People will always tell a star what she wants to hear, but I could show her. And I could say *I did this for you.*

Michelle is loyal. She had told people this plenty of times herself: Michelle's always loyal.

I would need her loyalty in return.

I couldn't burn the envelopes with their shallow bubble padding. Too messy, the plastic wouldn't burn properly, and all that would take too long. I shoved them with the charts into my handbag, and though the contents gave it an improbable bulge, I forced the clasp to shut.

That only left the tapes. By themselves, the demos didn't prove anything. *Drum* had already gone double platinum, and for all anyone would know or care, Morgan could have recorded the songs as covers to get singing gigs. I shoved a couple of the cassettes into my pockets and considered the rest. Then I impulsively began to tug loops of tape out of the spools and shred them.

I checked my watch. I had time. I carried the vandalised tangles, noisy like a pile of crackling cellophane, over to the fireplace and lit a match. The flame sputtered and died. I shoved in a section of *The Times*, but newspaper never burns as well as you expect, and I had to throw in a couple of pieces of kindling from Morgan's antique coal bucket.

The fire warmed me a little, but it wouldn't reach Morgan's body, cooling by the minute, its presence on the floor starting to tug at my nerves.

I could leave the fire. It had destroyed enough of the tape spools that they were beyond saving, and with the odds and ends I had tossed in, it would look like a regular small fire. Time to go. As I got into the freight elevator, I carefully peeled off the latex gloves and shoved them into my pocket. I had watched enough cop shows from *CSI* to the one Morgan had tried to write for, *Easy Death in Queens,* to be paranoid about the chance of fingerprints on the inside of gloves.

The freight elevator might as well have been a freight train for all the noise its steady *grennnrrrrr* made on the way down. If somebody had arrived even then I would have been sunk. Paranoia was making me shudder and itch. I was perspiring too much. I had been a cool customer with Steven, running on hate and adrenaline, but I had had to think too much about killing Morgan, especially when I was forced to do it so soon after the last murder. And now I was standing just inside the front door to his place, watching the street anxiously through the glass so that no one, *no one,* would see Michelle Brown or even Young Black Girl exiting victim's place.

Long exhalation of breath as I turned the corner.

By the time I reached the subway station, I thought I was safe. I even felt secure enough to stand on the platform, and though you know all these places are getting CCTV'd nowadays, I was curious about the cassette tapes I had preserved from Morgan's desk. I wasn't too worried about cameras, because, hell, I was entitled like anybody else to be at that subway station. If I happened to check a tape in my pocket, so what, but that's what fear and guilt does, it makes you hesitate over every banal thing you do, thinking it implicates you. When I reached down into my pocket, however, that wasn't what made me shudder, the idea of being watched. It was because I felt the glove.

There was only one.

One glove. My fingers checked again patiently, feeling

two tapes, feeling the texture of the latex and counting the fingers, digging around.

There was only one glove.

I looked around me. It hadn't dropped anywhere on the platform with my rummaging. It wasn't over by the steps coming down. *Shit.*

It could have fallen anywhere from the doorstep to the entrance of the subway, but the horrifying notion was what if I had left it in his place? Which meant I had to go back. And I could be late for Jill. Stupid, stupid, stupid.

And so I trudged back, almost in tears for being such a fool. Again I checked the street for precious minutes on end, praying not to be seen. God, how I waited in agony. And when I couldn't take it anymore, I jogged for the door and then remembered that he had *buzzed me in*. Panic was switching my reason off. How was I going to get back inside? Please, please, please. *Think.* Then I smartened up and remembered that I had brought along the spare set of Erica's keys, which included the key to his place, and with a great sigh of relief, I unlocked the door and rushed inside.

The freight elevator was another slow torture.

And when it came to a stop and I slid back the wooden guard with the same old squeak and rattle, there was a silence to the place that was almost unbearable. Finality of death, cutting off sound as much as life. He was still there, of course, just as I had left him. I couldn't stand this, and I tore my eyes away. I had come here with a purpose, and—

There. Thank God. In the dimness of the room close to where the floor dropped off into the elevator shaft. The glove had fallen in the darkness when I had left the first time. I picked it up in ecstatic relief. It might as well have been a diamond ring saved before it rolled into a gutter. One glove that made the difference between scandal averted and finishing my life in prison. This time I shoved it well down into my pocket and held the pocket closed. I took one last look around, telling myself this better be it, you damn fool.

I went through the same drills of watching the street. And then it was the subway and down to Midtown and Jill. When I showed up at the theatre, she was late. We still had time before the show, so we went for a quick one in an Irish pub across the street. To distract her from any questions about where I'd been earlier, I chose this moment to be the attentive new friend. Who was this new man who sounded so familiar in the background? Teasing her until she gave it up.

"You okay us talking about this?" She took my hand under the table and gave it an affectionate squeeze. "I know we haven't got together, but I'd still like to sometime, and if you're open-minded, there's no reason why we can't. Tonight was just a date."

"Jill, we're fine, honestly," I said. "How was it? What was he like? Who is the guy?"

"Okay, okay, it's Luther," she laughed. "Happy now?"

"What's going on?" I asked in a gossipy voice. "I thought he was finished with you."

"Yeah, but I wasn't with him," she said, taking a swig of her bottled beer. Arching her eyebrows, she told me, "The man knows how to scratch an itch." Then she quickly patted my arm. "So do you, sweetie, I just felt in the mood for him—"

I waved away any affront to my vanity. "I'm not offended. God, we're an incestuous bunch, aren't we?"

"You were right: he gets in his moods," she complained, barely hearing me. "I think in his head, he's actually cheating on her even if she won't give him the time of day! I know girls who wouldn't believe a guy could have that kind of devotion. He's great company, a fantastic lover, got loads of talent, and then he beats himself up over his relationship with her. I told him, 'Babe, you're a lot of fun until you get like this.' "

"He's in love with her," I said with a shrug.

"Yeah, Mish, I know, but after a while, the boy's got to take a hint. There are thousands of things you can't have in this world, and thousands of people you can't have. Get over it. Move on."

"Jill, we're in the pop music business!" I laughed. "If we listened to you, everybody would be mentally healthy, and all we'd have is songs from *The Lion King*."

"I'm not saying I don't 'get' passion or love," she countered. "But I don't believe in extremes."

"Aw, you got no poetry in your soul, girl."

"Some people have too much."

We talked about Luther for a few minutes more and never did get around to what I had been up to in the day. We walked into the theatre, got our seats and made fun of the previews for the latest Ben Stiller comedy, a cop feature with Denzel Washington and a picture with a bunch of anonymous French actors in a Nazi-occupied town. The only thing you learned about that one was *The Times* called it "A Triumph!" By the time Hugh Grant was doing his stammering charm bit, I knew I had nothing to worry about. It was over. I was safe. Erica was safe.

*I*t took until four the next afternoon before word of Morgan's death reached me. The manager of Stanford's Jazz Emporium had stopped by his loft to return a borrowed book, an old friend who had his own key and who spontaneously admitted he wanted to help himself to another volume if his pal was out. He was the one who called the cops. The news would take a while to circulate to Morgan's friends, and I was ready for it. I had rescheduled the more important appointments but left a couple of chores I hated to be cancelled on the spot when Erica made the call. And she would make the call. I could be certain of it.

I had finished my business with Morgan by ten o'clock that morning. In my office at Brown Skin Beats, I had opened a drawer in my desk and pulled out a FedEx pack. I shoved in Morgan's charts, now stacked and organised in my own sealed manila envelope. There was only one place to keep these goods safe. "Dear Karen," I wrote, "I've sent this to you because you're the one person I can trust. Nothing terribly interesting, just legal documents, but I don't have much privacy at the apartment. Just stash these away for me, will you? I love you. M."

I knew Karen wouldn't open the pack. Like many people who guard their privacy, Karen wouldn't dream of invading the privacy of others, even an old flame. And I could collect the package if and when I needed it.

FedEx came by, I signed on the proper line on the delivery guy's clipboard, and I stored the pink customer receipt in my desk so I could call the next afternoon to ensure it arrived okay. Simple as that. It was done. No more Morgan, and now no more Morgan's threat. I got on with my day. And by 4:17, I was sitting at my desk in my office with my feet up and let the phone ring three times before answering.

"Mish . . ." Pitiful sobs.

"Erica? Jesus, Erica, what's wrong? Tell me . . ."

Confession

Morgan made a reference once to how he had grand-children. It turned out he had an estranged mixed-race daughter in her thirties who lived in Queens, married to a Systems Analyst, with two little girls of her own. She graciously accepted Erica's help to pay for and arrange the funeral. She was pleasant to us all, but you could tell she felt alienated. At the reception, she listened politely to stories we told about Morgan in the studio or jazz clubs or simply jamming in the apartment. She volunteered none of her own.

"God, it's kind of like looking through a cracked mirror," Erica whispered to me in the reception hall. I didn't understand what she meant until she added, "I phoned my Dad this morning to let him know. He gave me a list of songs we ought to play. Morgan's favourites."

It sunk in about the cracked mirror. Erica had been watching our friend's daughter, how the woman's mouth betrayed no smile, no quiver for tears about to come, her eyes full of regrets and bittersweet emotions about what Morgan's life was all about and if he had left any legacy at all. Memories perhaps of when Daddy couldn't help with rent, when Daddy was away on tour with a band or was out that night playing. When it was so much easier to leave during an argument with Mom because smoky clubs were becoming branches of a second home. I could see from Luther's expression that the bell was tolling for him, too, thinking of his little boy. He said he visited Trey as often as possible.

Only a few minutes later, I made another circuit around the huddles of mourners and found Erica to see how she was holding up. And she said the strangest thing.

Staring at a wall, she remarked, "He could be a major prick. Morgan. He could lie to you shamelessly and tell you not to come over because he had people, and you'd drive past his place and know he'd be up there alone. He could be so selfish. He played piano like a god, and we got solid arrangements out of him on *Drum*. I loved that whiskey laugh of his. And when he made love to you, he took his sweet time... What do you do with a man like that? What are you supposed to think of him after he's done?"

I couldn't think of anything to say.

She turned and poured the last of her drink into a potted plant. "Maybe if he got out of that apartment once in a while, this wouldn't have happened. He was one selfish son-of-a-bitch up there with his books and his Scotch."

"Erica..."

"I'm okay, Mish. I just wish I knew what to think of him when I add it all up."

Erica sang "Late Night Promises" at the funeral. She said it was one of Morgan's favourites. I was the only one there who felt a disturbing irony, remembering how Morgan claimed to me once he had written this, too, but "let Erica have it." With *Drum,* he'd said, he had to put his foot down.

$\mathcal{I}$t should have been my time now. I hadn't killed Morgan to be closer to her, but I would have thought it just compensation if it happened. Luther disillusioned and distanced, Steven a memory, and her circle of friends available for condolences but not affection. Not love. I lived with her, worked for her. I was available practically around the clock, only a phone call away. *Turn to me now.* I confess part of me was selflessly moved by her pain, wanted to caress her away from this misery for her sake. It tore her up inside far worse than Steven's murder. I grieved, too. I walked around the apartment in a stupor of self-pitying shock, like a conscripted soldier who has killed his first man. In mourning, Erica didn't play jazz or the *Drum* album, reminders of her loss, she put a lot of Brahms and Chopin on the stereo. For the first time in ages, she talked about booking a flight to go home and visit her family. I told myself I had to give her space. Wait for this heaviness to pass.

Then Luther ruined everything. *Damn it.*

$\mathcal{I}$ say he ruined everything, but she started it really. She provoked him, looking to get a reaction even if she wasn't aware of what she was consciously doing. She skipped appointments to come into the studio to lay down vocal tracks. She had me call Brown Skin Beats and pull her out of doing guest vocals on an album for one of his visiting British protégés, a chore she was happy to do before and was actually looking forward to. The management at BSB dropped hints like cartoon anvils on my head that Erica must be taking diva lessons. They were losing patience with her.

The days of Brahms and Chopin were over, and she was

spending long hours lying on her bed in the apartment, listening to nothing. I was getting worried. I wanted her to turn to me, but she retreated into a dark place inside. She wasn't eating enough. I said maybe it was time she considered seeing her doctor and getting a short-term prescription for anti-depressants.

Sitting on the edge of her bed, I said gently, "Look, you loved Morgan, and now he's gone. I miss him, too . . ."

"Self-righteous prick," she muttered. "Hated A-B rhyme schemes. Probably laughing his fool head off at me right now as he burns. God, I do miss him, but . . . Mish, honey, this isn't about him. Okay, it is, but it isn't."

"Explain it to me."

"I can't. I just need you to leave me in the dark for a little while. I got to find my own way out."

I felt helpless. I had never felt helpless with Erica before. When she finally got out of bed at eleven on a Thursday evening, I asked if she was ready to go see the doctor tomorrow. Not at all, she replied. Tomorrow she would be fine. She was going out now "to return something." I learned later that she had headed over to Luther's. In the pounding rainstorm that sent sheets of water down on the New York streets, she demanded that Luther buzz her up to his place just to spend ten seconds outside his door.

"You can have this back now," she said, and she slapped the gift of his grandmother's gold watch into his palm, storming off towards the elevator.

A bewildered Luther stared at the watch, and then he ran down the hall to catch up to her. The elevator doors were closing on his protests. "Erica? Erica! What the hell are you doing this for all of a sudden? *Erica?*"

She must have thought I was asleep in my bedroom when she came home. I crept into the hallway and watched her quietly sobbing. She threw her jacket off, tossed her handbag in a corner and made herself a drink. Dark rum, a generous pour from the bottle. I would have gone out to comfort her if the buzzer hadn't made a shrill ring. Luther, of course. He had followed her home.

She didn't have to buzz him in. She could have told him to go away, leave her alone. Her choice to let him up. Neither one of them offered a greeting at the door, they just got straight into it.

"What is this supposed to mean?" he demanded, holding out the watch.

"Whatever you want it to," she answered. "I don't think it's right that I keep it. Not anymore."

"And why the hell not?"

She sat on an ottoman, tugging on one of her fingers nervously, staring at her baby grand. "You know I haven't worn the damn thing in quite a while, never did check whether it tells time properly. I'll bet if I open it up, there are no gizmos in there. I bet it's empty. Just like you."

"Erica, I think you better come out and say it. I don't know if I have all night to crack your code."

I hung back like a child hiding on a staircase, listening to Mom and Dad fight.

"I'm saying why haven't you called, huh? Morgan dies, and you go MIA when I ring you up. You're never around. What do I need your gift for? A reminder that I don't see you?"

"I gave that to you in friendship and—"

"We're not friends! And we sure as hell aren't lovers. I don't know what we are to each other these days—"

They're going to sense I'm here, I thought. Yet I had to keep watching. I advanced on tiptoe past the front lounge and crept down the hallway to what we called the sun room, what used to be a little office area but had been converted into the storage space for all the surveillance cameras and home-protection gear. I sat down and punched up on the control panel to put the living room on the main viewer.

"—Us to be lovers?" Luther, caught in mid-sentence as I brought up the volume. The sound from the webcams was a bit tinny, an afterthought. It was clear enough for me. He was laughing joylessly at her irrational whim. "I want you ages ago, and you say no, so now we play this game again, and what's going to happen this time, Erica? What am I supposed to—"

"*No!* No, you could have had me!" She jumped up from her seat, one hand on her hip, pointing a finger at him in accusation. "You could have me now! But I know better after all this shit! You always got to ask for more! It's like you want my fucking soul or something, Luther—"

"That's an excuse because you're scared—"

"Why you need this big commitment even before we get out of the starting gate and—"

"*I'm in love with you, goddammit!*" he thundered. "Erica, when are you going to grow up and take a risk? Have a real relationship? That 'playing house' you did with Steven was just bullshit, and you know it! Good ol' Steven, the pretty boy security blanket and combo insurance policy! And Morgan? You giving him his weekly rolls in the hay or however frequently you two got it on? What did you even get involved with him for?"

Erica looked ashamed for a brief moment. I watched her open her mouth to say something, to offer an explanation, and I thought *yes, do it*. Because her feelings over Morgan were so complicated, I couldn't make sense of them, and maybe we'd learn something now. Why she had felt she had to give herself to her mentor, sexy in his own way, I suppose, but Morgan had been her Dad's age—

"I don't have to explain myself to you!" she said at last.

"No, you *can't* explain! I'll bet you don't even know why

you do what you do. Big political singer, major talent throwing yourself into it when you perform! And then you play it safe. You do it with Steven, with Morgan, with me—"

"Don't you bring up Morgan! Not now!"

All of a sudden, Luther marched forward and angrily spun her around, his large hand seeming to vice her wrist and pin it behind her back, muttering something I couldn't quite hear like, "Don't you pretend with us..." He was kissing her neck, wrapping his other arm around her waist. Erica gave a short whimper of pain but didn't protest, grinding her ass into his crotch, and that was all the encouragement he needed. His left hand mauled the front of her blouse, tearing it away in a savage fury, ripping at the bra cups, and Erica's large tits bounced free, soon to be cupped and massaged and fondled by those strong fingers. I loved looking at Erica's breasts. I loved the way Luther played with them just as I would, tracing circles around their areolae, kneading them like dough, her nipples so thick and erect. Still pinning her arm, as if the jolt of mild pain was counterpoint to pleasure. He frantically took his hand away and unzipped his fly, and the fingers of her free hand were urgently helping, tugging at him impatiently—

She gave another cry of pain from the stabbing needles demanding attention in her trapped arm, and he showed her mercy at last, letting her go. I saw Erica's mouth open wide in shock as her knees slightly buckled, the two of them clumsily staggering near the piano, and her hand shot out to rest her weight on its corner. He had her trousers only halfway down her thighs before his fingers played with her mound, and he tentatively drove the head of his cock between her pussy lips. "Oh, God..."

Erica sighing, Erica making a sound through gritted teeth of *"Kkkkkehhhh"* as I saw the huge head of that cock linger with achingly light pressure and then dive between her vaginal lips. Warm wet beautiful folds of flesh I had dreamed about. I watched the map of veins and angry blood vessels on Luther's enormous cock disappear into her and emerge again, polished and gleaming with her juice, thickening and swelling even more.

Then, with a burst of tears and an extraordinary strength of will, she moved away from him, slapping away his hands as he reached in confusion for her. "No," sobbed Erica. "No . . . You want too much. And I can't trust you."

"What do you mean you can't trust me?" he asked in a hurt voice. He adjusted himself and zipped up his fly, letting out a long breath.

"You closed yourself off from me after you came back from London," she said quietly.

She looked at the tatters of her blouse and her sagging trousers, and I would have thought she'd duck into her bedroom to change. Leave him behind. Instead, she pulled her ripped top away and let it flutter to the rug, stepped out of her trousers and panties. She didn't care if she was naked in front of him, and in some personal instances, I think fearless, uninhibited Erica treated her nudity as her personal armour. Her voluptuous body could either beckon or insist a man keep his distance—the way she demanded he stay back now. Like Luther said, she could wear her political heart on her gown in front of thirty thousand fans, but to say what she was thinking to a man . . . She needed sex for that. She needed to be nude for that. To distract him? Embarrass or captivate him while she was vulnerable? Maybe all of those. She picked up her drink and downed the last of it.

"You want me to trust you, but you won't tell me what went on in London. You'd rather tell Michelle. You're great pals with her—"

"I *know* you can't be jealous of Michelle, Erica. Come on, she's—"

"She's my best friend," Erica cut through him. "That's

not what I'm saying. You're punishing me. That's what it is.
I *know* you wrote music in London, Luther. You wrote to
me about it, but you won't play it for me. You think I don't
have my own contacts in London? They say it's great, and
then ask me, well, haven't you heard it, girl? And I'm on the
other end of the phone, sounding like a fool, saying no, he
won't let me see the charts, won't play—"

"And what collateral are you going to put up, Erica? *No.*
You won't do it. Still playing it safe."

"Get out," she barked at him.

She turned to face him, still defiantly nude, tears running down her cheeks. "Go home, Luther."

"I'm in love with you."

"Get out!"

She took one skittish step back, thinking he might reach
for her again, and she wouldn't be able to stop herself this
time. For a moment, I wondered if Luther would try. He
only had two choices. Gather her up or walk out the door.

He invented a third option. He knew one of them had to
bridge the gap of trust, and he walked over to the baby
grand and sat down. He would play, making love to her this
way if he couldn't touch her with his hands. Two seconds
before they reached out to touch the keys, her voice was
ready to slam the lid down on his fingers.

"It's too late."

But of course, it wasn't. He began to play the songs he
wrote in London—snatches of them, opening bars of a couple and bridges of a couple more. I don't mean to over-blow
this, but you have to imagine how privileged I was, getting
the chance, not just once, but several times, to hear virgin
creations of Erica, Luther, a couple of other major names.
What would it feel like? If you were in a room when Elton
John casually played for you the notes of "Sorry Seems to
Be the Hardest Word"? Or somebody had a guitar and
played those signature chords of Peter Gabriel's "Solisbury

Hill" that make you recognise it right away? Or if you were in the room with Quincy Jones when he worked with Michael Jackson? I was down a hall, supposedly asleep, as Luther Banks played the opening of "Resurrect Me" for an audience of one, this woman he loved equal to his art. He played her what became his classic, "Brixton 2 AM."

Get out, she'd told him, and now she was a statue, riveted by his compositions. On the monitor, I saw her eyes shine with an epiphany. I covered my mouth with my hand, struggling, too, with my feelings. It wasn't only because of Luther's beautiful music, it was the revelation of how he had created it. He wasn't Morgan playing it safe. He wasn't Steven sampling and copying her. The songs were original, yet you can hear Erica's influence in them. I shuddered in my hiding place because I had killed for her, but he made Erica children of notes and chords. She had become an air bubble in his veins, but once it was extinguished by her callousness, he lived again, clean, whole. Every melody was a soundtrack for days of introspection, for the shit he had seen in Hackney, in Lewisham, and, at last, for a grief over her absence in his life, an absence he had forced on himself. They were songs as good as any she had written.

"Oh, my God," she whispered.

He didn't acknowledge this. He kept playing. And she listened.

She listened as I held back my tears down the hall. Her eyes were opened that night. You see, she didn't fall in love with him because she'd found her creative equal or soul mate—it was richer than that, oh, yes, far richer. Erica had been looking for inspiration all this time in her flings, searching for a man to be her muse. And now she found this gorgeous man who embodied something higher, who took creative sustenance from her and used his own palette. His music said we want to be made better than our normal selves through intimacy and company with our beloved, and for a creative person, to do your work and then discover you've provoked a rich tapestry of musical feedback...Joy.

I couldn't resent Luther in that powerful moment. I was a pedestrian mortal with a stash of high school notebooks full of scribbles and half-finished novel drafts. I had never written anything close to being as good as those songs. Hell, I had never finished a try at a novel. Even if I could, Luther's playing was a reminder that a page of words couldn't express a feeling so accurately, so *directly* as a few bars on a piano. Maybe that was why I never finished those stillborn books. Not only because I loved her but because of this simple truth: she made it easy, my abdication from my own creativity.

In my own soft, quiet way, I had competed with Steven and the others for Erica in terms of generosity, attentiveness, loyalty—I thought of her as my reward for being a good person. No one, *no one,* until now had ever assumed that Erica Jones could be incomplete emotionally in terms of the music. Because she was so gifted. But Luther understood. Oh, God, yes, we want to be more than what we are. And as he played on, I knew that love isn't a slow ballad. It's the exhilaration of the anthem.

I didn't resent him that night. That came later.

She interrupted his playing, lifting his hand to her cheek. "Oh, Jesus, baby, it's taken me so long to find you..."

"Do you want these?" he whispered to her. He didn't ask: *Do you love me?* They were the same question.

Crying now, his thumbs wiping away her new tears, her voice cracking with feeling as she nodded and said, "I want...I want more than having them...for you to... I want you to make an album out of them, *your* album..."

"All right then," he said.

"Okay."

Their foreheads dipped and touched, and then they were kissing again passionately, deeply. Erica's fingers on his face, his neck, Luther running his hands through her hair. She took him by the hand and led him away. In the sun room, I punched up the monitor for her bedroom. The only reason there was a digital camera in there was the short balcony off the sliding doors, but it took in the entire room.

They were away from the bed, but I could see their reflection in the full-length antique mirror near the vanity table. I heard Erica say *I made you suffer,* and Luther denying it. Erica saying, *Take me.* Luther shedding his trousers as quickly as he could to penetrate her from behind once more. She gripped the ends of the oval mirror as Luther slammed into her, thrusting harder and harder, and I watched the ripple of her ass cheeks with his momentum, the jiggle of her tits. She and Luther captivated by the reflection of their raw need.

In the sun room, I tilted my chair back and perched the soles of my bare feet on the sill of the desk. My eyes were glued to the screen as I slipped my panties off, already drenched, my inner thighs wet with my lubrication, one finger anxiously stroking my clitoris. So beautiful, so beautiful when you make love, darling...

Wishing they'd retreat to the bed, and they did, Luther stripping off his shirt to reveal his well-developed physique, shadows of abs and chunks of muscle on his forearms and biceps from years of his feverish, happy percussion, his legs almost feminine in their perfect shapeliness, smooth and strong. I felt a confusing mixture of arousal, Luther's balls in a ripe sack of hanging grapes, his ten inches of throbbing penis a dark spear, and I'd thought only one man could reach me, Steven, because of his psych games and his pretty boy androgyny, and yet here was Luther...My mind flashed on the gun barrel nudging into my pussy back in Steven's house, and I felt a quake in my legs. Erica lay on the bed, opening her legs invitingly, and the dim light of the windows picked up the slickness under her bush.

I had a zoom-in function on the camera.

Erica pounced on Luther as he came over, her thick lips smacking and slurping as she took him into her mouth. I could see the veins like forks of lightning along his girth, and, oh, to have that mouth on me. To have those fingers that played with his balls, cupping them delicately. Erica delighting as always in her own prowess when she gave head. Jerking him with her hand to bring him to a froth, sucking now on just the crimson tip, and he couldn't take it anymore. Neither could I. But they moved too fast for the camera, and it was a blur, my hand darting to the control panel to zoom out and see them. Luther pushing her down on the bed and hooking his arms under her legs, settling his cock between her pussy lips to float there in heaven on a membrane of her juices for a moment before he greedily thrust himself in.

"Make me come!" Erica cried out. "Make me come, honey!"

Luther thrusting in and out of her, Erica feeling her own tits as she lay there, her eyes closing and opening as the shadows played with the flex of muscles in Luther's ass.

"I ... need ... you ..."

Me. In the little room, rubbing my flushed breast that had popped out of my brassiere and shoving a nervous finger into my vagina, catching sight of my tortured expression in the black glass of a dead monitor on the side, the cords in my neck taut. I wished Jill were here, Jill tapping one of her magical secret pressure points to send me over the edge, but what I really wanted was down the hall, and, Jesus God, I want to fuck you, I want to fuck you so bad, honey, all this time, while on the monitor Luther was in my place with his dick inside her, prompting her hands to clutch the blades of his shoulders in frantic claps, Erica pumping her hips for *him* as she let out her banshee scream of "So good, so good, fuck me, darling, fuck me!"

"I love you, baby," Luther rasped. "Always loved you—"

"So good, so good—"

Watching her. On the monitor. Always so beautiful, I thought.

"I need you..."

Their passion so raw, so animalistic. Different from Luther with Jill, different from Erica with all her other guys, throwing herself into lovemaking with her usual abandon, but there was something more this time as she bit into his shoulder to urge him on and came in a sob, in a piteous, child-like wail. For *him*. And as I felt my orgasm shudder through me in my miserable loneliness of the sun room, my mind struggled with the new truth as naked as their sweaty bodies, the truth that was rolled out in strings of notes for Luther's compositions. She will love *him*. Steven had dazzled her, but it was a genuine article this time. God damn it, *she loves him*.

*T*wo days later, Jill called and asked me to come down and meet her at Morgan's apartment. I asked her what for, but she said she'd better explain when I got there. A bored uniformed police officer waved me into the building when I offered my name, and another cop waited just outside the freight elevator as I came up. Jill was alone behind a string of yellow caution tape. She always said she had pull with New York's finest, but this was impressive. I thought they only let civilians into crime scenes in the movies, but there she was, nosing around. She watched me as I pulled back the wooden slat door, and I had the presence of mind to hesitate before stepping off. Better make it look good. Subtle shock is best. My heels creaked with slow steps along the floor boards, as if I were entering a cathedral. *God, this is where it happened,* I wanted to show on my face, this is where our poor friend fell.

"Hi," I said almost under my breath.

"Hi," she said simply.

I reached out my arms, needing an embrace. She hugged me back, and I could tell her eyes were darting to the uniformed cop in the corner. I couldn't push for any more overt sign of affection between us. I squeezed her hand, one last small reminder we had been lovers. A telepathic demand of: please, no more of your amateur sleuth third degree.

"Jesus, Jill, why'd you bring me down here?" A soft cry caught in my throat as I saw the tape outline for Morgan's body.

"I'm sorry, honey," she said. "You're the strongest, I think, in some ways. Erica's a wreck, and the label people don't know him, and Luther had to go to LA on business—"

"Luther's here in New York," I said. "He's been back about a week." Which was true.

She looked blankly at me. "Oh. I haven't heard from him, so I just assumed . . ."

I gave her a look. Considering how she imitated Erica in doing her wham-bam-thank-you-sirs, did she expect a sunny invitation from Luther for brunch?

Then I stared at the white tape outline.

"I don't know if I can stay in this room," I told her.

"Take it easy. Look, I called you down here because I needed someone I could trust, someone who knew him. Do you know where Morgan would have kept his valuables, anything he wanted to protect with his life?"

I shook my head in astonished confusion. "But . . . didn't whoever did this to him already clean him out?" I gestured to the open drawers way off near his bed, the head of Beethoven I knocked over to make it look like a struggle. "You think they missed something? I mean, what could Morgan have worth stealing anyway? Look how he lived."

"You're absolutely right," said Jill, folding her arms.

"I am?"

"Yeah. Blood doesn't lie. And in this case, the evidence at the crime scene suggests somebody came here with a specific purpose." She shrugged. "The cops know this kind of stuff in a matter of hours."

"How do they, um, figure that out?"

"You sure you want me to talk about this?" she asked. "I mean, the guy was your friend, and this stuff often strikes people as a bit morbid or ghoulish."

"Jill, you had me come down here," I said impatiently. "Just . . . go ahead and tell me."

"There's a whole area of study around blood stains and drops. These forensics guys can actually figure out an angle of impact with blunt trauma using a trigonometry formula. Doesn't matter how far the blood's travelled. You take the width of a spot, divide by its length and you get the impact angle."

"Fascinating," I said in a monotone.

"What I'm saying is, from the blood stains and cast-off blood drips on the nearby furniture, they've figured out a bit of the physical profile of our killer."

"They have?" I asked cautiously.

Jill nodded. "Oh, yeah. We know from the angle of the wounds that the blows came down, and the person's right-handed. We also know the killer's shorter than Morgan was. This is a short guy or woman, I suppose, who needed to strike Morgan—a reasonably strong and healthy fellow—three times over the head to cause the hematoma that killed him."

"So you're saying they came to rob his place and panicked when he turned up?"

"No," she said very distantly. "Not at all . . . I do think they came to *steal* something from him, but they weren't your run-of-the-mill burglar. It's been assumed they panicked when Morgan showed his face, killed him and then took off in a hurry. Okay. But are we supposed to believe they killed him and then took the *time* to rifle his drawers? I don't think so."

"Well, how do you know they took his stuff after they killed him? Why not before?"

"Let me come back to that in a second," said Jill. "Let's say they did have time. Okay, why not take some of that snazzy computer stuff? At least the hard drive, you can yank the cables out and tuck that under your arm. Or the DVD? No, they were looking for something else. And they knew him."

"How can you be so sure?"

"The conditions are exactly opposite of Steven Swann, Mish."

"I don't follow you."

"Steven was richer than God, had a security system in a big townhouse. His killer lets herself in and sneaks right up to him in a soundproof recording studio. He never heard her coming. Okay. Here was Morgan. Lived in a loft space, cheap buzzer lock security, but you're *bound* to hear that freight elevator unless you're in the shower or deaf. If Morgan arrives after his robber, she hears *him* coming. *The first thing you do if you're going to ambush someone is put everything back in its proper place so that they don't suspect you're there.* Common sense."

All those careful steps I took, and I overlooked the foolishly obvious. I rode that freight elevator countless times with Erica and Luther to visit Morgan and got used to its rattle, but that's no excuse. I should have considered the sound. After all, on that night, I was terrified by how long the elevator took during my escape, and, still, I didn't think of the sound. I never once factored its noise into my burglar scenario. *Fool.*

"So my guess is that she didn't have time to rifle his drawers beforehand, she did it after," Jill went on. "At the very least, if you really want to stretch to the incredible, she was interrupted *during*."

"Hold on. Why? Why is it so incredible?"

Jill pointed to the intercom buzzer. "Like I said: buzzer lock security and no sign of a break-in. What burglar announces herself and gets buzzed in? So she gets past the front door, up the freight and rifles his drawers all with Morgan in his home and letting her do it? If it's a stranger, he would confront the person straightaway, right as she steps off the freight. If he lets her in, maybe they talk, whatever, and he steps into the bathroom or something and she goes for the drawers. He comes back and says what do you think you're doing. Either way, she went back to the drawers after he was killed. I just don't buy that it was a robbery."

"You're doing it again," I said softly.

"What?"

"You always use 'she'—it's like you always assume the killer must be a woman."

Jill waved this away with a shy smile. "Oh, that's probably me being gender-conscious. He, she—no big deal. What was I saying? Oh, yeah. She rifled the drawers after."

"You're so sure," I said, trying to control my exasperation. "He could have come home as it happened."

"Okay," answered Jill. "So why not kill him right as he steps off the freight? She's got the element of surprise. Why the struggle? And look where Morgan's body was found. Well inside the apartment. If he catches a burglar in the act when he comes home, all the debris from a struggle would be closer to the exit, but it's scattered pretty evenly through the living room. Staged. And the statuette was the murder weapon—which means the killer had to come *all the way over there* to get it. Sure, she could have picked it up when she hears him coming, but why not leave his body by the elevator? She didn't kill him there and move him. There's no need for that. Plus the cops say Morgan's body wasn't moved. And if there was a struggle, how did she manage to kill him with a blow to the *back* of his head? It was some-one he knew. And she waited until he turned his back on her."

I couldn't offer any rebuttal.

"You know people get foolish ideas in their heads, Mish. They want to make a murder look like a robbery. But they've never robbed anyone so they don't understand how robbers think or do their job. It's amateur hour, and you can see right through them. Check out Beethoven, for in-stance."

I glanced at the portrait bust on the floor, the back of its head caved in like a hard-boiled egg tapped with a spoon, shards of it not far away.

"What about it?"

Jill cocked her eyebrow and tilted her head a little. When she talked about these details, she became quite ani-mated. Gesturing with her hands, a whole repertoire of pensive expressions on her lovely face.

"Well, jeeze. Look at that cheap fake pillar where Morgan rested it. It's pretty unstable, and I'm surprised he both-ered. Point is, the bust's knocked over, but the stand hasn't moved. The lab guys lifted it. Dust perfectly settled and ac-cumulated around the base. You wrestle around with some-one, breaking furniture, and things get shuffled. The pillar wasn't."

"Oh," I said.

"*And,*" she said, "they put all the fragments together like a jigsaw and then dusted for prints."

"So did they get any?"

"Not fingerprints. But they did lift two perfect glove im-prints." She pantomimed the motion of casually knocking the bust over. *Exactly* as I had done it.

"When you point all these things out, yeah, I see what you mean," I said.

"So?"

"So what?" I asked.

"So can you think of anything he might have had that somebody would have killed him for?"

I turned my head and scanned the loft, taking in everything and weighing her question carefully. "No...Look, our friend's dead. It's not like I can think straight. I don't know how you detach yourself emotionally from stuff like this, but me, I..."

"I suppose it comes with the job," replied Jill.

"But this isn't your job," I said, betraying my frayed nerves. "I could see what you mean about Steven. He was a star. The wacko who killed him could come after Erica. But Morgan? He was nobody. No, I don't mean nobody, but—well, you know what I mean. He was the gentlest, sweetest guy. He wasn't perfect, but, shit, he deserved to go while he was asleep in his bed!"

"But, Mish, that's why I'm looking into it," argued Jill, resting a comforting hand on my arm. "Erica asked me to. She feels the same way. He didn't deserve this, and she's just so torn up inside that...Well, the best thing I can do to make her feel better is conduct my own small investigation."

"I guess."

"We might as well get out of here," she suggested. "Hey, I brought my wheels. I'll drop you back at the apartment."

"Thanks."

We said nothing as we left the building and got into her car. I was still silent when she turned on the stereo and sang along to the Sophie B. Hawkins hit playing: *I had a dream I was your hero! Damn I wish I was your lover. I'll rock you till the daylight comes...*

If I hadn't slept with her, if we hadn't grown close as friends, I would have sworn she was mocking me.

*W*hen I came home, I found Erica in a chair in the living room. Waiting.

"Mish, I want you to explain something to me," she said.

Her face was solemn with grief, the way it had been over Morgan, and I felt my heart send a battering ram against the inside of my chest. She was very upset, and I didn't know why. "I want you to explain . . ." Her eyes were moist with tears. I didn't have a clue what the hell was going on. Had someone else died? Was there another problem with her and Luther?

She picked up the VCR remote and clicked on it. My jaw dropped when the image flickered onto the screen. Me. In the sun room a couple of weeks ago, masturbating as I watched Luther and Erica make love.

Oh. My. *God.*

"You never knew there was a webcam trained on the sun room, did you?" she said quietly. "Home security guys threw it in." She anticipated the question forming on my lips. "The monitor is this TV, closed circuit feed on channel 72. I wouldn't have seen this, except I was changing the tapes, and the deck counter showed it was full. It hits 'Record' any time you bring up the monitors in there . . ."

I looked at her, my face burning with shame. Erica was staring at me not with righteous indignation but another kind of shock. I don't think she gave a damn that I had seen her making love. The girl wasn't shy with her private circle, and Steven was proof of that. No, she had figured it out. All she had to do was confirm it for me.

"I know you're friends with Luther, hon," she said, her voice cracking with feeling. "But you've never done so much as given a second look at him. So this . . . I mean, you tell me you're gay and there was Karen, and if you weren't getting off on seeing Luther then..." She couldn't bring herself to say it.

I ran from the room. Oh, Jesus, this can't be happening. She'd taken away my face, stripped me naked right there over my burden.

I raced into my bedroom, but she chased after me, opening the door as soon as I slammed it shut, calling my name over and over again. "Michelle? Michelle! *Michelle!*" Tugging at my shoulder as I buried my face in the pillows. "Talk to me! Please tell me what's been going on. We're friends! What *is* this?"

Me sobbing like a child, knowing I was going to lose my job, my home and most of all the person I loved more than anyone else in the world. She could have held my arm over the gas burner on the kitchen stove, and I couldn't have felt more agony than this. Shouting into my pillow:

"I love you! I love you! All right? I know I can't have you, and it tears me up inside!" Collapsing into spasms and more sobs, mewling in the pit of my own self-loathing.

I couldn't look at her. I heard her voice, calm, flat, almost respectful in the wake of this revelation as she said to me: "How long?"

God, I couldn't roll over and look at her.

"Michelle. How long?"

I sat up at last, sniffling, and Erica handed me a tissue from the box on the nightstand. I blew my nose and covered my mouth with my laced fingers, muttering, "Years. Does it matter?"

Another long pause as she grappled with this. "I... I don't understand, honey. We're like... like sisters to each other. You know I love you, just not like that. You've seen me with how many guys, and you work with me day after day and...? You must have known we—"

"I can still be a professional," I snapped. And then all my pent-up frustration and shame boiled over into open resentment. "Have I put this on you? Have I made it your problem? *No*. You can't say I haven't done my job, Erica. And I've been a good friend."

"Yes," she said quietly. "You have. You're my best friend, Mish."

"Damn it, I'm good at my job!" I said, letting it all out now. "It's just . . . it's just that sometimes . . ." Feeling my lip quiver again and a fresh flood of tears blurring my vision. "I look at you, and you make a joke or you're performing or something gets you down, and . . . and it gets too much, you know?"

I stole a look at her as her brow crinkled, still trying to make sense of me, this stranger she'd never met before I had replaced her good friend. "And you . . . want me? The way you want Karen?"

"Not the way I want Karen," I said, sniffling again. "Well, yeah, that way—yeah, I understand what you mean. Look, Erica . . . I would never have told you. Never. Part of me loves you, but, yeah, we are sisters. You're my best friend, too, and I didn't . . . I mean I couldn't . . ."

She stood up from the bed and began slipping off her jeans.

"What are you doing?"

She didn't answer me. She folded them in a neat pile and set them down on a chair. I watched her unbutton her blouse, a shy smile on her lips, and set that aside as well. Then her panties and her bra. Erica, standing in all her luscious glory. Mahogany skin, full large breasts with dark nipples, her wide hips and her wedge of dark pubic fur, the strong legs leading down to delicate feet with toenails painted a burgundy shade this week.

"Erica, don't."

She beckoned me with her hand, saying, "Come on." She stifled a mild shiver. She'd never been with a woman before. And her first would be me. If she had stopped to consider how it would affect her relationship with Luther, it didn't show. Maybe she thought being with me "didn't count." Like an idiot, I was the one who hesitated.

"Why do you want to do this? I know you don't feel the same way."

"Come on," she said simply. "One time."

"Why? Why do this?"

"For you."

I was wretched. My beautiful girl naked in front of me, offering me what I had dreamed about *for years,* and I couldn't touch her. "Erica, I don't need a pity fuck."

"It's not a pity fuck."

"Okay, a compassion fuck."

"Mish . . ."

Waiting for me. I sat there on my bed, struggling to summon a scrap of battered, shrivelled dignity, knowing I wouldn't win against my own desire. Then Erica said the words that sprang me into action, giving me a push. She always knew the right thing to say.

"Look, you know I've never been with a girl," she said. "Don't make me feel any more self-conscious than I do, sweetie. If I was going to sleep with a woman, I would . . . I would want it to be you."

I looked in her eyes.

"I'm not just saying that," she added.

I didn't undress, not right away. I rose slowly from the bed, and again she shivered. The first kiss was excruciating in its awkwardness, her mouth so tense, barely yielding to my lips. She watched me as I wrapped my arms around her, doing her best to return the embrace. I held her like a precious stone I had rescued from a mine or a deep forgotten pool, cradling her in my arms, running my fingers down her back to her ass and feeling its delicious curves. I massaged her breasts, grateful that I could tease her nipples erect, and she averted her eyes, looking down, perhaps embarrassed that I could stimulate her like this. Gently, gently, I kissed and sucked on one nipple, *Erica's* nipple, tasting her, working my way down her belly to pause at her hip and feel its roundness, brushing my fingers against the tight curls of her pubic hair . . .

She stiffened as I coaxed her with my hands to part her legs. She shuddered as my tongue made its first hesitant laps on her pussy, *Erica's* pussy, the taste of her lubrication the sweetest wine I've ever had, and when my eyes looked up to check her reaction, I saw her own were closed. I was making her wet. I was making Erica wet, feeling Erica's skin . . .

I asked her with my eyes to lie down on my bed. She was so passive. She didn't reach out to hold me or to explore my body at all. She would *let* me do things to her. And, God help me, I couldn't help myself. I parted her legs and ducked my head down, revelling in the smell of her, wanting this for years, and my greedy mouth covered her and my tongue probed into her vagina. She groaned in response, and I was thrilled. *You will love what I can do for you*, I thought. Better than any guy, better than any stupid man just invading you with his dick. I have softness and subtlety and I love you, really love you. I started a fast rhythm of sucking her clit in and out, and she was clenching her teeth, shutting her eyes as if she didn't want to let go, as if she wanted to postpone her orgasm. When I finally tore it from her like a prize with the skill of my tongue, she covered her face with her hand and wailed. I undressed in a rush, and she stared at me glassy-eyed, not moving, her hands in a kind of fetal pose over her breasts while three of my fingers dipped into the sweet well of her pussy. She didn't seem to know me. I kissed her, and she opened her mouth, tasting my tongue, but there was no passion behind her curiosity.

Her hand was in my hair, stroking me, touching my cheek like a benediction. She cupped my left breast, and I sighed with the pleasure of this small gesture. She gave me the saddest smile I've ever known.

"I can't, Mish . . . I can't."

"I can please you," I whispered, not ready to let it all slip away yet. "I can."

I didn't take my fingers out of her. I kept pushing them in and out of her vagina, my mouth coming down like a hawk on one of her breasts, sucking a nipple, teasing it with small bites between my teeth. Erica's hands grabbed fistfuls of the sheets as my mouth roamed over her belly again, and I started to rub my pussy against her thigh. A little more, just a little more now, couldn't she see how much I loved her? You give yourself to me, and I'll gorge myself on you, her thigh above her knee getting slick with my juice as she lay on her side, coming. I keened, a shiver fluttering up my back, my eyes wet with the cathartic release of at last reaching my goal.

"Oh, God, feel me, Erica, touch me, please . . ."

"Mish . . ."

"Please, please . . ."

She shook her head no. "I can't . . ."

"You're coming under my hand," I whispered bitterly. "I'm making you come. All those times you fucked those guys ragged! I can make you come, and I really love you. Fuck *me*, honey. Love me back . . . Please . . ."

She shook her head again: no. Still whispering *I love you, but I can't,* looking at me like a scared rabbit. Waiting for me to finish. I couldn't stand the weight of that look. I was beyond tears now, past hope, and there is a pitiful state when you are naked and rejected, a kind of sleepwalking limbo where you're not prepared to get dressed yet, but you can no longer go through the pretence of affection. I gazed at her beautiful brown body, so tense and uncomfortable with me as she lay there, knowing I would never get another chance at this intimacy. I wanted to pledge sacrifice in that moment. I thought I would have been content merely to sculpt her skin with my fingers, to let my breath mingle with the air that reached below that lovely triangle of fur. *I can please you,* I'd told her. And we both knew it wasn't enough for either of us.

I know why she gave herself up to me. She thought it would break the spell. She thought the reality of having her would wake me up like an infatuated guy who had got his taste and was ready to move on. She didn't understand: *I loved her.* She only had to see that. Luther had cleared a path for me in a strange way. He had shown her genuine caring, and when she responded to this, her libido followed. And I loved her better than Luther or Steven or Morgan ever could. She needed time. I saw that now. If there was nobody else in the picture, she would wake up and at last see me through the forest of male disappointments. And Luther will let her down eventually, I told myself. Didn't men always with Erica? No one ever measured up in the end. She'll think of me. She'll remember my mouth and my hands inside her. She can't deny the pleasure she felt. I would have her again, I promised myself. I would.

Crisis

I borrowed one of Erica's cars and drove out late that night to Jill's house. Through the lace curtain in the window, she peeked out at me and then quickly opened the door. I'd woken her up, and she stood there on the threshold wearing only a long-sleeve dress shirt, a memento perhaps from an old boyfriend. The open ends were like parted drapes teasing me with the swell of her breasts and the thatch of dark pubic fur below. Ridiculous, coming to her like a cry-baby over Erica and then aroused by the sight of her. "I need you . . ."

She took me in her arms, half-naked on her front porch, not giving a damn if anyone was walking their dog nearby. We made love that night, and it was incredible again. She asked me what was wrong, and I said I wasn't ready to tell her. She said okay, I'll give you a massage instead. I fell asleep after only twenty minutes under her clever, sensitive fingers. In fact, I slept till close to noon the next day. "Shit!" as I bolted upright from her bed, but there was a note left with a spare key on the nightstand. CALLED YOU IN SICK. HANG OUT AS LONG AS YOU LIKE. J.

I did. As a thank-you and a romantic gesture, I found a market nearby and picked up a few things to make her dinner that evening. I explored her place. One of these days, I thought, Jill should really get around to unpacking the boxes she had pushed against her bedroom wall. I checked out the books she liked, one impressive shelf devoted to African dancing styles and African art. Another shelf held what looked like textbooks from her police academy days with titles like *Cleaning and Maintenance of Standard Service Firearms*. On a wall down in the basement, not the most conspicuous place, she had hung a framed portrait of herself in her NYPD uniform.

I sat down at her desk and discovered a white envelope next to her computer. It was unsealed with my name on it written in her hand, big loops on the "l"s in Michelle. Had she left me another note? When I opened it, the envelope looked empty. But it wasn't. There were these tiny bits of almost transparent brown plastic, and it took me a long moment to figure out what they were. When it hit me at last, my spine went cold, and my forehead beaded with nervous sweat.

Oh, Jesus. *Bits of cassette tape.*

I knew where they had come from—souvenirs from the fireplace in Morgan's loft. What the hell was she doing with bits of tape? You could see how they were shredded, charred. There was nothing she'd be able to learn from these. So what was she doing with them? And why did the envelope have my name on it?

As she walked in the door after work, I greeted her like a wife, telling her I'd made dinner, bought her flowers. It took me three hours to work up the nerve to ask about the envelope.

"Oh, *that*," she said casually. "That's simple. I found these bits of tape in Morgan's fireplace, and my friends in Homicide let me hang on to them for a while. They weren't very impressed with my 'evidence,' but, hey, you never know. I jotted your name down because I was making a mental note to ask you about them."

"But—but why me? What would I know?"

Jill shrugged. "Maybe nothing, I'm taking a wild stab in the dark here. I figured since you're so organised and you keep Erica's schedule, you had to keep track of Morgan and the others when they were all working together on *Drum*. I thought, you know, maybe Morgan mentioned something to you about what he was working on."

"Not that I can remember," I said tightly. "And you're working on a false assumption. I didn't have to care where the others were. Just Erica."

She waved it away. "Worth a shot. Sometimes when I have a problem, I carry little reminders around with me to help me think. I know it sounds like a weird habit, but it really does help. I look at them, I study them, and it gets my brain working. I thought I'd do the same with those tape bits. You remember I told you the killer wanted to make it look like a robbery? I did say that his murderer must have killed him for something he wanted."

"You did say that, yeah."

"It's so strange these bits of tape in his fireplace. I don't think Morgan would have tossed his cassette tapes in there. You don't burn something unless you really want to get rid of it. Perfectly good rubbish bin in his kitchen." She closed the envelope. "These are worthless, I guess."

She put the envelope on her desk. She *wasn't* throwing it away.

"Whatever they wanted, they must have got it, and now we'll never know."

I couldn't think of anything to say to that. I wanted desperately to change the subject, so I asked, "What did Erica say? About my absence?"

Jill looked distracted for a moment. "Oh. Not much. She

said she knew you weren't sick. She said you two had an argument, and it was her fault. She said she'd been a real bitch to you lately, piling on the work, and that she'd smarten up and give you some room. She said that apartment's your home, and you shouldn't feel like you have to leave because you two had a fight. Oh, and she said she's your friend first, always will be, and she does love you."

I nodded, making no comment. So it was to be like that. I suppose I shouldn't have expected anything else. She was my friend, and she was telling me she would stay my friend, but she could offer me nothing more, certainly not what I wanted. I could, however, keep my job. I could keep my place in her life. Erica wanted things the way they'd always been.

"Look, honey," said Jill. "Maybe it would be a good idea if you showed up for work tomorrow *at the office*. Do it in stages if you like. Then, when you're ready, you can go back to the apartment. Crash here for a few days, I don't mind. I'll swing by your place to pick you up some clothes—"

"No, that's only delaying it. I should go home. I'll be all right. Erica's good to me—most of the time."

"She's the best," chirped Jill.

I hugged her and said I'd stay one more night.

As I lay next to her that evening, I couldn't sleep. Wondering if I had got too smug, if Jill was playing with my head while she played with my body. *No.* Don't be paranoid.

I actually worried more about Jill than Erica, knowing my beautiful girl would never speak of giving herself to me, ever, ever, ever, not until I won her completely once and for all. That would take time. For now, I had to go back to playing the good friend. I could settle for that temporarily. I closed my eyes and drifted off, determined to forget all about hidden innuendoes and shreds of burned cassette.

*T*wo weeks later:

"We need to talk," said Erica.

Oh, shit, I thought. Nothing ever good follows that phrase. And I was right. There was something in Erica's tone as she asked me to sit down that wasn't the voice of a friend, but an employer. She waved me to the sofa, and I sat in a very guarded pose, my knees together, hands in my lap. Erica sat forward on an ottoman, her own hands clasped together and her voice low, as if breaking the news to me that my dog died.

"Luther's asked me to live with him," she announced.

I couldn't say anything.

"I've been kinda re-thinking my career," she went on. "Steven's death kicked the crap out of Brown Skin Beats. They've got his back catalogue, and we know they'll squeeze every last goddamn thing out of the studio sessions to cut and paste together a last album. But the label is circling the wagons. They don't want to just throw weight behind the rest of their artists. They want to build a whole new producer team so they never have any problems with the talent going off the rails, performers overdosing or having breakdowns or just losing it."

"I—I don't understand," I said. She was all over the map, first talking about her and Luther then about her career and then about the business. "What are you saying?"

"I'm saying BSB is throwing a whole lot of money at Luther to be their new Creative Director for the East Coast division," she explained. "A *lot* of money. They were bowled over by his work on my new album and a couple of others. And they're talking about moving him to the West Coast in nine months to have him take over the main operation."

"But that's Luther," I cut in. "You're the one who always wanted to be independent. Remember how you tied yourself up with Steven and—"

"I remember, honey. But Luther's not Steven. And Luther's turned out to be right, you know? I've lost my way, I think. When I came down here after high school, I wanted to make music. I wanted to reach people. And lately, I'm on auto-pilot. I'm cruising on my name. I don't think my songs are as good, and it's not that I've run out of things to say, I've just moved further away from knowing what the hell I'm talking about! I got so much bling-bling and shit, and I'm caring so much about photo ops and promotion, and how the hell did I let myself get talked into thinking of movies?"

"Aaliyah did it, Samantha Mumba, Beyoncé Knowles—"

"Good for them. That's not me. I'm tired, Mish. I want to write my songs and record when I'm *inspired*. Luther's saved my ass on this album, he really has. BSB will probably throw me a dump truck full of money for two more, and after that, I won't need to push so hard anymore. I got to look to the future, and I want to try my hand at producing. Luther thinks I got good instincts for it. We'll make a good team."

"That's what you said when you hired me."

She frowned at that. "I'm not *abandoning* you, Mish. This could be good for you, too. Look, you're still technically on staff at BSB, and Luther's going to pull a few strings. You'll be Deputy Manager of the Promotions department for the East Coast division. You can even keep the same office there."

"Terrific."

"Well, be a little bit grateful, girl," she snapped irritably. "He *sold* them on you. They don't know how hard you work. They just look at your title as 'personal assistant.'

Luther's the one who told them about your great ideas for the album art, how you got *Vibe* to do that profile, the concert in Zimbabwe . . ."

I didn't say anything for a moment.

"I want you to know," she said, softening her tone, "this isn't about you and me, and . . . Well, how you used to feel. You know that, right?"

I tried to shrug it off. "Of course not—"

"Luther's asked me, and we're going good so—"

"No, I understand, you don't have to say—"

"We got to strike when it's hot, you know?"

She clapped her thighs, obviously relieved *that* issue was out of the way.

I shrugged and told her, "Sorry, it's just that it sounds like everything's happening so fast."

She reached out and took my hand in hers. "Oh, Mish, there's *time*. We got months to go! You're not rid of me yet."

With a nervous laugh, we hugged each other.

"All that's happening for now is I'm going to start using this place as more of an office. Luther wants me to move in with him as soon as I can, but, hey, that just means I pack a few bags of clothes. I got knick-knacks and CDs and my toothbrush there, it's like I'm already settled. Hey, look . . . This is still your home. You'll make good money in that new job, and I can lease this place to you at a friend's bargain rate. What do you say?"

"S—sure. You know I love it here."

"*Happy endings all around, Mish.* You'll see."

I nodded my head and smiled. Happy endings all around, Michelle. She rubbed my arm in friendly affection and said she had to get going, she was hooking up with her man for lunch. Hey, did I want to tag along? Trying to give me a soft landing. I gave her my bravest smile and said, "No, thanks, I'm good." I should pop in to the label offices to sign off on those promotions she'd agreed to. I watched her hurry out the door, and in the cold silence of the apartment, I heard the distant bell for the elevator. I sat and thought.

The one thing she said that stuck with me was that we had time. Months to go. I would have to be patient, very, very patient. Jill Chandler was still snooping around, and it didn't look like she was going anywhere soon. Luther's death would have to look like an accident, nothing suspicious about it at all. Steven could be written off as gang violence or a lover's revenge, and Morgan could be a break-in, but for Luther to go would stretch plausibility to an angry snap. Too soon right now. I had to think. I had to do careful planning. And as I sat turning it over in my mind, it occurred to me I didn't really wish Luther dead. He wasn't guilty of hurting her as the others were. You don't need Luther dead.

That was the answer. You don't need Luther dead, you simply need him out of the way. My solution, I thought, would have a natural tidiness to it, an elegance. I wish I had planned more carefully, but now I had to fit the pieces together that I'd been left with. I went and fetched my handbag, digging around for the business card in my wallet from Holland, the police detective. Don't hesitate to call in case you think of anything else, and I had. Jill had called the guy an asshole. Well, assholes had their uses, too.

*W*e were having drinks, ironically enough, at a club opened by Steven seven months earlier, still going reasonably strong after his death. It was called Slow Fade, and he had told his designers to unapologetically rip off the design from Toronto's legendary RPM. He must have been inspired by Erica's hand-me-down stories from our parents. Back in its heyday, a mini-bus would pick clubbers up at a certain stop on Front Street, I think, and whisk them over to the double-decker warehouse of a nightspot. You walked into the foyer of RPM, and there was a full-size biplane suspended from wires. The showpiece for the club floor was a suspended Cadillac at a down angle over your head with mannequins re-creating the assassination of John F. Kennedy. The lucky ones got to see the Rolling Stones do unannounced gigs there several times when they were in town—this was, of course, before they got truly mummified.

Slow Fade had all that, plus Steven threw in a modest working re-creation of the Trevi Fountain with a Marcello Mastroianni figure posed with a blond mannequin who was supposed to be Anita Ekberg. Didn't matter that most of the twenty-somethings who paid the exorbitant cover never got the pop culture reference. He knew they'd get the vintage Richard Roundtree figure in the tan coat giving the finger to the front end of a yellow cab. And not far away was a Tussaud-like representation of Steven himself, grinning and posed like an action figure from the video of one of his biggest hits, all fresh-faced blond boy-wonder. God, it was tasteless. Since those dummies never quite look like the real person, Erica, Luther and I could *just* tolerate it, though Erica had strong words for the manager. His reply was hard to argue with. He was right. Steven would have loved it.

They were playing his music at the moment. The mixes he'd been working on the night he died, all warmed-over and served up just as Erica predicted in a *Final Sessions* album. I heard something familiar. The snippet of bass line from "It Was a Pleasure to Burn" then the peculiar sound...

"What is that anyway?" Erica asked Luther. "An animal call?"

"Don't have a fucking clue," he answered. "Steven always did treat a mixing board like a blender."

"It's pretty distinctive," offered Jill. "Is it supposed to be a girl coming or something?"

"Would be just his style," said Erica.

I sipped my white wine spritzer and said, "I bet you anything it turns out to be something simple. I think it sounds like a baby or a kid."

"Doesn't sound like any kid I know," laughed Erica. "Unless you hang with some scary-ass *Exorcist* babies!"

I didn't press the point. Some geek on the Net would eventually post the breakdown of the mix, and I'd win a bet two months down the road. Behind me the Steven Swann tune blended into P. Diddy into a cut from *Pariah* into Justin Timberlake.

Strobe lights flashing away and bodies packing the floor for the remix of a Deborah Cox hit: *You've been cheatin' and tellin' me lies—*

Jill coaxing a half-hearted Luther to dance while Erica and I hung back. And none of us saw the brawny stolid types in suits doing a Red Sea parting of the crowd.

You've been creepin' while I'm sleepin' at night . . .

Until we noticed the two uniforms behind them, one still with his radio loudly squawking every code from dispatch.

I didn't let on how I recognised Detective Holland. Jill knew, but I wasn't her problem at the moment. We could barely hear the voice lost in the music announcing Luther Banks, you're under arrest for the murder of Morgan Draper—

I think the bastards did it here for the sake of embarrassment. It would have been easy enough to track Luther down. I think they cherry-picked their moment. I think they got their rocks off arresting a successful brother and a high-profile one at that, and I think I would have sincerely lost my temper along with the others.

If I hadn't set him up.

"What are you doing? This is bogus!"

Jill telling us all to calm down, it would get sorted out.

Luther's eyes on Erica as the cuffs were snapped shut on his wrists. His astonished denial was almost pitiful. Erica calling his name as he was led out the door.

I had called that afternoon to say, "Detective, I don't want to get anyone in trouble, but you asking me all those questions and the whole ordeal ... It got me thinking."

No, of course my name wouldn't be mentioned if he were brought in for questioning. What kind of argument did he have with your friend Morgan? Well, how heated did it get? Me, doing the loyal protests: Look, Luther is one of the good guys. He even trained both Erica and me how to shoot a gun because he was worried about our safety! *Interesting,* muttered the detective.

"No, you don't understand," I insisted. "Luther wanted to help Morgan. He signed off as producer on the higher fee for Morgan's arrangements. He didn't care at all that Erica had a thing with him."

With every word, I blew away a few more grains of earth that Luther was standing on, a very, very precarious foundation. I wished now that I had planted a piece of circumstantial evidence on him. But knowing the cops, they would go digging around and connect what scraps they could to fit their theory.

And Jill didn't know it, but she had helped me put him in their sights.

I had called her out to come see the movie that evening. A few sound effects in the background, and she believed I was downtown. I corroborated her alibi, and she corroborated mine. But she had ended her date with Luther to come hang out with me, and that left him alone. Without an alibi.

"Luther, we'll follow you down," Erica assured him. "I'll call my lawyers and get you out of there."

I thought, No, you won't, honey. And when he was gone,

it would be all right again. All of this talk of hitching herself to Luther's star would end because his light in the sky would go out. No doubt, she'd visit him for quite a while. She might even get more militant in her politics because of his case. But whatever they had would wither for lack of contact or hope. In grief, she'd probably compose her most moving songs ever, chart toppers every one of them. There would be men, lots of men. Carelessly, frantically loved and lusted after, easily discarded, but through all of that, I would be available. I would be needed again.

Jail was where they put him, and jail was where he'd stay. Rikers Island. Luther insisted Erica not come to visit him in person, but he could have phone calls. He urged her not to cancel any show dates in the city, though we talked a lot about delaying the mini-tour that was coming up in five weeks. I argued in front of her and the label brass that it wouldn't do a thing to help Luther, and, in fact, we'd get hit hard financially over cancellations. Secretly, I wanted Erica to lose herself in her work. I needed her to stop believing she could effect any change, to accept that things would happen to Luther, and there would be nothing she could do to stop them.

We flew up to do a couple of shows in Montreal and Toronto. No talking to the press at all.

I waited on a daily basis for Jill to come rattle my nerves, informing me that she was doing another "favour" for Erica—this time not investigating a death but trying to clear our friend. But she didn't knock on my door. She didn't sound me out in the wings of the stadium while Erica performed. I found it almost peculiar.

I couldn't resist testing the waters, suggesting to her, "Look, you always say you've got pull with the cops. Can't they tell you what's going on? How their case is developing? This is Luther we're talking about, Jill. He couldn't have done it!"

"I know," she said in a defeated voice. "But this time, I can't stick my nose in. They know I've slept with the guy. Don't ask me how, they just do. So they're not going to listen to me. Besides, Mish—" She lowered her voice to a whisper. "Can you really be absolutely, positively sure he didn't do it? The cops think he was pissed off that Erica got it on sometimes with Morgan, and, you know, Luther's been hung up on her for ages. *Ages.*"

"It's Luther," I said again.

"We can never know what people are capable of, Mish."

She's given up. If *she's* given up, the road is clear ahead, I thought. At last. No one in my way anymore.

Endings

A show at the Garden. The echoing whistles and claps as Erica's piano played the opening bars of "Late Night Promises" and then the tidal wave of grateful applause. It was all before us now, not just Grammys but all kinds of honours and challenges. I had managed to get her to re-think the movie roles. I had told her hey, why don't we pack up and hit a nice hot beach after the European tour? Give ourselves a rest, God knows you deserve it after this year. I was showing her brochures only minutes before the floor director said everything was ready. She seemed distant tonight, subdued. "Knock them dead," I'd told her. She nodded at me as if I were sending her off to a gallows. I told myself I had to make allowances. She had been remarkably strong with all that had happened, and as the spotlight hit her, you could see the familiar joy, all the required energy and more. Maybe on a subconscious level, I knew something was going to happen because I relished watching her that night. I watched her like a fan.

As she finished up and left the cheering and clapping behind, I walked with her into her dressing room. There'd often be too many people in here that I would have to shoo out: hairstylists, makeup artists, wardrobe people, production workers. But none of them was there, only a few catering staff for the buffet and snack tables. The star's dressing room was impressively huge when half-empty. And I knew something was wrong when I saw Jill. She wasn't alone.

"Luther!" I said, stunned. "You're out . . . ?"

His voice was solemn, curt. "Hello, Michelle."

Then I realised that Erica wasn't surprised like I was. She didn't rush over and wrap her arms around him, which meant that any tearful reunion scene had been played out beforehand while I wasn't around. *She never told me he's back.* And Luther could only be back because the cops didn't believe he was a suspect anymore.

"How did you . . . ? I mean, when did you . . . ?" I spouted questions but he didn't answer. No one was offering answers.

"It has to be done now, I guess," said Erica. I didn't know who she was talking to or what she meant.

It was Jill who answered. "Yeah. We waited until after the show."

Erica nodded, her face grim as it expressed thanks for this small courtesy. I felt the earthquake coming, but I couldn't bring myself to run. Jill sat next to a small boombox, and now she hit the play button. We instantly heard Steven Swann's last track, the very track he played in the studio just before I shot him.

"You know this one, don't you, Mish?"

"What's going on?" I demanded softly. But I didn't think my meek mouse routine was going to work this time.

Pressing me again: "You know it, right?"

"It's Steven. What is all this?"

The song came to the bizarre vocal sound effect, and Jill said, "There," stabbing out a finger to shut the music off.

"I remember us talking about this sound when we were

in the club," she reminded me. "The night they came to arrest Luther. Erica said maybe it was an animal, and I said it must be a girl having an orgasm, and no one was sure. Except you. You guessed it was a child."

I didn't like where this was going. In a scornful voice, I said, "Well, is it a kid or not? Don't leave me in suspense! You guys still haven't told me what's going on here. Erica, what's—"

Jill's voice rolled over mine. "Funny how you knew what that sound is and no one else did. I don't think anybody in a million years could have placed that."

"So what?" I said.

"Well, how did you?" she asked. "It's been cleaned up, and it's been recorded *backwards*. You got an amazing pair of ears on you to place that."

They were all staring at me—Erica, Jill, Luther, the anonymous types holding food platters and clipboards. We could hear the shouts and cheers for a third encore, making my friend's name a chant in three syllables: *Er—i—ca, Er—i—ca*... Clap, clap, clap with each part of the chant.

"Steven must have mentioned he was using an effect like that, and I forgot about it," I ventured.

"Oh, yeah? Well, he recorded that sound on the day he died. He was making a charity appearance at a day care centre, and witnesses saw him fooling around with his little tape recorder. If I remember correctly, you said you never saw Steven that day."

"I didn't," I replied, my eyes appealing to Erica. I looked straight at her as I said again with emphasis, "*I didn't*. You know how Steven talked about his ideas. He must have mentioned it to me before."

"Yeah, that's convenient," sneered Jill. "He must have played that tape, and when you shot him, you left the recorder right where he dropped it. The cops gave me access to all the stuff in his studio, and I played that thing a million times. I ran it backward and forward, backwards and forward, and you know why?"

I shook my head mutely, not understanding where she was going with this.

Jill laughed with no mirth in it. "Because I thought: this is fresh. No one's ever heard this before. Except the killer."

"All I did was guess a sound," I protested.

"That's right," said Jill. "That's absolutely right. It proves nothing. But it sure is strange how you can possibly know that sound, and no one else can. I can't prove you killed Steven Swann, Michelle, but I know you did. They all know you did now."

"Oh, my God," whispered Erica, starting to shiver. Up until this moment, she hadn't wanted to believe it.

"Erica," I said, my voice breaking, knowing I had lost her but still making my appeal, choosing my words carefully. "I've protected you. I've always protected you!"

"You can tell yourself that about Steven Swann," said Jill. "And who knows what he would have done? He was a callous little shit according to everything I've heard. But you killed Morgan for nothing."

"I didn't kill him," I insisted. "And what are you talking about?"

Er—I—ca, Er—i—ca . . .

The floor director rushed in, oblivious, not picking up a clue about the voices backstage raised in anger and shock. "They're tearing the joint up out there. You sure you don't want to do the Neneh Cherry cover or somethi—"

"Fred, *not NOW!*" roared Luther.

The guy cowered from the indignant rage, looking at each one of us in turn as if we would give him sympathy. He got none. He backed up a couple of steps, turned and then fled to the wings.

Erica was struggling to get to her feet, in shock all over again about the murders. My murders. She wouldn't look at me anymore. She said to Jill, "You tell her. I think . . . I think I'm going to go throw up."

I watched my best friend leave me, Luther sheltering her with one arm and taking one last look at me in disgust. And I still didn't have a clue how this great revelation of Jill's should rob me of my purpose. She couldn't possibly have any evidence. I watched Erica go while Jill kept up her lecture.

"You're nuts, Michelle. You killed Steven Swann out of jealousy, and you killed Morgan over what? A bunch of pop tunes?"

His claims over the songs. So she had found that out. Still nothing to connect me to his death.

"It's Erica's talent that makes her stuff rise above all the crap on MTV," Jill went on. "She'll be played for ages."

"And Morgan was going to rob her of all that!" I insisted. "He was going to—"

"Morgan was going to do no such thing," said Jill. "He couldn't. Sure, he did a couple of bar gigs where he got drunk and started spouting off, and there are witnesses to that. But did you ever *once* see a public interview with him complaining? Did you ever see him take her on over the issue? *No.* Why? Because he never had a case, and Erica knew it. He bitched about it to *you* because he saw Erica drifting away from him, needing him less and less, and that hurt his pocketbook more than his feelings. He thought his threat would scare *you,* but with your usual discretion, you wouldn't bring it up with her. You'd just hire him somewhere or buy him off the way you got rid of the dancers she casually fucked or the hangers-on who wanted to go spill their guts to the *Enquirer.*"

"How can you be so sure?" I demanded. "You're guessing what he thought! You're guessing what Morgan did! How could you know he didn't have a case? How could anyone know? How could Erica?"

"Oh, but she knew, Michelle. That's just it. Because Morgan never wrote those songs. He was blowing hot air. *Erica's father did.*"

Oh, no. No, no, no, my mind screamed.

"Didn't Erica tell you herself that her father used to compose? That he gave her a few bits of melody to use as she pleased? Never wanted any credit. She was his daughter after all. She could have them and change them, do with them what she liked. *He* wrote those original melodies."

"No," I whispered foolishly, still not believing it.

"You think you know Erica so well," said Jill. "You got it into your head that you're her confidante, part of her family, the person who should be the real love of her life. You feel so strongly you assume it's as simple for other people— love them or hate them, enemy or friend. But people aren't as evil as you think they are, Michelle. And they're not as pure. Erica went to Morgan as a teacher—*yes*, with her Dad's blessing—but she also went to get his work back. Mr. Jones couldn't be bothered to fight his old buddy over his tunes. Sure, he grumbled over who wrote what to his daughter, but all the fight had gone out of him. Erica knew what diamonds her old man had created. She polished them up, gave them new arrangements and hot producers, and there you are. Top ten hits. But Morgan had the only copies of sheet music for about half of what he and Duane Jones wrote for their band."

I couldn't accept it. Stupefied, refusing to accept it.

"Morgan did arrangements for the *Drum* album, didn't he?"

"Y—yes."

"Three tunes on the album had bits of melody originally composed by Mr. Jones. He wrote the bridge for the title track five years before Erica was born! I've seen the chart, one of the few scraps the man has kept. It was his."

Blood was throbbing in my temples. What she was saying...it wasn't possible.

"Erica never talked about it with you because she *did*
have feelings for Morgan. And she was embarrassed by
what she did to him. That's right—*Erica* actually embarrassed. Screwing the guy and then smuggling the music
back! She's not ashamed of casual sex, but she was ashamed
of fucking him for an agenda. She cared about Morgan. He
was a good teacher for her, and he did have talent in his
own right. He was only a villain for you, Michelle. He was
never a threat to her."

"You don't know that. He told me he had charts, he had
demos—"

"Didn't matter one bit," replied Jill. "Don't worry, we'll
come to that."

It couldn't all be for nothing. I was still denying it to myself as she hammered home the facts.

"Let me tell you what *you* did," said Jill. "After you
killed Morgan, you searched his place for anything that
might pose a threat to Erica. You murdered him, thinking
you were protecting her, and now you needed to cover up
for her—or so you thought. In his file cabinet or his desk
or his bedroom closet—somewhere, doesn't matter where—
was a whole bunch of sealed envelopes he mailed to himself, never opened. You *had* to know what was in them. You
had to. You tried to stay careful, and you had your gloves
on, so you opened them up. That's what sank you. That's
what made me sure it was you."

I didn't say anything. One word, and I would incrimi-
nate myself. Yes, I had torn them open, not knowing what
they were. All those song charts and the cassette tapes.
How could she know? *How could she even know they existed?* I had been so careful. I had been so very careful.

"You were very stupid, Mish," Jill went on. "You thought

at first you should burn any record of the compositions. Fresh ashes under the elements on his stove, *paper* ashes found by the police forensics. You yanked out the little cassette tapes from their spools. Why take them with you? You ripped them up and tossed them in the fireplace, then set them alight. They proved nothing in themselves, but you were scared. You wanted to be thorough. You know what? You left just enough to confirm my suspicion."

She pulled something out of her pocket. It was an old-fashioned reel for cassette tape, and she gave it a sharp rattle for emphasis. With two delicate fingers, she held the beginning of the tape and pulled out a couple of inches of it.

"See the splice?" she asked. "I did it with razor blades and this brand of tiny seal tape that's like a Band-Aid. You can still get all this in the production equipment shops. Here, have a listen—we burned it to a CD to make things easier."

A young white man I had noticed hanging back in the group pressed a button on the stereo. He had said nothing all this time, his hands clasped in front of him, his posture perfect. *Cop.* He was waiting for Jill to finish before he put handcuffs on me. From the wings, I heard fresh footsteps, and then Holland the detective, ginger hair, same bad suit, walked in. He looked to Jill.

"I'm almost finished," she said.

There was nowhere to run as I heard Mr. Jones's voice, a higher timbre from years ago, softly singing. My God. Duane Jones singing "Late Night Promises."

"You never bothered to listen to the cassettes, did you?" Jill asked me.

I heard the fragment of a verse. It had different lines written for it, but the chorus was the same: *Don't whisper to me any more in darkness, don't tell me you'll change in warm sunlight . . .*

I tried in vain to still bluff my way out. "Still proves nothing."

"Oh, I know," said Jill. "I'm just taking you through how I figured it out. Call it a dry run for when I'm a witness in court. You see I heard that voice on the tape, and I wondered why the killer would give a damn about destroying that stuff. It got me thinking. And it led me to the proof."

"What proof?"

"You didn't think about what all those envelopes meant, Michelle. You took everything that had any relevance to Erica's music."

Yes, I had. I had scooped up charts and tapes for *Drum* and the hits on the second album, focussing all my self-righteous energy on disposing of these damning goods.

"And you failed to pay attention to everything Morgan came up with *himself*."

Mistake. A fatal mistake.

"Morgan penned himself a little ditty only a month ago," Jill was telling me now. "A jazz thing he wrote for a cop show, but the job fell through. *Easy Death in Queens*. And he did his usual ritual. He made a demo tape—this one, he did on the ADAT that Erica gave him as a present. He burned it to a CD and slipped the disc and the chart into an envelope he addressed to himself. It arrived two weeks before you murdered him, and he had a printout clipped to the envelope with the details. You saw the page with the title of the show, and you *knew* this couldn't be something Erica was working on, so you ignored it."

"How can you know?" I whispered in disbelief. "How could you possibly . . . ?"

I wanted to finish the sentence, to demand how she could possibly know what I did and *why*—why should the envelopes and not the music be so goddamn important anyway? Why should they mean I had killed him for nothing? I still couldn't fathom it.

Furrowing her lovely brow, she looked at me in quiet amazement at how I could be such a fool.

"Didn't you ask yourself *at all* why he mailed the songs back to his house? You didn't, did you? You only saw the song titles and the opening chords, and it was Erica, Erica, Erica. Protect your great love. No common sense penetrating that obsession of yours. That envelope bothered me the very first time I got a look at the crime scene. Why did he go to the trouble of doing that?"

"You're so fucking clever, you explain it to me, Jill."

"Well, it's simple really," she said. "Songwriters used to mail their compositions to themselves all the time. They wouldn't open the packages as a way of proving what they'd done by the postal mark. But the US Copyright Office no longer recognises this method. It hasn't for a while, Mish."

I felt a trapdoor in my stomach give way.

"Morgan was scraping by with his jazz gigs and his occasional arrangement work," said Jill. "Anything he wrote for TV was bought outright, flat fee with no residuals, so he had no reason to claim the copyrights. He couldn't get a label to take him seriously anymore, and he had given up trying. Here was this jazz artist who hit his peak in the Seventies, stuck in his ways. What was the point in publishing his songs if he couldn't get them heard? He never bothered to keep up with changes in the legal or the business side. *But Erica did.* A beautiful, fresh young thing like her just starting out in the biz? She would learn all she could. And in all her time with that slimeball Easy Carson, you never thought she'd learn contracts and ownership? Or that she'd come to New York knowing a few things? That she would make sure to cover her ass?"

Oh, Jesus, I thought. She was right. All those times I had taken care of crisis management, negotiated with troublemakers or swept people out of her way, I had got it into my head that I was thinking for Erica. But Erica was always sharp. She could solve problems herself but had merely delegated the small ones to me. And Morgan...?

"Morgan didn't have a legal leg to stand on," said Jill. "Erica filed her copyright forms for 'Late Night Promises' and 'Pariah' her third week in Manhattan! He could never touch them, and he wasn't foolish enough to try. Oh, he was arrogant in the beginning. He played her Dad's old tunes right in front of Mr. Jones's little girl on his piano, claiming he wrote them. And if his old partner hadn't challenged him in thirty years over these songs, Morgan didn't figure he'd start now. He counted on Erica not having a clue. But she had done her homework. She checked everything under Morgan's name through the government's website. And she simply waited until she got her hands on the sheet music, then rewrote what she liked and sent it in under her own name. When the second album went big, all he could do was grumble. And try to con you, Michelle, because you were in the dark."

Nothing. I had killed him for *nothing*.

Jill was watching me as the blow struck. She wasn't finished. She hadn't told me yet how she'd sussed it all out.

"The police didn't connect the dots between the tiny shreds of cassette tape and the paper ashes because they weren't looking at music as a motive," she explained. "When I heard that splice of Mr. Jones's voice, the pieces fell together. Because it occurred to me that if Morgan sent one envelope to himself then he had probably sent others in the past—only they were stolen by his killer. And it had to be you."

"You're wrong."

"Morgan's threats were empty and Erica knew it, so she had no motive. But not you, her great protector! And you'll prove it for me."

"Like hell!" I said.

"Yes, you will, Mish. When I figured out there were more envelopes, I had a guess that you would do something *really* stupid."

She dug into her pocket again and held up the pink FedEx receipt I'd pushed to the back of my desk drawer.

"You have no right to—"

"You dispatched the Federal Express package on company time from the office at Brown Skin Beats," she cut through me. "You technically work for them, not Erica, remember? That means you have no right to privacy when you're using company funds in your work space. And I know what you're thinking: one phone call, and Karen Ogis will make that package disappear. Uh-uh. The New York police contacted the RCMP. Being Canadian, you know how their cops' search and seizure privileges and their warrants are a lot more flexible than ours. It's done already. The Mounties came to Karen's door, and she gave it up without a fight."

Karen.

"You sent that package off, thinking just like Morgan," said Jill. "You thought it was your insurance. If Erica ever turned away from you, you'd use it as blackmail to ruin her career."

"I love Erica!" I yelled.

"If your love was so selfless, you would have destroyed all those pages," she countered. "I'm willing to bet you even stuffed them into the envelope using gloves. Problem is, how is your defence attorney going to explain to the court Morgan's papers with Morgan's fingerprints taken from Morgan's house and mailed by *you*?"

She gave the receipt to Detective Holland. "You have to sign when you send FedEx. You might as well have autographed a confession."

"I . . ."

I had nothing, that's what I had. No comeback, no excuse or explanation I could summon on the spot. Everything was slipping away from me, and I moved a step or two closer to Jill so that only she could hear my whisper.

"Jill, please. Why are you doing this? I thought we could have something. I thought you and I..."

She clucked her tongue as if I had some kind of nerve. Whispering back, she said, "Michelle. You see what you want to see. I've been with girls before. I'm bisexual."

"All that talk about first times...?"

"Was just talk," whispered Jill.

"What did you do?" I said in a small voice like a hurt little girl. "Fuck Luther and poke around his life to check him out, and then you come to me?"

"I fucked Luther to get to you, honey."

Bitch.

"I did tell you the truth," she said. "I just didn't give you all our pillow talk. He was still hung up on Erica. We were having a fling, and I told him about me liking girls, too. Nothing gets a guy so hot as *that* idea, so when he broke it off with me, I suggested he tell you about us, every little intimate detail. He got a kick out of it, helping me with my seduction, thinking he was playing match-maker..."

Bitch.

"I knew I'd have you," she said. "And I knew you'd want me if I made myself interesting enough. I learned about you long before you thought you had me pegged. That little story about the frolics out in Santa Fe, you guys with those electric eggs—whoa! You do such a good job of keeping a lid on Erica's private life, you forgot about Erica, Mish. Get enough Tequila shots in her, and once you're in the club, she'll be candid with you. About everyone. She'll tell every tall tale. You did turn me on, Mish. But you also made yourself top of my suspect list."

Then she gave me a look of genuine pity. I couldn't stand it, but I stood there and listened.

"Okay, full disclosure? Luther's a catch, and Erica's goddamn lucky to have him. I'd take him in a heartbeat if I didn't love my work more. They belong together, and I always knew I couldn't hold on to him. And you? You really got me wet, Michelle. You *really* had me going. I dropped my guard for a minute, and like a fool, I thought you might be interested in me."

"I was," I said meekly. "I am . . ." As if it could still make a difference.

She shook her head. "Oh, no. Not me. The way you look at her . . . It's obsession. Karen knew, didn't she? It's why she's never come back to New York and why you're not invited back to her house anymore, isn't it? I had next to nothing on you over Steven Swann. You did as good a snow job on me as you did the cops. But then you went and killed Morgan. And then you tried to finger Luther."

"If you and I had got together," I started.

"If, if, if," whispered Jill. "You've lived your whole life on if, haven't you? *If* Erica will finally see how you feel. *If* you can just get her past this hurdle, she'll love you back. *If* you can get all the men out of the way. Here's one for you: if there's a God, they won't execute you. They'll only give you life without parole."

As Holland stepped forward to put the cuffs on me, I lost all composure and began screaming at her, *"You bitch! You fucking emotional vampire!"*

The detective tugged me back by the arm.

There was flint in her eyes as she took a step closer to me and said defiantly, "I'm a vampire? You killed Steven and Morgan. You killed two men, Michelle. You sucked the lives out of them. You preyed on your friends, and you call it love. You took me to bed just to distract me, and you nearly did it. You're a predator. You need a cage."

"Goddamn you, Jill! You fucking manipulative—"

"Goodbye, Michelle. I probably won't see you again until the trial."

———

$\mathcal{T}$here's music in here where they've put me. I don't know if I think of it as a blessing or a mocking reminder, but it's somehow fitting that music still reaches me here. The pop tunes blare through the fuzzy PA system and float down the hallways, past the doors with locks that buzz when they click shut like the crush of steel on a bank vault. You hear an insipid Christina Aguilera tune, then maybe P. Diddy and every so often Erica Jones sings out and mixes with the squeak of the mop slapping and washing the tiles.

In the beginning, her songs would come on and a couple of the women would shout things like "Hey, Brown, it's your girlfriend." The joke got tired soon. Somebody figured out for the rest of them that as young and reticent as I was, if I could beat one man to death and shoot another, it was probably not a good idea to piss me off. Even in the violent ward, most of the women here are up for assault. Few murderers in here, and most of those killed their husbands because they got sick of getting slapped and punched around. They're not women who hunted. They're not *obsessive*. I am left alone.

I wrote to Karen. My letters returned unopened. She changed her phone number, too. In the weeks before my trial, I know the New York District Attorney's Office sent a rude, imperious letter in which their request for her to come down and testify amounted to a demand. I know this because *The Toronto Star* and *The Globe and Mail* were all over a story involving a Canadian pop star with a Canadian personal assistant charged with murder. A columnist for one of the dailies wrote:

Once again, American law enforcement thinks it can stomp its big foot across our border. Miss Ogis's relationship with the accused was apparently done and dusted by the time of the events in question, and her involvement in the whole affair minimal. I asked her lawyer, Mr. Ram, what she told the assistant district attorney when he phoned and claimed she "must" come.

"Oh, that's easy," said Ram. "She told the guy to go f— himself."

That didn't mean Karen would forgive me.

The trial . . . Well, everyone knows the outcome of the trial. I'm here, aren't I? There was brief talk after six months about my being extradited to a penitentiary in Halifax, since Canada doesn't have the death penalty, but nothing happened. I kept to myself, and they gave me a job in the prison library. The days are relatively peaceful, except that you are a child again, with someone telling you when to sleep, when to exercise, when you'll shower, when you will eat. You go potty in front of others, your toilet visible through the bars. I miss single servings of food on my own plate. Everything here comes out of enormous pots and cafeteria trays. You have to struggle to keep your appetite after seeing mountains of yellow scrambled egg, troughs of gravy or goop that's supposed to be vegetables.

But there's music in here. The CD racks in the library are about three years out of date, but there's good stuff in there. I got a peculiar look from a fellow inmate when she saw me reaching for a Luther Banks CD—his first album that he always said never got any marketing department backup, that sank like a stone in Tower Records and never made it on the charts. Funny to find it in here.

Erica came to see me once.

You'd think I was having an audience with the President or the Pope. They cleared the room with the glass partitions and the chairs and the phones, reserved it just for the two of us because Erica's celebrity "might prove disturbing to the other inmates." Translation: they didn't want a scene.

I had been in here a year, so it was safe for her to come. I was yesterday's news.

She wasn't dressed flashily. As a matter of fact, she looked like she could have walked out of a Goldman Sachs office. Blue blazer and skirt, white blouse with a delicate ruffled collar and this diamond brooch on the lapel. She picked up the phone on her side of the glass, and for a moment, I only heard her clearing her throat, struggling to find words. I hadn't gushed when I saw her. I wasn't smiling. I was in mild shock that she had come at all. Hell, my parents had never come down to see me. And here was Erica.

"Mish. How you holding up, sweetie?"

"Well, it's not *Shawshank Redemption,* but it ain't the Plaza either. You going to tell me your news?"

My intuition surprised her. She stared at me and said, "How do you know I've got news?"

I shrugged, drummed my fingers on the narrow table countertop. "I'm the prison psychic. Spill, girl."

I didn't state the logic of the obvious—she wouldn't be here unless she had news. Despite all that had happened and our time apart, I was still reasonably sure of her nature and her habits. She had come today out of a vague sense of responsibility for me. I'll just bet, I mean I'm *sure* she thought that if she had been a better friend or had been more observant—picking up on how I felt—maybe she could have done something. Kept me out of trouble. Guilt can be such a self-indulgent emotion. What could I do with mine? Or hers? I couldn't bring those men back to life. And she couldn't save me.

"I don't know why I had to come tell you this," said Erica in a small voice, "but I'm going to have a baby. And I'm definitely getting out of the game now. Luther's job is really taking off, and they want him out west, so we're buying some property in California. BSB wants in on a label we want to start up. We can piggyback off their distribution deal through HMV and Tower and all the others, and it means I can 'retire,' you know? Develop new talent."

I said nothing.

She rolled her eyes and sighed, then laughed nervously. "I don't want to end up a joke on the charts, you know? Still trying to get people to love me when the music's getting tired." She looked down at her hands for an awkward moment, then said, "Luther says he'll make an honest woman out of me. Baby's due in June so we're getting married next month."

"Send me an invitation."

"Mish, come on."

"It's okay, Erica, I'm in prison. If I want to make a joke in bad taste at my own expense, just let me be."

We talked about inconsequential things. Then a guard stepped over to say our time was almost up.

Erica put two fingers on the glass, a gesture to imitate contact when it was impossible in here, and her voice cracked with feeling: "Oh, Michelle . . . We were sisters."

"I know," I said.

"We were sisters, Mish."

Vague, creeping doubts still with her that somehow she was partly responsible. Her eyes were moist, and we both knew this was the one and only time she would come to visit. She slid back her chair and rose to her feet. Then a thought occurred to her, and she tapped the window of the barrier. I picked up the black phone receiver again to listen. Standing there, opposite me on the other side of the glass, I heard Erica Jones sing. Not one of her own numbers, but one of my favourite songs from Alicia Keys's second album, "If I Ain't Got You." Erica's voice, loud and clear a capella:

Some people want it all, but I don't want nothing at all, if it ain't you baby . . .

We were over our time, and the guard didn't stop her,

transfixed. She finished the final chorus, replaced the black phone and mouthed a goodbye.

No, I don't hold her responsible. I don't. Honest. I'm in here, and I wish her well. They make me see a psychiatrist, even though I never instructed my lawyer to use an insanity plea, and I tell the doctor the truth. I don't dream about making love with her anymore, about us being together intimately and passionately. That's impossible now. Right now, at this very instant, she is getting on with her life. This will be my address for a long, long time. There's music in here, and I will be all right. The obsession is over.

You see, I understand now that I *let* Jill catch me.

No, I don't dream anymore about Erica and me. I do dream about her and Luther, though. They're good dreams, and they're frequent. Sometimes I think about them together even while awake, and I remember what Erica confided to me about how they make love. I remember little details from the monitor when I watched them. Erica is vivid in my imagination, her lovely dark skin shiny with perspiration, her full breasts swaying a little as she rides her man, arching her back and pumping her hips with him inside her. Erica looks down at him with genuine love, and she is happy. Erica is finally blissfully happy. I can let my obsession go because she's found her true man, and they'll take good care of each other.

I *gave* Erica to Luther. I see that now. I must have subconsciously made mistakes, left little clues, a trail for Jill to follow. Miss Jill Chandler thinks she's so smart, calling me a predator when my love is more generous, more giving than she can ever imagine. I had tasted Erica, finally had my chance to make love to her, and I know, I *know* given time she'd lose her inhibitions and give love back to me. But we ran out of time, and I had to make sure she'd be all right with a person who loves her almost as much as I do. I chose Luther for her and let Jill catch me.

It's the only reasonable explanation.

In my dreams, I see how Luther's biceps flex as he reaches up to touch her face, to let his fingers run down over her collarbone to those full brown breasts, cradling them, their nipples so hard. I see Erica's mouth open in a gasp as she moves, and there, his enormous dick wet and throbbing as he disappears into her again. Riding him, riding him as her forehead glows and she feels rapturous love. I see all the combinations, all the positions for them. I can almost feel Luther for her as he takes her from behind, his strong hands gripping the soft skin of her ass as he sinks into her up to his hilt, the tiny sensation of his balls slapping against the inside of her thigh. I know how her vagina contracts and *holds* him there. I visualise her on her back, looking up at him, her knees raised, Erica screaming as she begs her man to pull out and come all over her, jets of creamy white spunk flying across her brown stomach and her tits. I see her making him hard all over again, demanding he put it in, the way that crimson head just pauses before it slips into the wet, welcoming folds of her vagina, and, my God, she's got such a beautiful pussy.

She comes. She's so amazingly beautiful when she comes, and I did say right at the beginning that she is larger than life even in sex, didn't I? Erica comes again and again with Luther inside her, and I know now that everything's fine.

Erica is happy. That's all that's really important.

About the Author

AISHA DUQUESNE began her writing career working with network correspondents in Africa. In her twenties, she moved from London to New York, where she worked at a major publishing house and helped write several "tell-all" autobiographies by black celebrities. This is her first novel.